Acclaim for *The Ultimate Love Story*

The Ultimate Love Story is a profound re-imagining of a familiar subject that will provoke a new way of thinking.

Ruth Siegel, Ph.D.

I have read many humanizing texts about Jesus, but none of them really hit the mark. After reading The Ultimate Love Story, for the first time I felt that Jesus was a real historical personage. Jay Clark's novel takes the reader on a journey into an intimate and highly personal world of love, consciousness and devotion. A world where the lives of these important historical figures are clothed with new meaning and purpose set on a rainbow background of multicultural existence.

D. Mikles, MD

"Not being a student of literature, I wasn't sure my interest would be sustained reading such a lengthy book... But to my utter surprise, the text was so fluid that I couldn't put it away. I am in awe of the effortlessness with which the author wrote the whole text... as if somebody is nudging Jay to write this!"

JT, Artist

"I found this book to be a refreshing "spiritual adventure" story. The questions raised were a metaphysical journey in itself. The personal experiences of the hero and several other characters were sometimes enlightening, often touching and always about the development of awareness. It's a combination of magical journey, surprising romance and tour of the esoteric all in one. For me the delight of the book was finding Jesus in Krishna and Krishna in Jesus.

John Dore, Ph.D.

"It was with a feel of going on a joyful journey that I went on reading the manuscript of "The Ultimate Love Story." Facile style, lucid expression that could treat even a mythical/spiritual/historical theme imbued with reflective pieces associated with Nirvana, Bodhisattva, karma et al and characterization of Isa, Mary, Mani, Sriram and others. It's as if you've negotiated the 'mystical cosmos' of diverse faith-based thoughts and made them explicable, accessible."

Pravin Sheth, Ph. D.

The contents of "The Ultimate Love Story" so absorbed my mind, that, the "show" continued in my nightly dreams. I journeyed with Isa and Mira through India, lived the lifestyle, heard the haunting music and wore the colorful garments of that time.

The author writes eloquently about the way of life in India, Tibet, Greece and France and their important influences on the life of Isa.

Many Readers and Searchers will find clarification, inspiration and refreshingly different views to many profound doubts they may have entertained until now.

Felicitas von Ostau, Artist of Interiors

"An experiential journey into the lives of two most beloved icons; Jesus and Mary Magdalene"

W. Beauclair

More comments at www.TheUltimateLoveStory.com

the ultimate
love story

an imaginary tale inspired
by ancient truths

a novel

Jay Clark

 **TULS** ASSOCIATES

ISBN-13: 978-1456598457
E-Book ISBN-10: 1456598457
LCCN: 2011902097

www.theultimatelovestory.com

To My Parents

In Memoriam

Their wisdom and insight awakened in me
a profound awareness of the world and my
responsibilities to it.

The light of their love illumines my life.

Chapter 1

The sun was setting in Galilee. The intertwining twin light of day and night at dusk has always been magical for Isa. Even when he was only seven he used to wander off from his family under some pretext to watch the sky, feel the breeze, stare at the setting sun, and listen to a solitary bird coming home. Often he would be lost in some memories ... undefined, fragile but soothing. Now nearly sixteen, his sunset saunters are a part of his daily routine.

Isa closed the door of the work area behind his house. Today, from a special piece of wood he had carved a doll with glowing eyes and captivating smile. The wood was a left over piece from the table he and his father, Joseph, had been working on for a wealthy Roman consul, Joshaya. As the table was for display in the official reception room, Joshaya had especially instructed Joseph to create a masterpiece, "I have heard of your reputation as a master craftsman. I depend on your excellence. Don't disappoint me."

Both Joseph and Isa had worked for many hours on this exquisite table. Only the day before, Joseph, who did not easily smile, had patted his son's back in appreciation for his excellent workmanship, "You are meticulous, son. You poured your heart into creating this work of art." Isa received this unusual compliment from his demanding father with a gentle smile.

Tying the doll, his personal masterpiece, in the hem of his robe he left the yard. The dusk was calling him once again to watch the sun hurtling down the horizon. This magical moment pulled Isa to his usual solitary spot at the end of town. Eyes riveted on the sun, Isa marched on. Sunrays piercing his two eyes formed a brilliant triangle.

On his path was the village well. Gazing at the distant sky Isa did not notice a big rock that people used to rest or chat around. This late in the afternoon of course the well was forsaken, or nearly so. Isa heard a giggle as he nearly stumbled over the rock:

Eyes in the sky, feet on the ground;
Sure way to stumble down!

It was the voice of a young woman. She laughed at this handsome but curious young man. Usually, like other village women, she came to fetch water in the morning. But today she told her mother she wanted to wash the new cloth she had woven. It was only an excuse to go to the well in the evening, as once before she had seen this young man taking a walk at dusk.

Drawn by her musical voice, Isa turned his gaze from the sun. What he saw transfixed him. One hand on the rope holding the hanging water bucket, another on her hip, this beautiful young woman had the most enchanting laughter he had ever heard. Without taking his eyes off her, he turned, approached her, knelt, and cupped his palms saying, "I am thirsty."

Chuckling faintly, the young woman at the well pulled the rope. Her robe twisted around her body as she drew the bucket up. The light in her eyes poured into his upturned gaze as the water gushed into his cupped palms. Cool water sprayed his face and soothed Isa's lips, mouth, throat.

His eyes were riveted on her delicate feet; savoring the moment Isa closed them. As he arose his eyes gradually moved from her feet to the hem of her robe, reaching the twist at her waist, circling around her bosom, reaching her head and the lock of dark hair fluttering in the evening breeze. Finally, his hazel eyes rested in her dark-brown glowing eyes, interlocked in a wordless embrace.

Chapter 2

A few days later it was Friday, the eve of the Sabbath. It was a perfect time for Isa to amble around, despite Joseph's fatherly admonition against deviating from strict observance of the holy day. Praying and resting were the rule in Joseph's household for the Sabbath, the only exception was an urgent demand from a Roman customer, of course. Isa could easily manipulate his movement on the Sabbath, and an occasional fatherly admonition would not deter a teenager anyway. He had his own covenant with the Heavenly father....

Isa loved to wander in the market place, despite those noisy hagglers whom he despised. A couple of times he had become edgy with a trader who was making an attractive offer to take Isa to the court of an Emperor in the east: "With your good looks and balanced demeanor, young man, you have a bright future," the trader had said with a wink.

"Doing what? Do you plan to sell me as a slave?" Isa had walked away, disgusted.

At sixteen Isa was certainly opinionated. His thirst for knowledge and new experiences was insatiable. With unwavering attention he listened to the stories of vendors, scholars, and artisans from distant lands. Distinct traditions, beliefs, and customs triggered new insight. He would ask: Do they have more than one God like the Greeks and Romans? What are their names and stories? What are their rituals? If their gods get angry how do people pacify them? Isa knew the Roman ways, but he wanted to learn how people in distant lands settle their differences. What do they do if they disagree with their priests? Stories of mysterious deeds of wise sages called *rishi, muni, sadhu* fascinated Isa. He found the information uncanny, and yet it was strangely familiar. God's creation was intriguing; it was so varied.

What could be the significance of such distinct traditions, Isa wondered.

This Friday Isa spotted Sriram, his favorite vendor from the Himalayan region who brought, besides spices and herbs, scrolls of writings in a strange alphabet and mathematical formulae. Spicier were Sriram's stories of yogis and their fantastic accomplishments. Were these yogis performing miracles? Or was God speaking to them as He did to Moses? Or were these stories Sriram's fanciful creations? Whatever the answer, it was a perfect time to listen to Sriram. Today even James, Isa's brother, came with him. Isa wondered if James was checking on what he was doing on the Sabbath? Did their father tell James to watch his movements? Why was their father so anxious?

As always, Sriram was holding court with his favorite listeners. The story was of a sage called Gotama, the Buddha. It was nearly a 600-year-old story of how Buddha healed people. One young listener asked if the Buddha could revive the dead. Sriram said, "You know what, he could, but often would not because of the *karmic* obligation of the individual."

Isa said, "That is not fair. And what is this *karmic* obligation anyway?"

Sriram noticed the aggravation of this inquisitive young man whom he had spotted on his earlier visits and had thought was special. "Son, every living being is involved in some action. *Action*, in our language, Sanskrit, is *karma*. The *karmic* obligation is simple: you pay for what you do. Good actions bring reward, bad ones retribution. It is an individual's own choice."

Isa asked, "What if the choice is not so simple, neither good nor bad? I want to come to the market place on Friday evening. I break my religious rule, would I be punished?" People laughed at Isa's naïve question, and laughed at the religious observance that often led to financial losses. They knew some Jews had started breaking this strict rule as it hurt their business.

Sriram smiled, "I cannot tell you how *your* father, here or in heaven, would reprimand you for your slack behavior. But a person in my culture would be held accountable for his *intent* and not just the *action,* if he violates a tradition. If a person kills a mad cow hurting a child he would not be breaking the sacred cow code we observe in our land. He would be killing the cow to save the child. His intent would determine his *karma.*" Isa saw the logic of this theory.

Another intrigued listener, Paul, asked, "But how did Buddha comfort the bereaved if he did not revive the dead? Last time you were here you said Buddha was compassionate. How do you explain such lack of compassion?"

"It's not a lack of compassion," Sriram answered. "Buddha taught each person according to his level of understanding. Let me tell you a story: Once a poor woman with a dead child came grieving, 'Please, revive my child.' Buddha said, 'Sure. But there is one condition. Bring me a handful of mustard seeds from a family where no one has ever died.' 'That I can do,' the sobbing woman said with a smile. With revived hope she went looking for a handful of mustard seeds. Every household was ready to give her mustrad seeds; but she found no family untouched by death. At the end of the day, the bereaved woman came back to the Buddha empty-handed. Her own *experience* had enlightened her about the reality of death that no *words* could have. She became the Buddha's follower. In our teaching death and life are not opposites. Death is not an end. Death is yet another shape of life. The cycle of birth and death repeats incessantly, we call it *samsara.*"

Isa asked, "Did Buddha teach why we are born and to what end?"

Sriram laughed as he heard this special young man ask the anticipated question. "Gotama taught that to those who would comprehend deep philosophy. To others he said follow the Way. He said if you are hurt by an arrow, would you first try to heal yourself or ask questions as to who shot you, why, and in what manner?" The crowd laughed too.

Isa also smiled, "Didn't you say once before that Gotama was raised a prince who became a sage after he saw people suffering sickness, old age, and death? So how or what changed him?"

Before Sriram could respond, Paul called out, "Didn't you hear the man? Just learn what is needed now. Attend to the arrow shot in your body. Why ask how, what and why?" The crowd mocked Isa's slow comprehension.

Sriram came to Isa's rescue, "No, no, no! The young man here, your name is Isa, isn't it?" and continued, "Isa is asking a relevant question. After leaving his palace, princely life, parents, wife and son, Gotama became a renunciate, a yogi. After several years of yogic training and reaching the highest level of *siddhi,* attainment, Gotama gave that up too because he did not get what he was searching for -- the meaning of life. He then sat in deep meditation under a tree, determined to find the answer. Legend has it that he reached that ultimate knowledge he was seeking. When someone asked him who he was, he answered, 'I am *buddha,* awake.' Thus he came to be known as Buddha. The tree under which he sat is called *bodhi tree,* the tree of knowledge."

James was listening carefully to Sriram's strange words and was getting increasingly uneasy. He certainly was alarmed by 'the tree of knowledge.' How can it be sacred? Didn't God forbid Adam and Eve the fruit of 'the tree of knowledge'? Isa should avoid hanging out with this Sriram character. Before James could drag Isa away from Sriram's stall, he heard Isa's next question, "But what did the Buddha teach?"

"Buddha taught the four noble truths. He observed that life is *suffering.* He said *suffering* is caused by *desire.* And one can remove *suffering* by following the righteous Way. It is by practicing the eightfold path that one can ultimately reach liberation, *nirvana,* from the cycle of birth and death."

"So *nirvana* is *liberation?* Similar to what we call being with God?" asked Isa who had heard the word often used by vendors from the Himalayan region.

"Yes, in Buddha's language, Pali, it is *nibban,* in Sanskrit it is *nirvana.*" Sriram knew only Isa would understand this distinction. It was too subtle for the rest, perhaps. Slowly people were walking away. Only Isa and James remained, since Isa still had more to ask, "What did he say about God?"

"The Buddha did not consider god as creator, or essential to one's liberation either. God's existence is a personal belief, neither good nor bad, only incidental. Buddha taught one can reach liberation by one's own intent and discipline following the Way, without God's intervention. But in subsequent ages Buddhist followers started worshipping him as god. Even non-Buddhists called him an *avatar,* descent, of one of the Hindu gods, Vishnu," Sriram explained lest Isa should think Buddhism was atheistic. Sriram had no inclination to go into the dialectic of theism, atheism, materialism and other multiple philosophies prevalent in his land. It was time to close the stall, so Sriram stopped talking and got busy gathering his wares.

As James and Isa started to leave the market place, James was convinced neither the Buddha nor Sriram was good for Isa: 'Tree of knowledge' and 'no God'! Isa was unusually silent as the two started on their way back home.

After they were almost halfway between their home and the market, Isa spoke almost dreamily, "What a wide world with such variety of beliefs and stories? I wish I could go to the Himalayan valley someday." James rolled his eyes, somehow Isa could not stop fantasizing the impossible, "Always a dreamer," James mumbled.

The two brothers kept walking in silence: one nurturing his hope, the other his fear.

The sand under their feet echoed their inner musings.

Chapter 3

Lying in bed the next morning, Isa's first thoughts were about distant lands. He fantasized, as children often do, about multicolored turbaned men and bedecked women from far away, thanks to the journeys he had made to various market places with his father. Now that the Roman Empire had spread to distant parts of the world, people of varied cultures kept gathering at ever-expanding market places in Jerusalem, Judea, Galilee, Nazareth. Isa went with his father selling goods and services, at times as far as Babylon and Egypt. Today he wondered if making wooden dolls, like the one he carved a few days back, would be good for business. He looked at the doll still tied in the hem of his robe hanging on the peg. Maybe he could trade dolls or sell them? Not a bad idea; he lay in bed daydreaming.

"Time to go to temple, Isa," he heard his mother Mary's voice, loud and clear just as he was about to untie the robe to admire the doll one more time.

"Saturday...it is...no more daydreaming about a new business venture," Isa mumbled.

He enjoyed being in the temple, but only when he could pray silently. All hubbubs bothered him. Somehow Isa could not focus on the Divine with the ritual of chanting and praying around him.

"Yes, Mother, I will be ready," and he got up from his mattress on the floor.

Joseph, Mary and Isa started for the temple; James usually went with his friends to the temple separately. It was quite a walk now that the new elegant temple was built away from the populated town center. Actually the town had grown around the old temple that was now too small. And over the years, the high priests had cultivated quite good relations with the local Roman authority.

Walking behind his parents, out of respect, Isa had to slow down his youthful pace. With his head down he was intently feeling the stones under his measured steps, a kind of quiet 'getting out there' as he described it to his friends, who often teased him about his sudden spells of silence. He was lost in one such dreamy state.

"Hey, nameless young man!" Isa was startled by a musical voice close by his side. It was the young woman at the well on whom his eyes were transfixed not so long ago.

Smiling and surprised, he said, "It's you! Going to the temple?" not knowing what else to say, Isa asked the obvious.

"What else does one do on a Saturday morning?" was her resigned response.

"You too are complaining? I thought you would be religious." Isa said.

"Saturday morning temple visits are like going to a market place: meet new people and get the business going – business with the Heavenly Father too, I guess!" She watched Isa to see if her lighthearted comment evoked a smile or a frown.

Isa smiled, it was a sore point for him -- mixing business with piety. "I wonder how people do business in faraway lands. Or pray for that matter? Is it very different from here, do you think?"

"My mother and I move from town to town selling fabric we weave, along with gems, special curios and all. My mother has an eye for the artistic items and a sixth sense to know what the Roman aristocratic women desire. Everywhere something is different. I enjoy the variety in the region from Babylon to Egypt. We notice local peculiarities, learn new business strategies, make new contacts...But it is all about profit and praying or praying for profit..." she laughed again.

Isa's mother looked behind to see who he was talking with. "Mother, I met this young woman at the well a few days back. She gave me water when I was thirsty." Isa introduced the young woman taking care not to betray any special feelings in his words, tone or voice.

"That's so kind of you. They call me Mary. What is your name?" Mother Mary asked the young woman.

"Me too, I am Mary!" answered the young woman with a musical laugh; her voice was playfully charming, Isa thought.

They all smiled, including Joseph, who had turned around to see what was happening. Isa was tickled to know she too was Mary, like his mother to whom he was deeply attached. "Isa adores his mother," people always said about him. But adoring young Mary was *his* secret to be kept a secret even from, especially from, the object of his adoration!! Besides, it was so new, so fresh, so vibrant, and so different. This synchronistic meeting, on a Saturday to boot, made him ecstatic...blood was rushing fast in his veins....

"My mother walks very slowly," young Mary said looking behind to see how far back her mother was. "She talks a lot, and that slows her down even more. I cannot walk at her pace. You see the woman in the blue robe way down there talking with a woman with a child in sling? That's my mother Miriam." Young Mary was pointing way back at the end of the street to a group headed for the temple. The Joseph family tried to show polite interest in Miriam. Isa was just happy to be with young Mary.

"Do you happen to have a name? Most people do," young Mary's words were almost drowned by mother Mary's, "Father and I will keep walking, Isa. Why don't you two wait for Mary's mother? We will see you at home after service."

"So you are Isa," young Mary's musical voice enwrapped Isa's entire being. Mother Mary decided it was a good opportunity for the young ones to connect – a natural instinct for a Jewish mother of an almost seventeen year old son.

Chapter 4

This was the day Joseph expected Joshaya's slaves to come to collect the precious table. Both father and son had been busy from early morning polishing the table with a soft cloth to a perfect glow.

For the last couple of months Isa had been absorbed in crafting this masterpiece. Each stroke of his hammer and chisel was like music to his ears; it was like a dance in a trance. The wood became in his hands like clay in a potter's hand: living, pliant matter. One time, a few weeks ago, when Joseph called Isa from the other end of the shed, he had not responded. Absorbed in his creation, Isa was in another world! "Are you dreaming again, son?" yelled Joseph. But it was a loving reprimand. Joseph knew how thoroughly skilled his son had become in the family vocation of carpentry. This table was a testimony to Isa's passion.

By midday the table was ready to be dispatched. Joshaya's slaves arrived with a Roman guard in charge.

"Our master, the Honorable Joshaya, requires your young son to come with us to the palace," announced the guard ceremoniously. This was quite unusual; Joseph was not sure why Isa had to go. But one never questions the command of a Roman Consul. Isa was of course excited by this new adventure of getting into the interior of a palace!

Life is getting better...Isa thought. Promptly he rushed to wash his hands, face, feet, and ran into the house to put on a cleaner robe, comb his hair, and tie clean wooden sandals on his feet. Mary looked at her handsome son with joy and pride. Doesn't he look like a prince, Mary thought to herself as Isa came out of the house. Besides, he is getting recognition from the powerful Consul. Cautious Joseph reminded young Isa to be proper and polite. "Yes...yes... father... I will be careful," he could not wait to get going. Meanwhile under

Joseph's supervision the slaves had carted the table onto the wheeled carrier they had brought with them. The procession was on its way out of this humble neighborhood, under the curious neighbors' admiring, also envious, watch.

Soon the precious table reached the palace. With great care, Isa supervised its unloading and placement in the designated reception area as per Joshaya's instructions. Of course Joshaya had paid a pittance for this artistic piece. Such workmanship should have cost him at least four times as much; but a reputed Jewish local carpenter was happy to get a fraction of it.

Joshaya had yet another business angle. He had heard reports of Isa's arguments with the learned rabbis at the temple three or more years ago. He was told young Isa was intuitively wise. The Roman wanted to determine if he could exploit Isa's gift for profit during his foreign travels, even in his diplomatic service. A Roman ambassador had long arms and deep insight for profitable moves.

"Isa is your name, is it?" Joshaya asked sternly.

"Yes, my lord... your Honor," Isa fumbled as he was ignorant of the proper term of address.

"Soon my royal caravan will be headed to Persia and I would like you to go with us. Do you speak other languages?" Joshaya asked keenly observing Isa's expression, demeanor, and response.

"Yes my lord, besides Aramaic and Hebrew, I understand Greek, and speak some Latin." Isa was careful in his tone, not to emphasize any special talent.

"Where did you learn Greek and Latin? Not in a Hebrew school to be sure?" the note of sarcasm in the Consul's remark was clear.

Such treatment was not new to Isa. It was part of life. He was not upset. One never knows what comes next, he told himself and politely answered, "My lord, I picked up these languages in the market place, from traders, vendors, travelers, and soldiers. I am told I learn a new language fast." Isa politely recounted his sources, downplaying his unusual talent as well as he could.

"Do you have any other skills besides carpentry work? Do you sing or play an instrument?" The Consul was checking the worth of his investment. Of course he would make sure to maximize his profit.

"My lord, I sing a little and play the flute some. But I am told I tell stories well. I can make friends easily, they say, because I ask questions without offending people, I am told." The diplomat in the Consul recognized a valuable addition to his retinue. Isa may be worth a lot more than he had previously thought.

"How far have you travelled from Galilee?" Why was the Consul asking that? Most Jewish people did not travel far, except to earn a living or when they were pressured to relocate by the ruling authority. His parents had to migrate to Egypt when he was an infant.

"Not too far, my lord. But I came from Egypt with my parents when I was a little boy. Since then I have lived here, but hearing stories of distant lands I have traveled far and wide in my imagination. Stories of wisdom and valor fascinate me. And then I retell those stories in new forms. Often people invite me to entertain them." Isa was calculating furiously as he selected every detail, uttering every word carefully in a guarded tone, not to sound boastful.

"What do you know of our Roman culture, our gods and goddesses? I know you people believe in one unnamable god. Personally I think *that* keeps you poor. But that's not my problem. We have more gods and goddesses so praying to many we gain multiple benefits." It is good business too, Joshaya thought to himself. He asked Isa, "Do you know what our beliefs are?" The Consul asked a vital question after a bunch of innocuous ones. This was an important question as Joshaya did not want to take a defiant Jew in his retinue. He knew of those indomitable monotheists, young radicals, and such...

"My lord, I am well aware of your festivals and rituals. Stories of Jupiter, Phoebus, Apollo, Minerva, and others fascinate me. They add to what I believe as One True God. In my heart I know I have a lot to learn from many other traditions of the far Eastern regions too. What I know so far I have gathered in our busy market places where people assemble from everywhere in the world." Isa thanked God for sending him the right words at the right time. Or did He, he wondered? But when the Consul made the next comment, Isa knew his intuition was right.

"I am delighted, young man, by your sense of curiosity and ardor to learn with an open mind. In two weeks we will march to Persia and I want you to join my caravan. Tell your father I require him to come and talk with me about the arrangement for taking you with me."

Isa was stunned by Joshaya's order. It was a marvelous opportunity to travel, something he had always dreamt of but did not expect would happen. Leaving his parents would be difficult; Joseph needed him, mother Mary and he were virtually inseparable. Going as a part of the Roman contingent held the best possibilities for the future, although it was risky too for a Jewish young man. At this moment he was happy, but did not know if he should be.

Confused Isa spoke with a calm steady voice, "I am most grateful, my lord, and I will convey your order to my father. He will be at your service soon, I promise."

"You may leave now." The Consul got up and left the room even before Isa could bow.

He looked up and saw a guard approaching to escort him out of the room, and the palace.

Once on the street Isa trudged silently, staring blankly ahead. The only sound heard was of his wooden sandals tapping the cobbled stones. As he turned on the dirt road leading home, he gazed up at the sky to find answers. Where was he going? To what end? Excited, enthusiastic, but a little anxious for his parents, Isa was not sure what the future held for him.

Chapter 5

Mother Mary did not know whether to weep or laugh when Joseph came back from Joshaya's palace, bringing the earth shaking news of Isa leaving home and traveling with the Consul in his caravan.

"Is he going to be one of the slave boys?" Mary cried out as if her husband were deaf. Equally disturbed Joseph shook his head, not really knowing what would happen to his son, to his distraught wife, or to his carpentry business. Soon Mary recovered from her shock. After all she had some experience in overcoming shocks, as when that angel appeared before Isa was born and she was still a young virgin. Now she wondered what was going to happen to Isa. Could it be for his good? Will he do well away from home? She knew Isa would love seeing different lands and meeting new people, learning about their customs and beliefs. But ... but... what? Her mind refused to think. "Tell me exactly what the Consul said?" Mary asked once again.

Joseph repeated one more time, "The Consul said, 'Your son will go with us. To compensate you for the loss of his labor my treasurer will send you 100 *dinars* each month. I am not taking him as a slave. Your son is too smart for that. It's a fair exchange for his service. He will come back to you as long as he is under my charge and does not run away. He is still young and one does not know about today's youth.' This is what he said." Joseph stared at his wife helplessly.

For a few minutes both sat quietly, then Mary looked at Joseph intently and said in a measured voice, "Our son will bring a new teaching that is beyond our imagination when he returns, with or without Joshaya." To Joseph's ears, even to Mary's, the words seemed enigmatic. She blankly looked around to see where the words came from.

When Isa learned from a neighbor that his father had returned from the palace, he came running home from the village square.

"What did Joshaya say, father? Did you accept his offer?" breathlessly Isa asked.

Before Joseph could utter a word, Mary's commanding words poured, "We have no time for words, son. Let's get ready. You will be leaving soon. I have to get your food package ready. Prepare extra robes and head gear for you, mend your leggings and sandals," Mary was enthusiastic. Once her mind was in its natural positive thinking mode, all she could do was overwhelm others with her energy. Isa thrived on that. No need to ask her anything now. Let her get busy.

"Father, let's organize the work shed," Isa suggested.

"You are not leaving *tomorrow*...what's the hurry?" Joseph grumbled as he got up to take a drink, but really to hide his tears....

After a couple of days of strenuous work: cleaning the shed, rearranging tools, removing grease and dirt from corners, and re-thatching the roof, Isa looked admiringly at the shed. "Father, can I take a couple of small tools and a few wood pieces to make dolls in my free time, that's if I get any leisure time?"

"Of course son, why do you ask?" Joseph's words were unusually soft. He admired his son's respectful behavior.

"You have trained me properly, father," Isa looked at Joseph with deep love and gratitude.

At that moment James entered the house. He had been away to the neighboring village with the farmer he worked for to sell the produce in Nazareth. The deals went well; he looked happy as he entered the house full of activity.

"What's going on? Am I getting married without my knowledge or what?" James joked.

Mother Mary gave him a big hug, hit him gently on the head and said, "Go get cleaned. We have some important news."

That evening the Joseph household celebrated the turning of a new page in their family's saga.

The two brothers spent a long time out that night discussing everything about everyone in the family. At the end James said, "Isa, you have always been a special son. I cannot say I have not been jealous of father's fondness for you. Mother totally dotes on you. At times I have felt distant from you. I do not know when we shall meet again. God says we have to be honest, merciful, and just or be punished for our transgressions. So I want to admit some resentment I have felt for you. Will you be able to forgive me?"

Isa put his hand on James' mouth, "Brother, no need to ask for forgiveness. Love is all we have in this family. You take care of father and mother when I am gone, that's all. I know you will, but I cannot help saying it."

For long hours into the night Isa and James sat quietly, listening to the flowing stream. Darkness was receding into the dawn as they got up, embraced, and silently walked back home.

Chapter 6

Going by the well for his sunset walk had a special meaning for Isa today. He was hoping to see young Mary. Life in his sixteen long years, almost seventeen, had its quirks, crisscrossing unexpected turns. Why was he anxious to share the news of his journey with a virtual stranger? Ready for disappointment – expectations' invariable companion – Isa marched off.

Soon he heard her golden laughter from a distance. Certainly Mary was there, but not alone, Isa realized, as he neared the well. It was too late to turn around. He was noticed. The giggling of Mary's companions intensified as he came closer. Isa kept walking, pretending he was headed for his usual destination at the end of town.

"Hey Isa, could you help me with this bucket?" Mary's request rippled through the air. Why does he melt every time her words come rushing to him?

"Oh, is that you, Mary?" said Isa pretending he noticed her just then.

Ruth, the mischievous one, whispered, "See? The dreamer boy never knows where he is going or who is around." Laughter filled the air.

Isa, now a little red in the face, approached Mary, "You want me to help you carry your bucket? Which one is yours?" He looked at the buckets lined up around the well.

"Oh, my bucket is in the well. The rope broke," she said leaning over the well. Isa looked into the well. Her bucket was bobbing in the water.

"Let's go, it is getting late," Ruth signaled the other girls, "Mary's mother is used to her late visits to the well. I do not want a lecture from my mother." The girls took the hint, picked up their buckets, and chattering went their way.

Isa always carried a small curved knife in his robe. With it he would often cut a little piece of dry wood off a tree branch to make a toy, a doll, or some sort of artistic figure. These creative moments were his time to think or as he said, "not think" – a kind of contemplation.

Today the knife came in handy. Isa tied it to the dangling rope and dropped it in the well. With total focus and a few twists and turns Isa could hook the knife to the bobbing bucket. Both cheered, "Aha... we got it." He pulled up the bucket. It was empty. Now retying the bucket to the rope, dropping it in, pulling it up filled with water was child's play. Isa did it in no time. Mary was all smiles; she stared gratefully at Isa as he placed the water-filled bucket at her feet...Oh, she has to stop looking at me like this, Isa thought. But of course he did not want her to... not really!

"I have to tell you something, Mary. I am leaving home for a long journey to Persia with Joshaya. You know of Joshaya, the Consul, don't you?" Isa said.

"Who does not? Those Romans eye all young girls. So we have to keep an eye on *them* for our own protection. Why are you going with *him*?"

"I don't have much choice. It was his command. They eye young boys for similar reasons too. Fortunately, Joshaya is interested in me for what he calls 'my skills.'" Isa explained without going into too many details.

"You better watch out!" Mary seemed to have a wider experience of life, being a girl traveling with her mother from place to place. Isa did not want to waste these precious moments in discussing racial, political or moral issues.

"Listen, could we meet to talk before I leave, perhaps by the stream on the hill?" Isa spoke slowly, cautiously, lest he may seem too forward.

Mary stared at Isa, without a giggle, just smiling eyes, "No man talks with me with such gentleness, such tenderness, in such soothing words. I would love to see you."

"Tomorrow a little before sunset?" Isa asked.

Taking his hand in hers Mary spoke, "I will be at the stream on the hill; till tomorrow." She picked up the bucket gazing at Isa intently, turned, and started to leave.

Isa stood staring till she was out of sight.

* * * * * * * * * * * *

"Where do you think the sun goes when it disappears leaving us in darkness?" Mary asked, leaning against the tree by the stream on the hill. Sitting by her side, Isa was watching the clouds changing from pink to orange. The sun whirled hastening to the horizon.

"Maybe he has to visit other parts of this earth? Maybe leaving us in darkness, the sun arises somewhere else on this wide earth?" Isa was only guessing. He was not sure. The brightness of his hazel eyes was deepened by sunrays. "Maybe some day in my travels I will find out where the sun goes after leaving us." Isa was already dreaming of the new venture.

"I wish I could go far away to my real home." Mary spoke pensively. Her eyes captured the reflection of sunrays in the rippling water. Her voice echoed an intense desire to reach another reality, Isa thought, similar to what he often experienced when he would be lost in deep musings.

Isa was staring at the stream hearing its incessant gurgle. "These ripples look like they are breath-waves. Doesn't the stream seem to be breathing?" rapt Isa watched, with shining eyes and parted lips.

"I am happy for your chance to go to other lands, Isa. But I am also sad. Perhaps we shall never meet again," Mary spoke in an unusually somber tone.

Isa held her hands and without words kept looking at her. The sun set and darkness descended.

❉

Chapter 7

Being part of a royal retinue, or any major caravan for that matter, was a novel experience for Isa. Nobody he knew in his town had been in a royal caravan. Everything was new. Isa wondered perhaps Joseph, the son of the ancient Patriarch Jacob, felt that when he was taken to Egypt? Maybe not as a slave or in captivity, but when he became the Pharaoh's favorite. Isa too was becoming Joshaya's favorite and certainly Isa was not complaining.

On many occasions, Joshaya would consult him on enigmatic political issues. Isa was intrigued. How would Isa know what the host king was planning? But most of the time, Isa's astute, intuitive observations were accurate. As they marched in and out of villages, towns, and territories resolving issues, and facing new challenges, Joshaya was convinced more than ever before that this young boy had special gifts.

When they reached Persia, the grandeur of palaces, paintings, music, literature so absorbed Isa, he regularly frequented places of entertainment, culture, and learning. The teachings of Zarathustra (many mispronounced his name 'Zoroaster') deeply touched Isa. The dualism of good and evil was at the center of Zarathustra's teachings. Concrete descriptions of heaven and hell made both realities vivid for Isa. The supreme divine was the Fire, the Sun, who transcended duality. The holy *Gatha*, the divine songs, revived Isa's interest in singing. Other ancient religious traditions including animal worship, and nature worship fascinated Isa. His horizons were widening. Isa was enthusiastic to *practice and experience* new teachings, if only for a short time. Then he would move on to a new experiment. Since learning languages was his natural talent he easily cultivated new contacts. Being in the capital of the Persian Empire was like being in a gold mine and wanting all of it... Isa even started taking music lessons.

He decided to learn to play a special kind of flute, from Mummona, a highly reputed cultured woman of taste. She gave lessons on her balcony facing the sea. Tender notes of the flute were carried on the waves all the way to the horizon. "No one ever reached the horizon," Mummona said admiring Isa's magical flute playing. She was becoming fond of this young man's talent.

But not everybody in the royal retinue was happy with Isa's social ascendance. The rise of a good-for-nothing Jewish boy was a thorn in many a Roman's side. One such jealous Roman was Petrof, Joshaya's best friend's son who was also Isa's age. Isa's entry into Mummona's upscale circle was the last straw for him. He decided to poison the Chief's ears. Petrof bribed one of Mummona's slave girls, Pontu, to entice Isa. Such social intrigues and assignments were her specialty. When Pontu's usual tricks did not work to catch Isa in a compromising situation, she became more ingenious. She told Petrof to bring Joshaya's chief officer to the ocean front at a specific time the next day to witness Isa's fall.

It was Isa's usual time for a stroll on the beach. Pontu jumped into the ocean as if she was committing suicide right when she saw Isa approaching the beach. Isa saw a woman drowning and quickly dived in to pull her out. He carried her in his arms and laid her down on sand. Trying to revive her, Isa put his mouth to hers to help her breathe, a technique he had recently learned from a Persian. Just then, as planned, Petrof and Joshaya's chief officer appeared on the scene. Pontu jumped up and started screaming she was violated.

The next day Isa was questioned by the chief officer and expelled from Joshaya's retinue. He was ordered to leave the caravan camp immediately. The chief officer was using his authority and did not need Joshaya's permission to fire a proven violator of Mummona's slave. The day after Isa was dismissed the chief officer reported Isa's crime to Joshaya. The Consul was furious with his chief officer for his poor judgment of this extraordinary young man and ordered his soldiers to search for Isa.

But Isa had already left the Persian capital with a caravan going further east.

It was now more than two years after Isa left Galilee and he had grown immensely during that time absorbing and observing life. He would have chosen to continue to live in Persia since he was fascinated by its rich culture. But something nagged him to go to Sriram's Himalayan valley. Didn't Alexander the Macedonian go all the way to India in search of more land and material wealth? Isa laughed as he thought of this intriguing Macedonian who was about the same age as himself when he marched into India. But that was three hundred years ago. And unlike Alexander's insatiable thirst for land and material gains, Isa's draw was India's inner wealth of Vedic, Jain, and Buddhist philosophies. Sriram spoke of yoga, breathing, energy control, healing and such. Isa could not forget his stories of yogis' simultaneous manifestation in two different places. And what about shape shifting and healing? It seemed Sriram's India had much to offer. Isa wanted to know the rich source of many traditions that sounded similar to those of the Essene's, that he had learned as a young boy with his father's companions. Why not go to India or beyond? Such a thought would have been rated a pipe dream, outlandish, before Isa left the small world of Galilee, but now he was a seasoned traveler, well... almost.

After the dismissal by Joshaya's chief, in the city square Isa ran into a wise man joining a caravan going to India. Isa promptly approached the caravan manager and offered to work as a carpenter. He was hired. The wise man noticed Isa's musical and linguistic skills and his sophisticated demeanor acquired as the Roman Consul's favorite. Isa looked too talented for a carpenter. The wise man advised Isa to downplay his accomplishments, not to get into trouble. Didn't Isa know it too well? He was grateful for the wise man's counsel.

* * * * * * * * * * * *

When Isa's caravan was still on the eastern border of Persia, another caravan, also going east, joined them. Caravans often camped together after an appropriate mutual scrutiny by their leaders. It was a time for celebration. Dancing, music, feasting, and exchange of news -- the usual activities -continued into the wee hours of dawn. Isa was returning to his tent when he heard the familiar musical laugh from one of the tents. He stopped in his tracks...it can't be her...he told himself. Then again, the same jingling laughter rippled through. He waited behind a tree a few yards away from the tent. An elderly man came out of the tent and went in the direction of the central festivities where more prominent people had their tents. Isa waited to see who came out next or if anything happened. Would he dare walk in? That was too risky. For a long time there was no movement. All was quiet. He made a note of the tent's location and went to his own tent in the opposite direction.

Early morning activities in both camps started in a slow gear today because of the previous late night celebrations. However, Isa could hardly wait to get back to the 'laughing' tent. Sure enough, it was Mary standing outside the tent breathing early morning fresh air.

"Greetings, Mary", Isa said in a kind of deep baritone.

Absolutely astonished young Mary ran to Isa, held his hands tightly: smiling and staring, and uttering 'ooh...s', 'ah...s' for questions and comments! After the excitement settled, Isa asked, what on earth was she doing in Persia?

"Where are you going, Isa? What are *you* doing here in Persia?" when Mary found words after those monosyllabic interjections, she could actually form a question to answer Isa's!

He stared at her, even more upset that his question remained unanswered. Quite curtly he asked, "Who are you travelling with?"

"Well, with Papa, my step-father. He worries about me a lot after mother passed on."

"I am sorry to hear your mother passed on. What happened to her? She was so energetic and lively." Much relieved Isa spoke in a compassionate voice, "You must miss her so. Mothers are special, I know." A thought about his mother Mary made his words even softer.

"Yes, she was. But her health worsened. Many years of traveling, trials, and hard work took the toll. Soon after our return home to

Babylon from Galilee -- when we first met a little over two years ago -- she passed on. Papa regularly travels to India to trade merchandise. He has been my father since I was ten years old and now he does not want to leave me alone without mother. This time when he was planning his trip he asked me if I wanted to go. 'Sure' I said." In her rushed narration Mary did not notice the relaxed tenseness on Isa's face.

"So that was Papa here with you last night?" Isa asked to make sure.

"You mean you saw me before now? You knew I was here?!" Mary was incredulous; her voice rose in utter disbelief.

"Well, I did not see you before now. But I heard your laughter last night as I was going back to my tent. How could I be sure it was you till I saw you?" Of course he was sure.

"So have you been in Persia all this time? Isn't Persia absolutely fascinating? Did you learn Zarathustra's teachings? I cannot stop singing the holy hymns from his *gatha*." Mary said with a twinkle in her eyes. "I am attracted to sacred places. For the last two weeks I have been visiting Fire temples."

"I learned some of those hymns too from my music teacher," said Isa and asked the vital question,

"Where are you headed now? What's your next stop?"

"We are taking a boat to go to Magadallah, a port on the western coast of India."

"That's wonderful! I too am headed to that magical land." Isa could hardly suppress his enthusiasm at the coincidence of both of them traveling to India at the same time. In a serious note he recounted his objective, "I want to learn yoga, meditation, healing, walking on water, things that help awaken, I am told, one's inner consciousness." Isa's passion was evident. Did Sriram trigger the hidden urge Isa already had in him? Who knows?

"That's exciting. I wish I could learn about those ancient traditions. But I have to abide by Papa's schedule. Let's hope we meet again," her words rippled like a flowing stream.

Isa asked if they were planning to go up north to the Himalayan region, which was his destination.

"I doubt it. Papa is looking for business opportunities on the western coast. Inner growth, awakening of consciousness and all that is airy stuff for him," Mary said in a serious tone.

"Well, let's spend some time together if our caravans move together." Isa suggested hopefully.

"That would be absolutely delightful, Isa." Mary was joyous again.

"What would be absolutely delightful, little one?" said Papa approaching Mary's tent. He eyed Isa carefully, diligently, with a fatherly instinct that had become stronger after Miriam's passing. "And who would this young man be?" he asked.

"Oh, this is Isa. We met in Galilee, Papa. Mother met his family. We are old friends." Mary elaborated lest Papa's protective urge became overly acute.

"It's certainly an unusual circumstance to meet someone from your past in a caravan. But it's so delightful when that happens." Papa spoke a little officiously. Did Isa hear a note of caution?

"Would you like to join us for the evening meal?" Papa asked. Isa gratefully accepted the invitation.

That night Isa dreamt over and over of the scene at the well when he saw Mary for the first time in Galilee and quenched his thirst....

Chapter 8

Tracking those rugged mountain ranges at a high altitude in what is now Afghanistan Isa felt changes in his physical body. His eighteen, nearly nineteen, year young body was maturing. Long hours of strenuous walk helped him focus on changes inside of him, something he had not done before. Now he was *observing* not only outer changes, but he *felt* something inside that was quite different that he had not noticed before. A constant ringing in his ears was soothing. Often he looked around to see if there were some insects flying around. He asked an elderly man, with a servant and an animal carrying his goods, if he had ever heard this ringing sound in his journeys. The man stared at him in surprise and said, "Where do you come from? Is this your first time in this land?"

"My home is in Galilee, but I was in Persia for little over a year. This is the highest altitude I have experienced," Isa said, his eyes spanning distant snow streaked mountain ranges.

The man smiled, "Yes that is usual for people with heightened consciousness to hear the ringing. Some see beautiful colors. Others feel vibrations, like a tingling sensation in their body. Some perceive all three." Isa listened to this man with interest. *That's* what he had been feeling, Isa thought, all three – sound, light, vibrations -- off and on.

The man continued, "I am Manishankar. I frequent marketplaces where learned people come from varied lands along with vendors. I go to Egypt, Greece, Palestine, Persia, and exchange ideas about life, its purpose, gods, goddesses, nature, science, healing herbs and such. Many philosophers exchange their theories in these markets. It's a place for exchange of knowledge, not just material goods. Upon my return to my homeland, India, I visit sages, teachers and *rishis,* at different *ashrams,* schools to learn more about the questions raised in the marketplaces I visit. Often I return with answers, bringing home information gathered from peoples of other lands."

"It seems your mule is loaded with precious merchandise and manuscripts. I guess that's why your servant is carefully guarding it, I can see that." Isa pointed at the loaded animal lead by a young attendant.

"That's Arun. He is not my servant; he is a scholar on loan," said Mani breaking in to a loud laughter. "Last time I returned home a *rishi* suggested I could take with me one of his students on my next journey to Egypt. Students learn entire scriptures by heart. That is how knowledge is preserved in my land. The *rishi* said, when learned men abroad hear the detailed texts, they can go deeper. There could be further exchange of information that might lead to more insights for both. Maybe I can bring more knowledge and understanding to them, and in return learn more from them. Such exchange excites me even more at this time in my life. My particular search is in the healing sciences: herbs, potions and medicine. Most of the load on the horse is that. There are quite a few rare manuscripts too, making the load heavy and precious. Arun is a cautious assistant. Well young man, I talk too much, my bad habit. What is your name?"

"I am Isa, son of Joseph of the faith of Abraham. As you well know our belief is in One god, unlike our Roman masters' beliefs in many gods and goddesses." Isa waited to see how this Indian, who like the Romans, also believed in multiple deities would react to his comment.

"Many gods and goddesses in my system are only manifest forms of One god," said Mani in a mirthful tone. Evidently he had encountered this issue often before in his exchange of ideas. "Despite the apparent differences there are many similarities between your belief in one God and mine in many." Mani wanted to keep the tedious endless controversy between monotheism and polytheism to a minimum. He believed in simplifying complex theories.

Isa continued speaking of his personal quest, "Often I have felt there is more to life than what is apparent. I feel compelled to *experience* this deeper *truth*. On an evening by the water front, or in a deep forest, or on high mountains, such as these, close to the sky, or in the fluttering humming bee, or the petals of a tender flower, or the throbbing wind I have *felt*, and I want to *know* what that is. Therefore I asked you if you hear ringing. Or have my ears gone bad? Or is it my imagination?" Isa smiled at his own speculation.

"Listen Isa, I do not know what your plans are or your obligations. But you are welcome to go with me. I will take you to the *ashram,* hermitage, where Arun lives and studies."

For Isa this certainly was a god-send. His desire was to be in an *ashram*, perhaps many *ashrams,* of which this was the first. "Much obliged, Sir. I need to make necessary arrangement with my caravan leader Castos and join you at the next base if he agrees." Manishankar could feel Isa's excitement in his tone, the way he moved his body, and most of all in his sparkling eyes. Mani had noticed his shiny eyes the very first time Isa spoke to him about the ringing in his ear.

That night Isa ruminated over the day's progression: He re-lived the impact of the mountainous terrain of this Pashtun land, its altitude, the thin air in his body, ringing in his ears. What made him ask *this* particular man a question he could have asked any other? And see what it led him to? How does this happen? Why? Is there something beyond what one sees? Is life a random series of happenings? Or with God orchestrating all things, perhaps this was ordained? If one cannot control it, then why hold anyone responsible for one's acts, good or bad? Oh, Isa stop thinking and sleep, he mumbled.

He had to talk with his caravan leader the next day to let him be released.

Chapter 9

"Do you think you can just walk out? What about your agreement? You think you can forget your obligation? Leave me in the middle of the journey?" Castos, the leader of the caravan, thundered almost ready to slap Isa. This was not the first time Isa had faced a master's anger. He stood silently, intently looking at Casto's feet, a technique he had learned from a young man in Persia, also a traveler. Isa was told to focus his eyes on the man's feet as if he was *nailing* his feet to the ground. The Persian had no clue how this technique worked. But it did, he had said, that was enough for him. Isa, standing silently, was intently doing just that.

"Greetings Castos," Isa heard someone entering the tent. "How is your cough? Are you doing well?"

"Oh, *Vaidya* Manishankar, welcome." Castos' angered frustration was forgotten in the wake of courtesy to a friend. "Do you need more herbs, Castos?" Manishankar continued, "I wanted to check before I left. I know you always store my special herbs." For years now Manishankar had been running a sort of mobile pharmacy of Ayurvedic potions and herbs, and had made many friends along the way.

"It is yet too early in the morning to depart. Are you ready to leave?" surprised Castos was curious.

"I need to make one stop along the way to see a sick woman, a few *koshas*, a few miles, in the next valley. She must be well, but I cannot resist seeing her adorable grandchildren. The children are my excuse, honestly." Castos' eyes lit up, he smiled. Castos, the Greek had a soft spot for children, Mani knew that.

"Let me ask my assistant. Hey Petrus, do we need more herbs for my medicine chest? *Vaidya* Manishankar is here. Check the medicine chest, quickly." Castos was particular about the protocol, and used the formal title *Vaidya*, Physician, Manishankar..

"I will soon report, Master," came Petrus' response from the far end of the tent behind the curtain.

Manishankar opened his big chest to introduce new herbs and concoctions for chronic ailments, like heart palpitations or intestinal ruptures. Castos got engrossed in the description of the power of the products. A major part of Castos' travel to India was to find new cures for so many ailments. Here he was getting information even before reaching that land!

Isa was standing, waiting to be dismissed while *observing* the whole event –a new habit he fondly called *ruminating*. In fact, it was in the Temple in Jerusalem that he had perfected this practice. His wise God had blessed him with that gift. Once again Isa noticed varied cultures blending together, the synchronicity of it all. While he was using the Persian method to nail Castos' Greek feet, he, a Jewish boy, was rescued by his new Indian friend. He was now *ruminating* the Jerusalem way to emancipate himself from his employer's anger. He was simultaneously considering the importance of this cultural crisscrossing in *his* evolution. Was Mani's entrance designed? Did Mani know that Castos would create hindrance in releasing Isa? Did Mani show up deliberately at that time? Or were they all co-incidences? Well, before Isa could find definite answers he heard Castos, "What are you doing here, Isa? You have no work to do? Go help Petrus." Did Master Castos forget what I came here for, Isa wondered. He started to go to help Petrus.

"Who is that young man, Castos? Can I talk with him?" Mani asked

"Sure. Hey Isa, wait. This is *Vaidya* Manishankar, a well known man of medicine. In India they call it *Ayurveda*. You may not have heard of it. But you would learn a lot about it when we get there." Isa stopped as he reckoned another twist of irony. Politely he bowed to Mani and waited for him to make his next move.

"Are you interested in the healing science, Isa? It is both an art and science. You will learn about duality and its integration in every aspect of Indian life: medicine, yoga, art, literature, dance, music, religion, politics, and social structures --practically everything." Mani elaborated, as was his habit.

"Greeks have integrated many dual aspects in their culture as well, Master. Are your integral methods deeper? Or different?" ever curious Isa asked. His eyes shone even brighter the minute he reckoned a new concept.

"You have a smart servant, Castos. What are his duties? Perhaps, my *rishi* at his *ashram* can train him. Isa has great prospects I can feel his energy chakras. If you let me, I would like to check his *naadi,* artery." Effusive Mani was almost too fast for many...

Dazed Castos said, "Of course" without having a clue what he was agreeing to. Mani signaled Isa to come closer and put his finger on Isa's wrist. He then checked Isa's chest, back, and various points on his spine.

Looking at Isa ponderingly, Mani said in a deep measured tone, "I know not what glorious work you will do, but you *will* do *it* for countless people for millennia to come."

Castos and Isa stood silently staring into... nothing....just soaking in the sound of Mani's words. What was *it?* *It* seemed beyond anything known.

Isa was first to say, "Master, I feel *it*, *it* is here, but I know not what *it* is." Isa's face had an uncanny shine, his eyes were distant. Was there a gentle smile on his face? No one knew.

Chapter 10

"How did you convince Master Castos to let me leave him, Master Mani?" after a few days into the new phase of his journey with Mani, Isa was bold enough to ask. They were in Gandhar, modern Kandhar, Afghanistan, at Granny's, the supposed sick woman's, *Prem Kunj*, abode of love, full of delightful, prattling children.

"Many things in the universe happen unbeknownst to us. But nothing is at random. We may not perceive the connection because of our limited perception," Mani said pensively.

"Could I have that doll, please?" a little girl coming out of the house asked Isa pointing at the hem of his garment.

"Where is the doll? How do you know it's a doll?" Isa was totally surprised. He had not taken out that doll tied to his robe for a while. It had become a part of his robe and was almost forgotten.

"I know you have a doll there. May I have it?" the girl was persistent.

"Sure," Isa untied the robe and gave the doll to the girl, "Here you are. Take good care of it - it is very dear to me. You understand?" The girl took the doll, held it with loving care and stared at it as if she had known it for all five years of her life. Both Mani and Isa were amazed by the girl's intuition.

"What do you see in the doll, Sophia?" Mani asked

"She comes from afar. You know those twinkling stars at night. They sparkle in her eyes. She comes from there. That is her home." Sophia said looking into the doll's eyes.

Isa kept staring at the fascinating girl. Mani was struck by Sophia the first time he saw her during his last visit when she was two years old, an enlightened old soul. What was the purpose of her life now? Whoever knows the purpose of any life, anyway? Mani had long stopped asking such questions that used to bother him in his younger days.

Isa saw the girl run to show the doll to her playmates.

"What do you think she sees?" Isa asked, "What has she come to accomplish in this world?"

"Living life is its own purpose. Thinking about it is counterproductive. Isa, I used to ask such questions in my younger days. Now I *know* life is not about thinking, it is about living, feeling, and knowing," Isa was to remember these words for his entire life. He *knew* that right away.

Mani went into the house to see Granny. Isa walked to the edge of the hill. The sprawling faraway mountain ranges and the green valley with rolling hills down below rendered a spectacular panorama.

The uneven rocky edge made a hollow right under where Isa was standing. He sat there ruminating over every curve of the hill. The nearby tree gently shook as a cool breeze swept through its branches. The blue sky seemed frigid. Chilly air made Isa feel numb. He closed his eyes.

He saw the deep hollow under his feet filled with rippling light. Slowly the ripples rose to his ankles, then to his knees, they kept moving upwards. The warm glow enwrapped him totally as he breathed in and out deeper and deeper. He felt he was floating in waves of light. So soothing! Now he did not even feel anything. It seemed like he was melting into these waves of light. There was no distinction between the waves and him. Was he the wave or was the wave himself? He smiled within. The question was redundant. Allowing his mind to rest, he just enjoyed the feeling, going deeper, deeper, deeper... Then he was nowhere.

❋

Chapter 11

"Do you want to meet my old friend?" Isa heard little Sophie standing by his side when he was *nowhere*. The evening was descending; he was not sure how long for he was 'lost.' The girl stood there with her inseparable doll.

Looking with immeasurable serenity in his face, eyes, and smile, Isa rose slowly to his feet, held the girl's hand, and started walking back to the house. Apparently another group of friends had arrived at *Prem Kunj*. It seemed the old woman was a patron of arts, crafts as well as needy people, and divine souls. Her house was a sort of way station for passersby. Many of the children were left under her care by travelers who picked them up and dropped them off on their journeys to and fro. Some infants were left in Granny's care for years while the parents made a living in distant lands.

"How could a sick woman take care of all these children?" Isa had asked Mani when he was told of this arrangement.

"She is not sick really. Granny is a devotee of Lord Krishna, a Hindu god. To her everyone who comes here is manifest Krishna. Serving them she thinks she is serving Krishna."

"But why does she say she is sick?" Isa could not understand it.

"She is love sick for Krishna. That is her only sickness! 'Krishna's flute is the magic healer,' she says every time I ask her this question. Now I don't ask her anymore. I come here to give her herbs for all these children and be in her energy." For Mani, Granny was not only an honorable elder, she was an exceptional human being who had integrated the yoga of devotion, *bhakti*, and yoga of action, *karma*. For Mani, Granny was a wonderful subject of study: someone who had integrated spirit and matter in the evolution of consciousness.

"What a way to serve the Divine, and love the divine in all of us," Isa said with admiration.

As Isa and Sophia approached the house, she ran ahead. Isa heard laughter emanating from the house...No, it can't be, Isa thought. It can't be Mary! Isa wondered if he had started hallucinating because of the experience at the hollow of light.

He saw the little girl pulling a young woman by the hand out into the backyard to meet Isa. Both Isa and Mary stopped in their tracks, disbelieving what they saw.

"Greetings, Isa," young Mary was the first to de-freeze total astonishment.

"Greetings, Mary," Isa muttered.

"Which way are you headed? Papa and I will be boarding a ship from a port two weeks distance from here going south." Mary tried to say something.

"I am headed north with *Vaidya* Manishankar." Isa spoke finding his voice.

"How do you two know each other?" Sophia asked Mary, "Did he give you a doll too?"

Isa and Mary both laughed. "I promise, I will give her one someday," said Isa to Sophia, without moving his eyes away from Mary. "Oh is that you young man?" Papa came into the backyard as he noticed Isa from the window.

"Yes, Sir, it is a pleasant surprise to meet you here once again," said Isa, coming forward to greet Papa with a bow and a handshake.

"You are not chasing us, are you?" laughed Papa.

"If I did not arrive here before you, Sir, I too would have believed I was." Isa continued Papa's joke, looking sideways at Mary. Papa patted Isa on his back laughing still louder.

"Which caravan are you with? Where are you going?" Papa asked.

"I am visiting a few *ashrams* in the Punjab area with Maniji." Isa mentioned his immediate destination.

"So you plan to be a *pundit,* scholar, like Mani or what?" Papa asked mirthfully.

"No, Sir, I do not have any plans. But learning, experiencing, exploring urge me on," said Isa, knowing it was not a line that would impress a successful businessman.

"We are headed for the port of Magdallah in Gurjar Land (modern Gujarat) on the western coast of India. That is our destination. I will be doing my buying in the nearby city of Suryapuri (modern Surat), and Mary will explore the city."

* * * * * * * * * * * *

That night Isa and Mary both were bereft of sleep.

Chapter 12

The next day Isa got up with distinct pain in his heart. Was he imagining things? Mani greeted him, going on his morning stroll. Isa only casually waved back, but kept walking without the usual courtesies. Nothing escaped shrewd Mani's eyes.

Isa went to the same hollow on the hill he was at the day before, hoping to clear his head and regain his composure. He sat there soaking in the cool air and soothing rays of the early morning sun. Why were the birds quiet? Where is the wind? Why are the stones under his feet so cold? Why is the sky glaring at him so? Isa felt he was certainly in the pit. Why does it happen now? Only yesterday he was in Buddha's *Nirvana*. Today he is in Zarathustra's hell. What is happening? He was lost in his thoughts.

"Greetings, young man. You have come with *Vaidya* Mani, haven't you?" asked Granny, the hostess, approaching the hollow on her customary morning walk.

Isa stood up bowed and joined his palms to greet the most gracious hostess, "Yes, Ma. My name is Isa. My family is in Galilee." Isa was still distant, a little lost.

"Welcome, son. Your parents must miss you. Such a blessed man you are. They must be proud of you." Granny instantly sensed Isa's true essence, his inner being.

She was a perceptive pragmatic guide for souls on their journey, many had said. But she thought nothing of it. She would say, "I am no guide to anyone. All this is god Krishna's *lila,* play. He just keeps me dancing this *raas,* stick dance, as if I were his *gopi, a* cowgirl devotee! I have no choice but to keep dancing. Someday, he will say stop and I will."

To Isa she said, "Do you know the story of god Krishna? He was a mischievous boy, a young man, a great flute player, maddening all *gopis* of his village in Vrindavan. The *gopis* would leave their household work, husband, children, and run to hear Krishna's flute."

Granny's words eased Isa a little. He smiled at the exploits of Krishna, a god and a prankster, "My mother would admonish me if I did that. What about *his* mother?"

"Oh, Ma Yashoda, she would scold him, but Krishna's enchanting smile would melt her. She was not soft, mind you. Still..." Granny paused, kind of lost in a dream... "Let me tell you what happened once when Krishna was a toddler. He was playing out in the yard. Ma Yashoda saw him putting dirt in his mouth and she ran out screaming, 'Open your mouth, let me see what you put in it.' She raised her palm to smack the child to discipline him. Krishna opened his mouth. And lo and behold, speechless Ma Yashoda stood in total amazement, peering into her son's mouth. She witnessed the entire cosmos: the planets, stars, galaxies and universes in Krishna's open mouth."

Isa was fascinated, "Incredible...she must have been transported into another reality."

"She certainly recognized her child was special. She *knew* his divinity and *felt* blessed." Granny said with a smile on her face.

"Mothers are special. They see and feel what no one else can. My mother said she had an angel come to her before I was born. Perhaps my mother had a dream." Isa shared this story he had long forgotten. But Granny's narration of Krishna's mother reminded him of his own mother.

"Son, stranger things happen in life than one may reckon. It is one's essence within that one needs to touch. We need to open our hearts. Feel that divine within. When your soul is fully awake, keep playing the game till your time is up. It's all *lila*, a play, as I say. Krishna keeps me dancing. Ask *yourself* who keeps you dancing on this journey. What are you looking for? You will find answers right there." Granny pointed at Isa's heart.

Isa looked at Granny in amazement. How much she resembled his mother in directness, simplicity, and depth. He bowed to her touching her feet, the Indian way he had learned from observing people he met so far. "You are my mother in this moment. Grateful I am for this reminder. " Isa said. His eyes were wet.

They saw Sophia arriving with her two inseparables – the doll and Mary. "It's late Granny, we were waiting for you to have breakfast. Come, let's go." She started pulling Granny who happily joined her escort. In the process the little girl had to let go Mary's hand, as the other hand held the doll.

Mary and Isa walked a few steps behind. "You seem to know this place, Mary. How? I thought this was your first visit this far to the east." Isa showed his surprise at Mary's familiarity with this place.

"Years ago I too was Granny's ward like little Sophie. My mother left me here under Granny's care when I was an infant. This is my home. I grew up here." Isa was astonished by Mary's unusual background.

"What? I thought you said you were from Babylon," Isa spoke in total confusion.

"I lived in Babylon since I was five. Before that, since I was less than a year old, this place *Prem Kunj,* Abode of Love was my home." Mary looked around scanning the area. Her eyes were moist with delight. It was a homecoming for her.

Chapter 13

It was early afternoon. Isa was sitting on the patio absorbed in deep conversation with little Sophia.

"Where did you find this doll?" Sophia asked.

"I made her from a piece of wood in my father's work shed."

"Where is your home? Is it two villages away?"

"No, it is more like a hundred or a hundred thousand villages away." Isa said.

"Oh, *that* is very f...a...r...Who taught you to make this doll, your father or your mother?"

"Neither. Something inside my heart kept guiding my strokes." Isa tried to make it as simple and truthful as possible.

"Do you know this *something* inside of you? What is it?" the girl could be a good interrogator.

"Umm... not really. I *know* it is there. But I do not know *what* it is." Isa said. To the little girl Isa sounded pathetic.

"Listen. You need to keep your heart open, it is here," she said tapping Isa's chest, "If you listen carefully you can *know*. Granny says never let that place be closed. So you know what I do? For the last two years -- I am five now, you know that, don't you -- every night I stretch my heart like this." She put her two fists on her chest: her fingers turned in pulling in opposite directions trying to keep the heart open. "With my heart open I say my night *jaap*, recitation of god's name. And then I sleep. It works. I often see things before they happen or before anybody else is aware of them. That's how I *knew* you had a doll in your robe." She giggled shrugging her shoulders sharing her 'secret'.

Thoroughly amused Isa heartily laughed, loudly; something he had not done in a long time...

"Somebody is having a good time," said Mary approaching the two.

"This girl is amazing. At five she is wiser than I was at thirteen. My townspeople were amazed when they saw me arguing with the priests at the temple at that age. Look at this five year old." Isa was all admiration for the little girl's penetrating awareness.

"You know Isa, you can learn some more from Mary, too. She is a good teacher for young ones like you and me. You know." The little girl said in a serious tone giving advice to her classmate.

With appropriate seriousness, keeping his face straight, Isa conceded, bowing, "Yes, my precious little teacher, I will remember."

* * * * * * * * * * * *

The evening was descending fast in these magnificent Afghan mountains. The sun would set in half an hour or so. Mary and Isa stepped out of the house and started walking toward the hollow. It started to drizzle. Catching the rain drops in both his palms, Isa said, "Everyone seems to be visiting the hollow. Even I ended up there on the first day I arrived. Is there something special about that spot?"

Mary said, "You know all over the earth there are powerful spots connecting us with the Divine. The hollow is one such spot. You say you found it *accidently;* I call it *intuitively.*"

"So where were you born, Mary, if not in Babylon?" Isa was now eager to know more about Mary's intriguing past.

"I was born in India, in an ancient city, Suryapuri. That is where we are going now. Papa was going to India on his usual business journey and asked me if I wanted to go now that mother was gone and I would be alone. When I said 'yes' he changed his usual trip to north India, and said he would explore Suryapuri for a possible new business. It is an important market place for people from everywhere, because the river Tapi is wide and deep enough for big ships, Papa said. What a glorious opportunity for me to visit my birthplace." Mary's excitement was evident.

"Do you have a family there? Do you know them?" Isa was curious.

"Oh no, my mother had no contact that I know of. Now that mother is no more with us, it is only an emotional journey for me. No social connections. Besides, I was raised Jewish in Babylon; nothing in common anymore with Indians and their religious practices." Mary was casual. Her interest was to visit the place where she had her roots, other than that it was an adventure to an exotic land.

"But why did your mother go to Babylon from India? What about your father?" Isa was confused.

"Oh my father was killed in a century old rivalry between two families when I was only two months old, my mother said." Mary reluctantly shared a few sketchy details, "As a widow my mother's life would be reduced to nothing, she said. I don't quite know why or how. So she took me and ran off with a Gypsy family traveling from Magdallah, the nearby seaport. My mother stayed in Ur in old Sumer with the Gypsy family for a few years. Do you know that the Gypsies' origin is in India?" Mary gave a quick sketch of her background.

"So you traveled from Magdallah in India to Ur, then in Babylon, and were raised as a Gypsy?" Isa was putting various pieces of the puzzle together. Every detail was more intriguing than the other.

"Oh no...not as a Gypsy," Mary broke into a loud laughter. "But my mother was guided by the Gypsy family. We were like an extended family. It was actually the Gypsy mother who advised my mother to leave me here with Granny till she had established herself in business. My mother was creative and learned new skills in weaving and making jewelry. She used her skills in writing and singing in innovative ways. I stayed at Granny's till I was five. My mother came for a visit when she could. It was she who renamed this place 'Abode of Love' *Prem Kunj.* " Mary thought she had given enough details.

"That's amazing. What a courageous woman your mother was?" Isa was admiring Mary's mother's insight, wisdom, and above all her daring. "Little five-year-old Sophia is almost your mirror image. Did you too learn how to keep your heart open, Mary?' Isa asked with a mirthful smile.

"Yes, of course. That is Granny's lesson number one. After my mother took me from Granny's we lived mainly in Babylon, but travelled around, as you know. My mother knew a lot about surviving while bringing up a child on her own, and being on the periphery of society. She never cut off her connection with the Gypsy family."

"Growing up Jewish in the Roman Empire I know what you mean by living on the periphery. I know the hurt of being humiliated and not understood even when the truth is on our side." Isa spoke, his eyes scanning the distant horizon.

They had ambled to the hollow. Thick rain clouds were hanging low covering up the sun. Isa caught the rain drops in his palms as the drizzle became a little more intense. "Look at these raindrops. Feel the moisture," he touched Mary's cheeks with his wet palms. The little chill in the air, the warm touch, the sacred hollow, their interlocked eyes all coalesced as it started to rain heavily. Drenched, Isa and Mary sat like statues in that hallowed spot that would hold them in its sacred memory for time that would never end....

Chapter 14

Mani's caravan left the next day, with Isa, for the northward journey. Papa stayed a couple of more days as the weather remained wet. And Granny was delighted to have Mary a little longer.

It was a long arduous journey, a perfect background for Isa to ruminate on the preceding week's events at Granny's. The panoply of experiences and information was magical: from herbs to the cosmos in Krishna's mouth; from a five year old's unusual intuition to Granny's extraordinary wisdom; from his infusion into the light at the hollow to meeting with his dream woman Mary. And then there was Mary's exotic background. To crown it all, the last evening at the hollow in the rain with Mary...that was climactic; it cannot be un-etched from his heart...ever.

He lost count of the number of hours they walked or rode. People in the caravan alternated walking and riding a horse. Walking 'rumination' was very powerful for Isa, he had concluded that by now. Many questions got resolved. But many more lingered, or new ones arose. Isa wanted to talk with Mani about the meaning of all that he had experienced. However, by now he had learned Mani's style. He would often be silent in response to Isa's query. A smile and a look of... what was that look? Certainly he was not admonishing, not pitying, nor challenging. What was it? Isa wondered.

It seemed they were coming close to a Buddhist monastery. Isa was engulfed in powerful energy. If at the hollow at Granny's he had felt he was enwrapped in a pillar of light, now he was flying into space. He was light, swift, he almost stumbled. Mani brought his horse close to Isa.

"Are you well, Isa? Watch your step. The land here is charged by many holy footsteps. You have to be more conscious of the

energies in this place. Be more aware. *Dhyana,* meditation, will help."
Mani prepared Isa for the new experience.

"I do not know what *dhyana* is?" said Isa.

"You may not be trained in Patanjali's *Yoga Sutra* or any of the
Buddhist meditations of both schools, Mahayana and Theravad. But
I know that you have meditated in your own way," Mani said.

Isa had learned some of the Essene teachings but not practiced
any of its traditional methods or of the *kabbalah,* but he *naturally*
connected with the Divine. For Mani that was enough. As an
investigator of the inner workings of the mind and the heart, Isa
wanted to learn more -- that was Mani's educated guess. He
continued, "What these schools do is create a method to break the
old habits of the mind and create new ones for the mind and body,
and ultimately teach to give those up to gain consciousness beyond
the mind. Transcendence, not by rejection of the mind but its
integration into a higher consciousness, is the aim of life."

"Is that according to the Buddhist school or the Vedic school?"
Isa needed some clarity on these fluid statements he had often heard
before in conversations with Mani.

With a quizzical smile Mani said, "Isa, watch out for various
schools in India. The more the *rishis,* ascetics, and seers emphasize
giving up the mind, the more they or their disciples engage in them.
Over the years, roaming in different *ashrams*, I have realized that
reaching the *truth, Sat,* is a solitary journey. All masters, teachers,
philosophers, and *rishis* are sign-posts on the way. *You* alone know
who you resonate with. Some may want to stay with those teachers,
follow them, or even worship them as god. Some others learn from
all schools, creating their own path. The key aspect is *resonance.*"
Mani thought he needed to stop his usual lengthy discourse.

Isa was intently listening to Mani. "What do you think of those
exceptional body related practices of manifesting in more than one
place, or dissolving and manifesting one's body in a different place, or
healing the dead, walking on water and such?"

"Yes, many practitioners of yoga, *tantra*, can perform these *siddhis*, spiritual attainments, by breath manipulation and yogic postures that control their physical energies."

"To what end?" Isa asked.

"I still have not found a satisfactory answer myself. Maybe you will." Mani said with a sly smile.

They arrived at the monastery. Two very young boys in orange robes ran to meet the guests.

Chapter 15

Isa stayed in the Buddhist *vihar,* monastery, for a while. Mani went to his own *ashram,* hermitage, saying Isa could join him when he was ready.

Days at the monastery were rigorous. Regular practice and strict discipline marked every day, nay, every hour. Isa related well to this new facet of life. The quiet natural surroundings, the rhythmic sound of chants, and deep meditation suited him well. Dietary changes that now included fruits, vegetables, grains, *ghee,* purified butter, and honey were conducive to a healthier body. Exercise too helped deeper meditation. Isa wondered why he found many of these strange practices natural and easy. He had not yet found an answer.

Young monks around him were friendly. Technical questions pertaining to meditation, *dhyana,* were answered by the chief *muni,* monk. Other monks would not interfere with a new comer's query or training. They would be supportive in the *sangha,* community life experience. *Dhamma* or *Dharma,* the teaching that holds all, could be taught only by a qualified monk. Isa particularly cherished the sonorous chant:

Buddham saranam gacchami
Dhammam saranam gacchami
Sangham saranam gacchami

I surrender to Buddha
I surrender to the Teaching
I surrender to the Community

He often pondered over the affirmations in the chant. Did he truly feel them? Was he honest singing them? Was he truly a member of this community? He could not always find answers. But the inquiry drew him deeper into his consciousness as the sound reverberated in his being. The heavenly chant drew him into another space.

Quiet meditations were the best. Stopping the mind, even thinking itself, allowed him to enter into a no-thing space where he could connect with his own unnamable YHWH. It was simultaneously a full-empty state. Isa felt the Buddhist chant helped him connect with his own faith in the divine.

Two months of regulated disciplinary life was vastly different from the caravan life. Isa felt rejuvenated, centered, and calm.

* * * * * * * * * * * *

Was he going to Arabia so soon, Isa wondered when he saw Mani and Arun arrive at the monastery. It had been only two months.

"Greetings, Isa. How do you feel? Are you getting what you are looking for?" Mani was asking half jokingly. His cheerful voice delighted Isa.

"Greetings, Maniji. Hey Arun, are you well?" Isa greeted both with *namaste,* with joined palms, the traditional Indian way. Then turning to Mani, he continued, "This *vihar* has been a blessing. My meditations are profound and uplifting. I become stable and calm right away. They seem so natural to me." Isa looked more serene, a little grown too. Was he twenty yet, Mani wondered.

"Are you going back to the West so soon, Maniji?" Isa was surprised.

"Oh no, this visit is strictly for you. Are you ready to move on? We shall be happy to escort you to our *ashram,*" Mani announced.

Isa's face beamed. He thrived on journeys. They were not about going *away from* anything, always *to* something new. He was ready. The next day they started to go southeast to Mani's *ashram* a day and half journey away.

All three of them were riding horses. The terrain was varied, uneven. It was mountainous, with streams and tributaries of rivers intersecting their path all the way. Small forests were followed by fields full of crops, some ready to be harvested. Isa learned the names of many unfamiliar fruits, flowers, and grains. Largest were the fields of wheat. A pair of oxen pulled the plough as farmers sang love songs to them. It truly was an exotic land that he had heard about from travelers. It was called Punjab, the land of five, *punch,* rivers, *aab.*

Enchanting small villages nestled in lush greenery. Most of them had a temple at the center by a huge tree. Around the tree would be a little circle of brick and mud for people to rest, chat, or hold town meetings. Even the elders' court gathered around here to decide local disputes. It was a men's meeting place. In another section of town was the women's gathering circle, the well. But that was some distance away from the center for men. Isa smiled. It was just like in Galilee. He still had not figured out why men considered themselves superior to women and had their seat of power sufficiently removed from women's. He knew for sure his mother was wiser, but his father's wish was the command.

Isa soon was lost in his favorite reverie of time spent with Mary, their meeting by the well, their Saturday walk to the temple, the meeting of the caravans, and then at Granny's...All memories jumbled over, a bit here, a bit there... Isa wondered where Mary could be now at this very moment. He was in the northwest part of the land; she was perhaps along the midwestern shoreline, enjoying the ocean. Even if he did not know for sure where she was, it was a pleasant, sweetly soothing memory.

Chapter 16

Leaving Granny's abode of love, *Prem Kunj,* Mary cried. It was natural. Granny was the only mother she had known till she was five. When her mother Miriam came to take her almost fifteen years ago... oh, how time flies...she had cried bitter tears at the hollow.

Walking in the forest grove, Mary remembered those days when she had to leave *Prem Kunj.*

Hours of walking around Granny's grove with Miriam had finally reconciled five year old Mary to go with her mother. It was not that she disliked Miriam. In fact, she looked forward to the visits of funny, generous, and kind Miriam. The gifts she brought were so unusual and so many! But Miriam was no more than a loving visitor, that's all. When five year old Mary was told Miriam had come to take her, she was shocked. She cried, screamed, ran into the forest grove to talk with Mintu, the rabbit, and Mrug, the deer. Maybe they all could runaway! Mintu and Mrug sat silently looking at Mary as she narrated her story. She told Granny that her four legged friends were also crying.

Once again Mary pondered over those days, and smiled. Now she was a grown woman, and had endured many trials of separation. It was hard to bear the blow of her mother's passing two years ago. Sweet are those moments of union. Wasn't meeting Isa in *Prem Kunj,* in the abode of love, the most pleasant surprise! Thinking of Isa she smiled. She fondly looked around at familiar spots that stored recent sweet memories.

She looked up at the sun, it was time to get back to the house...Papa must be getting impatient. Oh, he had been the only father she ever knew for the last ten years and had been a loving protector, especially after her mother's death. She smiled. Uncanny, unexpected are the turns of life. She thanked God for her adventure of life.

Granny and Papa were relaxing over a fine brew of tea. This was Papa's first journey to Magdallah, the sea port near Miriam's home town. "I thought Mary might want to visit her birth place. Miriam had often spoken to me of Suryapuri, a thriving market center and a river port nearby. Big ships dock in its harbor. I thought it won't hurt me to explore a new business area in India either, although so far I have only explored the northern trail." He laughed with a twinkle of an adventurous businessman.

"You would profit well in Suryapuri. Travelers speak of kind, hospitable, honest people of the city, but most of all they rave about its food. I have gotten some tasty recipes and spices from these travelers." Granny was animated. Papa laughed at the prospect of visiting a thriving business town with a taste for life, literally.

"Do you know much about Miriam's life in Suryapuri? I am sure you know more than she told me or Mary. I only know Miriam and Mary use the name Magdalene derived from Magdallah, the port from where Miriam left her dear native land with her infant to go to Babylon. I certainly was not much interested in it then. Miriam was a remarkable woman, sharp, kind, loving. That's all that mattered to me. Now that I am visiting her native land, I am curious." Papa was a caring father, Granny could tell.

"Are you ready for an unusual narrative? Miriam was special indeed, even more than you know." Granny started, "Mrinal, that was Miriam's real name, perhaps you know that. Her father had two brothers; they belonged to a prominent Brahmin family of landlords for several generations in Suryapuri. Besides a lucrative spice business and land ownership, the family was known for community service, devotion, and honesty. Her father was a judge in his district with progressive ideas. He doted over his only child, Mrinal, and gave her the education usually available to boys, ignoring traditions. Social restrictions imposed on women, he said, had ruined the future for girls in their society. He even hired a tutor to train her as a scribe, to copy scriptures, a training that is normally given only to boys. Not having a son, her parents raised Mrinal as a son. A little spoiled too, if you ask me," said Granny with a sly smile. She took a sip of the brew, and continued, "From her mother's devotional stories and songs, Mrinal knew a lot about the epics, the *purans*, stories of heroic men and women, and ritual practices. One day Mrinal asked her father a question about farmers working on their land. That began Mrinal's visits to the farmland with her father. She saw the ramshackle huts of poor tenant farmers. You can imagine this independent girl growing up in luxury, suddenly was exposed to a different kind of reality."

"I thought she knew a lot about the business world too. Something that helped establish herself in Babylon." Papa was not sure how Miriam became a successful business woman in a new land.

Granny chuckled, "Well, her father started taking Mrinal to his family's port business, mainly run by his brothers, and his Judge's office as well. For a girl to be with her father in his work place was unheard of. People's raised eyebrows did not daunt Mrinal's father. As a matter of fact, that is where a young business man saw Mrinal and was smitten by her beauty, daring, independence, and confidence." Granny's energy was reflected in her eyes.

"This young man I presume was her future husband? I am not surprised, because that verve for independence and sharp intelligence is what attracted me to Miriam." Papa laughed heartily, till tears welled up in his eyes. Were they tears of joy or sorrow? Who knows?

"True. Both were Brahmin families of compatible resources. The families met, along with Mrinal and Parshva, the young man," Granny paused for a moment.

"Ah, Parshva. I would never forget his name because I often used to tease Miriam. It was our private joke: Whose love was more intense, Parshva's or mine, I would ask. She would fret and fume and I would laugh..." Papa said fondly remembering their romantic games.

"So you never knew her entire life story?" Granny was a little surprised.

"Not really. Miriam was understandably reluctant to open old wounds. She would much rather not talk about the tragedy: Parshva's cruel murder, leaving her parents, and so on... I never persisted, honestly. It's an alien culture too! I was happy with my Miriam." Papa confessed his self-absorption. "So what happened to these blessed families?" He could not wait to hear the rest.

Granny saw Mary entering through the back door. "We are in the living room, Mary, come join us." Mary looked refreshed, Granny noticed. Papa said, "Listen, I am checking out your family history. Do you know the details? Did your Mama ever tell you her entire life story?"

"Mama was moody, you know, Papa. She would bring up bits and pieces here and there about dressing styles, food, weather, but nothing more significant." Mary sounded indifferent. Young Mary was all focused on the present.

"Well, sit here. You are a grown woman now. It's time to know your family history," Granny said in her uniquely assertive, yet inoffensive, tone.

"Your father Parshva's family had more than a hundred year old political history, Mrinal said. His great great grandfather, a Brahmin, was a king, although traditionally most kings would be of the Warrior caste, if my shady memory serves me right." Mary smiled: nobody would suspect 'shady memory' in that razor sharp mind. "A century or so ago for a short span of fifty years Parshva's Brahmin ancestors became powerful kings defeating corrupt Warrior kings. It was relatively a small but powerful kingdom."

"So how was it related to Parshva nearly two hundred years later?" Papa was curious, now more than ever.

"One of the descendents of the Warrior caste, I will never forget his name, Sungish, was the same age as Parshva and held an important political position. Parshva and Sungish often met at social and cultural events, and were involved in business deals as well, like many young men of the upper echelon. But Sungish was vain and competitive – a kind of dark energy, if you ask me. He would always make scathing remarks about an old family feud every time they met. When Mrinal and Parshva got married, Sungish who had his eyes on Mrinal, considered it a personal defeat. It was *his* fantasy since there was no possibility of their marriage. Sungish was a *Kshatriya*, warrior caste and Mrinal was a *Brahmin*, priestly caste! According to social norms, such an inter-caste marriage would be highly unlikely, if not impossible; however, logical reasoning was not Sungish's strong point," Granny said with a sly smile and a raised eye brow.

"Granny, say it the way it was. He was crazy, right?" Papa was angry.

"So this cruel Sungish killed my father out of jealousy?" Mary was shocked. She had known her father had died a violent death, that's all.

"Yes. And Sungish made his vile act sound heroic. He said he was taking revenge for his ancestor's defeat by Parshva's great great grandfather, the last king of that dynasty."

"How atrocious, what a rascal! He killed Parshva for a personal fantasy, and called it an honorable act -- revenge for a hundred year old family feud? God save us from such heinous hypocrites," Papa was furious as he expressed his indignation.

Granny remained silent, tears welled in her eyes. "You were two months old then and when Mrinal arrived here you were six or seven months old," Granny said in a gentle voice to Mary.

"But why did she have to leave her family? Her parents could have taken care of us both," Mary was confused.

Papa had vaguely heard of the scourge of the Indian widow's plight in his earlier trips to this land. He had heard of the ritual of *sati*, burning of a widow on the husband's funeral pyre. He asked, "Miriam was not escaping from being a *sati*, was she?"

"No, no, no. fortunately it was not prevalent in her part of India and certainly not in her caste. But Mrinal said a widow's life was miserable, like a pariah's."

"But her family was so well placed, her father so progressive, they could have done something," Papa protested.

"Whatever support her father could give her was restricted within his household. Socially Mrinal would be like a caged bird with clipped wings. She was twenty-two when Parshva was murdered. According to the prevalent customs she would be compelled to wear nothing but unadorned white clothes. In some other areas of the land women wore dark brown or gray – just one drab color determined by an age old social custom. No jewelry, no shining sparkles that adorned other women. Traditionally, a widow would be labeled an unfortunate woman and was considered a bad omen at festivals, weddings or ceremonial celebrations. She could not actively participate in them. Above all she could not socialize freely even with women of her age, nor could she appear in public places. She could not go to her father's place of work, certainly not her husband's. She was fortunate that her father could prevail upon Parshva's family to let her live with the baby at his house. Any other traditional family would have rejected such a proposal by the widow's father. Often the widow would remain virtually like a silent shadow in her dead husband's family for her entire life," Granny was agitated sharing this inhuman treatment of widows.

"No question of remarriage for a widow in India, right?" Papa continued, "When we got married, I used to tease her about living in sin," Papa burst into a loud laughter lightening the thick air...

"In fact, Mrinal considered becoming a Jain or a Buddhist nun, a path many young widows chose to escape the scourge of widowhood." Granny continued, "But that meant leaving you, Mary, with her family. You would be well raised, but your mother would have to leave you forever. Mrinal spent a couple of months in total agony and confusion."

"That is horrible," said Mary, "I would never have imagined she went through such torture. Now I understand her occasional harshness in disciplining me, though I hated it then," Mary looked thoughtful and sad.

"So what changed? How did Miriam decide to leave her family and her land?" Papa was eager.

"Mrinal's father tried to do his best to ease his daughter's predicament. He often took her for a ride in their horse carriage after most people had retired for the evening. They would ride to the port of Magdallah a few miles from Suryapuri. He did the most he could for his daughter without openly violating social norms. Your grandmother would look after you, Mary, when grandfather and Mrinal went for a ride to the port instead of asking one of the servants to take care of you. She would protect the family name from the servants' gossip about the secret ride to the port that would spread like wild fire." Granny smiled at this universal social quirk, gossip.

"On one such evening Mrinal saw a troop of Gypsies singing and dancing at the port saying farewell to an adventurous Gypsy family that was embarking on a cargo ship. Even for those nomadic Gypsies it was an unusual venture. The departing family would probably reach Arabia after a year. They might have to get off at another port. The ship, or the family, might run out of resources. But you know, nomads are ready for anything. Such is the nature of all journeys, theirs and ours. Unpredictable." Granny stopped to see Mary's response.

"You don't say Mrinal learned her dancing and singing from the Gypsies?" Papa was absorbing new information, connecting it with his own knowledge of Miriam's accomplishments.

Granny smiled, "Not really, Mrinal had had tutors for music and dancing since she was three. But that evening she said she was struck by the *freedom* these men and women exuded. Their songs, their voice, their movements expressed utter freedom. It touched her at the core, when she had lost all of hers."

"Do you say my grandparents agreed to let her go with the Gypsies?" Mary asked a little intrigued and impatient.

"Good heavens, no, of course not! They would never allow their precious daughter to leave on such an unheard of venture. Witnessing the expression of freedom was inspirational. After a few days of intense agony and thinking Mrinal worked out a plan. She spoke to the trusted horse carriage driver, who drove father and daughter to the port. The old man had been in her family's employ from the time before Mrinal was born. She said, 'Uncle, I need your help. It's a secret. Please do not let my parents know.'"

"Was he her uncle, a poor relative?" asked Mary.

Both Granny and Papa smiled, "Oh, no. That is a term of respect for an elderly servant who becomes a part of the family," said

Granny, and continued her narrative. "Mrinal said, 'Uncle, please help me for my daughter's sake and mine. Could you make a trustworthy contact with a migrating Gypsy family next time they are in town? Ask them if they can take me and my Mira' -that was your name, Mary - 'with them. I can pay them well.'

"The old man was shocked, no way was he going to demean himself to talk with those Gypsies. How could anyone trust them? 'No, Miss, I cannot do that. Please, don't ask. You cannot be safe with the Gypsies!!' Mrinal felt helpless.

"But destiny had another plan, it seems. The old man relented. Mrinal said she was surprised at his change of heart. It seems that during a couple of months the old driver noticed how Mrinal suffered. Ostracism of widows was no news to the old man. But he could hardly bear to see a young woman like Mrinal live her entire life in a virtual prison. Suffocation of a vibrant, independent, accomplished Mrinal was too much even for the illiterate poor old driver to bear. He agreed to contact the Gypsies next time they came to town."

"So the old man had to wait a couple of months for the next Gypsy family to arrive for the next ship?" Papa was fast getting a grip on the narrative.

"Yes, when you were six months old, Mary, one day...Mrinal wrapped you in a blanket and left home without her parents' knowledge. The old driver took you both to the port and the Gypsy family who had promised to take care of both of you. Well you know the rest. The Gypsy family had to go by land after a short sailing, like you will be doing soon, in the opposite direction, going to Magadallah. The Gypsy woman advised Mrinal to leave you here with me, Mary, for your safe upbringing," Granny concluded her narrative.

"So she had to leave me? Why would she then not leave me with my grandparents? Isn't that safer? Better? I don't mean I was unhappy here; don't get me wrong, Granny." Mary was confused.

"Yes, she could have left you with your grandparents, but that would mean leaving you forever. There was no way she could go back to her parents, ever, after she sailed away. It would be a social stigma, while leaving you here with me was a temporary arrangement. You were here till you were five, right?" Granny said gauging her reaction.

"Well, judging from what happened to Mrinal and Mira -- Miriam and Mary -- one would say it was all good, won't you agree, despite a few challenges on the way?" said Papa trying to relax.

"Did mother ever contact her family? Or did her family try to find us?" Mary was curious.

"The last time I asked her that question was when she came to fetch you. It was more than fifteen years ago, wasn't it? But she avoided answering it. Mrinal was too ashamed to leave her loving parents without telling them. She had disappointed her exceptional parents who had given her unusual opportunities in life to grow. She knew they would not have allowed her to leave with the Gypsy family or with anyone else for that matter. That would have been asking for much too much. I do not know what happened after she left. That part of the story died with her, I guess." Granny sighed.

All three sat silently for a long time watching the sun set behind the distant snow-peaked mountains. The somber evening glow healed their hearts, minds, emotions in that abode of love, *Prem Kunj*. All felt a distinct healing wave of love for Miriam ...a friend, mother, lover...now only a spirit. Would this hole be ever filled?

Chapter 17

Between two villages, away from the daily routine of village life was the *ashram,* hermitage. Mani sent Arun ahead to let the chief *rishi,* ascetic, know they had arrived. Isa was amazed by the number of tamed animals and birds the *ashram* had. Vast orchards of fruit and enormous patches of land, with herbs and vegetables, were colorful. Of course, Isa remembered, Mani's passion was Ayurvedic herbs, potions, and *aushadh,* medicine.

Many students were specializing as *pathaks,* reciters. They, like Arun, knew entire scriptures by heart and were walking reference sources. Many hermits who were trained to be temple priests were chanting ritual *mantras.* Others were chanting *mantras* to perform *yajna,* a ritual fire sacrifice. The whole hermitage was humming. Isa was to realize later that except from 9:00 at night to 3:00 in the morning the *ashram* was buzzing with various sounds and activities all day. Of course since the peacocks, cows and other animals did not follow the yogic clock, they sometimes became restless when humans got busy long before the cock crowed.

Within less than a week Isa was thoroughly absorbed in all activities of the *ashram.* It amazed him how effortlessly he blended the *ashram* routine of activity with motionless meditation. One day Isa was lost in a trance tending to a young mango plant. Another *ashramite* tapped Isa's shoulder to 'wake' him up. Isa did not know how long he had been working on that plant or in the garden. It was amazing to Isa how naturally he was getting absorbed in activities of a Vedic *ashram* or a Buddhist monastery. Why did it feel it was something he had always done or known before, he wondered?

At the center of the *ashram* was a temple of Shiva. Wasn't it Sriram who spoke of Shiva? Isa smiled; it was years back in the market place in Galilee. Shiva, the ultimate in dualism, the god of destruction was also the god of creation. Did not Sriram mention a similar paradox regarding Shiva's wife too? He said, "One of her forms is Parvati, the beautiful dancer and nurturing mother, the other is ferocious Kali, with long teeth, who wears a garland of human skulls. Kali is also all powerful *Shakti,* energy, more powerful than the gods who approach Kali for help when they are in trouble. In this form she even vanquishes her husband, Shiva." Isa remembered the hearty laugh of the crowd when Sriram described one of Kali's images with her husband under her dancing feet.

Isa smiled as he remembered these stories on his way to the temple. It was amazing how so many Indian stories were inherently dualistic. Multiple forms and traits, often mutually opposing, represented varied aspects of the *same* deity. He thought the juxtaposition of opposites gave a balanced perspective.

Lost in his thoughts, eyes on ground, Isa did not notice a huge bull passing by brushing his tail on Isa's white robe. Mani, approaching the temple from the other side, laughed and alerted absent-minded Isa, "Watch out, next time the bull might say 'hello' with his huge horns."

Isa laughed and said, "An experiential awakening initiated by Shiva's personal attendant! Not bad."

Both walked toward the entrance of the temple guarded by a stone image of a huge bull. Isa was fascinated that each major god and goddess had an animal or bird as a personal totem or vehicle, and people showed respect to those animals and birds as well. Following the general practice of showing respect, Isa touched the horns of the bull's stone image and then touched his head as he entered the temple with Mani. Mani joyously laughed, "You are becoming one of us, Isa!"

They entered the temple. At the altar was Shiva *lingam*, a cylindrical stone image, set in a curved circular stone ring, *yoni*, open at one end. From a disk above water flowed on the *lingam* and then through the channel of the *yoni*. For Isa it was not the familiar image of Shiva, a multi-armed dancer in a ring of flames he had seen in other temple carvings.

"Maniji, Is *this* Shiva different from the dancing Shiva and his *tandava* dance of destruction?"

"No. This is the creator aspect of Shiva. The phallic cylindrical shape symbolizes life. The ring at the base is symbolic of *yoni,* the female genital. The constant pouring of milk or water from the disk above is the nurturing life force. By performing daily *pooja,* ritual worship of Shiva, people celebrate life. Shiva is one of the most popular gods in our tradition." Mani's scientific mind would cut through all mythical jargon focusing on the essential symbolism of the creation process.

Isa observed people coming in for the *pooja* ritual. "This is a part of people's daily life. Look at the men, women and children bringing flowers, milk and fruits as an offering and receiving Shiva's blessings. They sound the temple bells, bow, pray, chant, and go home to their daily activities feeling protected by Shiva." Mani explained.

"Do people know the symbolism of the *lingam-yoni* and their own participation in the creative process?" Isa asked.

"Of course, they don't. It's an ancient ritual people follow. People pay homage to the divine for peace, prosperity, and protection, as people of different faiths do all over the world. It is difficult for laypeople to understand the abstractions and symbolism of ancient traditions. Scholars like me *analyze* them. Evolved *rishis,* seers, *feel* them in their being. For laypeople *lingam-yoni* are not even images. They are personified Shiva and Shakti, deified energy, for them. People have faith that their sincere adoration, reciting mantras, and performing rituals will protect them and bring them happiness." Mani elaborated the power of faith and dedication.

Isa was amazed, "Why not one god and one way of worship? Aren't such variations confusing for them?"

Mani smiled and asked, "Do you mean to say the immensity of the Divine Source can be reduced to one concept, one image, and one way of worship?"

"I believe in one God, who cannot be described or named." Isa said, "And I have no problem praying to that nameless source."

"Does the fisherman or an artisan in your village have the same awareness you have?" Mani asked.

"Surely not, that is why we have rabbis and priests speaking of God to masses of people" Isa mentioned the obvious.

"Didn't you tell me you argued with scholars or rabbis or some important personnel in the temple? What was that about?" Mani was intently looking at Isa.

"Oh that was because they were misinterpreting the Essence of holy teaching," Isa said.

"Then you admit truth can be interpreted differently depending on one's awareness and intent," Mani wanted to make sure their thinking was linked.

Isa said, "Sure. God is beyond total human comprehension, I have to admit no one can describe God in *words*. One can only *feel* Him within, and pray in one's own unique way."

Isa continued watching the stream of people coming for the *aarti*, the waving of lamps, accompanied by ringing bells and beating drums. People chanted *Om namah Shivay,* my homage to Lord Shiva. The piety, faith and devotion of people touched Isa profoundly. Their melodious chanting, rhythmic bells and drums drew him into a deeper consciousness.

At the end of *aarati* people waved their hands around the lamps and then touched their heads, a symbolic act of receiving divine blessings. After receiving blessings Isa and Mani too walked out of the temple and stood under the nearby banyan tree watching the men, women and children go home laughing and talking.

"Do you know, Isa, there is another paradox in yet another image of Shiva? It is called *Ardhanarishwar*, half man, half woman, the androgynous icon of gender balance."

Isa had not, yet. He realized the ancient *rishis* of this land had perhaps not left any logical stone unturned. He smiled. He was getting a grip over many stories he had once thought were a little far-fetched, even meaningless, fantasies. This conversation was certainly breaking new ground for him.

Now was the time for Isa to ask Mani a simple obvious question and hope to find an educated answer. "Why do Indians and Greeks, Egyptians and Romans have so many deities?" Isa asked.

Mani laughed, "I thought you would have figured that out by now. Belief in multiple gods is a product of distinct human needs. A panoply of gods and goddesses is essential to cater to varied individual awareness and needs. In our land we have three hundred and thirty three million deities." Mani and Isa both laughed heartily.

"Each person is caught up in a distinct situation, has multiple needs, and is at various levels of consciousness. Each one resonates with a specific deity, depending on his situation in life at a given time, creating a personal bond with that deity. It is similar to having different angels that protect you in travel, in sickness, and so on. But in our land everybody, educated or illiterate, knows *multiple gods are only varied aspects of essentially one Divine.* Like other paradoxes we talked about before, people have no problem integrating the *human* with the *divine* either. You know Krishna is at once human and divine, both man and god. It is a slightly different mindset from the Greek's, I believe." Mani explained.

"It's amazing how distinct cultures can create varied beliefs. I understand how in your land the ancient *rishis* concretized their insights and abstract concepts, even paradoxical ones, in distinctive images so lay people could comprehend them." Isa spoke, keeping his eyes on a little yellow wild flower by his feet. "But I do not understand another element."

"What would that be, Isa?" Mani was curious.

"If multiple concepts of the Divine are accepted as *one,* how come there are so many schools and sects within the same religion: Brahmanism, Buddhism, Jainism? Logically should they not accept all as valid? Why should there be such divisions at all?" Isa had a vague understanding of it but he needed Mani's explanation.

Mani concurred, "For a long time I had asked the same question. Often I used to get angry about the hair splitting *vivad,* scholarly debates, and perpetual subdivisions of schools. After much studying and thinking I realized that it is all about the limitations of *words.*" Mani's voice was sad.

"What do you mean? The Word *is* sacred. In the beginning was the *word.* Language is of utter importance. You do not agree?" Isa interjected.

"True, the *word* is the only tool we humans have to express thoughts, emotions, and experiences. That's why it is sacred. The *rishis,* seers, experienced the deepest truth. That was an authentic experience for them. But when they tried to capture *their experience* in words, they knew it was often not accurate nor complete. *A mystical experience translated into words always falls short of the actual.* You know the limitation of language, any language." Mani was matter of fact. "Out of this limitation emerges a conflict about whose word represents the truth. This process gives rise to debates of logicians, thinkers, and scholars resulting in sectarianism. It then becomes a matter of ego, power, and all that....and of course the rise of a new religion." Mani had spent years studying various texts and found them partial. Most were egocentric, he felt.

"Wouldn't such intellectual process hurt the original teaching, its authenticity, and even its simplicity?" Isa wondered.

"Inevitably it did, it does. And even worse it creates factionalism in the community. Politics of religion runs deep, becoming a power game. It is a game to control credulous crowds in the name of religion and god." Mani then spoke of religious imposition by outsiders. Colonization by the Romans was a good example.

Mani continued, "You know how Romans rule over you. The Roman military power controls vast masses of people in various parts of the world. Do you think if Hebrew people of your faith had political power over people of other religions they would treat others the way Romans treat you?"

Isa knew too well his people left Egypt under the leadership of Moses from the Pharaoh's rule centuries ago, and the Romans are now persecuting his Jewish community in Palestine. How many times his mother had told him the story of their narrow escape when he was an infant? He would have been killed with so many other children, had they not escaped to Egypt. Life goes in circles, Isa mused. Exodus from Egypt, exile back into Egypt! He smiled. Isa knew politics within his own religion too well. The temple priests in Jerusalem have been using it over his own people. Had he not already debated the priests on the temple steps years ago as Mani reminded him?

Isa realized there was much to think about. *Knowing* the divine within *has* to be posited in the context of the real world. It can't be dissociated from everyday life. Meditating in a cave may be calming, but the turmoil outside must be confronted. One needs to be a diplomat besides being a visionary, Isa was learning fast. One may have to pay any price for one's belief. The revolution of ideas can be accomplished only by co-opting people, not by excluding them.

There has to be a way out of injustice, cruelty, unfairness, and persecution into peace and mercy. To reveal the Divine in everyday life has to be the focus of his life. Isa was determined.

Mani saw Isa was lost in thoughts. He left the young man to ponder alone.

Chapter 18

Sailing on the ocean was a new experience for young Mary. Full of curiosity, anticipation, adventure, she was once again vivacious and joyful. Papa was delighted to see this renewed life in her...She had been a happy girl since he first saw her when she was nine. Once again she looked a child on a venture to a fairy land...Was it, Papa wondered, because she was 'going home?'

Staring at the receding shoreline, Mary's sparkling eyes had a vacant look. Her heart kept pace with the rhythm of the shuffling oars. The sails of *Avantika*, joyously puffed up as the wind soared. Mary ran to the front deck and stood open armed mimicking the sails, feeling the wind on her face, arms, feet, her entire being. What a delightful embrace! She started humming a love song breathing the salty air into her lungs and out of her nose. Oh, how azure blue the sky was. She was flying up there. As she soared higher, she heard another sound mingling with her humming. It was coming from the shining star not too far. And then she found herself floating toward that star...

"Isa....!"She uttered a gentle surprise at what she saw.

With arms outstretched and indescribable smiles on their lips the two flew toward each other, starlight beaming from their eyes.

The Captain of *Avantika* came to send Mary back to the interior for her safety, but stood entranced by what he saw, heard, felt in his bones, in his being. Is she *Samudra Devi,* the goddess of the Ocean, come to bless his ship – he wondered.

"What on earth..." Papa stopped in his tracks as he came out looking for Mary. Words froze on his lips; open mouthed he stood enchanted by what he saw, felt, heard -- a confluence of energies.

None knew for how long they were on the deck...

* * * * * * * * * * * *

Days rolled by keeping pace with the ship's movement. The Arabian ocean was calm gently ushering *Avantika.*

"In a few days we will be in Magdallah, Mary," one day Papa said, "What do you feel now that your dream to visit your homeland is becoming real?"

"I cannot think what to expect, Papa. But all days on the ocean so far have been like floating in a dream. I lost count of days. Even while doing the chores of cleaning and cooking with others, I have been floating in some other world..." Mary said, "It has been like living in two worlds at once, Papa."

Papa noticed a new note in her laughter. Wasn't it more musical? Ah, she was now a grown woman, he smiled. Her laughter was...well, more enticing. Or was it more mature? Certainly it was more melodious. Of that Papa was sure.

"You know Papa, I want to just see, feel, whatever comes. No plans. Could I go with you wherever you go if I feel like it?"

"Of course, am I going to leave you alone in a strange land?"

"You know, Papa" whenever she began with this phrase Papa knew he was going to hear something he did *not know.* "I would love to dress like the Indian woman. Could I?"

"Sure, we will buy a few garments when we arrive at the port. I will talk with the captain about the market days here. He may know some reliable vendor!" Papa was ready to indulge her. In fact, this was a perfect way to get acquainted with the untapped market. How naturally things were falling in place!

"You know Papa, one more thing, what if everybody called me Mira as long as we are in India. That was my name at birth, wasn't it?" Papa conceded with a twinkle in his eyes, what would he not do for this girl? Well, Miriam would be happy he was sure. His beloved wife's image was never too far away on this journey.

❅

Chapter 19

Purnam idam purnam adah
Purnat purnam udacyate
Purnasya purnam adaya
Purman eva avasisyate
Om Shanti, Shanti, Shanti

This is Perfect; that is Perfect;
Out of that Perfection emanates this Perfection;
In the ocean of Perfection surge the waves of perfection;
Yet that Perfection is never lost.
Peace, Peace, Peace.

The sky was dark. The sunrise was still a few hours away when the Vedantic chant awakened Isa. He had had a strange dream. Musing about it he got up and was soon absorbed in his daily routine of the *ashram*.

Lately his meditations were getting deeper after rigorous yoga practices. Even before he would complete his cycle of *pranayam*, breath control, and *dharana*, concentration, he went into *dhyan*, deep mediation, effortlessly; and stayed in it far longer than the training of a new initiate demanded. Sukumar, the chief disciple, had to often awaken him from *samadhi*, trance.

This morning during his routine practice, Isa recalled that last evening his trance was long... he did not know how long. All he remembered was what he envisioned. He was not sure if it was deep meditation *extending* into a dream or something else. Truly he did not care what to call it. But the vibrations were still strong, Isa wanted to remain in that place. He knew in his meditation he could reach a higher level. He remembered flying high and even becoming bright, almost like a star. What a blissful flight it was! Deep blue evening sky stretched as far as he could see. And then he heard a voice; turning his face in the direction of the voice he saw another star and heard a familiar voice calling his name, "Isa...."

With arms outstretched and indescribable smiles on their lips the two flew toward each other, star light beaming from their eyes.

Was this a dream? Was it a vision, a meditative state? Or was he in *samadhi,* a trance? Whatever...Isa felt Mary and he were connected...at a higher level of consciousness.

* * * * * * * * * * * * * *

"How are you doing Isa?" When he was washing a cow, Isa heard Mani's words as he entered the cowshed.

Isa had been in the *ashram* for almost six months.

"Well, *Vaidyaji*" Isa used the Indian address to add honorific 'ji' to an elder's name. He could not call Mani simply by his first name either. It was rude to ignore Mani's age and his status as a venerated *Vaidya.* "I am well. Practicing *pranayam,* breath control, and *ashtanga,* the eight limbs, yoga has helped. But repeated listening to recitation of Swami Patanjali's *Yoga Sutra* by the *pathaks,* reciters, has helped me increase my inner awareness enormously. I feel the chant in my being while I practice yoga."

Mani looked happy with Isa's progress. But more importantly it was visible in Isa's demeanor. "You have been here for a few months, almost a year? I am leaving soon for Takshashila, Taxila, farther north." Takshashila was the renowned university where scholars from all over the known world came to exchange ideas, learn and teach. "I would like you to go with me, unless your heart guides you elsewhere." Mani offered a choice. His timing was impeccable, as always.

"Surely, I have more questions *now* that I know so much more," Isa spoke with joyous laughter. Takshashila was the learning center he had always wanted to go to. Ever since Isa heard Sriram speak of it years ago Isa had wished he could go there someday. It was only a fourteen year old Isa's pipe dream then. It was now becoming a reality! And to be at this learning center with Mani, a well known scholar himself, that certainly was a miracle. Isa could hardly contain his joy. Was this an auspicious day or what, Isa wondered. While he was still gliding in the last night's flight with Mary, he got invited to go to his dream place, Takshashila!

"You seem very happy today. Is there a story behind it?" Mani was curious about a new verve in Isa's sprightly voice and gait.

"Oh, it's a long story. And as I said I have so many questions I want to ask you. But we can talk while we travel. Do you want to greet Guruji, and ask for his permission for me to leave with you while I finish my work in the cow shed?"

* * * * * * * * * * * *

Later that day Isa and Mani were walking toward the stream at the end of the *ashram*. Isa narrated his dream vision of the night before in which both Mary and he were kind of star people. "What do you think it means?" Isa asked.

Mani was impressed, but not surprised. He knew Isa and Mary have an exceptional cosmic connection over millennia. "Isa, do not be bogged down by theories of vision or dreams. What it means to you is what it is. As I have often said, leave the mind out of it. Do not over analyze your experience. Physically we live in linear time; at spirit level time and place are irrelevant."

"That's what I am telling myself. It was so blissful. I don't want it to fade away." Isa sounded like a twenty year old. But Mani knew the words came from a lot deeper awareness, though yet unconscious. It was another aspect of Isa and Mary's evolutionary experience, centuries old, eternal, infinite, connecting their other lifetimes. Mani kept quiet. Isa had to recognize and realize it himself. Mani changed the subject.

"You will be exposed to varied traditions in Takshashila. Religious and philosophical traditions range from meditative *samkhya,* knowledge based *jnana,* to feeling based devotion, *bhakti* are explored, discussed, and experienced at this center of learning. Buddhist and Jain traditions focus on human effort, as you know, bypassing the divine intervention. Then there is *vijnan,* special knowledge, that includes the study of earth, sky, nature, human body, animals, plants, birds, everything humans can perceive. You know my special interest is in research in *Ayurveda,* the science of life. I also check out new findings in astronomy, mathematics, and geometry. I go there regularly to keep up with every possible branch of learning." Mani expanded on the nature of Takshashila Vidyapith, University.

Of course Isa had heard of this fascinating center of learning back in Persia and visiting it was god-send. He was excited. People in this land translated religious, philosophical approaches into everyday social life, much like his own Jewish traditions. The difference was that his people had migrated in different lands with Abraham, Moses, and the patriarchs. Did such migrations make a difference, Isa wondered. A long continuous history of cultural evolution is bound to be complex, he was sure. Oh, his questions for Mani were multiplying every minute. His eagerness and enthusiasm to know more was evident in his walk, his smile, but most of all in his eyes, Mani noticed.

Chapter 20

As the ship sailed eastward, the serene sunrise charmed Mary, now often called Mira. Every day she would get up early and stand on the front deck to pay homage to the source of light and life. The sun had become a living entity for her. She would be lost in its glory, feeling it was guiding her steps.

This morning the captain's assistant, a young *brahmin*, was offering a prayer of gratitude as the ship was nearing the harbor.

Om bhurbhuv svah Tatsavituvarenyam,
Bhargo devasya dhimahi Dhiyoyonah Prachodayat

May we meditate on the effulgent Light, the supreme,
All bliss, Source of Life, Dispeller of Suffering;
May he direct our intellect
toward the benevolent goal of our life.

Had Mira not heard this *mantra* before? She wondered. Where could it have been? Was it at Granny's? Or did her mother sing it? The Vedic mantra transported her into a trance. For a long time Mira was lost in an enchanted world.

It was Papa's hand on her shoulder, "We need to get ready to disembark, Mary...umm... Mira."

Opening her eyes from a deep dream, she smiled, "Yes, Papa."

* * * * * * * * * * * *

A few hours later...

"You look fabulous, Mira. Now I cannot even by mistake call you Mary. You look absolutely Indian." Papa laughed joyfully as Mira came out of the vendor's cottage where his wife helped Mira dress in deep pink sari, with red *choli*, blouse, over a richly embroidered deep green colorful skirt. On her arms bracelets spread three inches thick and a richly decorative necklace lay heavy on her breasts. The hanging earrings tinkled competing with the jingling anklets as Mira came nearly running, even stumbling a little on the way.

"On my life... you have even the red mark on your forehead, girl. Did you get married while I was looking the other way?" Papa merrily laughed shaking Mira's shoulders. "Let me look at you. Do I know you?" With Mira's giggle, Papa's loud laugh, and the vendor-family's smiles the first venture in Magdallah began.

"If you like this outfit so, maybe you will buy more to sell in Babylon, I can be your model sales girl," Mira joked.

"Let's not get carried away." Papa could not take his eyes off her. Mary had literally transformed into Mira.

"Let's explore this port town." Papa suggested. They went walking through vendor's stalls and into narrow streets with small houses of fishermen. Alongside the main street was a guest house with friendly owners. Papa found this humble abode quite comfortable to spend one night.

The next day he hired a bullock cart to go to Suryapuri, the famous commercial center in this region and his intended business center. The carter, Ballu, was a multilingual interpreter, not unusual in market places in port towns.

They passed by vast orchards lining the road with lush *papadi* beans, bananas, mango trees, and oranges, followed by groves of peanuts, eggplants and acres of fields of wheat, barley, and *juwar*. Unfamiliar colors, shapes, and aroma of vegetation excited Mira. Papa was impressed by the abundant crop.

The tinkling bells on oxen's horns and the loud ones around their necks became a bit quieter as they slowed approaching the city. On the outskirts of Suryapuri, houses were large with ample flower gardens and fruit trees. Both houses and gardens became smaller in the city but they were beautiful works of architecture. Carved pillars, decorated windows, and neatly tiled roofs made the houses charming. Watchmen and servants buzzed around, horse carriages came and went. Common people were on foot or in bullock carts. Aristocratic women were carried in *palakhi,* litter, by four men. Smaller litters had two carriers. It was a busy city.

Ballu pointed out family homes of famous men as they passed by their mansions. One *haveli,* manor, belonged to a well known *jamindar,* landowner, with a hundred contracted laborers. That was impressive. "Very rich," Ballu said, "and look at this beautiful garden here. The owner is a lawyer. He is very fair and takes care of poor people, not like those who always favor the upper caste and rich." Mira and Papa were getting a cultural tour of this town.

The king's palace was stunning. "Colorful marble decorates the floor and pillars. The main door of pine wood and iron is twelve inches deep. Do you see the image of Ganesh, the elephant headed god who removes obstacles, at the center of the floral carving on the front door?" Ballu was describing the palace with a native's zeal to his foreign visitors.

At the center of the city was a famous temple of Durga, the mother goddess. Its richly decorated carved pinnacle rose high up in a conical shape. Durga's *dhaja,* flag, fluttered atop a golden pot shining brightly in the midday sun.

"Could we go into the temple?" Mira asked. Papa was not sure if it was a good idea. Stories of caste restrictions made everyone wary.

"Oh sure, you can go in," Ballu said to Mira, "Let me check with the *pujari,* the chief *brahmin.*"

Without waiting for an answer Ballu pulled up the reins, stopped the cart, and ran into the temple.

Mira and Papa waited, they were engrossed in watching people in colorful garb coming for *darshan,* seeing, Durga Ma. They brought flower garlands, coconut, red powder, and fruit as offering. At the temple entrance they bent, touched the threshold and then their heads to show respect. They rang the bell and prayed. People came and went.

Ballu came back. "Yes *pujari maharaj,* the chief ritual priest, says you can come in. We will stand at the end of the jostling crowd to watch *aarati,* the waving of lights. After *aarati,* he will bring you close to Durga Ma. No one except the *pujari* can go closer." Evidently Ballu had arranged for a special treat with the chief of the temple.

Mira was excited. Papa was cautious. He had heard such strange things about Indian practices and customs. And everything seemed so confusing and different. He could never figure out what to make of such a plethora of information. But with Ballu's help everything went smoothly. Standing there in the open yard, slightly away from the huge crowd, Mira looked at Durga in all her glory, riding a lion, sword in one of her eight hands, blessing people with another, holding a water pot in the third... She had a shining crown on her head, was dressed in a beautiful red sari. Gold, diamond and pearl jewelry decorated her arms, nose, ears, and anklets. Even the crown on her head glittered with red, blue, and yellow sapphire. A radiant smile on her face blessed her devotees. The *pujari* waved the five lamp *aarati* in circular motion in adoration of Durga. Other *pujaris* rang huge hanging bells, metal rattles, and cymbals; drummers beat drums, people sang and clapped.

The rhythm of drums and bells and music opened up another reality for Mira. Light, sound, vibration transported her into a magical trance as she stood against the wall. With open eyes she was looking into another world.

Papa was speechless. He never knew bells, drums, and singing of the adoring crowd would move him. Frankly, he was expecting to be irritated.

When the *aarati* ended, Ballu who was singing hymns with the rest of the crowd approached them, "Do you want to go in the interior?"

Mira still felt a little dizzy, "Let's go, Papa." Papa followed.

The chief *pujari* explained various symbols of Durga, the achiever, a benevolent aspect of Mother Goddess. "Her eight arms suggest her multiple power and varied tasks she can perform to protect her children. The fierce aspect of the goddess is Ma Kali. She insists on our facing our fears so we may evolve. She looks fearful, the destroyer of evil. Here you see Ma Durga is seated on her vehicle, the lion, whom she controls, encouraging us to control our animal instincts. With a sword she defeats all adverse forces reminding us we can do the same. Often our own weaknesses are our adversaries. She is the gentle, nourishing mother giving us the water of life. That is her water pot." The *pujari* pointed at the decorated pot in one of her eight hands.

"Different names and forms of goddesses are only varied *aspects* of the same divine *Shakti,* energy. She is another aspect of Parvati, the beautiful consort of Shiva. She is also called Amba, mother, in her absolute love for us. All seeming variations converge into *One.* If you have any more questions feel free to come here any time. Ballu will arrange for a meeting. Jai Durga, hail Mother Durga." He folded his palms saying *namaste.* Mira, Papa, and Ballu did the same. Ballu bent down to touch *pujari's* feet the traditional way. Then they left.

Mira walked silently gathering her thoughts and feelings, nurturing her inner self. Papa was quiet trying to assimilate the wealth of information and experience.

Chapter 21

Once they set their pace on the way to Takshashila, Isa said, "That was quite an experience, Maniji. I now realize how deep *tantric yoga* is, amazing."

Mani was curious, "Tell me what was different for *you* in this experience."

"It was the depth of experience; reaching the maximum boundaries of my awareness through physical perceptions and sensations. It was not losing the body self. In a curious way it was merging of the body and spirit in total reality, a sort of expansion." Isa was looking upward as if words were floating toward him from outer space.

His words reassured Mani that the direction of Isa's journey was correct. The time too was precise, Mani thought. The conjunction of stars and planets influences individual's journeys on earth. Astrologically, perhaps at the time of Isa's birth stars and planets were in a significantly favorable place. Such intuitive knowledge had guided Mani to orchestrate Isa's journey ever since they first met in the caravan on the border of Afghanistan. Having recognized Isa's essence, without making it too obvious, Mani had been directing Isa's steps, though always letting the young man make the choice.

With a gentle smile Isa said, "Maniji, I used to get mad about people's incongruous behavior, especially the behavior of those who are supposed to guide others, like priests and rabbis. Now I am more tolerant, because I understand the true essence of dualism."

"It always helps to keep an open mind, Isa," Mani spoke, "Observe everything patiently, and you will find *your own* answers. I used to ask similar questions when I was growing up. But after many years of skeptical questioning, and yelling, and eventually growing, I concluded: One, *dharma* varies with each individual depending on each one's level of consciousness; two, depending on one's resonance each one chooses a personal deity and/or path. But know that all lead to the same goal, liberation.

"At this time this is enough for you to ponder, Isa. I want you to draw your own conclusions. You may reject some of my conclusions. I hope you do. That is good. Our Indian philosophies hardly discard anything totally. Your experience in Takshashila will further demonstrate this truth. There is no one central philosophical system to control us; we retain our freedom to think, debate, act, and create our path. The price we pay is confusing complexity. However, a divine order is the basis of this seeming chaos. To find it and live it is *my* journey. In you I notice a similar urge, fellow traveler." Mani's eyes sparkled with delight. Despite their difference in age, both felt deep connectedness in this moment.

"You are a real *vaidya,* physician, Maniji, a genuine healer. Your words are wondrous; your diagnosis of the disease of the body, mind, and spirit is so accurate. I feel healed," Isa felt light, some of his confusion dissipated.

Now to their onward journey....

Days rolled by...they camped, rode, ate, sang, told stories. Villagers came to trade goods, share the food, and receive herbs and advice from Mani for the sick in body and mind. Isa learned the ways of village life, not too different from those in his homeland. Details varied, of course. But the spirit of cooperation and mercy, or disputes, was similar.

Villagers were amused by Isa's questions, especially when he asked about their dress, temples, and gods or goddesses or their cows. Why does he ask? Some wondered. Doesn't he know? He is a grown man.

"He is like a child," an old man said in a deep voice. His eyes sparkled as he kept looking at Isa intensely.

❀

Chapter 22

Ballu had arranged for Mira and Papa's lodgings in Suryapuri with a family that took travelers as guests. That night Mira slept well. After a long time on the road and the ocean, she felt relaxed, at home.

It was early morning. The sun was not up yet; Mira heard sparrows twitter by the little terrace with a low roof hanging over it outside her room. She looked at the river Tapi gently splashing against the wall below the window. The small house was built high up on the rampart which was once a part of the city's active fortress wall built to fend against floods and foes. For a long time Mira vacantly gazed at the blue grey sky. The dawn was painting it pink.

The first rays of the sun hit her eyes, forming a triangle between the sun and her two eyes. She felt the vibrations of the river in her being; its flowing sound rang a constant 'hum...' She stared vacantly....at nothing.

Tap...tap... a light knock on the door brought Mira back into the room...A young servant boy was standing at the door with folded palms, "Breakfast is ready, Sister. Mother would like you to come downstairs when you wish."

"We will be down soon. Let me see if Papa is up," Mira went to check on the other side of the wooden partition. It was a huge room, as wide as the house, and was divided by an elaborately carved wood partition. Wasn't that a wonderful intricate carving of circles, hexagons and triangles? She liked it more than the usual flowers and bird patterns she had seen so far. Every time she passed by it, her eyes glued on it.

"I am ready. Let's go down. What a peaceful place this is, Mira," Papa was soaking in the cool, gentle, early morning breeze.

"You have such a beautiful house, *Sriman* (Sir), *Sriamti* (Madam)," Papa was elated by this regal cottage -- called a cottage because of its small size. Everything inside was regal, artistic, tastefully decorated and well preserved. Papa guessed, rightly, their hosts were special people.

"We are blessed by Krishna's grace and blessings!" Vallabhdas, the host, joined his palms in gratitude to Lord Krishna. Kunti, his wife, greeted Mira and Papa with *namaste*, and led them to their wooden seats on the floor in the dining hall. The seats had decorative carved backs, normally used in aristocratic homes.

"Malini, start serving breakfast," Kunti called the cook.

"Have you seen much of our city? There is a lot to know about this ancient place. It has a long history." As a leading member of the aristocratic community Vallabh knew the history of Suryapuri well. Princes and kings perpetually had land deals with aristocrats. Landlords were involved with tenants in any number of complex contracts. Inevitable were the issues of succession. Vallabh's father had acres of agricultural land, and a flourishing business at the port with contacts with ships coming from distant lands. Law and politics were Vallabh's specialty, over and above the joint family businesses he shared with his brothers.

"A long time back in Babylon I had heard of Suryapuri and its glory. It seems we have come to the most amenable and well informed, generous and refined hosts who can enlighten us." Papa's words kind of multiplied, as he found a compatible conversational partner in his host. Mira gave a knowing smile, ready for an interesting dialogue.

Kunti saw Mira was pecking, "*Beti,* daughter, don't you like *khir?*" It was rice pudding. "Shall I get something else for you? Malini, bring some *puri* and *khakhara,*" Kunti called for other items in the bread variety without waiting for Mira's response.

"Oh no, *Maji,*" Mira used the common term of respect for the elderly hostess, "I like *khir.* Please do not get me anything else. I am too excited to eat." Mira knew *khir* as her mother often made it. But, she kept quiet about that.

"It seems you like our kind of dresses and jewelry. I suppose you got them here?" Kunti was admiring this 'foreigner' in native attire and jewelry.

After breakfast the two men got busy talking about business, art, history, and politics as they moved from the dining room to the parlor.

Mira asked if she could go to the river bank for a walk. "Surely, Manek let us go to the river. Bring my sandals and another pair for our guest." She called Mailini's husband, Manek, who was the watchman, gardener, horse carriage driver rolled into one. Aristocratic women did not go out unescorted, a sign of class but also of security. Mira did not expect Kunti to go with her, "No *Maji,* please do not exert yourself because of me."

"It's my pleasure, *Beti.* I walk there once a day when Manek has time. Sometimes your *Pitaji,* (father)," referring to Vallabh, whom according to custom she could not address by his first name, "goes with me in the evening. We often watch the sun's journey to the west." Kunti sounded quite emotional. Or was it Mira's imagination?

Mira was tickled by Kunti's words "your *Pitaji* (father)." Ballu had once elaborated on this custom in this part of the world with great sense of humor. It is brash impoliteness for an upper class woman to address her husband by his name. The husband is always referred as "he," or "your master," or "your brother," or "your father" depending on who the woman was talking to. Depending on the listener's age, relationship or station, the term varied from: son, father, brother, friend, elder, master to numerous in-law relations. An older man is often addressed as 'father' for all.

Manek arrived with two pairs of walking sandals. All marched out by the back garden door on the walkway to the river bank. Manek was following the women, almost twenty feet behind them.

"That is the new city wall in the east." Kunti continued pointing at the extension of the fortress, "When this old rampart was in disuse, your *Pitaji* bought this royal cottage. It was built for the *sena nayak,* the army chief, when he needed to stay here on duty." Kunti gave a little peak into the city's history connected to personal story, "Your

Pitaji acquired it almost ten years ago. We have lived in it for five. We have had many visitors from distant lands." Kunti took a breather. The morning breeze was pleasing, but a little too cool for her. She pulled her shawl tighter.

"Are you comfortable, *Maji?* We can go back if it is chilly for you," Mira said.

"Oh no, I am fine, *Beti.* You took Indian name too with your outfit? That is cute." Kunti was amused by modern young foreigner's whims. Would an Indian girl her age do what Mira is doing? She wondered...she was lost in thoughts...fell silent for a while.

Mira too was lost in her reverie. How beautiful and broad the river Tapi was. Big ships sailed all the way in here. Mira wondered if their ship to Magdallah could have anchored here. As they walked more, they could see the active harbor. "Woohoo...Look at those big ships. So many! Suryapuri is a big city, even bigger than Petra, perhaps." Mira was thinking of one of the major trading centers she had heard of.

"You surely have travelled a long distance at a young age, *Beti.* I admire that." Kunti was curious about those distant lands.

"Let's go back, *Maji.* Next time I will come with Papa. He may even go visit the main harbor."

Chapter 23

It was easy to engage in a debate; it hardly ever remained a conversation in Takshashila. All who came there, from everywhere in the civilized world, were learned, or wanted to be. *Almost* all thought they were experts.

Isa was amused as he found himself debating every time he said anything to anybody. Mani had deliberately kept quiet on this point. As always, he wanted Isa to observe and draw his own conclusions.

"I am from the Platonic school, Demetrius by name, which school do you belong to?" a pompous young man accosted Isa near *Tattvajnan pathshala*, School of Philosophy.

"I am a seeker. Isa is my name. I belong to the school of life." Isa said humbly.

"Who is your *guru*?" Demetrius was not interested in this late bloomer, who looked nearly twenty-two and seemed to have no clue what he was doing.

"I have learned from many Essene teachers in my home land in Galilee, and eminent scholars in my travels through Persia, Afghanistan, to the Punjab and now Takshashila. Some of my teachers have been thinkers, rabbis, Socratic scholars, fire worshipper Persians, followers of Zarathustra, *yogis, sramans,* Jain monks, *munis,* Buddhist monks, *bhaktas,* devotees, or even an *ayurvedic* medicine man." Isa recounted his journey of almost six years. "In Persia, I was exposed to Greek learning too, although I have not yet traveled to your land," Isa gave his credentials.

Unimpressed Demetrius said, "Not adhering to one path you lay waste your energies, Isa."

"What brings you here away from your Platonic school? Are you not deviating in seeking knowledge from others? Or are you here only to impart what you know?" Isa asked noting the obvious contradiction in Demetrius' statement.

"I gain knowledge and information from many scholars. For philosophical mystical search I adhere to Platonic teachers." The Greek said with an air of one who knows. Did Isa notice a touch of ego?

"Demetrius, I am curious. Since you have many years of learning, have you found parallel ideas, methods, symbols, attitudes in different traditions? Something that you learned in Greece you re-discover here in India?" Isa was curious.

"That may happen because Takshashila is a world *vidyapith,* center of learning. Many scholars come here and then teach in different parts of the known world. Intellectual *exchange* in this place is incredible. Many Jain, Buddhist and Vedantic scholars, sages, monks I have been exposed to or have heard about are independent thinkers. Their logic fascinates me." Demetrius seemed genuinely impressed by the level of scholarship, investigative instinct, and mastery over complex systems of thought.

"Their annual debate sessions," Demetrius said, "are not restricted to Takshashila, but take place all over the land, in many a learned king's courts and *ashrams* of famous sages."

Isa was especially interested in the antiquity of scientific and mathematical aspects of yoga, He asked, "What do you think of *samkhya?* Sage Kapil elaborated it almost eight centuries ago, they say. Did Pythagoras in Greece also not teach similar concepts two centuries after that? Do you think Pythagoras could have learned the *samkhya* of *Sage* Kapil?" Isa was unsure.

"It is possible, since Indian and Greek scholars often met in Persia. That empire has been an influential seat of cultural and business exchange. My teacher in Platonic School believes, Pythagoras and Heraclitus both were exposed to Indian philosophers, mathematicians and theorists. Socrates, Plato, Aristotle regularly communicated with other scholars in this area. " It was obvious Demetrius was an eager researcher.

Isa said, "I am particularly impressed by the Indian thinkers' analysis of three aspects controlling human behavior: *sattva,* the truth, the essence, *rajas,* the force empowering action, and *tamas,* indolence. Human action reflects a continuous interplay of these three."

"Not just that but the two fundamental forces of creation: *Purush,* Spirit, and *Prakriti,* the primordial Nature, are elaborately analyzed by Vedic sages. *Purusha* and *Prakriti,* the masculine and the feminine aspects, reflect the all pervasive essential dualism of life. These r*ishis* are called seers and they truly are genuine scientists." Demetrius elaborated the interplay of dualism and non-dualism in Indian thinking.

"How do you adjust your Platonic theories with the Vedic and other schools of philosophy?" Isa was curious.

"In Greece before Plato the emphasis was more on the material world. Plato introduced the ideological reality claiming the real thing is in the universal mind, somewhere beyond the material world we know. The real thing is the 'idea' of the object. So in a way he was closer to non-dualism. I am inclined to see the reality in its totality, both the ideological and its material copy." Demetrius sounded very reasonable to Isa, despite his initial arrogant behavior. Perhaps he was cooled down by the genuine innate intelligence of Isa. Demetrius concluded, "That's why the theory of reincarnation that allows the soul to reach liberation through actions, *karma,* sounds logical and hence acceptable to me. Well, *mitra,* friend, you are in the right place if cultivation of the mind is your aim."

Isa was happy with this exchange, though cultivation of the mind was not his sole objective. They bowed to each other, Isa said, "Glorious be your search, Demetrius, *namaskar.*"

"May your path be smooth," blessed Demetrius. And they parted.

The next few days revealed to Isa an amazing world of learning in varied fields: astronomy, archeology, warfare, the military, physics, agriculture, medicine. Numerous scholars constantly interacted across disciplines. Isa visited each school and got engaged in conversations with teachers and interns.

But too much intellectual engagement stilted Isa's inner sensitivity. Each evening he went to the secluded grove at dusk to witness the sunset and ponder its beauty. His habitual dusk walks were his healers.

This evening as he watched the splendid pink blue sky, its vastness benumbed him. He was amazed by the wonderfully creative human mind, its skills and its persistence. What a tool humans have. With his mind he can traverse the outer world as well as scan the inner. Each human makes a little dent in this churning, pulsating life, he thought. But to what end?

He sat with his eyes closed...hours passed....he was motionless. The moon rose and set. The night was quite cool. Isa was still sitting, motionless. Hours later, Mani came looking for him. It was past midnight. Isa's body was cold. Had he stopped breathing? Mani checked his feeble pulse. Touching Isa's chakras in various parts of his body, Mani activated his pulse. Isa opened his eyes with a distant look. He was calm, unruffled.

"How do you feel, Isa?" Mani could only guess what Isa had experienced...

"You know where I have been, Maniji." Isa spoke with a voice emerging from immense depth. It came from another dimension.

Chapter 24

It was evening; Mira and Papa were having dinner with Vallabh and Kunti.

"How was your day, Pharaoh?" Vallabh asked Papa. Now that he knew Papa was from Egypt Vallabh called him Pharaoh. They had become quite friendly. Often their conversations went way into late nights over fermented barley brew or grape juice. Vallabh called the tender coconut palm fermentation *soma* juice, after the famous *soma,* the intoxicant of gods.

Today Papa was especially happy; he was all smiles, "The day was productive and special. Ballu, I have to say, is very resourceful." Papa admired Ballu's ability to produce intended results, be it sightseeing or business deals. Ballu's pragmatism suited Papa's work habits.

"I knew it the first day we met," said Mira laughing her ever enchanting musical laughter, "Ballu is a perfect match for Papa. I have to say we save time. Before Papa completes his sentence, Ballu and his oxen are on their way to run the errand. Ballu even thinks for Papa." She laughed again.

Papa burst into a hearty laugh as he narrated the story, "Especially today, Ballu surpassed himself, I have to admit. As you know Seth Ratanram deals in many expensive items including precious stones and fine muslin fabric. Both are favorites of Roman women; they crave these items. If I make this deal my entire trip will be a grand success. So I was thinking of walking to Seth's office, instead of showing up in a bullock cart and ruin my chances." Ratanram was an eminent business magnet in this area.

"When I was buying some ointments and perfumes," Mira sounded funny as she had a big piece of sweet *laddu* in her mouth, "Ballu went away for an hour or so, and came back with this stylish horse carriage and himself in a uniform with a turban and a scarf. I could not stop laughing. We did not recognize him for a second. 'Is that you Ballu?' I screamed."

"I had my ride to Ratanram Seth's *pedhi*, in full regalia of an Egyptian dignitary." Papa could not stop laughing.

"So did you strike the business deal, Pharaoh?" Amused Vallabh was eager to know.

"It looks good. We will know for sure in a few days. Do you have an important festival coming up? Some *pedhis* are closed for the celebration." Papa was not sure if such holidays were good for business.

"*Maji* , Ballu said tomorrow is a special day, Krishna's birthday. Can we go to Krishna's temple? It was blissful when we went to Durga's temple the first day we came to Suryapuri." Mira wondered if it was possible to witness another, perhaps different ritual.

"Surely we will go to the Krishna temple for *darshan*, and even more. We will have *pooja* ritual here in our home. We will put baby Krishna in a cradle at midnight, place toy figures of cows, peacocks, birds and such all around; some toy figures of *gopal*, cowherd, and *gopi*, cowgirl, too. Decorate Krishna's cradle with flowers, gold and silver ribbons. Put decorative lamps...We will sing *bhajans*, hymns, have *kirtan*, devotional music. And then we will offer a lot of goodies -- sweets, fruits, milk to Krishna which we will enjoy as *prasad*, grace, later in the day. Oh it is a lot of fun, you will enjoy it." Kunti was excited for this annual celebration. With foreign visitors the event would be even better: Kunti would do more, talk more. She was energized.

"So you will get up late next morning, I believe," Papa asked Vallabh, "It seems all businesses observe this big holiday."

"Oh yes, no business. But that does not mean a late morning. The day after Krishna's birth is the day of celebration. God is born to help humans. People, mostly young men, will pretend they are Krishna's cowherd friends. They will re-enact Krishna's childhood games in the street, pour colored waters on each other, scream, laugh, dance, and have fun. It will be a noisy morning with music and dancing in the street all over the city. You can't sleep late, even if you want to. Too noisy." Vallabh's eyes shone as he remembered all the fun he had on the streets as a young man.

"So people in every town do it all over the land?" Papa was amazed.

"Almost everywhere, however in important places like Vrindavan and Mathura, Krishna's birth place in north of India, the celebrations are even more elaborate. Pilgrims come from all over. To be honest, people here in Suryapuri are known for finding an excuse to celebrate anything and stretch a bit more for fun." Vallabh said with a twinkle in his eyes.

"Do you remember Papa, Granny said that people of Suryapuri are exceptionally warm, kind, fun loving, and friendly? Outsiders feel at home. She was right, I must say." Mira said looking gratefully at her hosts.

"Who is Granny? How does she know?" asked Kunti.

"Oh, that will take a whole evening- maybe some other time. I am exhausted. Are you ready for bed, Mira?" Papa spoke getting up from the *gaddi,* thick mattress, on a stone slab strewn with rounded pillows and a decorative sheet.

Papa and Mira went upstairs to their quiet room. Mira was full of excitement. The whole day had been one adventure after the next. It took her a while to quiet down. Suryapuri was a special place, she thought.

Listening to the splashing ripples of the Tapi, she slowly fell asleep.

She dreamt...

It is dark all around. She is flying. It is soothing. The farther she flies the darker it gets. Then all is pitch darkness; it cannot be blacker. Brilliant suns and stars in different galaxies are only dots of light in infinite darkness. All is right, though nothing seems as she knew it so far.

Light as breeze, she flies, though there is no air.
Light cannot lighten the dark surroundings,
Light in weight cannot shine, but can fly

Life is meaningless without death
Death is only another shape of life
Darkness is yet another color of light.

She keeps flying, humming these lines. On a shining planet hanging in space, she descends. In the middle is a gazebo with an altar at its center. On a crystal throne on the altar is an orb, neither solid nor immaterial. Multicolored energy strings constantly move in it. The orb is Shakti, energy, Prakriti, *primordial nature. She stands glaring at the orb. A beam of light* Purusha, spirit, *falls from the pinnacle of the gazebo piercing the orb.*

Amazed she stands. By her side stands Isa. Both are dressed in flowing shimmering gowns staring into this vibrant orb. A ray of light emanates from the orb and pierces into their eyes forming an interlaced dual triangle.

Chapter 25

Isa roamed in mountainous Takshashila for over a year. Mani was busy at the Ayurvedic School sharing his findings, teaching, and investigating new research. Isa often compared this fascinating place of exchange with those market places in Arabia and Egypt, centers of world trade in ideas and goods.

He smiled at the resemblance of activity in the most unlikely two places, the Arabian market place and the valley school of learning in the foothills of the Himalayan mountain range. Both were in the vicinity of the international trade route, of course, going all the way to China. Isa wondered how people of different lands cooperated, exchanging knowledge and goods. Such positive exchange can easily slide into areas of conflict, domination, greed for land and power. People repeatedly engaged in conflicts, battles and wars. How does one resolve such dualism of human nature? Can one? Isa was lost in thoughts of lust for power. Humans are perpetually suspended between the two polarities of divine creativity and demonizing self-interest. Is that not the constant struggle between good and evil that Zarathustra spoke of? Isa knew it as the strife between God and Satan within each of us. They are not two distinct adversaries. Both live in us. The trick is to choose whom we would allow to conquer.

All this time Mani was engaged in researches connected with potions, herbs, pastes, oils and such. He was specially focused on herbs for reviving the dead. Various kings, *ksatraps, nayakas* chieftains and vassals were looking to *revive* their dead, or nearly dead, warriors. Constant battles all over the known world had made this discovery an important object of research. These sages truly were *vijananis,* scientists, Isa thought once again. Their questioning minds never stopped amazing him.

Isa remembered one of the legends Mani had shared with him. The legendary guru Sukracharya, an ancient sage for the *Asuras*, demons -- *Devas'* adversaries -- had invented *sanjivani vidya*, knowledge to revive the dead. According to tradition, the *Devas* sent one of their heroes, King Yayati, disguised as a poor *brahmin* to learn this science.

Isa asked, "So did Sukracharya teach Yayati how to revive the dead?"

"Sure, he trusted this brilliant young *brahmin*. But Yayati could not use his knowledge."

"How so?" Isa was curious.

"As the story goes Sukracharyas' daughter Devyani fell in love with Yayati during his three years stay in the *ashram*. Both were deeply in love. So at the completion of his training, when Yayati had to leave, Devyani, insulted by his disguise and duplicitous behavior, cursed him, 'You will not be able to use this *vidya.'* Hence the *Devas* never profited by their secret ploy." Mani said raising his eye brows with a smirk.

"And you are trying to reinvent it?" asked Isa amusedly. "I am amazed by people's constant curiosity and ability to adapt, search, evolve, in matters of the body, heart, mind, matter, spirit." Isa continued, "I am happy we met and I decided to come with you to India, Maniji." Isa reiterated.

Mani was pleased. He had a deeper inkling about Isa's advanced awareness. That recognition had originally prompted Mani to get Isa released from Castos, the caravan chief, almost seven years ago. Mani was happy to recognize that varied experiences were converging to raise Isa's consciousness even more.

Holding debates with students was interesting and challenging for a short time for Isa. But he preferred to listen to the *sages'* discourses in various disciplines. Mani's connections made it possible for him to go to varied discourses of eminent scholars in all branches of learning. Sage Shankar's discourses on Consciousness -- *chitta* -- were substantial. He explored levels of consciousness as defined by diverse schools in Hindu, Buddhist, and Jain traditions. The list was long, and Isa thought, a little too complex, though he did not disagree with the underlying logic of each.

After almost six months of going to Shankar's discourses, Isa felt, he had to stop listening or talking. It was a lot of intellectual acrobatics. He needed to practice what he was drawn to, listening to the inner silence. Students were required to spend certain hours in the early morning *dhyan,* meditation. But that was not enough. He needed to calm the overcharged intellect. He withdrew from discourses to be in *dhyan* focusing on *shunya,* emptiness, as the Buddha did.

* * * * * * * * * * * *

At the assigned time of their meeting every two months, Isa met Mani in their favorite grove at the outer edge of town, away from the center of the *Vidyapith.* The early morning cool air and chirping birds announced the arrival of spring. All nature was celebrating this change, more visible here -- more welcome too—in this northern snowy terrain.

"How do you define *compassion,* Maniji?" Isa asked looking at the distant snow laden mountain ranges. These were some of the highest mountain peaks in the known world.

"You know the Buddhist texts..." Mani started.

"No...no...I have heard enough about all those teachings in discourses. I am familiar with Sage Nagasena's teachings in both Mahayana and Theravada schools, and their disputes. Some I know by heart. I want to know what *you experience,* not just *know* from scriptures. I feel compelled to translate *knowledge* into *action.*" Mani was elated. Isa was asking right questions, as he expected.

"So my *compassion* could be stretched farther and farther." Isa continued, "If I was a Buddhist my own *dharma, svadharma* would take a whole different turn on the mental, emotional and spiritual levels."

"But you are a Jew. So you have to create your own definition of *love* and *compassion* relevant to your time, place, and situation." Mani spoke of the inner intelligence, not of the mind but of the heart, the *being...*

Isa now looked at Mani, "So *compassion* does not mean one *agrees* with the other person or *feels* his emotions? Does it? I will have a hard time condoning, for instance, Alexander of Macedonia. True, it was more than three hundred years ago, but how do I show him compassion when I cannot empathize with his rampant ambition that ended in reckless killings, including his own people? How can I feel *connected* to him?" It was obvious Isa had thought on various aspects of compassion having listened to hours of intense debates for months. He knew Mani would help him simplify these vital concepts.

"True it may be difficult for you to connect with Alexander. But do not forget many others call the same Alexander a great hero of all times. That young Macedonian prince kept conquering, acquiring more and more territories till he found the world too small. When you look dispassionately, with a neutral approach, you may begin to understand him, without agreeing with him," Mani paused to see if Isa was with him.

"I guess I will have to accept that when I totally detach myself from my personal perspective," Isa said, curiously looking at Mani wondering where he was going next.

"First you *observe yourself.* Turn your lens toward you. What is the basis of your evaluation of Alexander's action? If his ideals and ambitions are irrelevant to *you,* does it mean they are wrong for *him?* If you say 'yes', you are not a neutral observer. So you have to say, 'no', and since those acts are not wrong for him, you need to conclude that Alexander followed *his svadharma,* actions inherent to his own nature. Isa, we have discussed *svadharma* before in regard to the *Bhagavad Gita. So you know each of us needs to choose our action according to our inherent nature,"* Mani concluded his argument, or so he thought.

Isa appreciated Mani's turns of concepts and phrases that opened up deep dormant knowingness in him. "You remind me of Socrates with your questioning, Maniji," Isa joked and both laughed.

"I hope not, Isa. I do not want to be forced to take hemlock and die, I hope to live long and do my research," Mani continued the good humored conversation, "I prefer to be like the *rishis,* seers, of the *Upanishads.* They taught by questions and answers. You know the word *Upanishad* literally means 'sitting by the side,' don't you? Students and teachers sat and communed like we are doing now." Mani added with a meaningful smile, "I am not sure who is learning from whom in our dialogues, though." Mani knew the depth of young Isa's wisdom.

Isa said respectfully, "Your modesty is touching, Maniji," and continued with his query, "I guess now I know the essence of compassion, detachment, and neutrality. What about *love?*"

"Isa, love is not an *emotion.* It is a *state.* A mental state created by *compassionate observation* as we established before." Mani spoke clearly and conclusively.

"Let me see," Isa spoke slowly, weighing each word, once again gazing at those distant mountains, "So, if I *understand* Alexander it means I *accept* his acts despite my personal disagreement with them, since he cannot or will not do otherwise. Such perception creates *equanimity* in me leading to forgiveness for Alexander. In the process I learn to *forgive* myself, not judging the other or myself, right?" Isa looked at Mani with his last question. "According to you *that* is *love?*"

Smiling, Mani threw the last Vedic arrow, "In that moment of *understanding* and *forgiveness* you see that both of you, however different, are distinct manifestations of One Brahman. The Vedas say, *tattvam asi, You are that. Experiencing* that cosmic connectedness is *love.*"

Isa *felt* it in his deepest awareness. Their profound and yet simple dialogue had enabled Isa to *experience* what he already *knew* in his being.

In that moment Isa listened to the silence of the air. His eyes were fixed on the distant snowy peaks. Breathing the cool spring breeze deep, he was thinking of his home, mother, father, and Mary; his inner intelligence focusing on love.

Mani watched Isa's face with paternal compassion.

❄

Chapter 26

"*Maji*, never in my life have I eaten so many sweets in two days," Mira's complaint sounded more like a compliment.

"That's why I made you fast on Krishna's birthday. So for the next two days you can eat, eat, eat..." Kunti said with loving mischief in her eyes. She seemed to take extra pleasure in treating this foreign young girl for whom everything was new. Yet, she adjusted to all aspects of daily life so easily. In fact, Kunti noticed, each day was new for Mira and therefore festive.

In the afternoon it rained. Mira asked Kunti if they could walk on the river bank. "Yes, today Malini can go with us too. She does not have to cook today after three days of constant cooking. Hey Manek, we are all going to the river. Get our sandals out." Upper class women went for a walk in sandals but took them off as they walked to the water. It was rude to touch the holy river with one's sandals.

Mira and Kunti walked a little ahead. Manek and Malini followed a little distance behind. They walked barefoot.

"This is my way to let Malini walk with Manek and enjoy the evening. It is not proper for them to be going out in public together. In their caste, such public display of love is not allowed." Kunti was telling Mira in a soft voice out of the servants' hearing. Mira was surprised, but thought she would ask more questions another time. Her curiosity about Krishna-Radha love story had been suspended for more than three days. She could hardly wait.

"Maji you said Radha was not Krishna's wife, correct? Krishna had eight other wives, right? So why do people worship Radha-Krishna as a couple symbolizing ideal love?" It seemed incongruous to Mira. A society which nearly sanctified the institution of marriage and its austere demands, especially for women, would *deify* a non-marital relationship! Consider it ideal *love*! Having more than one wife was usual in many cultures. So Krishna having eight wives was not an unusual issue. But adoration of a non-marital love relationship as an ideal! That seemed illogical for this culture.

Kunti paused a little, before answering. With intriguing surprise she looked at Mira. Had Kunti not faced this question before? The evening ray of the setting sun piercing through a slit in the hanging dark cloud shone on Mira's face. Kunti's heart started thumping fast. Is this Mrinal come back? The same eyes, the same nose line as hers. Mira's lips curled the way Mrinal's did especially when she was intent upon some deep inquiry.

Kunti turned away her face, controlled herself, and said, "I can give you my answer. I have thought about this deeply because I had a special reason to. Krishna and Radha represent the highest kind of ideal love a husband and wife can attain, should attain, but is hard to attain. The love of Radha and Krishna is an ideal relationship, without any expectation of security, prestige, progeny, or lust. The usual social bonds that hold a marriage together are irrelevant in Radha-Krishna's love relation. It is without condition or demand. It is the purest form of man-woman love. It thrives on total surrender to each other. It supports the other to grow without interference. No conditions: expressed or assumed. Just love. Pure love."

Kunti's eyes reflected the setting sun, as she pierced into that jagged golden line of the quizzically shaped dark cloud.

"So Krishna's love for Radha was of this kind, but not for any of his eight queens?" Mira wanted to make sure she had it right.

"Yes, that's true. Krishna loved all of them, but his love for Radha epitomized the love of *atma,* Soul, for *Paramatma,* the Supreme Brahman. Krishna's love for his queens was the usual social kind," Kunti smiled hoping she had not confused Mira even more.

Mira wanted to make sure she had it right, "So Radha-Krishna symbolize the mutual love of each Soul with the Divine. It is the ideal one hopes to attain." Mira was struggling but getting there, Kunti thought.

"Yes. The meaning of love deepens as it grows within one's soul. Some individuals get so enwrapped in this *bhakti,* devotion, to Krishna they do not want to end the cycle of birth and death. They want to come back to be Krishna *bhaktas,* devotees to gain his love," Kunti emphasized another angle in this love relationship with the Divine.

"I wonder if it is only an ideal or can two humans reach such an ultimate love relationship in real life?" Mira asked wondering if her vision of *aakash yatra,* space journey, to another planet and being with Isa in a gazebo meant anything...

"Well, that's the ideal one hopes to attain," Kunti spoke with a blank smile, "We must turn back. It is getting dark."

Chapter 27

In the company of ever inquisitive Papa, Vallabh regained his zeal for active life that had numbed some during his retirement. With Ballu's assiduous help, the three of them vigorously explored Suryapuri -- its political, commercial, educational history -- visiting different sites, monuments, buildings, temples, important people, and even lay people. Mira went almost everywhere with them except when they went to make business deals. She preferred to chat with Kunti.

Vallabh and Papa were lounging on *gaddi,* cushioned mattress, in the parlor when Kunti and Mira went for a walk by the river with Malini and Manek. All felt relaxed after three days of *Krishna's* birthday celebrations.

"What about your children, Vallabh? Do they live very far? Can they visit you for *Diwali* or other festivals?" Papa asked.

"Well, we have only one daughter, Minu. She is smart, beautiful, and ambitious. But we have not been in touch for many years," a note of sadness was obvious in Vallabh's voice.

Papa waited for Vallabh to continue. And he did, "Someday she may come, we hope. She was an exceptional girl. It is not customary for girls to go to *ashram* schools. Jain and Buddhist nuns run schools for girls, so at first Minu went to a Jain school. A music teacher came home to teach playing *veena,* the string instrument, and singing. I even sent her to the dancing school of highly respected Ambapali tradition. The school was a famous center for Kathak dancing. I sent Minu to this school much against her mother's protests. Kunti thought it was too radical for a *brahmin* girl to learn dancing. Among upper caste Buddhists families this was a well respected art, since Ambapali, a well known dancer, was a devout follower of Gautam Buddha himself."

"So she did not have the education she wanted, I suppose," Papa was aware of this unfortunate reality regarding women practically everywhere in the world.

Vallabh smiled remembering how Minu asked for the impossible and he always gave in. "It was not true for Minu. When she finished nuns' *vihar school*, she said, 'Nuns taught me about the teachings of the Jain *munis, tirthankars,* sages and teachers, singing hymns and all that, even painting. They said everyone must learn to write. So I learned to copy manuscripts of *sraman's,* holy men's teachings. It was good. But I want to learn Astronomy.' Her last statement was the final stroke."

"So what did you say? Very few women in any country have much education. This was quite a demand. You certainly had given her an enriching education. Besides weren't you ready to get her married? She must have been 16 or so already by then, I guess," Papa was curious.

"True. In fact, Kunti was getting impatient. She said I had done enough doting on our only child. Kunti was not opposed to my liberal ideas about her education. She even tolerated – I guess she had to against the two of us -- when Minu started to come to my office as a copyist of documents. Kunti, the ever wise woman, reminded me maybe we had to start looking for a suitable husband for her. I realized she was right."

"So you got her married to a man of your choice? Vallabh, I thought you would do something else, like *svayamvara,* where the princess chooses her mate from the gathered assembly, like princess Sita does in the *Ramayana,*" Papa was laughing loudly at his own joke. He was certainly getting interested in this story.

Vallabh joined in his laughter, "Would you believe, it came close. One day a young lawyer came to our office and saw Minu working there. The second time he found an excuse to talk with her since there were some corrections to be made in one of the documents for his client. Well, a few weeks later Parshva's -- the young man's -- father came to visit me. He asked for my daughter's hand in marriage for his son."

Papa suddenly became serious. Straightening his back, moving away from the reclining pillow he looked around to see if anybody was in the vicinity. Vallabh was intrigued. A minute before Papa was laughing, suddenly he was tense. Vallabh asked, "Do you need something, Pharaoh? Mira, Kunti and the servants are all out for a walk by the river."

"No, I am checking if I can talk confidentially. For a few days now, Vallabh, I have wanted to ask you something. It was farfetched, too many missing links. I did not want to jump ahead of myself. But when you mentioned Parshva's name I got my clue. Your daughter's name was Mrinal, not Minu, correct?" Vallabh nodded in consent, astounded. How would Papa know?

"Well then, are you ready for this? Mira is Mrinal's daughter." Papa declared with absolute certainty.

Vallabh nearly screaming, jumped out of the cushioned *gaddi* with utter astonishment, his eyes popping out of their sockets, "What?...You mean?...No way!" He was incoherent, almost losing his mind; his heart thumping fast...

"What happened, Papa?" Mira ran in hearing Vallabh's scream as she and Kunti entered by the back door.

"What's the matter with you, *Nath,* (husband); Are you not well?" Kunti rushed to hold Vallabh lest he should fall.

Wide-eyed Vallabh kept staring at Mira in total disbelief. After a few seconds, not taking his eyes off Mira, he came toward her, took her hands in his, "Long live *Beti,* my granddaughter -- may Radha-Krishna bless you." Tears were rolling down his cheeks as he gathered Mira in his arms caressing her head.

Kunti intuitively knew what she had felt on the river bank in the slanting ray of the setting sun in Mira's face, was true. It *was* Mrinal's face. Mira *was* her granddaughter. Nobody had to tell her that. She *knew* it. She stood shedding tears of joy watching this moment she had waited for her entire life. She had waited, waited, waited... She was afraid the day would never come.

Now Kunti was hugging confused Mira, kissing her forehead, "*Beti* may Radha-Krishna bless you. My Krishna heard my prayers and brought you home. May you live long!"

"They *are* your grandparents, Mira, the ones you were hoping to meet," Papa said to bewildered Mira.

"W...h...a...t...!" she hugged and cried and repeated, "I can't believe it...I can't believe it. I can't... I can't!"

After dinner that night, Papa did a lot of explaining. Facing a barrage of questions from three sides, what he said could be summarized thus: After Mrinal left home and dropped Mira at Granny's, following the advice of the Gypsy mother, she travelled through Persia, Syria, Greece, and settled in Babylon. In the beginning she sang with the Gypsies. Her training in singing and dancing came in handy. The Gypsy leader and his wife protected her from ill behaving strangers or members of their own group. In Greece, Mrinal worked as a scribe, a copy writer, though she had to disguise herself as man. People were reluctant to work with a female scribe. There was a great demand for Indian script writers, for business contracts, documents and such, almost everywhere. Legend was Indians had a long memory so their documents were accurate. Mrinal often taught basic religious teachings of Vedic, Jain, and Buddhist traditions to seekers and philosophers, of course that too was done in a male disguise.

Later, after she met Papa in Babylon she thrived with aristocratic Roman women customers who had become very fond of Indian jewelry, perfume, textile, animal skins, and such. Papa had a gem shop and other little businesses. At first Mrinal, Miriam, worked as Papa's employee, but after about six months they married. Meanwhile she had been visiting Mira at Granny's regularly till Mira was five. Born in India, Granny had faint memories of the land of her birth, except her ardent devotion to Krishna.

After Mary was twelve Miriam would take her to markets in Arabia, Syria, Galilee, Jerusalem mainly selling woven material and gems. Miriam loved to travel and had a very good business sense. It had become a part of her personal and professional life. She wanted

Mary to be exposed to the world of ideas, to knowledge of various cultures, and of course business. Miriam often spoke nostalgically of her childhood in India in bits and pieces: about food, customs, dress, and such.

Papa continued, "Vaguely she might say she would come to India with me, but she never had the heart. She retained enormous burden inside her heart, it seemed. Nothing she would want to talk about. However, years of irregular life affected her lungs. Travelling had to be curtailed. We tried all possible healing potions, herbs, roots, including those from Mani whom I had met in Egypt many years ago. He has been our good friend for years. But even he was helpless. A little over two years ago Miriam passed away.

"One thing I do not know is this. Did Miriam, Mrinal, ever contact you after she left you? I have to tell you she loved you both and regretted leaving you the way she did. She was so proud of the exceptional life and opportunities you had given her. But given the social conditions a widow faced here in India, she said, she had to do what she did. She could not have convinced you to let her go either. She knew that. Whenever I would ask her if she ever let you know about her, she avoided the answer. It seemed she felt terribly guilty about hurting you. Then I stopped asking because it pained her so," Papa concluded.

"The old coachman, who helped her, told us three months after she left. Mrinal had instructed him to tell us at that time, after she was well out of our reach. The coachman said she had gone to Arabia. That was the Gypsies' destination," Vallabh said.

Kunti spoke in almost a whispering note, "I knew in my heart that some day she would come back. Our hope never died. That is why we host foreign visitors hoping someone would bring us her news. But she never came back."

They would never see her again. All sat silently, grieving...reminiscing their time with her...

❁

Chapter 28

Isa met Sriram almost half way between Takshashila and Kashmir. Using the services of inter-caravan messengers they communicated with each other. Mani was to spend a few more months at Takshashila before leaving on his westward journey to Arabia. Sriram was to stay in Kashmir before he too would be heading west. Isa's plan... well, he had no specific plans other than learning....knowing... evolving. Of course there was no end in sight....the more he knew, the more he felt....he would keep exploring the innermost worlds....

"Sriramji, I have so often dreamt of going to the Himalayan valley of Kashmir since I heard you mention it years ago in Galilee. Finally, I am headed that way and with you. I can hardly believe it," Isa's exuberance was visible in his gait, voice, and most strikingly in his eyes.

"Being in Takshashila must have been quite an education, Isa," Sriram spoke noticing Isa's enhanced energy.

"It was quite explosive- even useful. But I am glad to be out of that intellectual circus." Isa smiled. Sriram noticed a distinct sign of maturation in Isa. He remembered having seen Isa for the first time in Galilee when Isa was 11 or 12. "I always remember your stories – Hindu, Buddhist, Jain, and even Greek stories," Isa continued remembering his younger days in Galilee.

"Well telling stories is our cultural heritage. We have Brahmins who specialize as *kathakars*, storytellers. Did you have a chance to listen to any?" Sriram said, "People go to them every evening, especially the masses who cannot study scriptures themselves."

"What do you think is the difference between Indian and Greek gods and goddesses in their relationship with humans?" Isa asked a question that was nudging him.

"You mean you did not listen to those debates in Takshashila on that question?" Sriram chuckled.

Isa rolled his eyes. "I want to know what you think. I have had enough of theories."

"The Greek pantheon, as I see it, favors or despises humans as per their own whims. Indian deities have to qualify their ire or favor for humans. Hindu gods, *devas* and goddesses, *devis,* cannot ignore individuals' actions, *karma or* inherent duty*, dharma,*" Sriram was succinct in simplifying a complex issue.

"What about Indian deities taking birth as humans? Didn't Vishnu have nine incarnations, *avatars,* descent on earth, as they call it, and a tenth yet to come?" Isa's information was new and fresh from school. But Sriram detected another level of inquiry in Isa's face and his tone.

"Indian gods and goddesses descend as humans subjecting themselves to the process of birth and death. To my knowledge, Greek gods and goddesses visited the earth, begot children with humans, but were not *born* as humans. They always were immortals." Isa admired Sriram's cutting through complex issues. "But why do you still ask? Takshashila is behind you. I know it is not an intellectual inquiry, is it?"

"You are right, as always. It's personal," Isa said, "Didn't the five heroic Pandavas, the five sons of King Pandu, have various gods as fathers? Evidently since King Pandu was unable to procreate, his two wives invoked major gods by *mantras* to beget five sons. I am trying to understand what happened to my mother before I was born in this lifetime. She had an angelic visit which confused her, I am told. "

Sriram laughed aloud, "Young man, there are so many unusual stories of personal experiences that may sound like miracles. Know that many mysteries *seem* magical. Life is a constant dance of subtle energies un-reckoned and unparalleled, absolutely unique." Sriram's language was becoming more abstract. Isa too was getting pulled into the magnetic energy of the land.

"Your words match the surroundings, Sriramji. Look at this valley. The music of running streams, meditating tall pines, colorful flowers, and quizzically fluttering butterflies make this little corner resemble paradise. Everything is magical..." Isa turned to look at Sriram after absorbing the panorama in front of them.

Sriram smiled and remained quiet absorbing the surroundings. Both continued to walk without words.

"How could heaven be more beautiful than this?" Isa asked Srirram as they viewed the panorama of snow peaked mountains and deep valleys of Kashmir. "Nature seems to meditate, and so do all who live on this land. Fish, flowers, birds, humans, trees, animals all breathe in unison with Mother Nature." Isa's question about heaven obviously was rhetorical.

They kept walking in the mystical valley, silently absorbing its energy. Isa felt it was like a walking meditation. After a three hour walk over undulating hills and valleys they came to a solitary hut.

"It seems this dazzling grandeur has befuddled my brain," Isa said smiling, turning to settle down in the hut in the village along the road from Takshashila. They decided to sleep in that night...or many nights...nothing was planned...they were floating in the energy flow.

"Brain is what you put aside. It's the greatest interference in your conscious evolution, Isa," Sriram said laughing.

"True. But I need my mind to function in the material world. I cannot totally discard it, Sriramji," Isa continued in a lighthearted tone.

"Have you ever watched a child poking its head into everything? Running mindlessly to the danger he knows nothing of? What do you think about his brain?" Sriram asked.

"That it is undeveloped, yet," Isa said the obvious. "The kid has to grow up," he added.

"After it is 'grown' as you say, do you think the child, now a man, can keep up his exploration, his curiosity? Run to the danger knowingly?" Sriram asked, "How would you describe that person?"

"A compulsive explorer or a fool- depends," Isa was not sure where Sriram was headed with such simple questions.

"Depends on what?" Sriram asked

"His ultimate goal, if he has any. Without a goal he would be a fool."

"What is the goal of a compulsive explorer?" Sriram was not giving up.

"To find the Ultimate Truth. He cannot stop it no matter what the risk, what the price," Isa said in one breath *without thinking.* He was amazed by his own words. Where did they come from?

"Where did your words come from?" Sriram echoed Isa's unspoken words!

"Certainly not from my brain," Isa said.

Both broke into a loud laughter. "Well that is your search, the source of thoughts, words, Truth. But without using the brain."

They ate fruits, nuts, and *roti,* flat bread, tied in their satchel. Drank cool water from the stream by the hut, and lay on the straw mattress. Soon both were asleep.

* * * * * * * * * * * *

Walking, touching the earth, feeling her energy in his being Isa was transported into another world as it were. Eerie surroundings created uncanny physical sensations. His eyes were open but he did not seem aware of the trees or the snowy patches, or the colorful flowers. He was a part of them. It was like walking in a dream. After what seemed to be a long walk, he came to a hut. He knew he lived there. He fed the fat sheep outside the hut, went in and sat smoking his *hukkah,* the smoking water pipe.

The rest was a big empty blur.....

"Wake up Isa," Sriram had his hand on Isa's head.

"Oh...Is it night time already? How long were we gone? I do not recall going to bed," Isa asked totally confused.

Sriram, "We were not out at all. You were tired, so the minute you lay down you fell asleep. It is early morning, Isa."

Isa described what he experienced, "Was I dreaming? It seemed so real."

"You were not dreaming," Sriram's voice was clear.

"Sleep walking?" Isa grinned.

Sriram laughed shaking his head.

"Then what was it?" Isa was intrigued.

"Let's find out. Let's walk the way you went," Sriram suggested.

Isa got up and started walking, Sriram followed a few steps behind. They kept walking. Silently. Isa's feet seem to know the way. After a couple of hours of walking they arrived at the hut he had seen in his vision, dream, whatever. Without a word or question Isa fed the fat sheep, walked right into the hut and sat down to smoke the *hukkah*..

Sriram asked, "Isa, do you know this place?"

Isa 'woke' up from his trance. Amazed Isa looked at the hut, the *hukka* and asked, "What place is this?"

"Didn't you say you came to this hut last night?" Sriram said, "That was an out of body experience."

"Did *you* activate it? How did it happen?" Isa had heard of it.

Sriram laughed, "No one else can activate it for you. It is the heightened energy of this land that triggers your inner energies. Isa, you are blessed with the finest of vibrations. On this land your vibrations intensify even more. So your body can manifest outside of you."

"But I seemed to know the place. Like it is the hut I once lived in," Isa was puzzled.

"Well, that seems like memory from another life. Maybe you lived here before as a *rishi*, an ascetic, in this hut," Sriram was smiling, but certainly not joking. "Isa, you gathered a lot of intellectual and philosophical information in Takshashila. Practiced meditation, learned many techniques. Now is the time for you to let that effort oriented practice rest and *feel* the surrounding energy," Sriram was helping Isa open deeper perception.

"I thought I had mastered quite a few techniques that did take me to contemplation and trance, *samadhi*, for a short span, perhaps. So I knew I was not brain stuck, as you name it. A couple of times I even flew into outer space, *aakash*. How is this different?" Isa asked.

"Let me see if I can make it simpler. Techniques that you learned are important to bring you to a certain level. Then you have to let go all that *doing* technique. When you are in that *being* experience, you float, you let your *brain* and conscious *effort* sleep. Remember yesterday you said something, but knew not where the words came from? It happens when the brain rests. Yesterday when you slept in our hut at the base, your fine tuned vibrations resonated with this land's energy. It catapulted you into an out of body experience of another life time," Sriram could explain complex concepts in simple terms to laypeople. Talking with an exceptionally advanced Isa was easy.

Isa put aside the *hukkah* he was still holding, though not smoking. He said getting up, "So one can cultivate a technique to use this inner and outer resonance at will? That is how sages manifest themselves in two places at the same time? And that's how they go out of body at will anywhere, I guess."

Sriram remained silent. They started their return journey.

Chapter 29

Kunti and Vallabh laughed more, moved more swiftly, engaged in more socializing with people of town. Everyone said they looked younger. Mira was endlessly entertained by new found relatives, extended family, and at social gatherings. Her frequent joyous outbursts at every gift she got became louder and louder. She was twenty-one going on ten, Kunti thought. Malini was a good companion who explained current fashions and various uses of cosmetics, exquisite jewelry and garments.

"You know so much!" wondered Mira knowing Malini's meager possessions as a servant.

"I have worked for *Maji* ever since I was a little girl. My mother worked for her till she was too old. I have seen *Maji's* family and friends and their rich treasures for so many years. So I know all that. *Maji* gave new and some old things of her daughter's to my mother." Malini explained that she was virtually family despite her humble background.

"Where does your mother live now?" Mira was curious.

"She lives in our village. *Maji* and *Mahashaya,* the Master, got a little hut built for her when she needed to rest. They said she had worked for many years. "

Parshva's mother was glad to see her long lost grandchild return. However, the senseless murder of her young son had broken her spirit beyond repair. Three years ago her husband too passed on. Her other son and daughter were too busy with their own families. Seeing Mira brought tears of joy, but she soon withdrew into her silent melancholy. Of course Mira received appropriate gifts from her paternal grandmother, uncle and aunt. Everything was socially 'proper,' but the genuine warmth was missing. Parshva's family seemed to have not forgotten the scar left by the scandal Mrinal's escapade had created. Such are the ways of the world, Kunti solaced herself.

The conservative response in the community to Mira and Papa was guarded. Mrinal's daring was too radical for them to ignore. In fact, some of Papa's business deals were being 'reconsidered' by a few in light of the new information. Papa was the second husband of a widow from their prestigious city! And he was Egyptian! Not even Indian, much less of their caste. It was unheard of. Some men even contacted *pundits* to determine if it was acceptable to engage in business deals with those who violated their social code. Ballu's resourcefulness impressed Vallabh, when he successfully re-negotiated Papa's deals with quite a few reluctant vendors. Surreptitiously, Ballu would contact commercial *pundits* who would produce favorable results for paying clients.

Now, Papa was ready for his return journey. Mira was sad to abandon her new-found home and family. Ecstatic Vallabh and Kunti had to calm down to face parting again from their newfound treasure. What will they do now? What will hold their life together?

After lunch all were relaxing in the living room. Kunti was preparing an after meal digestive with exotic herbs and *paan leaf.* Papa had become fond of this traditional routine. It was customary for the lady of the house to prepare *paan,* leaf, for guests after meals. He had seen elaborately carved tools, beetle nut crackers, and *paan* carrying-boxes in royal and aristocratic families. Papa had even acquired a few *paan* boxes of different designs to sell. It was a new item for business that might catch the fancy of his Roman women clients, he thought.

"Well, Vallabh, this was quite an experience of life for me," Papa said, "You got your lost granddaughter. I wish it had happened when Mrinal was still with us."

"Life tests us in many ways," Vallabh said. "We are grateful to Radha-Krishna for bringing Mira to us. We do not know what we will do after you leave. It seems our life's purpose is fulfilled."

"Radha-Krishna will guide us by opening new doors for us." Kunti said, cutting beetle nut with a *soodi,* nut cracker.

"Traveling has opened such a wide world for me," Mira said, "It has brought me all treasures of new experiences, lessons of life. Now I have a whole new family, blood family! It's almost like a miracle. *Maji,* Malini was saying things happen when you pray to Radha-Krishna. Is that true?"

"She is right. When you connect with the divine Essence of the universe," Vallabh said, "and intensely wish for something, align yourself with the Essence, Radha-Krishna, it happens."

"So what's your next wish, *Maji, Dada,* after Papa and I leave?" Mira was in a playful mood.

Kunti looked at Vallabh, smiled and said, "Who knows, we may go on a pilgrimage. That is what *bhaktas,* devotees, do if they can." She said casually, to keep the conversation going. Travel was hard, expensive and physically challenging. She did not know where these words came from. Neither she nor her husband had ever even mentioned going on a pilgrimage before.

"Where would you go?" For Mira travel was a way of life. Vallabh and Kunti had hardly ever gone more than fifty miles around, and that was more than most of their friends and relatives had done.

"I don't know...I am teasing..." Kunti laughed. She was only prolonging the prattle with the child.

Vllabh and Papa were enjoying the prank. Papa continued, "Well, I have heard travelers talk about Amarnath, Shiva *lingam* in Kashmir way up north."

"Perhaps we may consider a pilgrimage to Mathura and Vrindavan, Radha-Krishna's land," Vallabh added chuckling at the impossible prospect.

For Mira no talk of travel was just a joke. "Oh, let's all go, shall we Papa? You want to go to Kashmir. Can we go to it after visiting Mathura? Please, Papa," Mira was giggling once again, Papa noticed it was this giggle that had always defeated Mrinal's resolve, as well as his... Somehow, the giggle now had more sonorous quality to it. It sounded mature and...blissful. It exuded, *ananda,* bliss, as people here in India would say, Papa thought.

"I need to get going back to Babylon if I want to work on the new deals I have made in Suryapuri. If *Maji* and *Dada* are serious about pilgrimage, *yatra,* you can stay back, Mira. Spend some more time with them. On my journey in a couple of years or so, you can go back with me. We can even go to Kashmir then," Papa was half joking. He thought this was a clever way not to say 'No' to Mira.

"Oh that is wonderful," the only person serious about this dream travel cried out joyously.

Chapter 30

Long hours of walks, some treacherous, some dreamily hazy, had brought Isa and Sriram in contact with many: sages, *siddhas*, highly attained, *sadhakas*, disciples, *sramans*, ascetics, *munis*, silent ones. They opened up a new world of *experiential* awareness for Isa. Sriram jokingly termed the happenings 'brainless excursions.'

"Every time I meander into the Himalayan Mountains, I discover more *tantrics* practicing varied techniques. They defy ordinary norms of the visible world. Like acrobats in entertainment shows, who ply their bodies in unusual, even unnatural positions, these *sadhakas* twist their minds and brains with conscious control," Sriram explained this impossible exercise with an analogy.

"I am amazed by their *siddhi*," Isa was stunned by their nearly super-human accomplishments. "You know what interests me is their full faith in the mind's power to control the body," Isa said. "But that is not the end. The mind then catapults consciousness. Or is it the other way round?" Isa was convinced of the strength of mind and consciousness working in unison. But the picture was still somewhat hazy. Was it consciousness controlling the mind or the other way around? What was controlling what?

Sriram laughed, "Isa, for the hundredth time, let your brain sleep. Be brainless."

The next day found the two travelers in a remote valley. Sriram stopped by to admire the grey blue sky scraped by snowy mountain peaks. Isa saw him lost into 'cosmic escapade' – that was Sriram's description of his deep meditation, often open-eyed, like right now.

Isa walked on magnetized by the stream that was a tall water fall before it became a gentle flow. It still was babbling as it flowed on. The deep gurgle of the fall mixed with the babble of the brook creating a deep sonorous giggle. Instantly Isa heard young Mary's giggle. How long had it been? Days, weeks, months! Time did not matter. Or did it?

He heard young Mary's giggling laughter in this stream. Each ripple gushed freely, fearlessly, mindlessly, not knowing for what or to what destination. It was enjoying the moment in utter bliss. Isa stood there, staring, engulfed by the free, fearless mindlessness of the ripples, they enwrapped him in their vibratory energy field.

Light as a breeze he was floating, though there was no air. All seemed right, though nothing was as he had known so far. There are no twos, though they appear so.

Light cannot light the surrounding darkness.

Light (in weight) cannot shine, but can fly

Life is meaningless without death

Death is only another shape of life

Darkness is yet another color of light.

He kept floating, humming these lines emanating from him. On a shining boulder by the next fall he landed. On it was a gazebo with an altar in the middle. In it was a crystal throne with an orb at the center. The orb was not solid, nor immaterial. In it were many colored energy strings constantly moving, shining. It was Shakti, *the feminine energy, matter,* Prakriti. *A beam of spirit, the activating seed, man,* Purush, *fell from the pinnacle of the gazebo piercing the orb.*

Amazed Isa stood there, by his side was standing young Mary, both in flowing shimmering gowns staring into this vibrant orb. The ray of light from the orb reflected in their eyes forming interlaced dual triangles.

* * * * * * * * * * * *

"Could there be simultaneous out of body experiences for two persons?" Isa asked when Sriram and he started to go back to their overnight resting place.

"There are no limits to what can happen, Isa. I told you many times. Experience every moment; only *you* set your own limits," Sriram reiterated.

When Isa briefly narrated his vision, Sriram said, "This is a lot deeper than out of body experience, Isa. Young Mary and you are twin flames. In the cosmic energy field your journeys are intertwined. At some point you two will connect to fulfill the purpose of your lives. What it is and how you accomplish it *is* to live your lives. Just as you naturally and freely floated like the ripples, without asking why and whereto, you need to march ahead. Do you understand?"

"I understand," Isa said, wondering where Mary could be now. How were they ever going to meet again on this wide earth? And then he laughed. He was already asking the wrong questions.

"Fearlessly, freely float ahead like those ripples....." Isa muttered to himself.

Chapter 31

Malini, Manek, and now even Ballu, were constantly busy. Vallabh and Kunti were going on a pilgrimage to Mathura and Vrindavan the holy places of Krishna's childhood.

In Vrindavan Krishna played pranks with *gopis*, cowgirls, and was imbued in a loving bond with Radha that became the epitome of divine love for his devotees to aspire- Krishna also became a source of absolute fulfillment for his foster parents, Nanda and Yashoda. For Balram, Krishna's brother, life became a constant celebration, be it at play or a heroic venture. Devaki and Vasudev, Krishna's birth parents, adored Krishna's exceptional deeds from a distance.

Kunti and Vallabh could not believe they actually decided to go on this pilgrimage. Their granddaughter unknowingly became a catalyst for this unprecedented journey.

Preparations ranged from preparing food and collecting appropriate clothing for northern territories to medicines and torches and tents. What about protection against robbery and theft? Before leaving, Papa, being a seasoned caravan traveler, gave helpful tips as well. With his ingenious resourcefulness Ballu was a great asset in taking care of all details, including Mira's probable eccentric wishes. It seemed Ballu thrived on challenges. He was in his element.

"Do you think we are being too bold?" one night Kunti asked Vallabh after Ballu left for the day.

"Why, are you afraid I may die on the way?" Vallabh tried to make the topic light. He knew Kunti was concerned about safety, especially Mira's safety. "Mira has travelled more than we have. She will be a help. You do not have to worry about her." Vallabh reassured Kunti.

"Can't we take Ballu with us?" Kunti asked. They would feel more secure, she thought.

"That's a brilliant idea," Vallabh agreed.

Letting Papa go without her was difficult for Mira. Papa too was sad. He had witnessed the vagaries of life as a traveler. Uncertainties, insecurities, were an everyday affair. One had to immunize oneself. But he left with a heavy heart. Vallabh and Kunti recognized the bond between their granddaughter and Papa. He was the only father she had known.

After a few days, Mira got busy with preparations for the pilgrimage. Ballu's going with them lightened her anxiety considerably. As the monsoon ended, floods receded, and the river Tapi regained her composure, after going crazy in heavy rainfall. Vallabh's family was leaving in a week. Besides good wishes for the family's safe return, friends and extended family brought gifts to be offered in various temples on their behalf. People flocked from nearby villages to see them off. It was an exceptional journey few could afford.

Mary was surprised by the stream of visitors that started weeks before their departure. "Not only is it a special occasion for us because it is rare, but it is a vicarious participation in pilgrimage for those who cannot go themselves. All who come to meet us with even token gifts earn some merit, even though they can't go on a pilgrimage themselves," Vallabh explained.

"We are all dependent on each other in society. So it is a kind of collective merit for all," Kunti expanded.

"So, you going on a pilgrimage will benefit all your family and friends? That's a beautiful concept of communal oneness." Mira saw how deep the community identity could be. Of course, it was the same identity that harshly judged her widowed mother's behavior too. Talk about a two edged sword, as they say. A pilgrims' caravan was quite different from the one she had been on, Mira thought. Unlike other caravans, common faith and devout spirit knit all pilgrims. Yes, there were those aggressive, self centered people who always complained, wanted more amenities, found fault with others...But then those who smiled and helped others were many more.

As they marched on, they sang devout songs, played musical instruments, especially the flute, Krishna's favorite. It changed the atmosphere. Mira was so used to unsettling elements in her other travels she took those rifts as natural totally ignoring them. But on this journey she was entranced by music and hearing stories of Krishna's *bal lila,* childhood games. His childhood pranks with his brother and other *gopal,* cowherd, friends were hilarious. Young cowherds got into elder cowherds' homes, stole butter and curd, distributing them to others, and enjoying themselves. Elders' wives who came to complain went away laughing when they saw Krishna's delightfully pouting smile when mother Yashoda scolded him.

It was his flute. Krishna's flute was the real charmer. *Gopis* left their housework and ran to listen to Krishna's flute. They forgot it was the same mischievous boy who often broke their earthen water pots by slinging stones. One time when several *gopis* were bathing in the river, Krishna stealthily took all their clothes and went up a tree nearby. A while later, the g*opis* found him happily playing the flute up in the tree as they stood naked, entranced. When he finished playing the flute, they asked for their clothes, covering their body with their crossed arms in vain.

Mira was amused and amazed; she asked Kunti the next day after she heard the story, "*Maji,* Krishna was quite a boy, I tell you. I am enjoying these stories, but am a little confused."

"What confuses you, Mira? They are innocent child's play," Kunti was intrigued.

"He breaks into people's homes, steals goodies, makes a mess. Takes away *gopis* clothes, makes them feel ashamed standing naked. And still he is worshiped as the beloved god!!! A real person in life would be punished for all these violations, wouldn't he?"

Kunti laughed loudly, louder than Mira had ever heard her. Mira was surprised, "Why are you laughing, *Maji?*"

"*Beti,* you have to understand Krishna is teaching the *gopals* and *gopis* to share – which you call stealing. The g*opis* standing naked face their real selves; they stand in front of god as they truly are, naked. He took away *gopis'* clothes under which they were hiding.

Their self is revealed as they face the divine," Kunti explained the inherent mysticism of outward action.

"Hmm...that's fascinating. *Gopis* surrender to Krishna to find their real selves!" Mira understood Kunti's words.

Vallabh, who was silently hearing the dialogue, said, "That is how the two, the *atman,* the individual self, and the *paramatman,* the Supreme self, unite. It is called *dvaita vad* –the principle of two-ness."

"The two become One?" Mira asked.

"The two *remain, knowing* they are inseparable. *Beti,* there have been and will be many debates to explain these *dvaita/advaita,* dual/non-dual theories. Each school gives a different name to its special brand. Do you know why?" Mira shook her head wondering why.

"Because people cannot stop their brain activity," Vallabh laughed. "Brainless musings alone would help arrive at this *knowing* within. Too many theories are just words. They are meaningless." Vallabh was silent for a long time.

For a while Mira too was silent. She was ruminating, walking with her head down. Was she hearing the earth talk? It was a long time before she slowly looked up into the sky.

A solitary dark cloud was hanging above them. "Isn't one of Krishna's many names *ghanshyam,* dark like the rain cloud? Look isn't he up there playing his flute?" Although a question, it was not; Mira *knew* it was Krishna.

Chapter 32

"Often these 'brainless' wanderings you suggest feel like craziness, Sriramji," Isa said one day. They had been in Kashmir valley for almost three months. "I wonder about things I see and feel when I go brainless. Am I mad or what?"

Sriram was tickled, "Do you have doubts? You *are* mad." Both laughed heartily, loudly. "So what do you see?" Sriram asked.

"I see shapes: triangles, circles, five pointed stars, in different colors and combinations. They get so intertwined, I cannot describe them."

"What happens next?"

"I am floating, but I am not sure of my bodyline. Am I diffusing? Disappearing? I do not know if I can describe what happens. There are no adequate words," Isa seemed totally confused.

"Intertwined energy forces constitute what we call the universe," Sriram continued, "You know the universe is endless. We see its horizon, but there is none. It constantly expands. Yet all its parts are connected. However, we cannot comprehend the pattern because that reality is in another dimension; our brain is incapable of *comprehending* it. Brainlessness however lets us *experience* its constant changes." Sriram tried to clarify the inner workings of energy forces.

"Floating like a ripple I felt I was connected with my surroundings, but I did not know my shape—it did not remain the same, anyway. I was like a constantly changing cloud of light waves," Isa described it the best way he could.

"Nor can you describe your connection. Isa, do you know that our body is made up of *anu*, atoms. Jain sages have described *paramanu*, sub-atoms. They classified animals, plants and humans in different categories such as those with one sense, two, three, etc. We humans have five senses, of course. Such categorization is already more than 300 years old now. Logicians believe that the next stage of evolution for humans will take us beyond five senses."

"That question came up in Takshashila once. What about it? Someday we will have six senses?" Isa said casually. Was Sriram joking, he wondered.

"You already have the sixth sense Isa. That allows you to feel, *experience*, what you call madness," Sriram explained. "You know *tantrics* have mastered the technique to reach such deeper awareness. All beings are like mechanical devices, *yantra* that can be orchestrated by an individual to reach a higher level of consciousness."

"Wait a minute, you mean I am a *yantra*, a device?" a little peeved Isa wanted clarification.

"*Tantra* is a technique to cultivate the body to attain higher consciousness. *Tantra* is derived from *tantu,* literally a string, connecting *all* in the cosmos. Once you cultivate it you can master many *siddhis* yogic attainments. The concept is *vaignanic,* scientific, and has been proven and practiced for millennia." Sriram looked at Isa who was staring at the ground beneath him, "Am I making any sense for you?" Sriram asked.

Isa looked up, focused at a distant horizon and said, "So it is a mechanical process that can be manipulated with rigorous practice. Once I learn the basic mechanism of the body and its connectedness within the scheme of the universe, I can learn to disappear, or appear in two places at once, or be buried underground and come up alive? And a dozen more things that *tantrics,* yogis, *sadhus,* ascetics, or *siddhas,* highly advanced ones, do. Is that what you are saying?"

"You may laugh at this, calling it a magician's tricks or a hoax. And some charlatans are doing just that to befuddle the innocent." Sriram continued smiling, "But people like us have a different goal, *you* know that."

"Of course, Sriramji," Isa wanted to get back to *his* mad experiences. "When I see those shapes, in fact, I am seeing *tantus,* connecting strings. I can then use appropriate *tantric* technique to manipulate energies. Correct?"

"What is your goal, your intent, to manipulate energies at that point?" Sriram asked.

"My goal is to reach that ultimate Oneness, the ultimate bliss, *param ananda,* as you call it. But honestly these concepts are other people's descriptions. I will know what it is when I arrive. After my forays into intellectual, meditative, and experiential *tantric* fields, guru Sriramji, where do I go next?" Isa was in a teasing mood. He always enjoyed light hearted but deep talks with Sriram.

"What do you think you have *not yet* fully explored?" Isa knew he could not pin Sriram down to a definite answer.

Isa will have no questions when he *arrives,* smiling Sriram thought to himself.

Chapter 33

"How do you think these migratory geese know what their destination is?" Mira asked Ballu as they saw a flock of large birds flying from the north. "I have seen many such migratory birds but never asked how do they know where to go?" Mira and Ballu were walking ahead of the bullock cart. They were quite close to Mathura. Kunti and Vallabh walked some, but mostly rode the cart. They had been travelling for almost a month. For Mira this was an easy path.

"We do not see too many of those migratory birds in Suryapuri. But my teacher said birds have inner understanding, like a little energy spot, a spark within." Ballu was smiling.

"You are joking right?" Mira said.

"No. In fact, I thought if birds have a little *spark*, what do we humans have to guide us?"

"Did you find out?" Mira asked, still smiling.

"I used to go to a Jain swami's discourses on living beings. I asked him that question. What he said made a lot of sense to me. He said, we humans also have a spark, but it is covered with rust and dust. If we remove the dirt by discipline, learning, fasting, purifying our mind, and meditating, we might find the spark and then we would know *our* destination too," Ballu was pretty serious.

"Well, how come birds don't have to work at it and we have to? Why don't we naturally *know*, as birds do?" Mira was insistent.

Ballu laughed, "I too wish we could. Had we kept our natural condition! But chances are we would be still in caves or living nomadic lives. It seems our complex human system developed the whole mind/brain /desire component. I think it is a brilliant evolution of humans. Look at the daunting world of music, art, architecture, literature, philosophy, science, religion we have created."

"You are right. It's a stunning world we humans have created. So are you saying that spark in us made us creative?" Mira asked. She was serious, not joking anymore.

"Yes, but we paid a heavy price. Our intellect, logic, thinking power enabled us to be innovative, creative, and productive. But the same talent made us killers, conquerors, acquisitive, power hungry, and self-centered." Ballu seemed to enjoy the sound of his voice. This travel was opening up yet a new dimension in him...it seemed.

"What was the price for the spark spot? Our killer instinct?" Mira was not sure where Ballu was going with his dialectic on positive and negative human traits.

"No, the price was we were separated from our divine source. The intuitive knowingness of our connectedness was lost. Now we have to learn ways to re-discover it. And all the time it is in there; the way it is in these birds," Ballu said.

Vallabh was intently listening to the conversation between Mira and Ballu. "That is very well said, Ballu. I did not know you had an interest in philosophy and logic," Vallabh's voice echoed his pleasant surprise.

Ballu smiled gratefully acknowledging Vallabh's compliments. "I had a reputation for arguing too much in *pathshala*, school."

"You could have been in the legal profession, Ballu." Kunti joined in gleefully laughing.

"My father had that plan for me. He wanted me to be a lawyer. But when he died very young because of *vaat dosh,* gastric complications, I was 15 and the oldest of four children. I had to look after our family farm. When my younger brother was able to take over the farm, I left that restrictive field to work as an interpreter. Being fairly good in languages, logic, and of course *vanijya,* business and marketing, helps. Someday I hope to travel to other countries. Maybe do some profitable business," Ballu was smiling, he was half joking about foreign travel. Ballu is still young, Vallabh thought, he had a chance to realize his dream.

"It seems we are almost in Mathura. That seems to be the Radha-Krishna temple. Look at that *dhaja,* flag," Kunti pointed.

Every temple had its flag that would reveal its affiliation to a specific deity. Many other pilgrims, arriving from different directions, were converging toward the main track leading to Mathura.

Everybody was excited to reach the destination. Ballu could not resist. "Well we *must* have our spark after all; we too reached our destination. Not only those geese." All were amused by being compared to birds. They roared into laughter, Mira's was the loudest.

"Is that you, Mary?" Mira heard her old name in a familiar voice.

She turned around in the direction of the voice that came from behind a small group of people. Her eyes wide open, eye brows raised, mouth open, her palm on her mouth stopping a loud scream, "Isa...! My word...How did you get here, Isa? How could you be here, of all places in the world in Mathura?" Mira was laughing, screaming, jumping, and clapping, all at once.

Isa came forward, the two held hands, and stood silently staring at each other with teary eyes.

Chapter 34

"It's incredible to see you here, Isa," Mira said barely being able to suppress her joy. "These are my grandparents, Dada Vallabh, Maji Kunti, and our friendly organizer Ballu. And I chose Mira, my name at birth." She then introduced a strange looking Aramaic young man to the totally surprised family, "Isa and I met a few times over the years, just like this: first in Galilee more than ten years ago, I guess," she was looking at Isa remembering that chance meeting by the well, "then at a caravan crossing in Persia, was it? And then at Granny's." All greeted each other with *namaste*, joined palms and a bow.

"I did not think we would ever meet again, Mary...Mira," said Isa not taking his smiling eyes off her.

"Nor did I. Well all our meetings have been unexpected anyway," said Mira with her delightfully musical laughter. Isa found her voice deeper, sonorous and mature....ever enchanting.

* * * * * * * * * * * *

That evening the pilgrims were busy settling down. All were making arrangement for their lodgings. Ballu got busy, negotiating with pilgrims' group leaders. Vallabh's position certainly carried weight. And Ballu even exaggerated it to get the best accommodation for his party.

Mira had told Isa to come to their *dharamsala,* pilgrim's inn, after he settled. A few hours later when Isa arrived, Vallabh suggested Mira and Isa could go for a walk if they still had energy; Kunti and he were exhausted and were ready for quiet restful time. "Ballu may join you, if he is not tired," he said. Was he being a cautious grandfather? Ballu said he had enough running around for the day.

Isa and Mira walked around the temple. Not being able to hold his curiosity any longer, Isa said, "I did not know you had Indian grandparents, Mira!" Mira said she had nearly forgotten her Indian heritage, but the way she found them was totally incredible. She briefly narrated her story. "And now I am Mira, as long as I am in India," She laughed. It was the same musical laugh Isa felt.

"Where have you been, tell me, tell me..." Mira was eager to know. They sat under a tree by the river Yamuna not too far from the newly raised tents for pilgrims.

Isa briefly spoke of his stay at Guru Arjan's, Takshashila, and Kashmir. "Sriramji said I had learned the mental, meditative, *tantric* yoga. But for the most important path of *prem bhakti,* loving devotion, I must stay in Mathura and Vrindavan, the land of Krishna's younger days with his parents and his cowherd friends, *gopals* and *gopis*. Sriramji especially emphasized the Krishna-Radha tradition of loving devotion. Then only, he added, I would comprehend, *experience*, and internalize total *surrender*. Sriramji thinks it is important for me to integrate the two major paths of devotion and meditation. *Bhakti* is inclusive and easily accessible to masses of people and he thinks it will help me in my work when I return home."

"He is right," said Mira. "I witnessed Krishna *bhakti* in practice in Suryapuri, my home town. It's very powerful, if you grasp its inner core. Even if you don't, and most do not, it still works because of faith, trust, belief, and total surrender," Mira spoke with utmost conviction. She narrated how she saw Krishna in that dark hanging cloud on her silent walk, feeling the dirt under her feet.

Isa was pleased, but not surprised. He recognized their deep connection and *felt* Mira's essence in his being. How diverse their paths had been, yet how close their emergence into new awareness was. He held Mira's hand in his, both kept looking at each other in silence for a while...The Yamuna witnessed a divine confluence.

After what seemed a long time, Isa said, it was getting late, she must be tired. They should walk back.

They returned to the inn. Isa went to his sleeping area at the end of tent ground.

* * * * * * * * * * *

As Isa lay on his mat, staring at stars in the sky, he envisioned his entire journey so far. And then he thought of Mother Mary. Perhaps Mira's grandmother evoked this memory. Whatever, he was happy.

Isa was standing at the door. Joseph was in his work shed fixing a small table. Mother Mary was cooking. She was blowing into the smoldering fire. The wood smoke made her eyes teary. Isa entered silently; sitting behind his mother and bending, he blew into the fire. The flame brightened up. Surprised Mother Mary turned around and saw her long lost son. "Oh my son... it's you. Let me look at you. May God in heaven bless you," Mary uttered, not knowing if she was laughing or crying. She flung her arms around Isa's neck. Holding her Isa got up and led her near the door saying, "Let me show you something." Pointing to young Mary standing by the door Isa said, "I am going to marry her."

The dream was over. Isa woke up, laughed, turned on his side, and lay there thinking for a long time before he fell asleep.

Chapter 35

The Radha-Krishna temple was busy with morning activities. *Pujari,* the ceremonial priest, and his helpers were preparing for early morning *mangala darshan,* viewing the gods waking up. For this annual *Diwali,* festival of lights, pilgrims had arrived from all over the land. Routine *darshan,* viewing, of daily activities of Radha-Krishna would be more elaborate for this biggest annual festival. Their images would be decked with precious jewels and festive attire. Literally hundreds of delicious dishes would be cooked. Some of them were prepared only once a year at *Diwali* time.

The doors of the sanctuary were still closed. Devotees had started gathering singing early morning hymns, *bhajans,* requesting the gods to wake up. Isa came early to witness devotional practices. He sat on the steps close by a pillar enjoying the music and singing. The lead singer's sonorous voice aided by a *veena,* a string instrument, a flute, drums and cymbals created a magical mood. The crowd accompanied the singer's lead. After a while, Isa too joined the crowd.

Isa realized why Sriram said *bhakti* touched the heart...feelings. Krishna has been worshipped as an epitome of ultimate love, divine love. Each devotee as it were becomes a *gopi* symbolizing a total loving surrender to Krishna, Sriram had said.

Soon Isa saw Vallabh's family arriving led by Kunti's devotional hymns. Her melodious voice promptly overpowered the crowd which quickly followed her lead in singing. Isa saw Mira, in her sparkling Diwali outfit and jewelry, singing closely following Kunti. Was she dancing too? Isa wondered. Or was that the way she walkeds? Isa was not sure.

The temple corridor was packed by singing, praying, and dancing devotees. Each line of the hymn ended with the refrain:

"*Radhe-Krishna-Radhe.*" After a while Isa felt he was receding into a meditation, of a different sort. It was a kind of collective rapture and he was a part of it.

As the doors of the interior opened, people rushed for *darshan,* viewing, of Radha-Krishna in their full glory. Isa stayed on the steps watching the crowd rushing in.

"Greetings, old friend," someone was tapping Isa on the shoulder. Isa turned around and his mouth fell open. A tall man in native outfit and a *tilak,* a symbolic mark on his forehead, was standing by him.

"Oh, Demetrius, is that really you? Fancy meeting you here! I thought you were going back to Greece from Takshashila. What are you doing here? When did you come to Mathura?" totally surprised Isa was full of questions.

Demetrius, the Greek scholar of Plato, was glowing and looked happy. "Isn't Mathura a special place?" he said in a cheerful voice, "I have been here for nearly three months. You must have just arrived."

"Three months? Then you know a lot about Mathura. I got here only yesterday. Everything is new for me; now you can educate me," Isa laughed.

"Let us go for *darshan* before the doors close," said Demetrius leading Isa up the steps.

Both of them proceeded toward the main lobby. The door to the sanctuary was not as wide as the hall, where people had congregated. Throngs of people, praying with joined palms touching their heads trying to get a glimpse of Radha-Krishna's image were jostling with each other. People kept moving to make room for others. Constant jostling and pushing separated Isa and Demetrius, but later they met outside the temple by the wall and stood watching people in festive garments and jewelry, coming and going, chatting and singing.

Demetrius asked, "Are you doing anything right now? If not, let's walk to the *ghaat.*" The *ghaat* was a built up walkway with steps leading to the river. "The holy river Yamuna was Krishna's favorite. Now she is mine too. She is a good friend who listens." Demetrius laughed loudly and added, "Sometimes you get an answer from her too!"

Finding their way through the street full of stalls of food, clothes, shawls, rugs, jewelry, toys, lamps, and trinkets was a slow process. But people made room for the tall Greek and the charming foreigner.

"This is *Diwali*, a major annual festival of lights. You know that, don't you?" Demetrius asked Isa.

"Sriramji, one of my two Indian mentors," Isa said, "told me to come here at this time. But I need to know more about it. Is *Diwali* not a harvest festival?" Isa asked.

"Well, we *pundits* would say that," Demetrius smiled, "For lay people it is celebrating the victory of gods and goddesses over evil. People seek divine blessings for prosperity, health, and liberation. For most agricultural societies harvest is the propitious time of thanksgiving, I guess. Their granaries are full. It is time for celebration and relaxation from hard work. People are happy, have good food and festivities. Business people settle their old accounts, and start another year with new deals. This is an appropriate time for a new year for their calendar; they honor the goddess of wealth, Laxmi in a special ceremony. The fierce goddess Kali is propitiated to protect oneself from dark forces. Millennia ago those perceptive *rishis,* who guided kings and commons, determined this as an appropriate season for gratefulness and festivities. Mind you in this land nothing is done without astrological calculations. They have accurate timings for all *pooja*, ceremonies determined by the positioning of stars, planets and constellations."

"The harvest festival is common in many cultures. Do they not do that in Greece? We have Rosh Hasahanah and Yom Kippur, our harvest festival in the Jewish tradition, and that is also the newyear," Isa observed.

"True. But my discussions with *pundits*, as well as my research, indicates that the practice was much older here in what we know as the ancient region of the river Indus. Could others have adopted it, perhaps? There has been a lot of cultural exchange over a long time," Demetrius evidently was totally charmed by Mathura.

"Cultural exchange does impact people's traditions. But all humans are connected with nature's seasonal changes. Seasonal festivals could arise independently in various regions, like sun-worship, for instance. Almost all ancient traditions have it. There is so much we all can learn from each other," Isa was getting more and more curious.

"You know well, Isa, the more you find, the more you want to know. I thought spending four years in Takshashila was enough. But now I know I could spend four more. It is endless. I guess I will be headed to Greece soon," Isa heard a sad note in Demetrius' voice.

"But you will continue in the Plato-school, won't you?" asked Isa.

"Yes, that's the plan," Isa heard a note of resignation in Demetrius' voice.

When Isa and Demetrius reached the river bank it was crowded too. Pilgrims were bathing in the Yamuna washing away their sins.

"We will soon arrive at the secluded end, if it is still secluded. This is the holiday season after all," Demetrius said to Isa who seemed kind of lost in the crowd.

"Sure, you lead the way. I am enjoying the smells, the chatter, colors, everything." Isa said with a delightful grin on his face. On the promenade there were more stalls, mainly food stalls. They saw people going down the steps for the dip in the river, coming up and eating.

"Hey... Isa," it certainly was Mira's voice. But where was she in this crowd? Isa looked in the direction of the voice. There she was in a group of women having a holy dip in the river. Mira waved, came out of the river, and started walking up the steps. Her clothes were dripping, revealing every curve of her elegant body. Isa was mesmerized.

Mira's voice, her smiling eyes and the sanctified body emerging out of the holy river literally entranced Isa. He waved back and stood there, his waving palm frozen in the air.

"You have to take a dip in the holy river Yamuna, at least once. It's mandatory," Mira laughed coming up the *ghaat*. It was the same endearing musical laughter.

"This is Demetrius from Greece. He is showing me around," Isa spoke, his eyes still riveted on Mira. Then turning to Demetrius Isa said, "Mary is from Babylon. We first met in Galilee. But not too long ago she found her Indian origins. Here they call her Mira."

"*Jai Shree Krishna,* Mira-*ji,*" Demetrius greeted her with joined palms, the way *Bhagvat* and *Vaishnava* devotees do. Demtrius had adopted the local traditions in almost all respects and was at ease. "I will make sure after Isa's Mathura orientation he will have the Yamuna *snan,* holy dip in the river," he laughed. Was that a laugh of a devotee or a cynic, Isa wondered.

"You will catch cold, Mira. Get dried and change your clothes," they all heard Kunti's gentle command as she came out of the river.

"Yes, *Maji,* I am coming," turning to Isa Mira added, "please bring your friend to our inn. *Dada* would love to talk with you both."

She ran down the steps to the pile of her dry clothes and Kunti.

Chapter 36

After the evening *aarati,* waving of lights ritual, at the bank of Yamuna, pilgrims assembled in the Radha-Krishna temple courtyard. Ample food offered to gods would be distributed among devotees as *prasad,* grace of god. At this temple and especially at this festival time all pilgrims and anybody else who shows up would get a full meal. Rich and poor, men, women, and children, regardless of rank ate at the temple. The outcastes too would get food, but they ate in a separate corner.

"Why are they considered outcastes and why do they have to be separated in the temple? A temple is a holy place," Mira asked Vallabh when they came back to *dharmasala* with Isa and Demetrius.

Vallabh needed to think a little before addressing the sensitive issue of the untouchables. Centuries of practice had made this custom seem natural to the natives, but for a newcomer it was inscrutable. In fact, the inhumanity brought to bear on the untouchables was abominable to many sensitive natives as well. Although originally the caste system had rational roots, the system had degenerated.

Vallabh spoke cautiously, "The caste system has intrigued many people. Originally it had a valid, justifiable, organizational principle. For the smooth running of a society, one needs organization, division of work according to one's skills. That is what *rishis* advised kings, chieftains, and common people almost 3000 years ago."

Demetrius quickly summarized the system he had studied, "True, one can validate four castes in their original concept. The caste system was a brilliant organizational principle for the smooth running of a society, as you say. Philosophers, teachers, priests, thinkers were called *Brahmins;* kings, courtiers and warriors were *Kshatriya.* Landlords, agriculturists, traders, and commercial people were classified as *Vaishya*; *Shudra* were the craftsmen, builders, artisans, and such. It was a brilliant classification." But he had not yet found an answer to one question, "Why *Mahashaya*, Sir, is the caste now determined by *birth* and not by vocation as it was originally conceived?"

"It is sad but true. Originally a *Brahmin's* son could become a warrior and he would be considered *Kshatriya*. But that principle did not last long in practice. Four castes developed a hierarchy which did not exist in the original system. *Brahmins*, who mastered learning and were religious preceptors, became powerful. They were considered superior to other castes. Even a king, a warrior, would bow to a *Brahmin*."

"*Dada*, you mean the all powerful king, a *Kshatriya*, warrior caste, would bow to an ordinary *pujari*, a ceremonial priest in the temple?" Mira intervened. It was inconceivable.

"Yes, *Beti*, centuries later such notions of higher and lower castes became a part of social behavior. Commercial people: *Vaishyas* who were probably the richest of all, were considered third in ranking. The fourth were the artisans and manual workers: *Shudras*. So the lowest who were scavengers, cleaning the streets and handling dead bodies, were considered 'outcaste,' the untouchables." Vallabh summarized the structure where knowledge ranked higher than wealth, but humans were treated as pariah.

It was Isa who readily grasped the source of discrimination. He had personally experienced it under the Roman rule. He observed, "So a *Brahmin* naturally would not want his son to lose his social ranking by being an artisan or a trader or a warrior."

"Or even if he became a prime minister, he would be called a *Kshatriya* and therefore socially below a *poor Brahmin*," Demetrius completed the circle.

"I get it," Mira was incredulous, "So you hope your son follows your vocation; but if he cannot, regardless of his vocation he does not lose his caste of birth, right?"

"Yes, *Beti*, soon the caste was determined by birth, not by vocation. We have followed this for thousands of years now. So it is ingrained in people's heart." There was sadness in Kunti's voice, "So entrenched these traditions have been over millennia that people forget they can be challenged." Kunti was thinking of another cruel tradition which ruined her daughter Mrinal's life. Despite their superior *Brahmin* caste they could not save their widowed daughter from social ostracism.

Isa observed, "Even the Buddha's teachings did not make a difference?"

Demetrius pointed out, "*Technically* the Buddha opened a window of liberation for all, including the lowest, the outcastes and the women – who were also left out of religious privileges, despite the tradition of worshipping the Mother Goddess! But there is no evidence of the Buddha *advocating* for them. In fact, there is a story that Buddha was reluctant to establish the order of nuns similar to the order of monks. One of the Buddhist stories narrates how women insisted on getting the order of nuns established to have a chance for liberation, *nirvana.* Many women, led by the Buddha's foster mother, marched miles and miles to reach Buddha's monsoon abode. Their clothes were dusty and torn, their feet were bleeding, but their resolve was unflinching; this was the first demonstration by any group, men or women, nearly 500 years ao for the opportunity to attain spiritual liberation. But the Buddha, according to the records, rejected them three times. He said it would shorten the life and practice of his teachings. Finally, his chief disciple, Ananda, pleaded for the women, and the Buddha established the order of nuns." Everybody was amazed by Demetrius' narration. Even Vallabh was not aware of this episode. A long time in Takshashila had its rewards.

After a few moments of silence Isa spoke, "Maybe the untouchables will someday become Buddhists in droves." Was Isa seeing a distant future?

Vallabh spoke, "That may come to be. In fact, the condition of the untouchables is similar to that of serfs and slaves in cultures you both are familiar with. In all power games -- business or war -- the winner exploits the conquered. It is the victor's world, his money, his religion, his political system are imposed on the vanquished. But someday the oppressed will rebel, rise in revolt."

Isa said in a pensive voice, "An awakened radical voice eventually brings a change from any overbearing power structure." Isa was thinking of his people under Roman rulers.

Ballu, who was silently listening, could hold his aggravation against social injustice no more, "But such reforms have been short lived. How many thinkers we have had who opened people's minds for a brief time? Three hundred years back Buddha did; Mahavir did. We have innumerable stories of radical reformers in our scriptures: the *Purans, the Bhagavatam, the Ramayana, the Mahabharata,* and such. But eventually in the name of the same reformers, their followers exploit others, repeating the same game of greed and power. I ask you more experienced and better informed people, does that happen only in our land? Or is it a human trait prevalent elsewhere too?" Ballu's passion surprised everyone; they stared at him.

Snatching a brief gap in the discussion of the sociology and politics of religion men were discussing, Mira jumped in with her question, "*Maji,* you told me a few Krishna stories. It surprises me that people worship him in so many different forms: he is worshipped as child, *Baal* Krishna; he is also the Divine *lover* of Radha and the *gopis,* he is the great *visionary* of the *Bhagvad Gita.* And he is the ultimate essence, *God.* He blends these seemingly varied aspects; they do not contradict each other," Mira was intrigued by the multiple aspects of the same god.

Kunti was making a garland of jasmine buds for Krishna with all her attention focused on her movement. The next morning she would bring the garland to the temple. It was her usual *seva,* service. In *bhakti* tradition such immersion into *seva* would be equivalent to one pointed meditation. She spoke in a gentle note, "They are all diverse phases of the same Krishna. We humans are limited. Some of us can show our love as mother, some as beloved friend, some as seekers of knowledge, or as ardent devotees. One person can have different roles, and varied approaches. Krishna knows who needs what."

Mira, "So Krishna fulfills all those worshippers whose needs and abilities are totally different, even unique?"

Isa observed, "What a powerful perception that is! Krishna loves and is loved by a cowherd or a king, by a mother or a thinker, by a self-absorbed damsel or a brave warrior."

Demetrius intervened, "Well, every religion has diverse followers. But Krishna worship is not thrust down your throat with one teaching like 'one medicine cures all' attitude. Krishna has a connection to each individual on one's own terms. It is a *personal* bonding of love that is at once *unique* and *universal.*"

Vallabh added, "And the best part of it is that you can focus on one or more of his aspects or only on *one* that resonates with you, ignoring all the rest. And you still would not miss *any* of Krishna's *essence.*"

Leaning against the wall, Ballu sat twiddling his thumbs and fingers, "Have you heard one of the verses of the *Ishavasya Upanishad -- Purnam idam purnam adah?*

This is perfect

That is perfect

From the perfect emerges perfection

Perfection still remains.

To a true devotee Krishna is this Perfection. All devotees derive *ananda,* bliss, from him, and he still remains undiminished perfection. Therefore he is called *purna avatar,* 'Perfected Incarnation.'"

Isa was intently listening to Ballu, "That's a fascinating integration of the two separate traditions - Upanishadic and devotional. But does a devotee emerge as a perfect whole himself?"

Mira asked a rhetorical question, "Isn't Radha a testimony to the love of a Perfected devotee, *poorna bhakta?*"

Kunti was happily surprised by Mira's extremely sensitive, deep perception. "*Chiran jive,* may you live long, *Dohitri,* granddaughter."

She touched Mira's forehead with both palms turned inward in a traditional blessing.

Isa, "Then Radha-Krishna would epitomize *the supreme love of the soul with the divine.* Would that be *the ultimate love story?*"

Vallabh, "And that is *mukti,* final liberation from *samsara,* the cycle of life and death."

Kunti, "However, do not forget. Some *bhaktas* are so enamored by this divine love of Krishna that they wish to reincarnate repeatedly to be in *love* rather than be a *jivan mukta,* liberated."

All kept silently looking at Kunti knotting the garland for a long time.

Her words flowed, gently touching their hearts. She kept threading one jasmine bud after another. It was an act of complete surrender. So unflinching was her faith, yet so soft was her voice, so tender her touch; she could be lovingly massaging *baal,* child, Krishna's divine feet.

Chapter 37

"Why do you look a little lost, Demetrius, are you not well?" asked Isa.

They were walking on the Yamuna *ghaat* very early the next morning. It was a proper time for *Suryanamaskar*, the yogic salutation to the sun. Except for a devotee's gentle hymn and an occasional cock crow, all was quiet.

"You are perceptive, Isa. I keep busy, learn, observe, practice, but am confused about integrating varied 'truths.'" Demetrius was a logician and idealist of Plato's tradition, a *jnani,* a pundit, who was enjoying Mathura, the capital of *bhakti,* devotional path. "Do you realize what an amalgam of traditions, schools, practices, and philosophies of the entire world could do to your head?" Demetrius' voice sounded like he was headed for a mental break down.

Isa recognized Demetrius' pain since he had known what a curse a plethora of information could be, "Oh I know what you are talking about. Didn't I go through it in Takshashila? Listen Demetrius, trust your heart, not your brain."

Demetrius said with a wry smile, "That's simplistic, isn't it?"

"Maybe, but some kind of shutting off of the brain is essential in *sadhana,* spiritual search, brother," Isa spoke with conviction of someone who had experienced the truth.

"Did you shut off your brain? Could You? It seems you did," Demetrius was curious, even envious.

"Well, at first it was a partial success. Sriramji was a great help. He taught me yoga techniques to quiet my intellectual chatter. But curiously, and quite unexpectedly, it happened here in Mathura for me," said Isa.

"How did it happen? What do you mean?" Demetrius was eager.

"I have been watching this throng of lay people and their tremendous faith. Most of them do not have the intellectual burden we carry. They hear Krishna's stories. Many of them literally believe them. That strength of faith, of belief, appeals to me. How animated they become as they enter the temple, the energy field of Radha-Krishna. It is almost magical," Isa was envisioning ecstatic moments of singing and dancing crowds of people.

"So you are saying that *knowledge* and *faith* are incompatible. That is my dilemma," Demetrius admitted.

"No they are not incompatible. In fact, last night it was like an epiphany. Kunti ma's words, her faith, and action were all of one piece, I noticed. Her total absorption was in service, *seva,* as she threaded the garland. Her silence *spoke* of her one-pointed bliss. But then her words revealed a deeper level, when she said a devotee would reject even heavenly liberation to experience this perfected love and joy again and again. It is a sort of total immersion, when two beings love each other they find themselves, instead of losing their identities in the other. In that moment *surrender* and *victory* are not opposites. Better still surrender *is* victory. *Knowledge* and *faith* are not incompatible either. Faith evokes true knowledge, ultimate knowledge," Isa spoke as he visualized Kunti threading the jasmine garland, flower after flower, one at a time.

Listening to Isa's compelling words, Demetrius was lost in thoughts. The two seekers saw the sun rising; it was time for their yogic salutation to the sun, *Suryanamaskar.*

* * * * * * * * * * * *

The town had come to life while Isa and Demetrius were meditating. They started walking toward the temple. Isa was relishing people's exuberance. This busy place reminded him of the active marketplace in Galilee, but Mathura was different in its energy and appearance.

"Hey, where are you two headed?" They heard Mira's musical voice from a bullock cart passing by. Both were surprised.

"It seems you are going out of Mathura," Isa noticed a few neatly packed bundles with Vallabh's family in the cart.

"It's a special day in Vrindavan today, don't you know? Aren't you two going?" Mira was amazed they did not seem to know about this special day.

"I totally forgot, Isa" said Demetrius, "It seems our deep conversations have distracted me some." The two men approached the travelers.

Ballu stopped the cart. In an excited voice Mira said, "It is *deva-diwali*, the celebration of Krishna's wedding with Tulsi. It's a lot of fun. Ballu says *Raas lila,* the dance play, is the best, an experience of a life time, he says," Mira's voice, her demeanor, her musical laughter were enchanting, even evocative. Isa was charmed. He looked at Demetrius.

"Well jump in, there is enough room in the cart, if you want to come," Vallabh suggested, and they did. Isa sat next to Ballu in the driver's seat. He just loved the jingle of bells around the bullock's neck. Demetrius was sitting next to Vallabh in the back.

"I still am lost about all these wives of Krishna," said Demetrius. "I reckon Tulsi is a kind of basil plant, right? What is the significance of Krishna marrying a plant when he had eight wives? He loved Radha the most but was not married to her. And yet, devotees all over this land worship Radha-Krishna. And I see a Tulsi plant in everybody's yard." Demetrius was light hearted.

"You are from Greece. You have stranger stories than Krishna's playful exploits. Why are you bewildered?" said Vallabh laughing loudly. Everybody joined in the laughter.

Ballu turned his head and said, "Krishna's connection extends to the non-human world. The cow, the *pippal* tree, and Tulsi, the medicinal herb, all are sanctified because of their importance in people's daily life and well being." Ballu's expertise was not faith based; it was knowledge based and fairly accurate.

"What is the significance of it all?" Mira was ready for more stories. Sanctification of an animal, a tree and a plant sounded interesting. Krishna certainly was a charmer, she thought. Isa, sitting next to Ballu, was feeling his zeal.

Ballu continued, "Krishna's divinity has relevance to all creation human and non-human as I said. The cow nurtures us with her milk. She also produces more cows and oxen. We use her milk and milk products for nourishment, the ox to cultivate our farms and pull carts, transport people and goods. Cow-dung is used for fuel, flooring, roofing; the cow's urine has medicinal value. When she dies her skin can be used for leather goods such as horse reigns, straps for armors, shields, and such. A cow is wealth. Killing her would be equivalent to burning gold coins." Ballu did not speak much. But when he did, his explanations were thorough.

"I did not know all that!" Mira was impressed.

"That explains a lot to me," Isa continued, "So what is the significance of the *pippal* tree?"

"Almost every village has a *pippal* tree at its center. Village elders meet there to solve disputes or make new rules for the community, or just to have a smoke. Youngsters meet there to socialize. *Jnanis* meditate under it. The Buddha is supposed to have gotten his ultimate knowledge under a *pippal* tree. It was by that tree that Krishna played his magic flute that enticed *gopis*. You probably know that nearly 500 years ago Jain scholars established that plants and trees have life. We may conclude there is innate wisdom in that *pippal* tree."

"So what does Krishna's marriage to Tulsi signify?" Demetrius was eager to get to Krishna's wives.

"Tulsi symbolizes all plant life with medicinal value. By the way, there is a legend connected with a woman called Tulsi too. For physical well being, people have to honor herbs and roots, since there are no other remedies to cure our ailments," Vallabh said.

"I certainly believe that after being with a much respected physician, *Vaidya* Mani, for a few years," said Isa.

Kunti added, "Tulsi is a sacred plant we grow in front of our house. It reminds us of Krishna all the time. Coming and going all pay respect to it. Some neighborhoods have a community Tulsi plant in a central place. Everybody takes care of it, waters it, and nourishes it." Her words revealed Tulsi's importance in everyday life.

Isa listened to the significance of traditions and learned how everyday common items can evoke deeper understanding of life. Maybe a piece of bread or a cup of wine can be sanctified. He mused over it as he watched people walking in the direction of Vrindavan. They were singing wedding songs.

Demetrius seemed lost in thinking. On one hand the Krishna *bhakti* tradition had captured masses of people. It entwined distinct aspects of everyday life. In Krishna's *Bhagavad Gita* the traditions of knowledge, devotion, action, and yoga converge. The scripture blends them all, rendering a deeper understanding of life and its purpose. What a comprehensive god Krishna had become. After all, people of India have been always re-hashing old traditions and reviving them in new shapes to meet new demands of changing times. That has been the Indian people's strength. Demetrius wondered if there was a similar figure in Greek tradition. Maybe Apollo! Someday he might research the issue. Such a figure would help sustain the dwindling hold of Greek traditions.

Chapter 38

Vrindavan was not too far from Mathura, but it was certainly more festive today. People looked happy, treated visitors cordially, were ready to help them settle, or find a place to have a meal. They were dressed in red, green, deep blue and mauve. Men had headbands of yellow, orange, red, and green. Their cows' horns were colored red and the tips of the horns had little bells on them. Around their necks the cows had larger bells. Cow bells and the silver anklets on women's feet created a refreshing jingle. Men played flutes, pipes, and *dholaks,* small two sided drums hanging by a strap across the player's shoulder. Music and laughter mixed with the confused questions of newcomers. All settled soon in the central ground by the main Krishna temple.

The sound of Mira's musical laughter mixed with the din in the temple square. She asked questions about curious items in vendors' stalls. For Vallabh and Kunti too many items in the market were new.

For the first time, since the days of caravan festivities, Isa was getting caught up in feverishly joyous communal activities in Mathura and now in Vrindavan or Vraj. Ballu got busy managing for the accommodations at an inn, *dharmasala.* Next he made sure he talked to the right person in charge to get front row seats for his group at the *raas lila* performance.

* * * * * * * * * * * *

After *darshan* at the temple and the *prasad,* Ballu guided the whole group to a designated special area. He led Vallabh and Kunti to a comfortable rug in the front circle. Behind them he had seats for Mira, Isa, and Demetrius. Ballu himself sat at the edge for easy communication with the organizers, in case anybody needed help.

The evening of *raas lila,* the legendary dance-play of Krishna with Radha and *gopis* of Vrindavan, was reenacted by the villagers.

The performance began with the blessings recited by the chief *pujari* of the temple. Young men in multicolored jackets, yellow *dhotis*, garment tied at the waist, and bandanas of varied colors; women in bright colored saris, flared skirts and jingling anklets, entered dancing with *dandia*, a foot long rounded wood sticks, in each hand. They struck the sticks keeping the beat of the music and drum, *dholak*. The songs were about Krishna, Radha, and the *gopis*. They also sang stories of Yashoda, Krishna's mother, and Nanda, his father. Brother Balram was always with Krishna in the songs celebrating games they played with other cow boys, *gopals*.

Isa was sitting between Mira and Demetrius asking Demetrius questions about r*aas*. Mira sat close to Isa leaning forward to be able to catch Demetrius' words with all the singing and music around them.

"*Raas* is the name of the stick dance," he said. "Evidently, Krishna usually played with many *gopis* of Vrindavan. But Radha was his favorite. Like most *gopis*, Radha too was married," said Demetrius in soft words, making it harder to hear. He did not want to offend either his hosts or others in the audience. "Everybody knew Radha was older than Krishna and married to someone else. But that was evidently not objectionable to this socially conservative society," Demetrius said. His tone reflected surprise at this paradox of social behavior. "The whole issue of the teenaged Krishna playing with *gopis* is not a moral, social, or ethical issue. It was *love* in its purest form," Demetrius stopped with his eyebrows still raised in wonder about people's uncanny behavior.

Isa laughed, "It's amazing how rigid people are in their everyday life about the sanctity of sex, marriage within the same caste, or supposedly guarding widows by ostracizing them. The same people worship Radha-Krishna's love relation?" Isa was curious. Mira was listening intently, trying to make a connection with what she had learned from Kunti walking by the river Tapi back in Suryapuri.

Demetrius said, "There is no question of sexual intrigue with regard to Krishna's ventures with *gopis* or Radha we have in our Greek myths. Radha-Krishna love is sensuous, without being sexual;

the connection remains a play, *lila, a game of the perfected divine love.*"

"*Maji* said, '*Love* is an emotion and also more than an emotion,'" Mira spoke, leaning over Isa even more to be audible to Demetrius; Isa put his arm over her shoulder to help her lean further, "It is an awareness of consciousness, *chitta,* of the connection between the soul, *atman,* and the supreme soul, *paramatman.*"

Isa asked, "So does *raas lila,* the dance, celebarte this divine connection?"

Mira explained, "Yes, each *gopi* is *atman,* the soul, who dances individually with Krishna, *paramatman,* the *s*upreme soul."

"This I have to see. Love is a state, a *connection;* not just an *emotion,* right?" Isa needed clarity. He remembered his mystical talks with Sriram on this subject. Isa continued, "It seems *love, compassion* and *oneness* -- the abstract concepts -- are demonstrated to people in concrete images of Krishna, Radha, and their actions. People have unflinching devotion to Krishna as a symbol of Absolute Love; but that love is personal too – as for a child, a lover, or a god. Since it is for Radha as well as all *gopis,* it is at once personal and universal. What a brilliantly conceived concrete image of an abstraction! It is a perfect way to reach masses of people who cannot comprehend abstractions," Isa was elated.

"Well said, Isa," Demetrius appreciated Isa's astute observation.

Dancers were getting more and more vigorous in their movements, carrying the audience with them into a deeper rhythm of awareness with every beat. Mira, Isa and Demetrius stopped talking and got absorbed in the rhythm of dance and music.

After vigorous dancing the group receded; another set of dancers entered. They were all women; colorfully dressed *gopis,* with smiling faces and ringing anklets, hitting wooden *dandia* sticks. On their faces was an expectant look. As the story goes, Krishna, always partial to Radha, had promised all *gopis* he would dance with each one of them individually, simultaneously. The legend was that Divine Krishna had multiplied himself to dance with each *gopi.* Each one danced with *her* Krishna. That occasion is celebrated by the devotees over the millennia.

At the center, eager *gopis,* each anticipating one's own Krishna, were in full swing. They turned around in frenzied swinging, vigorously waving their wooden sticks.

Suddenly the rhythm changed. The movements became more and more eerie. Beating wooden sticks, male dancers entered, each attired as Krishna. They all wore a *pitamber,* yellow *dhoti* garment, a flower garland, a crown with a peacock feather, and carried a flute in their waist band. Each *gopi* had her Krishna. The audience swayed with the movements of the dancers.

Isa and Mira sat entranced in the singing, music, and the rhythm of the dance. Isa's arm was still on Mira's shoulder. At the center was Krishna with his arm across Radha's shoulder, their eyes interlocked. Around them danced *gopis* with their own Krishna, also looking into each other's eyes. Music and movement made them lose their sense of the self.

So powerful was the rhythm of singing and dancing and music, Isa and Mira felt their identities merged. They were conscious of their physical closeness, yet unaware of each other as a separate person, feeling only a part of the *one* divine. It was a confluence of inner resonance. With Isa's hand on Mira's shoulder they were submerged into Radha-Krishna on center stage. Both fused into *one.* Despite the huge crowd around them, Isa and Mira felt the proximity of just the two of them alone. They *knew* only *one in the other.*

Slowly the rhythm slowed, so did the music and dancing. Gradually all came to a complete stop. Intense vigorous music followed by total silence transported everyone into another state. The audience of thousands was speechless. Each one was subsumed in silence.

Isa and Mira simultaneously remembered their past visionary experience: they had seen a gazebo with an ethereal energy orb at the altar; it was pierced from the pinnacle by a light beam; the bright light from the orb had reached their eyes, forming twin interlaced triangles.

Vallabh and Kunti were lost in bliss; Demetrius was in profound peace; Ballu kept staring into the empty space as if the dancers were still performing.

Chapter 39

"*Hare* Krishna...*Hare* Krishna," Vallabh awoke from a dream. His body was shaking, he was perspiring. What he saw in the dream was at once thrilling and scary.

He was one of the young dancers in raas on a full moon night by the bank of river Tapi. He enjoyed dancing with his friends around him. Young Kunti was his new bride. They were singing songs of Krishna's childhood exploits. Their raas movements became more vigorous as they sang of Yashoda and Nanda, Krishna's parents, celebrating Krishna's birthday.

The scene shifted, Vallabh was one of Krishna's cowherd friends playing ball with him. Krishna, no more than ten years old, jumped into the river to scoop out the ball that had fallen into it. Vallabh and the screaming team mates were asking Krishna not to jump. The river was poisoned by a snake, the seven headed Kalinag. Soon they saw an astonishing sight. Krishna, pulling seven ropes from each head of Kalinag, was standing on top of this giant serpent in total control, with a victor's smile.

Vallabh woke up, still shaking, repeating, "*Hare* Krishna...." Now that the terror of a ten year old was gone, he laughed. Well it was only a dream! But then it was funny too. Why did he rope Kalinag as if the kingb serpenthe was a bull? Isn't that funny? He lay in bed thinking of the dream enjoying dancing with young Kunti, and then being a ten year old playmate of Krishna..."That's who we are, Krishna's playmates, only if we remember,"...he mumbled, turned on his side, and went back to sleep.

Being one of all those *gopis*, Kunti dreamt, she was dancing all night with her own Krishna.

It was a dark moonless night, amavasya, the night of Diwali. Totally absorbed in her Krishna, she lost sense of her body. It seemed Krishna's energy subsumed hers. But she did not know nor could she tell what was happening. All she felt were these joyful vibrations, spandan. Her steps moving in rhythm became lighter and lighter. It felt like she was swimming, more like floating effortlessly in the river with Krishna, both becoming ripples of the river Yamuna. It just continued...endlessly...

When she awoke she touched her body to feel if she was really there. What a vision of total immersion it was, she muttered.

She heard Ballu saying something. He was sleeping on his rug by the door 'being a doorman' as Mira had said, 'even in his sleep.' Ballu's words were not audible, but he seemed to be arguing with somebody. Kunti turned and fell asleep.

"You confuse us so, Krishna," Ballu was arguing while still striking his sticks as he played with his own Krishna in the raas lila dance. He was thrilled to dance. His young body moved automatically, as if he was a keyed toy. But Ballu focused on questioning Krishna about things that remained unresolved in his mind. He had his own Krishna tonight. How much better could it be, he mused.

"What confuses you friend?" Krishna asked with a smile, striking his dandia sticks onto Ballu's and turning around. Following orchestrated movements both turned around, struck again four times, and took another turn. Playing the raas was fun. Krishna was energetic. His eyes, face, and every limb expressed joy, sheer bliss, ananda. Ballu was elated having his own Krishna as playmate.

"Arjun asked you all the questions he could. And I totally relate to him, and to his confusion as well. But what still bothers me is this detachment and desire you speak of. How can I put my energy into whatever is my duty, dharma, unless I desperately desire to attain results? 'Detachment from desire' you said, didn't you?"

"Well, actually, I said desire for 'the fruit of the action.' You have to admit I said it so many times. How could you miss it friend?" Krishna responded with a gentle smile on his lips.

"Granted," Ballu hit that last stroke heavily before taking yet another turn around, "if you want to split hairs on a phrase, granted *you are right. Whichever way it is, 'desire' or 'its fruit'; where do I get the energy from, if I abandon the desire for the result?"*

"From ME, priya mitra, *dear friend," said Krishna with that ever present smile. "Remember my cosmic universal form I showed to Arjun, the* visvrupadarshan?"

"Oh, your form that scared Arjun? How can I forget it? It was gruesome. You multiplied into hundreds of gigantic shapes-both divine and demonic; snakes sticking out of your mouth and ears and all that? Arjun could not take it and asked you to become his old friend Krishna again. You did shake him up, I admit," said Ballu with a sly smile.

"Don't you think Arjun needed it after all those repeated questions such as you are asking now?" Krishna could hardly hold his merry laughter. "If you keep asking more questions without hearing my answers, I will show you my overwhelming ultimate form I showed to Arjun. It might scare you too. But if you trust my universal image, you would be better able to enjoy the raas *dance of life. You did enjoy watching it last night and are dancing with me now."*

Krishna disappeared; so did the dream. Ballu woke up. He was still shaking, having vigorously danced and argued with Krishna.

* * * * * * * * * * * *

"No, don't pull my hand so hard, Krishna," said Mira faking anger, "it hurts." Krishna let her hand go and pulled her from her waist, close to him and burst into laughter saying, "Why don't you tell me you really want this?" Krishna teased her, embracing her, their lips nearly touching.

Both sat leaning against a tree by the river. Krishna pulled out his flute; one arm encircling Mira's shoulder pulling her even closer, he started playing a sprightly love tune. Birds started flying into the pippal tree above. Cows in the fields perked up their ears and kept grazing. Were they keeping in tune with the rhythm as they chewed their cud? Mira thought wild flowers at her feet turned their heads toward Krishna. Or was she dreaming, she wondered. She felt light within. Being with beloved Krishna was...indescribable. Was it bliss, peace, utter happiness? She looked at Krishna who was intently staring at her with a smile in his eyes, and flute at his lips. Why look for words? You feel what you feel, Mira said to herself.

To Krishna she said, "Make me the flute at thy lips, O Krishna."

"Priye, may you have whatever you wish," Krishna was willing to fulfill every sincere wish of his beloved.

"Be within me, and let us fly into endless space. Explore the universe, feel and be one with its floating energy," Mira was in ecstasy.

"So be it, beloved," Krishna said. Mira looked up at Krishna; their eyes were interlocked.

Absorbed in Krishna's energy, Mira saw Krishna's face turned into Isa's and felt his arms around her as they flew into space.

Chapter 40

Time seemed to move slowly as pilgrims began to pack and leave for home. Most pilgrims wished this journey would never end. But life has to be faced, Ballu said. Kunti seemed transformed; she was joyful, "We are returning as new persons. All burdens of life are lightened. Don't you feel younger, *Swami?*" She asked Vallabh.

"Younger? I am not sure. But I certainly see things more clearly. What do they say, the veil of illusion, *maya,* is lifted as it were." Vallabh had a clearer perception of Krishna's triple connections: the loving cowherd of Vrindavan, the victorious prince of Mathura, and the ruler of Dwarka who taught the *Bhagavad Gita.*

Before this journey, Ballu had thought that various facets of Krishna were paradoxical. The innocent child of Vrindavan had nothing in common with the killer of giants in Mathura; the ideal lover of Radha in Vrindavan was eons away from the teacher in the *Gita* and the lord of Dwarka. And still it was the same Krishna. Now the debater in Ballu was more reconciled than ever before.

Vallabh said, "The world is *maya,* an illusion. The seeming separateness in our lives is just that, an appearance, in essence all is One."

"I am not sure I want to leave this land of love," declared Mira. She was yet not fully on this earth after last night's dream of flying into the cosmos with Isa. Or was it Krishna? Does it matter? Did *Dada* not say it is all an illusion, *maya?* She smiled. Kunti asked what she meant by not wanting to leave this place.

"Oh, I don't know. It seems a Gypsy's life suits me well." Mira's comment touched a soft core in her grandparents' hearts. But both regained their composure. Their newfound equanimity helped.

"You want to stay here till Papa returns, whenever he does?" asked Vallabh, hoping she would stay back in India.

"Certainly you do not plan to travel all on your own in this land?" Kunti was protective.

"I can arrange for travel with caravans or pilgrims, if you wish," Ballu relished the idea of organizing another venture. He thrived on his resourcefulness and was usually a step ahead in any game.

Mira laughing her musical laugh said, "Oh no. I do not know yet what I want to do. All that has happened in the last few weeks is overwhelming. I need to calm down and think."

"Well, you have two more days to think before we start heading home." Vallabh continued, "You can stay with us as long as you wish. And we hope you do. But neither Kunti nor I will stand in your way, *Beti.*" Vallabh's words echoed the memory of Mrinal's departure from home twenty some years ago. They would not pressure Mira in anyway.

* * * * * * * * * * * *

Later that evening the Yamuna *ghaat,* the embankment, was much quieter. Many people had left for home. For dusk-walker Isa this was a perfect time. He headed toward the western end. The Yamuna waters were chatty this evening. Isa stopped to listen. He heard the Yamuna sing:

We flow and flow and flow unmindful of any interference.
We see an opening and we stream through;
Come to a precipice and we fall;
We glide gurgling by huge rocks.
Nourish all, fish and fowl, vegetation, or humans.
But we have no time to tarry to tell our stories.
We are never in one spot, ever.
Try stepping into our waters,
Touch the same spot twice, in vain.

Isa heard Yamuna's gurgling laughter. He touched the waters, scooped some and let it run over his head, splashed some on his face, feeling her cool gentle touch. What a blessed moment it was! Isa stepped into the Yamuna's gurgling waters.

The sun had started turning orange. "Till tomorrow, Isa," he heard. Was it the sun talking? Was it not smiling? Isa stood in the river with joined palms staring into that ever turning orange orb and its radiating light. What a comfort it was. How soothing was this evening. Isa remembered, as a young boy he often cried at dusk if he was in a noisy crowded place, away from the sun. He had shed bitter tears, feeling lonely in a crowd.

Isa knew that the twilight sun has been special for him. People in this land observe *sandhya,* a twilight ritual of dawn and dusk; Isa now understood its significance as he stood in the river bowing to the sun. The twilight, a propitious time, when day and night, light and darkness meet, is pregnant with deep energy. Isa had probably known it life after life, he muttered.

The Yamuna rejuvenated Isa as the last rays of the sun left a little speck of light on the curving river bed. Against that light Isa saw a silhouette. A figure was coming toward him from the sun, it seemed.

"*Suvarna sandhya,* golden twilight, isn't it?" said the musical voice.

"*Suvarna ghadi,* a golden moment, too," Isa said, smiling, recognizing the familiar voice. "How are you Mira? Getting ready to leave this magical land of love?"

"It is difficult to leave especially now when it is so quiet and peaceful. You can hear the Yamuna sing to you," evidently Mira had heard Yamuna's words as well.

Isa stepped out of the river, covered his body with his dry robe lying on the *ghaat.* Both sat staring at the Yamuna.

"What is your goal in life, Isa?" Mira asked.

"Does one have to have a goal?" Isa questioned.

"No, but most do. And you look like the one driven by something, what is it, Isa?" Mira intuitively understood the deeper layers of Isa's heart.

"On this journey for almost eight years now, I have learned a lot, experienced a lot. Now I know that learning never ends. So I am stuck in it," Isa chuckled. He was feeling elated, light, with Mira by his side at sunset.

"So you hope to be one of those *pundits,* eh?" Mira sighed.

"I hope not. *Pundit, sadhak, siddha* - are varied spiritual practitioners. I have tasted them all. Attained quite a few *siddhis* myself; and I grew with each. But I know there is something else, a unique spark within. Mine will guide me to the next step, and the next ... I do not want to let the spark diffuse. I will await its signal for the next step and follow it," Isa spoke still looking at the rippling surges of the Yamuna.

"I am glad you are as mad as I am. When I speak of the spark within people look at me like I am empty up there," gently tapping her head Mira laughed. "My family will be returning home in a couple of days. I will have to make up my mind by then if I want to go with them. My spark within is smoldering right now," Mira said contemplatively, also staring at the Yamuna.

"Yesterday, that *raas lila* awakened everyone's awareness. I know *we* were awakened," Isa was now looking intently into Mira's eyes which reflected pink clouds quickly turning grey.

"That was the most exhilarating experience I have ever had, Isa. Maybe if I stayed in this magical land it will do some more tricks on me! I dreamt I was flying with Krishna into space. In fact, he fulfilled my desire to be connected with the cosmos," She laughed charmingly.

Isa stared at Mira in utter amazement, "*You* asked for it? Don't tell me. I also dreamt I was flying into the cosmos," Isa's voice was ecstatic. Mira was speechless, amazed. Isa continued,

I was flying humming these lines as if they were emanating from me but I did not know their origin.

There are no twos, though they appear so.
Light cannot light, it is surrounded by darkness.
Light in weight cannot shine, but can fly
Life is meaningless without death
Death is only another shape of life
Darkness is yet another color of light.

Then I landed on a shining globe hanging in space. In the middle of this globe was a gazebo with an altar in the middle. On a crystal throne was an orb, not solid, nor immaterial. Many colored

energy strings constantly kept moving forming it. It was Shakti, *energy, matter,* Prakriti. *A beam of light,* Purush, *fell from the pinnacle of the gazebo piercing the orb."*

Isa felt Mira's intent gaze on him. Mouth open, her hands holding his, Mira was incredulous.

"It can't be, Isa, I know these lines by heart. They were *my* words in a vision. The orb at the altar in the gazebo has been a constant in my repeated visions. *Purush,* the spirit essence, and *Prakriti,* the primordial matter, unite," Mira uttered, staring at him in total disbelief.

Isa smiled and continued, "I have seen it as well before now. I saw that again after *raas lila;* the vision continued:

In place of the orb Krishna materialized with his arms around Radha. From his flute flowed gentle notes awakening the universe. A new energy rippled. There we were. You and I striking dandia *sticks were dancing* raas *to Krishna's flute. Divine tunes filled the air. Then I saw Radha and Krishna dancing raas with us...the four of us kept dancing, dancing, dancing ...moving to the most unearthly, arousing music ever heard.*

And then I was fully awake."

* * * * * * * * * * * *

Isa and Mira sat gazing into the river for a long time, their shoulders touching close, their fingers intertwined, listening to the Yamuna's song of love...

Chapter 41

"Ballu, could you find me a devout family in Vraj I could stay with?" Mira asked Ballu the next morning. She had talked with Vallabh and Kunti. With sad hearts they had agreed to let Mira follow her desire. She would have no life in Suryapuri. The grandparents had to let go their new found treasure.

"Ballu make sure it is a devout and loving family. Give them money for Mira's stay for at least a year," Vallabh instructed Ballu. "When Papa comes again to India, you can decide what you want to do," Vallabh told Mira. He showed loving concern for his granddaughter and planned for her future. Was it another attachment? He knew life's energies flow in inscrutable ways. His plans were irrelevant, but habits die hard. Who knows how subtle the attachments can be? How short sighted one's plans could be? Krishna must be laughing, thought Vallabh.

Parting from Mira deeply saddened Kunti; she remained silent. Caressing Mira's head, holding her in an embrace, she sat quietly. Was this one more expression of Krishna's will? She knew it was *right*. What else could it be? The whole world is, *Krishnamaya,* absorbed in Krishna. Had she not internalized that truth? Now Mira has to go her way, Kunti and Vallabh have to go theirs. If Krishna so desires, they will reunite someday.

Since Mira announced her decision to stay in Vraj, after she returned from the river walk the evening before, Kunti had struggled for the whole night with similar thoughts. After a great effort Kunti regained some composure in the morning. Now she was at peace. She kept chanting, silently, *Sri Krishna sarnam mamah,* 'I surrender to Sri Krishna.'

Later in the evening, Isa and Demetrius came to say farewell to Vallabh's family.

"Jai Sri Krishna, Mahodaya, Maji, Mira," said Demetrius, "Are you all set for the long journey home?" All exchanged appropriate greetings.

Vallabh said laughing, "We make our preparations. That's our duty, obligation, our *dharma.* What *happens* is Krishna's will."

"Do you think the two are different, *Mahodaya?*" Isa asked.

"We often think that they are," Kunti replied, while Vallabh was still finding a response. "Our human thoughts are limited. But when our hearts are suffused with devotional love, *bhakti-prem* for Krishna, we automatically *do* what we have *be-*come." Kunti spoke slowly, deliberately. In her words was conviction of faith, ardent belief. Vallabh and Ballu were surprised at her clarity and equanimity. Isa and Demetrius were impressed by her faith. Mira hugged her grandmother with loving joy.

"Will you Isa, Demetrius, look out for Mira? She is not going with us. She has decided to stay in Vraj," Kunti continued. Demetrius looked at Mira in total disbelief. Surprised, Isa stared at her. He felt a strange stirring within, a sense of contentedness, an unraveling of inner connectedness.

"Certainly, as long as I am here in Vrinadavan," said Demetrius, "Mira, will you please keep in touch? Let me help in whatever way I can."

"Our paths have intersected so often Mira," said Isa, "we do not need to make an extra *effort* to connect. It will manifest on its own. Our internal sparks will direct our paths, our journeys. *Maji,* your unflinching faith in Radha-Krishna has activated our faith." Isa said turning to Vallabh, "Mira is well protected, *Mahodaya.* Please do not worry about her."

Isa then extended his hand toward Mira, "Be yourself, Mira, I am here."

Mira arose, leaving Kunti's side and fixing her intent look into Isa's eyes she approached him and put her hand into his extended palm.

At that very moment Radha-Krishna temple bells started ringing for the evening *arati,* waving of lights. The sound of conch shell, *shankh naad,* reached higher and higher into space, *antariksha,* and thence deep into the inner sky.

Each one remained absorbed in the energy of the sacred moment.

Chapter 42

Days and weeks rolled into months, months into years.

Demetrius was planning for his return to Greece after nearly twelve years of being away. Isa and Mary had been away from their homes for nearly ten.

After that memorable convergence of travelers in Mathura-Vrindavan, Demetrius had gone west to Dwarka where Krishna spent his mature years as the King. Dwarka was Krishna's royal seat. It was as *Dwarkadhish,* King of Dwarka that Krishna went to be Arjun's charioteer, *sarathi,* in the war of Mahabharata, and gave his deep teaching, known as the *Bhagavad Gita,* the Song of the Lord.

Sitting by the ocean, Demetrius smiled as he recognized the irony: almost a thousand year later, Demetrius thought, Krishna was remembered more for his teaching than his kingship.

Posterity remembers poets and teachers more than emperors, Demetrius pondered. Isn't Homer, the Greek poet, a part of Greek memory more than Hector, the heroic warrior? Better still, Hector and Achilles, his adversary in the Trojan War, would have been forgotten were it not for Homer's epic, the *Iliad.* Demetrius wondered if Alexander, the Great conqueror, will be remembered for long. No doubt for 300 years to date, Demetrius thought, Alexander had retained his reputation for his wild appetite to acquire more and more land. And what about that other Macedonian, Cleopatra, the queen of Egypt whose recent death about twenty some years ago, idolized her as Egyptian goddess Isis. How long wil her memory last? She certainly had made a deep impact on Romans and Greeks.

How religious winds push people and politics in diverse directions, Demetrius mused. Politics and religion are joined at the hips, and will be joined forever. Will there be any people on earth who would ever even think that religion and politics could be separated? He could not help laughing aloud at such an absurd thought.

In Dwarka Demetrius was hoping to find some clues to reconcile the seemingly opposing aspects of the same god: the kingly Krishna with the cowherd, the teacher with the lover. He wondered if he could find in Greek god Zeus' exploits a similar blending of opposites. Greek gods and goddesses, he thought, were embroiled in *worldly* turmoil of their own and of their favorites. It seemed none of the Greek pantheon reached deep mystical or spiritual underpinnings, except perhaps Apollo. Why was it so, he wondered. Was he missing something? Could he find anything here that would help him unearth the root of inner divine awareness? Of course the Greek philosophers like – Pythagoras, Socrates, Aristotle, and Plato – made significant contribution to the world of the mind. It seemed gods, goddesses and philosophers walked separate paths in Greece. In India they intertwined.

Interesting, Demetrius thought. But why was it so? Will he ever find an answer? Can there be any answer to such questions? He needed deeper research...

He sat on the steps of the *Dwarkadhish* temple lost in thoughts looking out on to the ocean. He felt a draw toward his home, Greece. Too much thinking is not good for the soul. 'Intellectual acrobatics' that is what Isa used to call it. Demetrius had not thought of Isa in a while. He wondered where Isa would be; what could he be doing. When they last met Isa was planning to go to Varanasi, Benaras, the holy city of Shiva -- the most ancient city of temples and rivers. Where could Mira be, he wondered?

Demetrius stretched out on the steps in the gentle ocean breeze feeling relaxed, watching the blue sky above. After a while, the bright tropical sunlight created a haze; the waves of the ocean called him; he got up and dreamily walked...

He was headed deeper into the water. What was he looking for he did not know. But something was guiding him, he felt. He kept swimming further and deeper. It was dark and cold at this depth of water; even the sun did not reach here. Demettrius touched something. It struck him right in the head. He could vaguely identify stone steps and a steeple, *shikhar*, of a temple. Simlutaneously he heard, *"Deep are truths, buried in water and sand; Search and seek to heart's content."*

He heard the words clearly? But what do they mean? Where did they come from?

He swam back to the shore.

* * * * * * * * * * * *

Unrelenting funeral pyres burnt constantly on the *manikarnika ghaat,* the holy burning site on the bank of the Ganga in Varanasi, Banaras. Isa frequented this place, not out of morbid impulse to commune with death. But the longer he sat and watched the burning of the dead bodies with holy chanting and funerary rites, the deeper they touched the core of his being.

What is death? Is there another life? Is there a reincarnation? Theoretically he had all this information. He wanted to *feel* its reality. And being on the cremation ground would help, Isa was told.

The image of the presiding god of cremation grounds, Shiva, the Cosmic Dancer of destruction and creation, constantly kept flashing in his mind.

In one hand Shiva plays *damaru,* the rattle, tied to his trident, *sounding* the creation of the universe. He dances to the tune of cosmic rhythm. Another of his four hands carries the fire of destruction; his third hand bending gently over his raised foot blesses the world for peace; the fourth carries a rosary of *rudraksha,* seeds of the-eye-of-Shiva tree, for meditation. Under his foot he has the body of the demon, ignorance. The burning ring of flames around his dancing figure symbolizes the ring of life.

How pervasive, and persuasive, was this image? Nothing was left unsaid. This icon said it all: life, death, struggle, peace, creation, destruction -- all is Shiva. He is the Ultimate, the Cosmic Dancer, the Lord of all. He is worshipped by masses in temples in his symbolic form of *lingam,* the phallic symbol, signifying creative life force. Isa remembered Mani's scientific explanation. And then even his androgynous form of half man half woman, *Ardhanarishwara.* Isa was amazed by all inclusive concepts in one god. It seemed seers in this land habitually aimed at inclusions and integration, not exclusions. Philosophically, that is, Isa mused.

But social codes thrived on rigidity: exclusions reflected in caste distinctions, adherence to customs and traditions. *Spiritual freedom jostled with social restrictions.* That was the controlling force of the lives of the people of this land. Isa had to laugh at the ironic twist.

For hours Isa would meditate at the sacred burning ground. Sriram had spoken of the immense energy pull of this sacred place. Often Isa was transported into other dimensions.

* * * * * * * * * * * *

Where do the dead people go from here before they reincarnate? To different planets called *lokas,* Sriram had said. *Pundits* and *munis* have offered varied answers. Who was right? Isa by now had known that the right answer always came from within.

"Whose within are you talking about?" Mira had asked him once.

"Only *you* can see within *you,* none else," Isa had answered.

"So then there are as many truths as beings? Each has *one's own* truth?" Mira liked to go to absurd lengths. She did not care if she did not get *the* answer. Often she felt there was no *one* answer for anything.

Why was Isa thinking of Mira in this cremation ground? Could Isa and Mira have been together in another life before now? Who were they then? What was that life – or lives -- about? Is there any connection between then and now? There has to be, he inferred. Otherwise the whole concept of reincarnation falls apart.

"A soul's journey through life cycles is not about retribution, reward and punishment," Sriram had said once. "It is to *learn* and *evolve.* The trials of life are opportunities to learn lessons of right behavior, right thoughts, right intent."

"So when you wash off your *karma,* the cycle of birth and death stops for you?" Isa had asked Sriram years ago in Galilee where they first met. Isa remembered how embarrassed he was by Sriram's deafening laughter. "You make it sound like *karma* is a disease, young man. The body has to be cured of *karma*, as it were. No, no, no, *karma* literally means *action*, deeds and thoughts. Is there any living being who can refrain from actions or thought? The trick is to control your actions and thoughts and raise your consciousness," Sriram had explained the misunderstood concept in the simplest possible way. Of course that was so long ago.

Isa had by now understood the deepest level of *karmic* connections after his years at Takshashila and his own heightened awareness in the monasteries and hermitages. After experiencing Krishna-Radha devotional tradition in Vraj, Isa was sure Mira and he had had lifetimes together. And they were again together in this life for a purpose. What it was, he did not know yet. It did not matter either. Life was about living, not speculating.

Isa left *manikarnika ghaat* and walked toward his abode on the outskirts of Varanasi.

Chapter 43

For Mira, Vraj had become another heaven. Before dawn she was up with Sushma, the mother in the family she was staying with. Mira would go to the well to fetch water while Sushma swept the house clean. Then both, singing devotional hymns, *bhajans*, went to the Yamuna to bathe, the morning purification ritual that was now so much a part of Mira's life. As a child she used to complain when her mother insisted on mandatory morning baths. Mira smiled thinking of her mother whose cultural ties with her native land had remained.

Songs of Radha's fake complaints about Krishna's lateness, or his paying more attention to his flute, or about his pranks, filled Mira's heart with joy. She seemed utterly blissful to be all absorbed in Krishna, being *Krishnamaya.* After her bath she would rush to Sushma's garden to pick up *parijat,* the tender white flowers with orange stems and most heavenly fragrance. The maddening aroma spread all over the house, even to the neighbor's house. *Parijat* was one of the multiple gifts the gods acquired from the legendary churning of the milk-ocean. "That's why *parijat* has such heavenly fragrance," Sushma added, after telling Mira the long story of the cosmic feud between *devas* and *danavas,* gods and demons, to get *amrita,* the drink of immortality.

While Sushma cooked, Mira made garlands of *parijat.* She brought them to the temple and stayed there fluttering around doing *seva* – cleaning, cutting fruits and vegetables, preparing jewelry, decorating Radha's saris, Krishna's yellow garment, *pitamber,* or singing *bhajans*, hymns. Krishna-Radha were not mere idols in the temple, they were living entities for the devotees. The line between material and spiritual experience had vanished for Mira. It was all one, whether she danced or prayed or cooked or cleaned. It was all one blessed existence, constant Krishna consciousness.

Months passed by...

"Jai Radha-Krishna, Mira. How are you this morning?"* Mira heard Isa's voice on her way to the temple.

"Oh, Isa! How are you? You are back from Varanasi?" Mira's singing had stopped, but the questions still sounded musical to Isa. She was carrying a basket of *parijat* garlands to the temple.

"I arrived yesterday at *godhan,* cows' homecoming time," Isa used local expression. They kept walking toward the temple.

"What was Varanasi like? Did you find what you were looking for?" Mira asked.

"You know Mira, I never know *what* I am looking for. I go to *experience* whatever the place has to offer," Mira knew Isa's balanced perception of life. It had grown sharper as years rolled by, she observed, but did not say anything.

"So what did Varanasi do for you, Isa?" Mira was laughing. Had Mira's musical laughter become more contemplative, Isa wondered?

He looked into Mira's curious eyes. The morning sun made them shine brighter.

"*Kashivishvanath,* Shiva, the Lord of Kashi and the Universe, helped me experience the ultimate truth of life from yet another perspective, death," Isa said summarizing his total experience in a cryptic image.

Isa and Mira had reached the Radha-Krishna temple. Both went in through the side door. Mira handed over the basket of two thick *parijat* garlands with beautiful fragrant roses strung as pendants. The *pujari* held them up from the basket admiring the artistic knotting.

Isa's eyes sparkled, "How gorgeous they look. What divine fragrance. Where did you learn this artistic knotting?" It was a superfluous question, genuine admiration, though. Mira accepted the compliments from the *pujari* and Isa gracefully, with joined palms.

Isa and Mira walked around the temple and sat in the compound waiting for the doors to open for morning *darshan.*

"I am so happy to see you, Isa," Mira's voice reflected a deep feeling of contentment.

"Words cannot quite describe how fulfilled I feel seeing you, Mira," Isa's words exuded tenderness she could almost touch.

They briefly exchanged the details of their activities and experiences. Like a long-parted friends' converstaion, theirs was fragmentary. Mira jumbled half finished stories about Krishna, Radha's complaints, Sushma and her family, and on and on. Isa could not keep up with where Radha's stories mingled with Mira's. Isa's stories of the cremation ground were drastically edited for Mira's hearing. This was neither the place nor the time, Isa rightly thought. Varanasi was a complex, messy, chaotic city, but with deep layers of sacred energy. "Much like Lord Shiva and his multiple phases," Isa said.

He concluded, "I *feel* I *know* all I have been guided to."

At that very moment they heard the temple bells announcing opening of the doors for *darshan.* Both looked at each other recognizing the synchronicity of the moment.

172

Chapter 44

"Mira, I feel it is time for me to start my return journey home," Isa said one evening as they sat to view the sunset by the Yamuna, to commune with the river, the sun, and each other.

"It is Papa's time to come to India soon. So I may be returning with him," Mira continued, "Perhaps we will meet again?" That was a wishful question with an unmistakable sadness in it.

"I feel we certainly will," Isa said with eyes on the distant horizon. "Mira, have you ever felt that we have been together in other lifetimes?" Isa needed to know what Mira felt.

"Oh, truly I have, so often," Mira spoke looking right into the setting sun, "In visions and dreams, Radha-Krishna often get fused into you and me. At first I dismissed them as a young girl's fantasies. But then I am not 13 anymore. I am 25," Mira was still not looking at Isa, but directly into the setting sun.

"What do you make of your visions?" Isa asked. He had had some that he had not considered sharing with her, at least yet.

"Sushma *didi,* sister, and I have become very friendly, as I told you. One day she was talking about other lives. She said we meet other souls with whom we have lived before to complete our experience. She said that you and I may have had other lives together, that's why we met in this one. Do you wonder why our paths crossed so often without our planning?" Mira was looking at Isa.

"So have you figured out what we are supposed to do next?" Isa grinned.

"Don't joke about it, Isa," irritated Mira's voice was raised a bit.

"I didn't want to upset you, Mira," hurting Mira was already melting his reserve. "I have often felt our connectedness in visions and dreams. Remember we have had often similar visions and dreams. They have deep roots."

"So what do *you* make of our connection in this life?" Mira kept looking at Isa.

Isa stared at Mira, wordlessly. Their eyes interlocked, were searching deep within. No clear answer came. But they did not want to stop seeking or staring. They sat for a long time hearing the Yamuna's whispers as they saw her rippling by. In her flowing waves they heard their stories past and present. Neither of them noticed when Mira's hand, like a bird returning to her nest, gently rested into Isa's, her head resting on his bosom.

The sun had long been to the other world. It was quite dark. A solitary bird chirped in its nest. With a slight jerk, Isa re-focused his open eyes. Mira wondered why Krishna was abandoning her as her waking dream dissolved. The bird had broken their trance.

They arose leaving the river Yamuna and her deep ancient wisdom...

Chapter 45

After the first *darshan* Isa would walk to the open courtyard lean against the wall and be in meditation. No noise ever reached his ears, despite continuous loud chatter, singing, chanting, and clattering bells all around. Mira continued with her busy devotional service and singing *bhajans*. The day would end as usual on the Yamuna *ghaat*, their rendezvous at sunset.

One day, Mira announced that Papa was in Suryapuri finalizing business deals, and would be returning through Dwarka by sea to Arabia. Would she want to go back with him Papa wanted to know. Ballu had arranged to get the message to her through the caravan messenger service.

"I think I am ready to leave," said Mira quite happy to make a move. "It is not that I am tired of Vraj, but I am ready for Arabia, enriched and fulfilled."

"I relate to that feeling. Mani just arrived in Vraj last evening. This time he is planning to go back by the sea, from Dwarka. He asked me if I am ready for the homeward journey." Isa spoke realizing how such synchronicities multiply.

Sriram had spoken of the acceleration of co-incidental happenings once consciousness is awakened. The process of growth intensifies. Sriram had said, "Isa, one of the Vedas declares 'you are that,' *tatvam asi*. You *know* it, but won't admit it. But that won't stop synchronicities...try as you may...." Sriram had doubled up laughing.

"Are you also leaving?" Mira's question was rhetorical. Both knew they were ready to move on.

* * * * * * * * * *

Mira and Isa traveled from Vraj to Dwarka with a group of Krishna devotees, pilgrims who sang and danced, with drum cymbals. It was a joyful journey. Mira was in her element for more than one reason. There were her favorite activities – song and dance; there was her most favorite person in the world, Isa, as her companion; and she was going to another holy place of Krishna's, Dwarka. Best of all she was to meet her entire family; her grandparents were coming to see her, perhaps, for the last time.

Pilgrims assumed Isa and Mira to be a married couple. The two complemented each other, exuding a kind of made-for-each-other image. There was nothing to ask. So nobody did. Mira and Isa enjoyed this un-intimate intimacy. There was the usual communal sleeping at night, women and young children in one tent or a house, and men in another or out in the open under the starry skies. So there were no questions asked, no embarrassing moments to encounter.

Isa felt the depth of absolute love for Mira: all temporal lines, like marriage, caste, and such dwindled. They were irrelevant. Even in other areas whether he was meditating, or helping the pilgrims, or chopping wood, he could simultaneously *experience* all realities – material, ethereal, and spiritual.

Absorption into devotional *seva* had helped Mira blend the material and the spiritual seamlessly. Now she believed that her love for Isa resembled Radha and Krishna's love: divine, pure, unobtrusive, and totally absorbing.

It took them almost a month to reach Dwarka from Vraj. Upon arrival in Dwarka, Mira was thrilled to see Ballu in the busy market by the port. The Suryapuri group had arrived in Dwarka a couple of days before the Vraj group was expected to arrive. Ballu's planning as always was impeccable.

Mira shouted aloud, waving, "Hey Ballu, here we are..."

Ballu grinned from ear to ear. He waved back and started walking in her direction. What a beautiful woman Mira had become, so elegant, he thought as he approached her, "*Jai Sri* Krishna Miraji. How are you? *Maji* and *Mahodaya* are eagerly waiting for you. Papa will not recognize you, I am sure. Let's go," Ballu looked around for Isa and saw him approaching them. On his way Isa had stopped to help an old man struggling with the load he was carrying.

"*Jai Sri* Krishna, Isaji. Let's hurry to the inn. Everybody is eagerly waiting to meet you." The three made their way through the crowded road.

Ballu pointed at the two storey building as they turned the corner, "There is the inn, most clean and comfortable place in town." He could not help show off a little about his finding the best accommodation.

"Here they come," said Kunti who was eagerly waiting in the upper level balcony. She spotted the trio coming out of the market road. She rushed down the stairs, ran through the room, darting out on the street, ignoring Vallabh's words, "Don't run you will fall." Throwing caution to the wind, she ran to meet her granddaughter. When Mira saw Kunti, she rushed toward her with open arms. As they embraced, Kunti collapsed in Mira's arms. Isa dashed to their rescue, held both of them tightly to prevent their fall on the dusty rocky ground.

Carrying half conscious Kunti in his arms Isa entered the inn. Mira followed crying, "What happened to *Maji?*" Ballu had run ahead to spread the mattress for Kunti. Isa gently placed Kunti on it. Confused Mira was crying telling anxious Vallabh and Papa what she saw happen. Isa asked everybody to move a little to let some air come in. Then he laid his hand on Kunti's head and sat with his eyes closed. Mira was leaning on Papa, sobbing, looking at her grandmother.

After a few minutes of total silence, Kunti opened her eyes. She saw Isa's glowing face close to hers, with his hand on her head and eyes still closed. Slowly Isa opened his eyes as he felt Kunti's steady breathing. She had never seen such shining eyes before.

Kunti said to Isa, "Today you saved me from Yamraja, the god of death, son. I saw his fierce face when I fell out there in Mira's arms." Isa kept looking at her calmly. All eyes were focused on Kunti and Isa. "You carried me, snatching me from Yamaraja. I *saw* that," Kunti's voice was steady. She was not delusional.

Amazed Mira looked at Isa with admiration. Vallabh expressed his gratitude in silence, gently pressing Isa's shoulder. Papa and Ballu stared at Isa wondering what Kunti's words meant.

Faintly smiling, Kunti turned her head and saw Mira crying on Papa's shoulder, "Come here *Beti*. Let me see you well." Mira approached, Isa tried to move to make room for Mira. Kunti held his hand, "You don't move, Isa." She asked Mira to sit on the floor by her. Holding her head and kissing it Kunti said, "May you live for hundred years." Kunti then looked with a smile at Vallabh, then at Papa and Ballu. Everybody was relieved. A great danger had been averted.

Holding Isa's hands in both of hers, Kunti said, "Will you promise me to look after Mira? Will you take care of her, son?" Isa kept gazing at Kunti for a short while; then looked at Mira who was intently staring at her grandmother, amazed and intrigued. Such a promise meant only one thing, marriage.

After a few moments of silence, looking intently at Kunti, Isa spoke, "I will never abandon Mira or displease her. She will have my love forever." Isa then set his eyes on Mira. Astonished Mira turned her teary eyes from her grandmother to Isa. Joining both their hands in hers, Kunti said, "May Radha-Krishna bless you both."

Kunti was still holding hands of Isa and Mira when she breathed her last. Happy and contented, she left her mortal body.

A pilgrim passing by the inn was singing a hymn to child Krishna. It was Kunti's favorite she sang every morning.

Awake, O Kaniya, awake
Cows are hungry
Who will lead them to graze?
Your morning food is ready
Time to awake, Kaniya
Awake, awake, awake....

Chapter 46

Demetrius almost missed a step when somebody grabbed him from behind as he was walking on the port of Dwarka, "Hey *Punditji*, how are you?" When Isa saw Demetrius' tall figure from a distance he ran so fast he was breathing hard, as they hugged in sheer joy.

"It can't be you, Isa. Is that really you?" incredulous Demetrius had his mouth open as he turned around and saw Isa. "You have changed so. Look at this long hair and beard. My...my...my..." Demetrius was all gleeful, almost yelling at the top of his voice, his hands tightly holding Isa's shoulders.

"Are you going on this ship to Greece?" Isa asked unnecessarily when he found his voice. It was obvious. On such a busy day to be at the port meant only one thing unless you were a vendor, of course.

"I was wondering if you were still in Dwarka," Isa continued, "I am so happy to see you, Demetrius." Isa was excited, elated, to see his old friend.

"Well, obviously you are also homeward bound. We will have splendid exchanges of ideas and information." Was Demetirus still as head-bound as before, Isa wondered?

"It seems we have other friends on board too. Mira and Papa will be on the ship. Mira's grandparents came with Ballu to see her off thinking this might be the last time they will see her. Unfortunately, her grandmother died the day we arrived."

Demetrius was shocked to hear of Kunti's death, "If it is any consolation, she died in a holy place; a devotee's dream death."

Isa was intrigued by Demetrius's *heart-felt* observation.

"Any rewards of isolation in this holy place for you, brother?" Isa asked.

"Absolutely! I felt a shift after an extraordinary connection with the ocean here. It seems I touched some submerged holy relics of antiquity. I guess I swam too far from the temple into the ocean not realizing how far I went," Demetrius described his experience of touching the huge stone slab and a conical structure that, he learned later, was a steeple of an ancient temple.

"You may have traveled into another reality, another life may be?" Isa was always eager to expand the unknown dimensions of reality. "Let's sit somewhere. It is difficult to concentrate with this noisy crowd around."

"Good idea," said Demetrius. They found a quiet spot away from the port. He continued, "It opened up another dimension as it were. I started hearing sounds, seeing magnificent colors, and people's auras. It was confusing at first. Then I spoke with a sage who focuses on archaeology. He said 900 years ago, or even earlier according to other scholars, there was an ancient temple here. That would be Krishna's time. He thought I may have touched a long lost relic of his time. Perhaps it was the wall of Krishna's temple or a palace." Demetrius narrated his significant experience.

"This would be then a charged place, Krishna's kingdom. It was the time of his wisdom and maturity, the time he taught the *Bhagavad Gita,* wasn't it?" Isa speculated.

"True. I have been overwhelmed since touching the stone in the ocean. The overarching ideal in the cosmic mind that Plato speaks of is *real* for me, more than just an idea. *Knowledge* becomes an *experience,*" Demetrius was elated. There was the strength of *experienced* conviction Isa had not heard before in Demetrius' voice.

Joy and appreciation lit up Isa's face.

* * * * * * * * * * * *

A few days later the ship from Dwarka sailed off. Papa and Mira said good bye to grieving Vallabh. Kunti's passing had made a hole in his life; and now he was saying farewell to his granddaughter, his only family, whom he will never see again. His composed exterior hid his inner turmoil. Was it a habitual manly facade? Could it be a legacy of his professional life? Maybe Vallabh had cultivated a spiritual detachment to be practiced in *vanprastha,* the traditional third stage of life of contemplation. Whatever it was, when the ship sailed away,

Vallabh kept looking at the receding ship for a long time, till it became a dot on the horizon. A part of him was gone forever.

Ballu was moved by this family falling apart. His harsh pragmatic exterior carried within it a genuine sadness. Mira's departure touched Ballu's young heart. Her vibrant exuberance had often magnetized him. With Vallabh, he too stood watching a precious part of his life disappear. Both Vallabh and Ballu were like empty shells.

For a few days on the ship Papa and Mira were busy exchanging stories of their time when they were apart for a little over two, nearly three, years.

Isa was often away from his fellow travelers. He contemplated the water energy now that he was on the wide ocean. At Granny's hollow Isa had felt the earth's power; in Varanasi, it was the power of the fire; in Kashmir he had traversed into the air; now it was the power of the water. He was initiated by four out of the five elements. The fifth, space, *aakash,* was yet to be.

It was a confluence of Isa and Demetrius' energies creating another vibrant level of awareness. This awareness rippled through the waters of the ocean and spread into thin air.

Demetrius strongly felt the vibrations from deep under waters. It often shook his entire body. A few passengers even tried to help him, worrying he had an epileptic attack. He saw the earth's ancient treasures, contained in deep waters, manifest on the surface. He could feel the energies of furiously active gyrations in the watery bottom. The sound emanating from this gyration was like a thunder exploding upward in purifying flames. He felt he saw the water on fire.

"Are you alright, Demetrius?" Mira asked when she saw his other worldly look.

"Heavenly, Mira, I am ecstatic," Demetrius smiled.

"It seems you *have been to heaven,* I am happy you are back," Mira said with her alluring laugh. She was having a wonderful time, endlessly chatting with Papa and enjoying this watery journey which enormously helped her in soothing the pain of her grandmother's passing and leaving her grandfather alone. Besides, she was re-living the memories of Mathura and Vraj as she shared her stories with Papa. It helped her in regaining her natural blissfulness, *ananda.*

"What's that?" she saw a bright shiny pillar by the prow of the ship. Her eyes dazzled. She kept staring at it.

"What? Where?" Demetrius and Papa both looked in the direction she was pointing.

For a fraction of a second Demetrius saw a streak of bright light, "You mean where Isa is standing?" he asked.

Mira blinked, "Yes, right where he is. It's strange. Let me ask Isa," she walked toward him.

Wonder still lingering in her eyes, she asked, "Did you see a pillar of light a couple of minutes ago, right here?"

Isa laughed, and with a deliberate joking note said, "The only pillar of light I see is right here," he stretched his hand to take Mira's, drawing her near.

"Don't make fun of me, Isa. I am serious," Mira protested.

"Come, stand here. I want to show you something," Isa said, drawing her close to the railing. Both were standing next to each other staring at the ocean.

"Focus on any one point in the water. Do not lose that point."

Mira spotted one point twenty yards ahead on the water. "It keeps moving with the waves, I can't keep it in focus," she complained.

"Try some more."

After a few more seconds, she repeated, "No I can't. The waters move constantly. I cannot focus on one point. It is the same place, but the spot has moved. How do you do it? I can't," Mira was frustrated.

Isa suggested, "Now visualize Krishna at that spot. See if you can focus."

Mira saw her favorite image of Krishna with his flute, standing cross legged playing a magnetizing tune. Soon she was focused, calm, "Yes, there it is. The spot moves, but I can focus on it."

Isa put his arm on her shoulder, "All is transient. Only Krishna is constant. When you *see* him, *feel* him, *know* him, you *become* him."

Mira knew Isa spoke in pithy images. "So you *became* light? It was you I saw as pillar of light?"

Isa did not reply, he smiled and said, "Let's go back to Papa and Demetrius."

Chapter 47

One fine morning, Isa asked, "Demetrius, I have been pondering over my experiences in India and want to ask you something: in what way did the experience in India affect you? Did you have to shift your Greek way of thinking?" The ship was soon to anchor in a small port to take more passengers and disembark a few.

"Since my special interest is in Plato's teaching, my mind tuned into many of the yogic theories and practices without much difficulty. Both schools entertain a theory of two realities – *dualty* -- so that was not so difficult, despite other variances. It was interesting to learn, and it was new for me, that Plato was exposed to ancient Indian learning through itinerant scholars who came to Greece centuries ago, or Greek scholars who went to India. So I did not have to wrestle as much as some other Greeks," Demetrius said.

"So what would be the other Greek scholars' dilemma or difficulty?" Isa was curious.

"From what I have gathered, many of them have to shift their approach to stories of gods and goddesses in relation to human affairs. You and I talked about the Greek pantheon's preoccupation with the material world. The Indian 'divine contingent,' as I call their gods/goddesses," Demetrius joked, "fuse the human and divine worlds admirably. At times this is problematic for Greek scholars. They have a hard time accepting Krishna as god and human, mortal and immortal, at once. Many of my colleagues would have a hard time passing this barrier of thinking of a mortal god."

"I am wondering if Greek schools, or even the Egyptian schools, would further expand my awareness," Isa said.

"The best way is to try and find out. Why don't you go to Greece with me? You may reach Galilee a few months later." It seemed to Isa that Demetrius now spoke with greater surety about everything than when Isa first met him. Isa was sure Demetrius had experienced a transformation in Dwarka.

Mira was a little disappointed when she heard of Isa's resolve to go to Greece. But then she thought it was no different whether Isa was in Galilee or Greece. She would be in Babylon with Papa. She laughed. Sushma had said a long time back: Radha had only Krishna; Krishna had all those *gopis*, his parents, Yashoda and Nanda, and the cowherd *gopals* in Vraj. Then in Mathura and Dwarka he had his eight queens, the hosts of Yadavas, Pandavas, and Kauravas.

Sushma's words were, "Men's world is wide as earth; woman's world is her home." Of course Mira did not agree with Sushma. Mira's own world was as large as Isa's, she argued. But that was then. Now she was so close to Isa. Did she think differently, now?

A couple of weeks later the ship reached the last port in the Persian Gulf. The land journey began for all going to: Persia, Arabia, Egypt, Greece, Italy...and so on.

Papa was busy supervising the unloading of his merchandise and making arrangements for his onward journey. His trusted port helpers were busy.

Isa came to Mira and spoke in a comforting note, "Mira, we shall meet in a few months or a year. I made a promise to your grandmother. I will come back, I will never abandon you. Don't look so sad." He tried to cheer her up.

"What makes you think I am sad? I am looking at Papa. Maybe he needs my help," Mira protested and started to go to the unloading area. Pulling her by the hand Isa said, "You don't have to pretend, Mira. I too am sad to leave you."

He looked into her teary eyes, "I know there are deeper layers of truths we will explore together. It is our divine obligation in this life. But we need to be patient, Mira."

Isa was intently looking into Mira's teary eyes reaching deep into her soul. In his eyes and in his words Mira felt sadness, hope, and peace.

❋

Chapter 48

One evening Isa was lost in deep thoughts in a grove shaded by olive trees, not far from Athena's magnificent temple. Demetrius saw him from a distance and started walking toward him. It was a good time to chat with his reclusive friend.

"Hey Isa, have you been avoiding me? We have been in Athens for over four weeks and you have been unusually quiet. What is happening?"

Isa smiled faintly, looked at the pebbles on the ground and said, "To think and contemplate is our habit, isn't it? This quiet time in Greece has helped me immensely. I am connecting my past, present and the future -- where I was, have arrived, and what may be my next step when I return home. It is our usual search, my friend."

"Tell me about it. A similar search was the catalyst for me to travel to India, to understand the human mind better. Now I am trying to understand my own mind!" Demetrius' words mingled with his hearty laugh.

Isa looked up admiring the Acropolis, "How glorious has been the history of Greece! Thinkers, artists, musicians, painters, writers, scholars, archaeologists, architects, have created such a magnificent world here. It is mind boggling. Emperors and chieftains have supported them, encouraged them to build a glorious world. But I still feel sad within. Something is missing. What is it?"

"You mean besides the Roman conquest of Greece and the expansion of the Roman Empire abroad?" Demetrius' sarcasm did not go unnoticed.

"Oh that's a given. Political strife is a part of life. You and I are interested in the evolution of the individual mind and spirit. What happens to people's inner world when they live through times of conflict, conquest or defeat? Or conversely, when they enjoy conquests, power, and prosperity? " Isa clarified his focus.

"Have you found an answer?" Demetrius was curious.

"Not yet. I got a glimpse of what humans lost in their collective, acquisitive march. That's the way of the world. But whether it is building an Empire or a temple like Athena's," Isa pointed at the glorious Parthenon above, "the leaders have to use common people. Each hand that carved that pillar had a heart, mind and spirit – unique individual awareness. What happens to that spirit?" Isa was struggling to find a way to open people's inner awarenss, be they rich or poor, informed or ignorant. "You and I know all individuals can evolve and gain cosmic awareness. In Takshashila we gained *knowledge* of the workings of the human mind..."

"But that knowledge, though precious, was not enough, as you always said," Demetrius could not resist interrupting, "It was only in Dwarka that I finally could let go of what you termed the 'intellectual acrobatics' of Takshashila. I told you before, Isa, it happened when I touched that sacred steeple of the ancient temple in the waters by Dwarka. I *experienced* the beyond. It opened my inner awareness." Demetrius' eyes became dreamy as he recalled that life changing experience.

"How do you help others to reach a similar awareness, or do you think you can? Can you awaken it in others? Have you found an answer to *that?*" Isa was curious, even eager.

"I was mulling over that all the way on my return journey home. I still am searching. Teaching and discussions with perceptive seekers at school helps, but I have not yet arrived, Isa, not yet."

Isa noticed the same sadness in Demetrius' face that he had seen before.

"I am sure that the contributions of poets and playwrights such as Homer, Sophocles, Aeschylus and others help. And then giants in a long tradition of thinkers -- Pythagoras, Socrates, Plato, Aristotle – enrich the human soul. At Takshashila, you and I witnessed the wealth of the Vedic *rishis*, seers and thinkers from all over the known world, Demetrius. Such a wealth of ideas and attainment! Humans are a wonderful creation of God. And I feel, being made in his likeness, humans can reach divinity. That I *feel*, I *know*, is God's plan," Isa was trying to sort out his own thinking as much as encouraging Demetrius.

"True, but in Greece a radical Socrates was poisoned, in India a radical Buddha became a founder of a religion." Demetrius had fallen into seeing the half empty cup, Isa realized.

"So people need an open mind to deal with change, wouldn't you say?" Isa asked. "You said you personally gained an insight, a wisdom that freed you. Do you think you can help people change their rigid thinking?" Isa was curious.

Demetrius thought for a while, "I reckon that it all boils down to one thing: making choices. That is the human predicament in any culture. No choice is simply good or bad, right or wrong, material or spiritual, individual or collective. Krishna emphasized *svadharma*, one's own duty, one's unique obligation in life. What do you think of that?"

Isa kept quiet. For a few years now he had dreamt of cultivating peace and love among people, regardless of their race, creed, or belief: Roman, Greek, Egyptian, Persian, Jewish, Hindu, Buddhist, and all others. Isa had faith that peace could be attained if people understood and honored each other's beliefs and traditions.

Isa continued, "I believe in God, but I believe in the power of the human spirit even more. I honor human effort. I can even make room for those who do not believe in God. In my mind atheism is only an extension of the human spirit, the *essential* element. There is hope, Demetrius, do not despair," Isa laughed.

* * * * * * * * * * * * *

A few months later Demetrius and Isa were in a learning center run by Demetrius' school. It was in a small town on the shoreline of the Mediterranean. As the evening approached, both friends walked to the shore to watch the sunset.

Bright orange clouds painted by the setting sun scattered against the deep blue sky.

"What an enchanted moment this is!" said Isa breathing in the salty air.

"What are your plans now that you are returning to Galilee, Isa?" Demetrius asked.

Isa kept his eyes fixed on the horizon. The sun was hastening to the water's rim, "I want to find a way to awaken people much as the Buddha did." Isa took a few deep breaths; keeping his eyes on the horizon, he said, "I do not know why but I relate to Buddha." Demetrius listened with his eyes on the roaring waves dashing against the shore. Isa continued, "I have no plan; but I know I will be guided." His voice had a ring of absolute trust, faith.

Isa knew that awakening his community to the *truth* of inner reality would be a slow and patient process. It would be an uphill struggle. The subordination of his people under Romans had depleted their spirit. To this was added the self-centered authority of the power hungry high priests of his own tradition. People missed the real essence of life in their daily struggles.

After what seemed to be a long time of contemplating in nature – the sky, wind, waves, and the setting sun -- Isa said with utmost clarity, "It will require an enormous effort to create a new language for our time. I have an irrevocable resolve to do it, and I shall." Uttering these words Isa felt a stirring within, as if he had done this before, perhaps many times...before...in other lifetimes.

The rays of the setting sun illumined Isa's eyes. He continued in a dreamy, measured voice, "I have experienced reality beyond this world, and peered into the essence of Truth....the Ultimate Love connection of the Soul and the Divine. I have *felt* it in my *being*. I know, I have faith that if I can do it, so can others. I have faith that I will find answers no matter what the price. Even death would not deter me. I will do it. It's God's will, and also mine."

He had *known and touched* the acme of human potential, the supreme divinity, and now there was no looking back.

The two friends sat listening to the breaking waves of the Mediterranean long after the sun's tiny rim of light dipped into the ocean.

"That is the Way."

Demetrius heard it. So did Isa. Neither knew if it was Isa's voice or of the waves. Without blinking Isa kept staring, his gaze fixed on the horizon of eternity.

Chapter 49

"What was the most significant experience for you in India, Mary?" Papa asked.

They were back in Babylon. Papa had settled all his business deals successfully. With the approaching festival for Eostra, the spring goddess, the Romans were dancing, and feasting, and Papa knew his business would flourish. But Mary was not keen to join in the festivities. Papa found that unusual, different from the Mary he had known a few years back. She had grown into an elegant young woman. But there was an undefinable inner elegance too, Papa noticed.

"Hey, girl, where are you? Come back," Papa snapped his fingers to call Mary back from her reverie.

"Oh I am sorry, Papa," Mary said, "What were you saying?"

"Dreaming as always! That has not changed," Papa laughed and repeated the question about her significant experience in India.

"Oh, that's a hard question. Everything was so exciting, I cannot pick and choose. I am still reliving the sound, smell, sights, places, people, incidents...Experiences pop up randomly. I relish them all; I can't choose any one, Papa," Mary said with a gentle smile.

"So do you want to restart weaving your specialty, your Mary Magdalene wraps? Or have you cultivated other skills you can use? Or maybe you are looking to find a husband and start a family?" Papa was partly serious, partly teasing.

Mary broke into a peal of laughter, "Mary getting married? What a joke Papa!"

"Why what's so funny? I saw how close you were with Isa. What's wrong with that question?"

"That's true. We became very close. But that was on an inner level, soul level, truly bonded in love. But..." Mary fondly recalled, for the thousandth time, Kunti's last ritual before she passed on.

"But, what?" Papa insisted...

"Isa and I never talked about marriage, family, and all that. It seemed his heart was set on a much wider path. A divine purpose propels his life's journey. Such domesticity may not be a part of his life," Mary shared what she thought was on Isa's mind.

"What about you? What is your path? You found your old roots in India, your family ties. You look like you are a new person, Mary," Papa spoke with unusual seriousness.

"That's true. I am still adjusting to all these changes. Applying new ways in an old world is confusing. It is exciting, but also challenging," in Mary's face Papa could see what she did not want to admit.

Mary remained silent and for the umpteenth time recalled Isa's promise to Kunti, "*I will never abandon her, or displease her. She will have my love forever.*" She still *felt* the vibration of Isa's hand holding hers when he uttered those words.

"I am not sure what to do next, Papa," Mary had no answers. She was hoping to be with Isa, Papa saw that clearly.

* * * * * * * * * * * *

It was now more than a year after her return to Babylon.

"Still remember me?" Mary heard a familiar voice as she was returning from the well.

She nearly dropped her pot, as she turned around and saw Isa's smiling face. Isa rushed to rescue the pot, and found both Mary and the pot in his arms.

Time froze for a few moments in that embrace...

"How are you, Mira... umm...now Mary, right?" laughing Isa asked, balancing the pot in Mary's grip.

Flicking water from her robe, Mary, hardly able to control her excitement said, "When did you come? I thought you were in Greece? What are you doing in Babylon?" Mary was overjoyed to see Isa. All questions were redundant. But she had to say something.

"I returned from Greece last week," said Isa without taking his eyes off hers. Words spoken were idle, meaningless.

"Papa is home. Let's go meet him. He will be happy to see you," Mary said, needlessly. They had already started walking toward her home.

Their words filled up space and time, but their hands, gait, voice, and eyes were in total bliss...

"Papa, look who I found on the way," excitedly Mary called out from the front door.

Papa peered out of the window saying, "Now what new trouble have you brought home today?" and noticed Isa standing there with his 'ever enchanting heavenly smile.' That is how Papa always described Isa.

"Oh young man with the ever enchanting heavenly smile, it's you. Come in, come in. You are the best trouble I can hope for," Papa's uproarious laughter filled the house.

Isa felt happy and relaxed. After the usual questions about business and current happenings in Babylon and the surrounding area, the two men were ready for tea served with *laddu,* a favorite sweet of all three.

"Oh, look I told you Isa you are the best trouble I can have. I get *chai* in your honor," Papa teased Mary.

"So wonderful to have my favorite, *laddu,*" Isa said, picking a piece and savoring it.

"It's Krishna's favorite too, remember?" chimed in Mary.

"For how long will you be in Babylon? You are not starting a revolution, are you?" Papa laughed loudly at his own joke.

"I don't know if it is a revolution. But I am certainly seeking new ways of thinking. I have been listening to peoples' stories in my travels trying to understand how their minds work. Things I learned and observed in the east are helping me immensely," Isa gave a short version of his activities and potential involvement.

"Does Krishna's devotional tradition help you at all?" asked Mary, since that was her focus. She had been thinking how she could use those devotional stories to help people feel a deeper reality, as she did.

"It's a huge jump for *our* people to see God in such human terms. For Romans, Greeks, and Egyptians it is not that difficult. They have their own stories of gods and their dealings with humans," Isa said, half in fun, looking at Papa, remembering his Egyptian heritage.

"So what do you do? How do you convince people?" Mary was curious.

"I am not their teacher, Mary. I seek to understand who they are, where they are, what their daily life is. What are their needs? In the process, I give them practical advice or assistance. Then I will see how I am guided to turn them to the divine truth, of love, mercy, peace, and oneness."

"Who will guide you in this work, Isa?" Papa was listening carefully to gauge Isa's plans for the future.

Isa quickly glanced at Mary, and said, "Something inside of me, God within me shines as a *spark*, and I follow that guidance."

Papa was skeptical, "You mean they believe you when you say God is inside of you? Come on..." Papa smiled in disbelief.

"I don't tell them God is within me. I tell them He is within all of us. We have to recapture this forgotten truth," Isa spoke gently bypassing Papa's skepticism.

"How do you help them recognize that truth?" Mary was particularly interested in that process.

"I often remind them of the stories from the *Torah*. Narrate stories of Adam, Noah, Abraham, Moses, or Job, Jacob, Joseph. I even add stories of *bhaktas,* devotees, from other traditions that they can accept easily. I emphasize that devotion to God can be in *obedience* to Him, but also in *love* for Him. But I am *not* their teacher yet, Mary. I focus only on learning about who they really are. And often feel their *truth*. I am their companion walking with them," Isa spoke in the soft tone of a seeker, a learner.

"I admire your insight, patience, above all your calling," Papa's appreciation of Isa's intent and ability was genuine, despite his skepticism about the process or the result. "So what is your immediate plan now? Will you be staying in Babylon?" Papa geared the conversation in another direction.

Isa quickly glanced at Mary before answering, "To know if Mary will be willing to join me in my journey, Sir, and if it is acceptable to you," Isa spoke with clarity and directness, though he was unsure of the response from Mary or Papa.

Papa burst out laughing, "You mean I can dictate Mary to do or not do anything?" He chuckled some more, and then turning to Mary said, "What do you think? Does Isa's suggestion resolve *your* confusion?"

Mary looked at Isa's questioning eyes for a few moments. In those eyes she saw dew drops shining like diamonds on a rose petal. She saw herself marching with Isa to the horizon of eternity.

Chapter 50

"Do you think your mother will like me?" Mary asked Isa as they were nearing Galilee.

"What is there not to like about you, Mary?" Isa laughed so hard, a scared bird in the nearby tree flew away. "I haven't met anybody yet who says anything but the best about you," Isa continued looking at her blushing face. "My brothers may tease you though when you share your Radha-Krishna stories." In fact, Isa's teasing worked. Mary started hitting Isa with her satchel.

"Sh....sh...we preach *love* not *violence,*" Isa laughed loudly, wrapping his arms around Mary to hold her hands down.

Mary had been traveling with Isa from village to village from Babylon to Galilee. Talking with people was quite informative for them. Isa had a new way of looking at traditional Judaic teachings. He spoke of it in a language which caught people's attention: the just God was also loving and merciful.

It was early afternoon when they reached Isa's parent's house. Isa saw Joseph, really old now, napping under the idle work shed. His mother Mary was in the kitchen, trying to get the wood fire going for cooking. The fire was slumbering, getting smoky; she was blowing into it with her feeble breath. Tiptoeing, Isa went in, bent on his knees behind his mother, and blew hard into smouldering fire. The flame immediately started burning high. Mother Mary turned, saw her nearly unrecognizable long lost son, screamed "Oh Isa," and threw her arms around his neck; smoke and joy made her eyes teary. "My Isa, my son, you have arrived," she kept repeating as if to reassure herself Isa was truly there.

Joseph, awakened by Mother Mary's near screaming, came in the house and shouted, "Oh, it is you, Isa, why do you always surprise us? We are old people. We may die of sudden joy." And he laughed aloud releasing the shock of pleasant surprise. He coughed some...laughter caused the spasm.

Isa led them both to young Mary standing by the door, "Father – Mother this is Mary. I plan to marry her. Would you bless us?" Isa asked.

"What?!" All three shouted, Joseph and Mother Mary in pleasant surprise, young Mary in absolute disbelief. Wide eyed, young Mary was staring at Isa. Was she happy, angry, stunned, or ecstatic?

Joseph and Mother Mary could not stop alternately crying, laughing, and hugging the young couple. Young Mary knew not how to show her joy and anger at once. She allowed Joseph and Mary to hug and kiss and bless...

* * * * * * * * * * *

Later after an early supper, walking to Isa's favorite sunset place, young Mary's angered self was in charge; she asked, as soon as they were out of anybody's earshot, "How dare you announce *your* wish to your parents without asking me if I wanted to marry you?"

"Don't you?" Isa calmly asked, teasing her. That made her more furious. She hit his back, stamped her feet, pouted and kept quiet. When they reached a quiet spot to sit, Isa repeated his question with a smile, "So tell me don't you want to marry me?"

She looked away, tears falling down her cheeks. Mary could not stop crying. Isa drew her close not understanding what was bothering her. She hid her face in his lap and started sobbing...Isa kept caressing her head...mystified. Isa wondered if he lacked an understanding of a woman's mind. After a few minutes, Mary was quiet, her head still resting in his lap.

Looking at the setting sun, and continuing to caress Mary's head, Isa said, "It was your grandmother's dying wish; she virtually blessed us as a couple, wouldn't you say? Your grandfather expressed a similar desire he shared with me before we left Dwarka. Perhaps he did not think it was necessary to tell you about it. Papa blessed me when we left his house in Babylon. It was your wish to join me in my work. Now wasn't it time for me to tell my parents I wished to marry you?" Isa's logic was clear. Mary was still quiet.

She was of course extremely happy to be with Isa forever... But she was hurt that Isa did not tell her he was going to make this announcement. She felt left out in an important matter related to her. No men, including Isa, realized a woman could think the way Mary did.

After a long silence, and what seemed to be a long *contemplation,* Mary asked, "How do you think Radha would feel if Krishna told his parents about his intention before asking her to marry him?"

"But he didn't have to. They were never married to each other!" Isa protested. Mary's question was hypothetical. Any answer of Isa's could be challenged. "Why do you ask, Mary? What's the relevance of Radha-Krishna here?" Isa was really confused.

"You know how Radha-Krishna's love had absorbed me. They have become my role model. I almost became Krishna's Radha. Their love was pure, serene, sheer bliss. I endlessly sang those songs of love and joy, separation and sadness. When Radha complained about Krishna's behavior, you could tell it was a pretense. She never was really angry. Whether it was separation, indifference, uncertainty, breaking a promise, or unalloyed joy of togetherness, Radha loved to the point of total *surrender* and yet kept her *independence. The surge of their love never receded. They are the epitome of absolute love between a man and a woman. Marriage is irrelevant in such relationship.* Isa, people of Krishna's land still celebrate it almost a millennium later. Could our union, our love also be like theirs? I want to be your Radha could you be my Krishna, Isa?" Had Mary gone crazy? Not in Isa's eyes.

What sublimation of love in its purest form, Isa thought. Mira – she was always Mira when they were alone -- was talking about *reaching total union of the soul and the divine through love.* She wanted to transform *their* personal love into a form of *surrender* which is at once *freedom!*

Total immersion into each other in body, mind and spirit without losing one's identity is the ultimate love for her. In such union the *immanent* becomes *imminent*. It was a giant step to the true essence of Love.

Isa *surrendered* to that immanence in her.

Speechless, holding her close, Isa stared into Mira's eyes for what seemed to be eternity.... an ecstatic moment of fusion.

The sun had not witnessed such confluence of perfect love...perhaps not in a millennium...

Chapter 51

The road from Galilee to Capernaum was paved with total love and joy.

On the way Isa and Mary spoke with farmers tilling land and herders minding their cattle. They listened to their stories, shared their joy; helped them relieve their pain or sickness. A blind child began to see, the lame young man started walking. A woman in difficult child birth got tender care. Tears of woe turned into smiles and gratitude. Some villagers thought Isa and Mary had a magic touch for healing. Some people came to resolve conflicts with family and townspeople before the disputes would end up in the Roman justice system. Isa gathered a reputation as a counselor and people fondly called him 'rabbi.' His words did not deviate too much from the conventional religion, but his interpretation touched their hearts. .

Whatever people thought, Isa and Mary did not think consider it special. They were just being, well... Isa and Mary, loving, insightful, caring, energized humans who *knew their spark guided them.*

Their inner eyes had opened to envision the *cosmic truth.* All they saw around them was a remote twisted aspect of the ultimate reality, an *illusion* of sorts.

"Mary, wouldn't it be easy to explain to these folks that this world is an illusion, *maya?"*

One day Isa was pondering about bridging the gap between *ignorance* and *knowledge.* "These fishermen do not have the burden of learning that many educated urban people carry."

"It's true. You told me about the old goatherd woman in Greece, how easily you could convince her of the *illusion* of life. But you had a hard time with Demetrius' colleague, what was his name?"

"You mean Andreas?"

"You know, it is all about connecting with daily life," Mary said slowly, weighing every word like she was unwinding an endless cocoon trying to get to its core. "I felt the connection of *this* world with the *other* through my everyday service, *seva,* in Vraj. It is easy to *feel* the connection when you are absorbed into the Divine."

"*I* need to *feel the way* to transmit it in my words and action," Isa said pondering. He lay in bed for long hours that night contemplating the *way to total surrender.* Several of his experiences flashed before his eyes and took him into his innermost *being.* Some flashes were of his yogic practices in the Himalayan ranges, others were visions on the banks of the rivers Ganga and Yamuna, or on the ocean by Athens. It was strange, the place did not matter, but it inevitably was there when he recalled the experience. He laughed, that was like Plato's cave. The shadows spoke of the substance out there. That's it.

"I found at least one compelling image, Mary, to share with the villagers," Isa could hardly wait till Mary awoke next morning. Mary smiled with an expectant look. Isa continued, "I would tell them Plato's story of the man in the cave. And *ask* them what was real, the shadow or the substance. People may choose one or the other. I hope someone in there would say both, since there can't be a shadow without the substance, and every substance has a shadow."

"What's the point about *illusion*?" Mary could not wait. She often said, "Hurry up enough of the preface."

"If you put light on top of the substance, the shadow would disappear."

"Isn't the shadow still there, hiding under, but not visible?" Mary asked.

"Good. I need a sharp observer like you there, in my Socratic approach," Isa made his usual quick response, hurrying on to his final finding.

"My conclusion would be 'By manipulating *light* we can focus on real substance; and the shadowy image would disappear, would be recognized as an *illusion,* that is, not *real,*'" Isa was pleased.

"But how would a grieving mother with a dead child consider her son as an *illusion*, Isa?" Mary could intellectually accept Isa's analogy; whereas the emotional angle was altogether another matter.

"I could perhaps use Buddha's story? You know how he handled a similar situation to teach the woman of the inevitability of death," Isa knew he had to recognize the readiness of each person. And no ready-made tool would work in all instances. Mary and he had discussed this before.

"What worked on Andreas, eventually?" Mary asked.

"I touched his left thumb, that shifted his energy vibration," Isa said.

"You overpowered him with your will? Is that not unethical?" Mary could not believe Isa would do that.

"It was not *my* will controlling his. It was awakening *his* dormant energy and letting it go where it would. My work was to help him awake. Mary, you know how I work...Why are you so nagging this morning?" Isa smiled, "Let's get going."

They started the day's routine.

Chapter 52

In Capernaum, Isa's center, Peter and Andrew became Isa's initial helpers. They always joked about their work when Isa introduced them as his helpers. "We are trying to figure out who is helping whom." People enjoyed their good humor. They were competent, casual, and funny. They began as Isa's helpers, and then became his companions.

More and more people gathered around Isa. Stories of healing spread fast. Some considered him a miracle worker; some called him a wise man. Others just came because it felt good. He was serene. His young age and good looks did not hurt either.

One day a man, apparently from another town, asked Andrew, "Is Isa an ordained rabbi?"

"If he was, I would not be following him. I guarantee you that," Andrew replied with a loud laugh.

"So what is he: a magician, the Messiah? I come from Judea now. But a while back in my travels I heard a man speak of the appearance of the Messiah. Of course, one cannot know for sure. There are so many false prophets these days," the man continued.

Simon was busy mending tools for a customer in town, "Did you like the stories of the Messiah people told you? Did they sound true? You must follow your heart; that is, if you found your heart," Simon said with a chuckle. Being close to Isa for almost a year now, Simon had adopted some of Isa's words in his parlance.

Andrew rejoined, "Simon, the man first needs to know he has a heart. How can he find it if he is too busy with his mind, Isa would say." Andrew kept working at the fishing net for another villager. Both brothers helped villagers whenever they could. Often villagers brought food for them in gratitude.

Both fell silent as Isa arrived. "Isa, this man comes from Judea and has a question for you."

"What is your name, friend?" Isa asked intently looking at him. Was he measuring the newcomer?

"I am Thomas. I heard a man called John speaking of the coming of the Messiah. I arrived here and heard people talking about you. So I was curious. Are you the Messiah?"

Isa looked at Thomas and suggested, "Why don't you come to our gathering this evening and listen? You will know." Thomas left.

Andrew said, "Isa, more and more people are coming. Do we want to gather on the hill instead of the market square?"

Simon added, "Isa, first we began with my house. When it was not big enough, we started meeting in the market. Now the market place is too small. It will be better on the hill, Isa. In the market they come to kill two birds with one stone — buy fish, vegetables, cloth, and listen to you." Simon certainly did not care for casual listeners who combined shopping with spirituality.

Isa smiled, "That's how we reach them; why would they want to come without knowing what it is, Simon. But you have a point. The market place is too small for the increasing number of listeners we now have. And I agree the hill by the lake is an ideal place."

"To the hill tomorrow, then..." Andrew shouted, full of joy, raising his hands, and dancing.

"You are merry this morning, Andrew," remarked Mary, who was on her way to the well.

Simon told her, "Andrew is celebrating, Mary. Isa accepted his suggestion of meeting on the hill."

"On the hill? By the lake? That's a good decision," Mary too was pleased.

The Lake of Galilee was one of the major reasons for Isa to select Capernaum as his home base. Going to the lake with Mary to watch the sun set and contemplate had continued. The hill had become their favorite spot. Another important reason for selecting this town was its people. Hard working fisherman, farmers, artisans, made a living in this sprawling town along the lake. Isa's focus was on the ordinary average people. Not many aristocrats, temple authorities, or Roman centurions lived here, except of course a contingent of Roman soldiers because the town was close to the major trade route, extending to other countries far and wide. Even that was convenient since interested travelers and traders often stopped to listen to Isa's words, were impressed, and many stayed back. Capernaum was ideal for his work.

Mary asked, "Isa, did you meet a man who was looking for you? He said he arrived from Judea."

Isa was looking at the sky above, lost in thoughts; he heard Mary's words, but gave no answer. Mary touched Isa's shoulder, "Did you hear a word I said?"

"Yes, I met the man," and Isa was silent again. Mary went her way.

Chapter 53

"As God's children we carry his blood in our veins, just as your children carry yours. God's divine blood flows in us as energy. It keeps us breathing and functioning. So you can say his kingdom is your body." Isa was concluding his talk on cosmic connectedness of all beings in layman's language. He was addressing the crowd of listeners on the hill.

"Are you the Son of God?" someone asked loudly. Mary turned to see if it was the same man who was asking for Isa.

"No less or more than you are, Thomas." Many laughed.

There were men, women, and children of all ages. All sat on the slope of the hill facing Isa who was sitting on the peak of the mount. Isa stared at the sun for a while. All, close to a hundred, sat silently looking at Isa.

Isa asked the crowd to turn around and intently look at the setting sun. "Try looking at the setting sun. Remain absolutely quiet. See its incessant turning, and anything else you observe."

The Lake of Galilee reflected the trees on the shore line. The low hanging white clouds were turning pink and grey. Gentle breeze touched people's cheeks, hair, and mixed with their quiet breath. All eyes were on the sun, some at peace, a few teary, many quizzical, most full of wonder. In the magic moment of dusk the sun connected them all. An exhilarating sensation passed through many. Silent moments grew into seconds, seconds into minutes. A solitary bird, coming back to its nest, chirped breaking the silence.

So did a five year old girl who said, "Mama, I saw a king in the sun. He was riding this big eagle and took me for a ride in the sky."

"Be like the child. The kingdom of heaven will open for you. This little girl is my witness," Isa spoke in a sonorous voice coming from afar...

* * * * * * * * * * * *

The gathering of Isa's close followers, now known as companions, had grown to twelve. Isa would share with them deeper findings about life, soul, relationship with the divine, and such. Many questions, Isa had asked in the past, came up again and again. Mark was most inquisitive and asked intelligent questions about life as illusion, *maya*. How does one go within and where does one arrive, always puzzled John. Isa elaborated on the companions' inquiries with diligence. He was guided from within to answer each query, each problem, each dilemma.

That guidance from within was the voice of God for Isa. It had become his second nature now. Whether he was questioned by crowds of friendly or challenging people or his close companions, Isa's words came from inner awareness – an intuitively wise *knowingness*.

Isa had invited Thomas to come to the group of companions. The thought, "How does one know who is the Messiah," was nagging Thomas. Every companion started asking what would convince Thomas if a person's claim was legitimate. Luke gave examples of promises the so called prophets made in the countryside. Peter warned about accusations of the high priests against any claims by others that would threaten the Temple's authority. John quietly listened. Matthew spoke of contemplation, searching inside one's heart for an answer. John reminded the others of Isa's repeated instructions of how to open oneself to listen to truth. Thomas was elated by the level of interaction among Isa's companions. Isa listened quietly to the companions' comments.

"What do you think, Thomas?" Isa asked

"This is an unusually enlightening discourse. If I had some doubts before," he added with an ironic smile, "I have more questions now." All were amused, except Peter. He did not like too many questions.

"How would you distinguish your teaching from the Essene's, Master?" Thomas asked.

"Much of what I have learned comes from many sources, including the Essene brothers. Truth is One. Its many faces may delude us. But know that all teachings speak of One Truth. The Essene brothers spoke of One God. Their mystical message remained true for a few in a small community. We, God's children, have to bring the light of Truth to everybody." Isa looked at Thomas to assess him, his energy.

Mark was curious, "Do you think, Master, the Essene brothers learned their worship of One God from the Egyptian Pharaoh Akhenatan's adoration of Aten, the Sun God?"

"What if they did? It does not matter. That it is the Truth, I know in my bones. The sun gives us life, light, and food. Understandably, all cultures have some form of Sun worship. Mark, I have taught you *yogic* salutation to the sun, *suryanamaskar*. And you benefit by it in your meditation." Isa looked around and continued, "All of us have to know that the question 'Who did it first?' is futile. Time and place are human concepts. They do not matter in God's reality. And God within us knows that. We consciously have to learn to accept that fact." Isa was tired of endless debates regarding the comparative time frame of the Greek, Egyptian, and Judaic teachings. "Who impacted whom or when are moot questions. Ever since the beginning of trade and migrations of people, all have learned from each other. Even when people fight and kill or rule over others, they impact each other, both the conqueror and the conquered."

Thomas was elated by Isa's expansive approach, and he declared, "I am certain *you* are the Messiah, Master."

"The true Messiah may not claim that title and he may come from an unexpected corner," Isa said gently with a somber look. "He knows what he *is*, or has become, can be attained by everyone else. He realizes his self-hood as an expression of the Divine, and shares it with others, encouraging them to do likewise. What he has done, he believes, others can do, too." Isa's words were simple but profound. His companions were absorbed in the music of his voice.

Mary entered announcing the arrival of one of Isa's friends from distant lands.

"Oh Maniji is here, let me go meet him..." Isa hurried to the door. He hugged Mani. Both were all smiles and kept looking at each other wondering how nearly ten years had matured both.

"No Maniji, you do not have more wrinkles, only more light; you are beaming," Isa said.

"You look *totally* awakened O *param, buddha,* great Buddha," Mani said laughing, looking at Isa with admiration.

Isa lead Mani into the room to meet his companions. Soon John brought food and wine for all.

* * * * * * * * * * * *

"So Maniji, tell me about your findings regarding *sanjivani,* the reviving technique. Did you make any headway?" Isa asked Mani as soon as they were alone.

"We made tremendous progress. One sage from Brahmaganga region agreed to let us use his cadaver for further research. After four years of intense experimentation and research we have succeeded in two areas. We have an absolute cure for healing most treacherous wounds on the battlefield and thus save lives. Also we have found yogic practices to control energies to revive the dead within less than twelve hours after they are considered dead. Both are independent researches."

"What do you mean? You cannot use both on the same person?" Isa asked.

"What it means is that the soldier fighting on the battlefield does not have the luxury of yogic manipulation. So he can be healed only of his wounds." Mani explained, "Besides we cannot help the warrior who has been dead on the battle field for more than twelve hours."

"What about less, say, six hours?" Isa was curious.

"That's very successful. Obviously, the shorter the time, the better it is. We are still working on all that. I stayed in Persia to consult with some of their physicians. Now I am headed to Egypt. They have ancient knowledge of dealing with the dead." Mani smiled referring to the funeral rites of kings and lords.

"Their Mummies were prepared under the assumption that the dead would arise some day, right?" Isa wanted to make sure he understood the connection.

"From what we have gathered, the process of mummifying involved taking out some of the inner body parts. But we are not sure of its underpinning principle. Hopefully, that may throw light on what *we* can do. What we have found is very encouraging. But learning more is even more exciting."

After finishing her chores, Mary came to join their conversation.

"So you are going to Egypt? I hope you will stay here for a while. Sriramji may be arriving soon. Papa plans to visit here for a couple of days. He is from Egypt, you know that, Maniji, don't you? You will enjoy talking with him. Mother Mary will be coming for the holiday." Mary was excited about gathering her family and dear friends.

"Oh, I plan to spend more time learning the new yogic practices Maniji was talking about earlier," Isa told Mary. To Mani he said, "You must stay till the holiday season. My companions will have many questions for you," Isa insisted.

"Yes, I plan to talk with a few Greek scholars before I go to Egypt," Mani wanted to touch all possibilities before he left this area.

"Why has Judas not been seen for a few days, Isa?" Mary asked. She had an errand for him. Mary trusted Judas for his practical ways.

"Judas has to talk with a few centurions regarding our meetings in Jerusalem. It seems temple authorities have lodged a complaint. You know how well he manages those officials." Isa trusted Judas for all such dealings. Judsas had a keen business talent, everybody noticed it.

Mani asked, "Judas is one of your companions, I guess. Perhaps he can help me set up some contacts in Judea and Jerusalem?"

"Sure, I will speak with him. You can trust Judas," Isa said with certainty.

❋

Chapter 54

Talking with Mani was stimulating for Isa's companions. Their interests ranged from the caste system and the holy cow to Buddhist and Jain teachings. Hours of conversation became a routine, that is, whenever Mani was available. Isa was exuberant. Once again he was learning new yoga techniques from Mani. He could control his body sensations and even hold his breath much longer than he had ever done before. This was a totally different technique, Isa thought. It came close to physical manifestations in two places at once, a technique he had mastered once under the guidance of Sriram. But now he could remain in another dimension longer.

"All these techniques require constant reinforcement. Learning it once, or accomplishing a certain level once, is not enough," Mani said smiling when Isa complained how much he had forgotten."You know that, Isa."

"It's true. I was shocked when almost fifteen years ago I heard Sriram mention the first time that the body is a *yantra*, a mechanical device. 'If you fine tune it, it can work miracles,' he said. I was not ready to accept being compared to a device!" Isa laughed aloud.

Mani asked, "All your companions have such varied interests and levels. Have you been teaching them much of what you learned?"

"Yes, but not much of yoga, except to John and Matthew. Our teaching resembles the way of devotion, *bhakti,* since it suits the ordinary people's nature. You know Mary is well immersed in devotion, so her words reach their hearts. Most of our companions also relate to devotion more than meditative yoga. When I say 'the kingdom of God is within you' or 'what I can do you can do and much more,' they understand the deeper meaning. For larger crowds of people in public, I have to adhere to stories, much as the Buddha did, with large masses of people," Isa elaborated on distinct styles he had to adopt for varied listeners.

"Isa, tell Maniji, what you did the other day in your sermon on the hill," Mary suggested.

"What was it?" Mani was curious.

"Isa made the crowd take a step forward in their growth by asking them to *experience* the sunset. They had their first glimpse of *within*," Mary laughed contentedly.

"Oh! that child helped me. I got lucky! She became my witness when she said she saw a king riding an eagle emerge out of the setting sun and take her for a ride," Isa said modestly, laughing loudly.

Peter came in leading Sriram into the room.

"*Jai, Jai,* Sriramji," Isa jumped up from his cushion, all smiles and vigor, bending to bow. But Sriram held him in a friendly hug.

"Finally, you arrived! I was hoping you would be here soon." Mani and Sriram greeted each other bowing with joined palms. Mary got up and bowed to Sriram, "This is a blissful moment for us, Sriramji. We have two *gurus* in our house," Mary's musical laughter filled the room.

Mani and Sriram almost simultaneously protested. Mani's words: "Me! A *guru?*" and Sriram's, "*Guru* is an illusion, Mary," sent everybody into a burst of laughter.

"We will have a great time together. Mary and I have often spoken of the old days. This will be a special reunion." The animated exchange of greetings and stories of travel kept them busy for a while.

* * * * * * * * * * * *

A few days later...

Mother Mary arrived from Galilee for the forthcoming feast of the Passover. She often came to be with her son now that Joseph had passed on. In the beginning she had complained about why young Mary would only be a companion and not a wife. "These young people -- nobody can understand their ways," she used to grumble. She gave up arguing as Isa smiled and remained silent on that subject. Meeting Sriram and Mani, Mother Mary was overjoyed. With added enthusiasm she got busy in the kitchen, relieving young Mary to 'help Isa.'

Ever since Mani and Sriram arrived, Isa's activities had been conveniently curtailed, leaving him much needed time for practicing new techniques of yoga and meditation. A constant awareness of the spark within was vital for Isa at this special time. His companions had so many questions for Mani and Sriram, the two experts, they did not have much time to listen to Isa!

"This is becoming a feast of *knowledge*," said John.

Sriram and Mani answered the companions' endless questions.

Mark asked, "If the Buddha did not consider God as relevant, what is *nirvana*? Isn't it similar to being with God?"

Sriram said, "It depends on how you define God. If God is a supreme being, a super human, but separate from us, then *nirvana* has nothing to do with it. But if God is transcendent Supreme Source, a non-being, then yes, *nirvana* is to be a part of it. Both Vedic and Buddhist traditions would accept that notion, each adding its *specific* commentary on it."

"Our logicians have to split hairs and make marginal differences. Such is the nature of all scientific inquiry," Mani laughed about the complex world of the mind.

Thomas had to get a clarification, "So do you think yoga is a science like your study of *Ayurveda*, herbal and medicinal science, surgery, and such?"

Mani laughed even more loudly, "Why do you ask? Of course, they are all connected. Yoga connects the physical body, focuses on the mind, and activates inner awakening which relates to consciousness. Like herbal science and the study of the human body are material sciences, *rishis*, seers and yogis are scientists of the *inner* world."

Matthew was fascinated by the categorization of living beings the Jains had developed. "You said that the Jains believe in extreme non-violence, even fan the ground they walk on so they may not step on insects, or tie a mouthpiece lest they kill invisible insects in the air.

Even fasting till death is considered a pious act. Is that not anomalous? Is that not violence against one's own body?"

Mani responded after a few seconds of silence to this unfamiliar question. In his land nobody considered fasting as suicidal though some highly advanced Jain sages abandoned their earthly bodies by fasting. "Fasting is primarily to regulate the body system. It purifies the body and the mind. It is not considered torturing the body. There are regulated fasts for certain days, where strict routine has to be observed. The mind is engaged in pious thoughts and prayers connecting oneself with the absolute reality. However, fasting till death is undertaken only by those *munis*, sages, monks and nuns who have attained the highest awareness. They have attained total control of the body and mind and are called *siddha.*"

"Well, talking about fasting, I am getting hungry," Isa laughed.

Chapter 55

It was later that night. There was no moon. Darkness was pervasive, intrusive, and even offensive, inside and out. Isa was waiting for Judas' arrival from Jerusalem where he was sent to inquire about important matters and make necessary arrangements. Only Judas, with his pragmatic approach and integrity, could be trusted for this important assignment.

As soon as Judas arrived, Isa and Mary lead Mani and Sriram to the loft of the house. Judas followed them up the narrow ladder. Joseph of Arimathea, Isa's uncle, was already waiting. The loft was narrow and musty. Only a small hole for a window up by the roofline let some air in. Although each one had some idea of what they had gathered for, none knew the specifics of what might turn up.

Earlier in the day Isa's companions had discussed the rage and discomfort Isa's popularity had caused among the Temple and State authorities. Either or both of these powers could punish Isa and his companions, each in its own way. No one could be sure what that could be.

"We cannot allow *fear* to control us." Isa started in a voice a little higher than a whisper to his private circle of trusted friends. "But we cannot be naïve about the reach of the authority either. Judas, tell us about your findings." Isa had sent Judas to assess the situation in relation to Isa and his companions' forthcoming visit to the Temple for the Passover.

All eyes and ears focused on Judas. "Master, these are vicious people. But I succeeded in reaching the weakest links within each base, both at the Temple and the Roman Court."

"What do you mean?" Sriram was not sure, "You bribed them? With what? Heaven does not interest them, does it?" Sriram joked. Only Isa smiled, the rest were very stern.

"I had told Judas to find out all possible venues to protect ourselves against any dire contingency," Isa said. "We need to be prepared, be a step ahead of them."

Mary was anxious, "Are you sure of your strategy, Judas?"

Judas shrugged, "That's the best I could do. Who knows what may transpire!"

None could predict the future.

"We have to be ready for the worst including being declared a criminal," Isa said in a controlled tone.

"That would mean the worst punishment - the cross," Joseph of Arimathea nearly shouted, but lowered his tone as Judas signaled to him with his hand to keep his voice down. The tension was getting thicker.

Mani was quietly listening while carefully watching Isa's body movements. "You have mastered many yogic practices, Isa. Sriram can even make himself invisible or be in two places at the same time, if need be. You all should know." Mani looked at each one making sure they absorbed the information.

"I am sure we can work something out. With Mani's knowledge dealing with life and death we may be able to work out a rescue plan, if need be." Sriram gauged the enormity of the situation, but was still relaxed.

"I will see what pressure I can bring with my position as the member of the Sanhedrin Council," said Joseph of Arimathea.

Isa said, "I have strengthened some of my old yogic practices that would allow me to better control my body. The new yogic practices Mani taught me recently have extraordinary powers."

"A part of me says, things will happen as our Father has ordained, but I cannot help worrying, Isa," Mary was nearly in tears.

"You will know, Mary, you will," Isa comforted her putting his hand on hers.

"Keep all herbs, oil, and potions I have given you, Mary," said Mani to make sure her bag was ready.

"Isa, could the four of us go ahead of the rest of the group to Jerusalem for any last minute arrangement?" Joseph of Arimathea asked.

"Of course," Isa said with utmost calmness.

It was a contingency plan, in case....the worst happened...

Chapter 56

The next day after lunch, the companions were lounging. Judas was leaning against his satchel.

"Isa, those priests are upset with you because you draw huge crowds of people."

"They have no problem with my words, my teaching?" Isa was curious.

"Only words like 'king' and 'kingdom,' upset them." Judas shrugged his shoulders, "Both Roman centurions and the high priests seem to be focused on your Kingly claim. They think you want to be the king of this land or God in the Temple. That threatens them," he added.

Andrew was nearly shouting, "Are they dumb or what? Even a fisherman understands Isa is speaking of one's mind and body. Not *their* kingdom." All laughed at the implied denouncement of Andrew's own vocation! Andrew was laughing the loudest.

"Why are they worried about large crowds? They are ordinary people living their daily lives. They are not power hungry centurions. A few Romans who come to listen, only come to check, I guess. Don't they, Master?" Luke wanted to know.

"They are scared of numbers. Larger groups of people are becoming aware of what is wrong in the claims the Temple high priests make. They do not want people to hear it. And then there is the issue of taxes for our Roman rulers!" Judas said the obvious.

Isa seemed lost in deep thought. In fact, he was in his open-eye-meditation, despite the impending questions, doubts, fears around him. He had cultivated a practice of being in two worlds simultaneously, even when he was in big or small groups of people.

He said plaintively, "Often I have spoken of the real world and the *illusion* of life. You all know that in India they call such illusion *maya.* I have talked about it before. Masses of people who come to listen to us cannot understand it. But you, my close companions, can. Andrew, I am very pleased that you understand it. Once again I remind you all of the *duality* of life. That is our human condition. To know the true nature of duality is to awaken to *life*. John, you mentioned how the butterfly flaps its two wings to balance its moves. Likewise we need to balance *our* two realities, the world within and without."

Isa continued, "But the butterfly establishes another, vital truth of life. Once a grimy, heavy, crawling caterpillar, devouring leaves and snoozing inertly in its cocoon, becomes so light! It is now a blazingly colorful butterfly flying gently around. Who would imagine that? I want you all to know that we too can be such butterflies. Mired in our material world, we can transform and reclaim our Divinity of light. We need to meditate in our cocoons of this world. Even if we sleep for a while, we have the spark within that will transform us. And awakened, we shall soar into heavenly skies."

"Master, do you suggest we go into caves, cocoons, like the *rishis,* seers, of India you spoke of?" Luke wanted to know.

"How would we then serve our people who need our help?" Peter was confused.

Mary felt she had to intervene, "Hasn't Isa so frequently told us about different kinds of meditation. Didn't he tell us to focus on the Divine Father in our everyday activities of life? Never divert our attention from the Divine, he frequently says, no matter what we do."

"Consider life's activities as Divine play, you call it *lila,* Master," reminded Mark.

Isa looked approvingly both at Mary and Mark and continued in a grave note, "Listen, all of you. The time for the test of our faith in Truth, our Way, has arrived. You have heard me for a while now. You will witness dire times and tests. The most severe will be for me. In my absence I do not want you to give up what you have learned and practiced. Spread the Truth about God, Love, and Mercy to all."

All companions fell silent. They were stunned by Isa's serious tone. His deep sonorous voice seemed to come from afar. After a short period of silence, John, closest to Isa, hardly able to control his tremulous voice asked, "Isa, it sounds like you are leaving us. What do you mean by your absence? Who will guide us?"

Looking intently at John, Isa spoke in a slow measured tone, pausing after each sentence, "John, we have often talked about this. Look after my mother, when I am gone. Of all, you understand me the most. You know my thoughts even before I utter them. Often I do not know where I end and you begin. Why do *you* ask? You will see me, touch me, despite the hardest violence the authorities may inflict on me," Isa's whole *being* seemed to pour into his words.

Isa turned his head and continued addressing everybody, "To testify my presence within you all, I pass this bread as my flesh, and this cup of wine as my blood. May you all take these and feel my presence within you, always." Isa held the cup high and then passed it with the bread to his companions sitting around him.

Isa spoke slowly, emphatically and with clarity, looking intently at each companion as he received the bread and the chalice. The last was Mary sitting next to him; their eyes interlocked, they remained silent for a long time.

Then Isa looked at his brooding companions, "All of you have learned well. I urge you to ponder and record your experiences to instruct future generations. You may be hunted for being my friends and companions. Maybe you will all want to be less visible for a while but quietly teach others in your own way. That is God's will as I understand it. Mary, Judas, you have served God well. I know you have your stories to share. Philip you grasp the depth of my words. Share them with people. Thomas you are new, but you learn fast. Wherever you all go, hide or flourish, bring the message of God's Love and Mercy to all. There is strength in community and in discipline. All of you remember the special *knowledge* I have shared with you from my *experiences* in many lands. Use it well with discretion. And as I said before, and I repeat once again, what I have done you can do too, and much more. Call on me and I will come to your aid."

"I am not really leaving you," Isa made the concluding remark looking meaningfully at Mani and Sriram. They were leaning against the wall in a corner witnessing a significant event.

Everybody knew crucifying criminals was the Roman way. But none could imagine any such thing would happen to them, much less to Isa.

* * * * * * * * * * * *

Lately Isa had been spending long hours in virtual isolation. Mary understood him well and kept the other companions' intrusion to the minimum. Mother Mary's arrival with sisters Martha and Ruth allowed her spare time to attend to some of Isa's work. She knew Isa was in deep contemplation. Their love had 'sensitized her to perfection' as Isa called it. Without verbal communication Mary would know Isa's mind, his thoughts, and his feelings at the deepest core.

Later that day, their routine dusk walk on the hill by the Lake was time for *their* communion.

"Has the time arrived, Isa?" She asked as they sat on the slope of the hill by the Lake, leaning against their favorite rock.

"I believe it is close," Isa spoke gently, looking across the Lake, his arm around Mary's shoulder; her head resting on his.

"I am sure you are prepared," Mary said, almost complaining in a 'how could you?' tone.

"But *you* are not, Mira," using his term of endearment now that they were alone. He raised her head, looked into her teary eyes with deep compassion, "You have to be bold, Mira. This is *our* work. We agreed to do it in this life: for Truth, Faith, and Love -- that is God, the Divine within."

"But we did not agree we would not cry, not feel sad, nor not scream," Mary protested. Isa heard unprecedented sadness in her voice. Could her musical laughter vanish completely?

With a sad smile holding her hand in his, Isa spoke, "True. We shall come out victorious despite all misgivings, cries, pain and torture." Isa knew his predicament.

"Isa, why is it that you have to suffer unjust torture, although Truth is on your side? Why can you not speak aloud and declare the Universal Truth? Defeat them. God will help you," Mary was still clinging to the last straw.

"Truth before its time cannot be spoken. Nobody hears it," said Isa slowly, deliberately, his head resting on the rock, his eyes piercing into the empty space above. The words came from his mouth, but he knew that was not where they were formed. Did Mary utter those words long ago? He was sure she did. They lay buried in his subconscious.

Mary broke into soft sobbing. Isa caressed her head in his lap. For a while he was lost in a trance staring into the water. Those days on the bank of the river Yamuna flashed afresh in his mind. Hands intertwined, they had chatted with Yamuna endlessly, often forgetting how late it was. After a while Isa saw Mary was calmly looking at the Lake, her head still in his lap. The water reflected the setting sun.

Whirling fast, turning orange the sun was reaching the horizon.

"Look up, Mira, the sun is ready to go to another world, but will not leave without greeting the full moon coming up on the other side."

Mary raised her head, tear tracks on her cheeks, hair fluttering in the wind across her forehead, she looked up. Her moist eyes reflected the orange pink sunrays. As she turned to see the full moon of the spring rise on the opposite side, her teary eyes filled with serene calmness, "Isn't this a magnificent moment? Isa, don't the sun and the moon look almost the same size? Look." She was turning her head in both directions to watch this celestial meeting of day and night, the sun and the moon.

"They do. You are right," said Isa turning his head from the sun to the moon. "Like two lovers they constantly move to catch up. But they can't, except for a few moments like now they can see each other at a distance. How blissful is this viewing, *darshan*, of twin love flames!" Isa had his hands around Mary.

Their faces looking up in the sky were close. Isa looked into Mary's eyes. Their eyes interlocked in fervent embrace. Moments became seconds...seconds turned into minutes...they sat motionless, interlocked.

The sun and the moon tarried a little longer today witnessing the rare union...much like their own...distant yet close. The sun smiled and casting his last ray of blessing on the lovers continued his journey on the ordained path.

A little later, the moon, now dazzling bright in the dark sky witnessed the blissful joy of the intertwined young couple by the Lake.

The moon watched the couple for a long while....

Riding on the winged Unicorn, Isa and Mary were scanning the starry firmament. Were the blinking stars and planets greeting them? "Look at the flowing waves," said the Unicorn. Isa and Mary became aware of the floating waves of light rushing around. "These waves are where the stars are born," the Unicorn was flying so fast it seemed stationary as the firmament sped them by.

A long span away, passed planets, constellations, and galaxies, Isa and Mira saw big boulders, stars, and other strange heavenly bodies rushing into a huge dark hole. The Unicorn flew into an indescribable dark range of aakash, space. It then started its descent back toward earth.

Isa and Mary passed by the stars and planets of the Solar system. "Isa, look, doesn't the earth look like a beautiful blue green pendant in the Sun's necklace?" Isa agreed, "It is magnificent."

Momentarily, the winged creature landed on a snowy mountain range. Gently gliding Isa and Mary off its back, the unicorn said, "In the valley down there, is your new home."

Isa opened his eyes, looked at Mary resting her head on the same rock by his side.

She turned toward him, and said, "I had a strange dream."

"So did I," mumbled Isa.

※

Chapter 57

The Passover was approaching.

Mother Mary was fussing about preparations to go to the New Temple in Jerusalem for the holiday. She was quite excited, but was pensive. She had no specific knowledge of the impending risks for her son, but she was uneasy. In fact, during her stay in Capernaum she was delighted by her son's increasing popularity. She was the proud mother celebrating a major holiday with her son. How much more does a mother wish for? She will march with her widely admired son tomorrow at the head of the procession! "Pride is sin," she checked herself. She humbly thanked God for blessing her son, and smiled remembering her vision of the angel before Isa was born. "Well, my son has been God's favorite from the beginning," she muttered comforting herself.

Mother Mary was sitting on a bench in the backyard, lost in her thoughts stroking the head of the sacrificial lamb. She had cleaned the lamb herself to be taken to the temple for the Passover ritual the next day.

Isa came into the backyard, "There you are, Mother. Are you ready for the journey?" He approached her and sat on the ground winding his arms around her back, gently resting his head in his Mother's lap. One hand on the lamb, Mother Mary started caressing Isa's head with the other.

"Yes, son, I am more than ready. I do not recall when I was so happy in my life! God has been so kind to you and me. He has made you His true Son. He will always look after you. That's Mother's blessing to you, my dear son."

She bent to kiss Isa on his head, her other hand still on the lamb.

Young Mary entered, looking for Isa, and froze in her tracks seeing this divine statuesque of absolute love.

* * * * * * * * * * *

The next day Isa's companions were ready to leave for Jerusalem.

Mani, Sriram, Joseph of Arimathea, and Judas had already reached the destination for their appointed assignments. Mary had her sack ready.

With his companions Isa marched to Jerusalem on Sunday.

Chapter 58

Howling winds, lightening, and thunder mixed with the cries of the crowd on Golgotha. Thunder still echoing in his ears, lightening dazzling his eyes, Sriram stepped backwards. He nearly bumped into a stern guard in charge of the Golgotha crucifixion site.

Today there were three culprits. Earlier in the day the guard had wondered why there was such a huge crowd on a stormy day. Living close to "the cross hill" –as the guards called Golgotha -- he had missed the commotion in Jerusalem for the last three days. He had not heard of Isa, the self-styled king, bearing the cross to this spot, till he arrived on Golgotha, almost half dead.

It was Friday; the Jewish Sabbath had made everybody's work day shorter. The guard had originally planned a relaxed evening with his family.

But now having witnessed the earth shaking event, literally, the guard's eyes were glued on the center cross. Instead of the woeful cries of the two other criminals, this man in the center was really kingly in bearing his pain, the guard thought. In his long career as the crucifying guard, he had never seen anybody retain his dignity as the man on the center cross did. When Sriram bumped into him, both were gazing intently on Isa's face against the dark agitating clouds. Each glared at the other. The guard was dazed; Sriram walked away, sad and contemplative.

As prearranged, Sriram headed toward the tomb on the property of Joseph of Arimathea. At the end of the crowd he saw Judas leaning against a tree tears rolling down his cheeks. He was staring at Isa on the cross. Sriram went to Judas and put his comforting hand on his shoulder. Both looked at each other meaningfully with understanding and determination in their looks. Sriram left Judas and walked pensively to the designated place.

A loud shriek of renewed terror spread through the crowd as the Roman soldier's spear pierced Isa's *left side near his heart, blood oozing out.*

At that very moment there was another agonizing scream virtually drowned by the collective shriek of the crowd. It was Judas' scream as he fell on the ground with a deep dagger wound in the *left side near his heart, blood oozing out.*

A few minutes earlier a young man in the crowd saw Judas leaning against the tree. That morning in town he had heard a rumor that Judas had betrayed Isa for a sum of 30 dinars. The man was raging mad witnessing Isa's crucifixion. When the man saw Judas...he rushed to the betrayer with a dagger and stabbed him to death.

It being the Sabbath, Joseph of Arimathea could get Isa's body released early for funeral rites. It seemed the guards had prior instructions from the authority to honor that request. Without much hesitation the guards complied. Mani, Joseph, John, Mother Mary and young Mary gently gathered the motionless body of their beloved Isa. Mother Mary held her son's body in her lap. She was in extreme agony, young Mary was stunned in a speechless daze, Joseph was stern, John was bereft, Mani was intent.

As the group made its way toward the tomb with Isa's body, it started raining; the wind blew making a swooshing sound, but was not fierce. It seemed nature after its earlier howling agony was now comforting this loving assemblage with a gentle drizzle.

Life and death were held in balance.

Chapter 59

Three Roman guards stationed to watch the tomb on Joseph of Arimathea's property noticed Isa's body being carried toward them. They were relaxed, not anxious.

One of the Jews had come to their barracks a few days before asking who was assigned to guard the tomb site on Joseph's property. The Jew had a cask of wine and 30 dinars. The chief among the three, Secundus, had joked about an unusual incident of a Jew bearing gifts. Today Secundus thought there was nothing wrong in going easy, look the other way; allow them to do whatever for their dead king. After all he was dead, how much trouble could a dead man be, he wondered?

The group carrying Isa entered the tomb. After what seemed to be hours of cleaning or praying or whatever else they do, the guards noticed that all went away, still crying. The old woman, the mother of the dead man, was supported by a man and a woman on each side. The poor woman was really broken down, Secundus mumbled.

The guards went in to check the tomb, saw the dead body wrapped in a cloth that had oils and some powdery stuff. It "kind of smelt funny...but not bad; better than the rotting body," Secundus said and all three laughed coarsely. They looked around "nothing but the dead body," he muttered. After checking the tomb, the guards rolled the huge stone to close its entrance. "Always follow instructions," Secundus said, "No matter what you do, don't upset your superiors." He enjoyed his seniority over the two freshmen guards.

They returned to their position and had a goodly drink from the gift-cask. "This wine is good. It's different. Sharper than anything I have ever had. What do you think?" Secundus was babbling away

228

and drinking...They all laughed, joked; soon they fell asleep, deeply asleep.

As was arranged, Sriram had already been inside the tomb before Isa was brought in. After everybody else attending to Isa left, Sriram had become invisible when the guards came to check. For the whole time Sriram worked on Isa applying herbs and potions that Mani had given him with detailed instructions.

In the early morning when Joseph of Arimathea arrived with his trusted servants, the guards were fast asleep. The servants removed the stone at the tomb's entrance and left. Soon young Mary and Mani arrived. Everything was working out as planned. Only Judas wasn't there. Where was he they wondered?

As they entered the tomb, young Mary saw Isa seated on the stone slab. Overjoyed she ran to him, sat by his feet caressing them, kissing them, her tresses of hair hanging low soothing the healed wounds on Isa's feet. Isa bent and raised her to sit next to him. The two shone like twin flames in that dark tomb.

Isa looked around. "Where is Judas?" he asked.

Nobody knew. It was strange.

Sriram mentioned his brief meeting with grieving Judas on the crucifixion ground.

Isa closed his eyes for a short while. He *knew.* He said, "Let us carry on with our plan. We cannot tarry too long. Before Sunday we must accomplish all we need to."

All walked out of the tomb.

Only the cloth remained.

Chapter 60

"Oh, my dear son!" sobbed Mother Mary, and fainted. Yesterday she held his motionless body in her lap, today he is alive!

Isa sat gently caressing Mother Mary's head in his lap. He was thinking of the scene in his backyard in Capernaum with his head in Mother's lap. It was the day of their journey to Jerusalem.

"Wake up mother, I am alive, I am re-born. You cannot faint every time you hear of my birth!" Isa said in a faintly laughing tone, still tenderly caressing her head.

Slowly Mother opened her eyes, kept staring at her son, tears running down to her ears. Isa's smiling eyes were riveted on her face.

John, who had not left Mother's side since their return from Golgotha, was dazed by Isa's return to life. Blissfully happy John was still mystified as to how such a miracle could happen.

"John, call all our companions. Before Mary and I leave I have to speak to them. You all must know what happened."

John hastened to gather all companions. Mother Mary was quite composed by the time all the amazed and happy, still bleary eyed, companions assembled. Their excitement was palpable.

Smiling Isa looked around, comforting each by his serene eyes. Then he began, "Yesterday you saw my wounded, motionless body on the cross. Today I am here, alive in my healed body. I want you to witness my resurrected body. Bear witness to the power of intent, yoga, and control of energies that I have often spoken of before."

Isa looked around, "Where is Judas?" he asked.

All looked around, except Peter. He began, "Master, I do not know how to tell you. I am ashamed. It is my fault." His voice trembled as he started sobbing, "Yesterday I saw Judas by a tree, weeping, while you were nailed on the cross. I started going toward him to comfort him, but just then I saw a raging young man running to him with a dagger. Before I could reach Judas, the man stabbed him. It was exactly the same time when the Roman soldier pierced your chest and the crowd shrieked. At that very moment Judas fell dead on the ground, blood oozing from his body."

A cry of disbelief spread in the room. Everyone was shocked. Some were staring at Peter in total disbelief.

Sobbing Andrew tried to speak. Only broken phrases came out of his dribbling mouth, "I can't...believe it. How can...wise Judas die? ...He always saved me...Peter...why do you say...you are ashamed? You did not... kill him. Did you?"

"Brother Andrew, I did worse. After I saw the man kill Judas, I was so scared that I did not go to his rescue. But even worse, when some people recognized me as Master's follower, I denied it. Not once, nor twice, but three times. I am ashamed of my cowardice...fear is the real killer, brother," Peter sobbed. Hitting his head repeatedly with his fists, and could not speak anymore...All were unsettled.

What a cruel end for a devoted, loyal, and efficient companion Judas was the one thought in everybody's mind.

Isa was in an elevated state since his transformational experience on the cross. His raised consciousness could envision other dimensions. In a gentle voice he began, "Judas has been the most faithful, trustworthy, and loving companion for all of us and our work. He had been a special friend for me. He gave his life for us." Isa looked up for a few moments, closed his eyes and remained silent, gratefully acknowledging Judas.

Then Isa turned to Mother Mary and held her hand. With immense love in his eyes he started to speak, "I want you all to be a witness. I am arisen from the dead. You all see me. You can touch me. Know me as real person with the same body. You are witnesses of my resurrection, my coming back to life from the dead. We live in difficult times. Some of us have to pay with our lives, as Judas did. All of you have to be cautious. Peter, I do not admonish you for your denials. All of you can learn from Peter to be practical. Life demands intelligent, pragmatic decisions. Never waver from your *intent set in love and mercy. Be compassionate.* Manifest the power within you. The kingdom of heaven is within you as I have spoken many times before," Isa spoke slowly, with clarity, weighing every word and remained silent watching each of his companions.

"Master you are not leaving us?" Philip was not sure he had a clear picture. Why did Isa sound as if he was going away?

"I cannot live in this land anymore. In the eyes of everybody I am dead and buried. Only you know and believe I have resurrected. We live in troubled times, the world is not ready for such tidings. But you are eye witnesses. Choose your path. What I can do you can too. But Mary and I will be leaving before daybreak tomorrow." Mother Mary tightened her grip on Isa's hand.

"Will you be going to Egypt, Master?" asked Luke.

"Maniji suggested that we could go with him to Egypt. But that is not wise right now. The Roman centurions look for all 'troublemakers' from Israel in Egypt. The high priests will worry about my missing body. And if as per the prophecy, I am considered 'resurrected', they would feel they killed the Messiah, and therefore may look for me even more eagerly." Isa smiled gently and continued, "The high priests will make sure to prove that some of you are responsible for my missing body. They might even question you. Or punish you. They might help the Roman authority to look for me in Egypt. So Mary and I will go eastward with Sriramji to finally reach India."

The companions sat dazed by the events: Isa tortured, nailed, revived, and leaving again...none could think clearly through this maze of intricate politics and possibilities. They remained quiet, sad, grieving for the impending loss...once again...!

"Son, how do I face another separation from you? I just got you back," Mother Mary was incredulous. "Are you in a condition to travel after what you went through on that horrible pole?"

"Mother, I was on the cross only for a little over three hours I am told, and Sriramji healed me in the tomb for the whole night. I had enough time to recover," Isa laughed loudly trying to lighten the sadness around him. "I wish, Mother, I had another option, a different path. But times compel us to make hard decisions. It pains me a lot to leave you once again, Mother. And I do not wish to part from all of you, my companions. We live in tumultuous times. Mother, John will be like your son when I am gone. He has promised me. We all will have to decide what to do, where to go, and what to say. There is a wide world out there. Take God's message wherever you can and will. May we all be blessed! God will protect us all."

Everybody was trying to let reality sink in.

Mother Mary was the first to speak, "Look after my son, Mary," she said to young Mary touching her cheeks and caressing her head.

"I will never forget how kind and loving you have been to me, Mother," young Mary spoke gently. Isa looked at her and knew she was thinking of her own mother.

"You be happy and fruitful my children," Mother Mary blessed them the traditional way. Both Isa and Mary looked at each other, intrigued.

They all stood up in silence. A few moments of prayers enwrapped them all.

"May the winds be gentle and your path smooth, Master," said Mark.

"We will communicate in spirit, Master. I will look after Mother Mary as my own," John reassured Isa once again.

"We will find some way to connect, Master," said Thomas.

"Why are you quiet, Peter? You are strong like a rock. Life will have many challenges, and you will face them successfully," Isa reassured Peter.

Isa and Mary walked around greeting each companion, holding hands, hugging, kissing, and blessing.

As Isa held Thomas' hands, both kept staring at each other for a brief moment before Thomas spoke, "I have never thought of going away from you, Master. Who knows, now I might go to India, as you suggested once." Isa held his hands tightly and gave him a gentle hug with a smile

In a tremulous voice, Andrew said, "I will miss you, Master," and hugged Isa tightly. He turned to Mary saying, "You were the best teacher I had. Take care of my Master."

Isa held Simon's hands, "But for your faith I could not have begun my work. Keep up that faith and spread the word." Simon was unable to utter a single word. Isa embraced him.

* * * * * * * * * * *

Teary eyed companions watched Isa and Mary walk with Sriram to the end of the hill, till they could see the travelers no more.

Chapter 61

Two years later....

Sunrays reflected on the snowy blue peak of the sacred mountain created an ethereal aura. Intently staring at it, she saw the peak slowly turning brighter, lighter, turning into shimmering turquoise. Watching it intently for a long time she *felt* her eyes and the peak become one. The sun came up in full view from behind Mount Kailash. Serene blue grey ripples of the lake Mansarovar reflected the sunrays in its expansive lap. It was a spring morning in the extreme northeast of India, on the fringe of the area now known as Tibet.

"Wavy ripples of the lake seem to laugh as the light reflects on them. They laugh just as you do Mira," said Isa intently staring into this play of sunrays on the water.

"Do the sunrays laugh? They jiggle on the ripples, Isa. You have become a poet," Mira broke into a loud joyous laughter rapt in the scenery and fresh air. They were sitting by the lake to watch the rising sun from behind Mount Kailash, legendary home of Shiva and Parvati, the ultimate divine pair --- *purush,* spirit, and *prakriti,* the primordial nature.

"I thought I have always been a poet," Isa spoke mirthfully, "a little crazy, perhaps!"

"Aren't we immensely blessed, Isa?" Mira's eyes reflected the sunrays as she lay on the ground looking up in the sky. Isa extended his arm to support her head, himself stretching out on the cold earth. Both stared into the sun, un-blinking, absorbed. The sunrays reflected in the eyes of Isa and Mira formed two overlapping triangles. A lone eagle flying high in the sky noticed the shiny formations it had never seen before. It dived to catch whatever it was.

"Isn't this just like what the little girl said that day on the hill?" said Isa as he watched the eagle approaching them almost from the sun, "She said she rode the bird coming from the sun."

"I feel I am a little girl," giggling like a child, Mira turned her face to Isa.

The eagle flew away as it saw the strange shiny formation disappear, sighing, "It's only those humans on the ground!"

* * * * * * * * * * * *

Since leaving Jerusalem a little over two years ago, Isa and Mira had endured a lot.

Much had happened to the young couple as they traveled in disguise with Sriram. Of course, the Roman Empire had strong and long arms to catch them if they were identified. Fortunately, for the Roman officials Isa was dead. The disappearance of the body after the crucifixion bothered the high priests, but not Herod. Pilate had washed his hands of Isa for good. So no Roman officials were looking for Isa. Travelling with two Indians, Sriram and Mira, in her Indian outfit to avoid any suspicion, Isa had been safe.

The destination was Kashmir in India. It was Sriram's suggestion.

Since Sriram first met thirteen year old Isa in the market place near Galilee, he had consciously recognized Isa's essence, his spark. Sriram also knew of their inner connection and his role in Isa's life. Since those early days Sriram had kept a watch on Isa's journey. It was Sriram's *dharma*, the purpose of this life time, he once told Mani, who was another guide on Isa's path.

The appearance of Sriram and Mani in Jerusalem at the time of Isa's trial was not consciously orchestrated by anyone. The events had synchronized. Mani had arrived in Jerusalem en route to Egypt where he planned to learn more about the techniques of mummification. That might help him, he hoped, in his area of interest: prolonging the life of cells in humans. Sriram's intuitive knowledge guided him to plan his market trip to Jerusalem that holiday season. The events in Jerusalem: the earth shaking crucifixion and its aftermath, made Mani wonder if he too should return to India with Sriram, Isa and Mary, to help them reach India safely.

"Do not worry Maniji, you proceed to Egypt," Sriram said, "Do your life's work. Mine is to be Isa's guide. You played your part in Isa's healing. I am confident, the worst is over. Go in peace and be blessed in your findings. The world needs you."

Sriram, Isa and Mary travelled their way back through Syria, Persia, and Afghanistan to the borders of modern Pakistan, without much hardship. Isa and Mary went through the Swat region of Punjab to Kashmir. Both instantly recognized the valley they had seen in their simultaneous vision, years ago, at the end of the space-ride with the unicorn, who had said, "there is your home down in the valley."

After they had spent a few months in their new home, one spring day Sriram appeared.

"Isa, are you ready for the next journey?" Sriram asked. Isa, who was watching a little rabbit coming out of hibernation, joyfully turned to Sriram who had shown up from nowhere. This was no surprise as Sriram had materialized and de-materialized naturally, mostly unexpectedly. They greeted each other with a bow, *namaste*, and a friendly hug.

"As your *chela*, disciple, I am not supposed to know when I am ready. You, the *guru*, knows. Am I ready, Master?" with a twinkle in his eyes Isa asked. Both broke into a loud laughter. They knew it was not the usual *guru-chela*, master-student relationship. They were dear friends.

Mira came out of the house, "*Jai, Jai* Sriramji." Sriram blessed her, "Live long, dear girl. You have a great blessing and a huge responsibility here," merrily pointing at Isa.

"Don't I know it?" came Mira's musical laughter. "So what's next, Sriramji?" Mira knew Sriram's appearance indicated some move. It always excited her.

"In Mathura and Vraj you *experienced* the Love of the *soul* with the *divine* in Krishna–Radha." Isa and Mira glanced at each other with a meaningful look. Weren't they conscious of it every moment?

Sriram continued, "Now is the time to *experience* the ideal divine love of Shiva and Parvati that integrates the physical and the spiritual, the ultimate cosmic connectedness of *purush* spirit, and *prakriti,* the primordial matter, nature."

Isa was curious, "In Varanasi, I experienced Shiva's duality -- his dance of *life* and *death.* Now this is about the *love* of Shiva and Parvati -- the totality of *love* in all its aspects. So where in the Himalayas do we go, Sriramji?"

"Mount Kailash and the Mansarovar, the home of Shiva and Parvati."

Mira looked at Isa, then asked Sriram, "To what end, Sriramji?"

Sriram somberly said, "*You* have to find that. I only point the direction."

Isa asked, "Will you guide our steps to our destination, Sriramji?"

"Follow the spark within," Sriram said.

Before Isa or Mira could say any more, Sriram was gone -- had disappeared.

Chapter 62

Isa and Mira traversed the rugged land, met people, communed with them, and visited several Buddhist monasteries on their way to Mount Kailash In Lumbini, the birthplace of the Buddha, in modern Nepal, every step they took enchanted them. The place seemed to vibrate in their beings; it was uncanny.

Isa spent hours in the monastery, talking with the monks. Younger monks in training were at hand to transcribe their conversations on palm leaves. Precious sayings were carved on copper plates. For ready references monks in training would recite Buddha's teachings by heart. These monks were *walking* scriptures like Arun, Mani's assistant, whom Isa had met years ago.

Isa was familiar with some of the Buddhist scriptures from his years at Takshashila. In fact, he had used quite a few teachings from the Buddha's eightfold path in his own teachings back home in Galilee. But the discourses with the chief monks of monasteries were on a deeper level. Isa became more aware of the significance of the rituals and traditions.

"Isa, do you feel you have been here before? I know it sounds strange," asked Mira one morning as they were walking in the forest in Lumbini.

Isa breathed in deeply, drinking the air in. Looking around silently he felt the vibrations of energy. "Mira, we were here in another incarnation. We naturally do not have active memory of it. But the place does invoke faint stirrings, doesn't it? Long talks with Anand Muni at the monastery triggered buried awareness in me too."

"How does one know for sure?" Mira wanted to believe it, but was not sure.

Isa remained quiet for a while, then looking intently at Mira, said, "In my deep meditation last night, I was transported into that time. Everything was clear. I remember being born as Prince Siddhartha Gotama, the Buddha."

Astounded Mira almost tripped over a small boulder saying, "What?!"

Isa spoke with absolute certainty. His eyes were on the mountainous horizon. "Do you recall Buddha's mother Mayavati's dream? A white elephant entered her body before Siddhartha's birth, remember? I saw that vision clearly and felt I was entering the womb. You were Mayavati," Isa's words seemed to flow from another dimension.

Mira was grappling with the enormity of this statement. Holding Isa's hand, she sat down on a rock nearby. Isa sat on the ground by the rock. Both kept looking at the mountains. After a long silence, Mira spoke, "Does that mean we have been reincarnating time after time out of compassion for people to help them?"

"True. Being humans we are limited. We forget other lives. To fulfill the purpose of each life we are blessed with open eyes, hearts, and minds, and unlimited love and compassion for all," Isa simplified a complex process in a few words.

"Thus we connect with the Cosmic Divinity!" Mira completed Isa's thought.

"Truly that is the fusion of the Cosmic Self with the individual Self -- the only reality there is. No separation. *Nirvana*, Liberation, Salvation: different names for the only real Truth. *Soham*, I am That, as the ancients declared."

Isa and Mira were silently staring at the sky for a long time unmindful of their surroundings, till they noticed the setting sun.

Their eyes reflected the sunrays vanishing behind the mountains.

Chapter 63

"Isa do you remember the story of Shiva and Parvati's marriage? Being an ascetic, Shiva was always in penance, *tapas*. Fascinated Parvati often came to see him; but he was always in meditation hardly noticing her. You know, maybe Shiva was meditating on her. What do you think?" It was obvious Mira was partial to love-sick Parvati.

Isa was amused; he continued in the same tone, "Maybe you are right; Shiva was meditating on her. Parvati was so beautiful. She did not walk, she danced, her smile sounded like jingling bells, she walked like a graceful deer, her eyes were like lotus leaf, and...."

"Hey...hey... wait...you are borrowing your fancy similes from *kathakars,* story tellers?" Mira was amused by Isa's stylized poetic description from popular epic stories.

"Why do I have to borrow from anyone when you are here? I can just describe you," Isa's eyes were mischievous.

"I was happy when I heard that part of the story when Kamdev, the god of love, came to help love-stricken Parvati. But Shiva was impervious to the abundant beauty in front of him. Oh how gorgeous was that spring Kamdev created with fragrant flowers, buzzing bees, chirping birds, colorful butterflies, and gurgling streams. In the middle of it all Parvati danced with such joy," Mira was recollecting the stories she had heard.

"But when Shiva opened his eyes, witnessing that *untimely* spring, he was enraged. Opening his third eye he burnt Kamdeva who had disturbed his penance," Isa completed the story, "everything has its proper time. *Absolute Love* cannot be hastened." Isa looked at Mira anticipating a rejoinder.

"True, Parvati certainly learned that lesson to be a suitable spouse for an ascetic Shiva. She started her own penance of austerities, *tapas*. She became a *tapasvini*." Mira spoke with a trace of determination resembling Parvati's.

"And then the two, Shiva and Parvati, were a real match to create a suitable warrior child, Skanda. The gods needed a powerful hero to defeat their adversaries, *daityas,* demons." Isa underlined a collective humanitarian objective behind the personal union of Shiva and Parvati.

"But I still feel a little sorry for the other son, Ganesh, with his elephant head and human body," Mira bemoaned the ugly head.

Isa was in a cheerful mood today, "Listen Mira, I would not mind being Ganesh, if I were worshipped *first* before any of the three hundred million gods and goddesses people adore in this land, ugly head or no." Isa laughed heartily, and added, "Fancy being considered God, when you are only another human!" Isa was amused by the thought.

Mira also laughed aloud at the notion of Isa being worshipped as God..."Do you think any of your companions would start adoring you as God?"

"No way, our companions would never indulge. But one never knows what the future holds," Isa laughed and laughed at the idea till tears started flowing from his eyes.

Chapter 64

At midday when the sun came to its zenith, Mira usually swam in the Mansarovar. Did Shiva and Parvati play in it, she wondered. The waters of Mansarovar were heavenly, literally. They sanctified both body and mind as Mira floated in its chilliing waters. She felt lighter as she stepped out of the cool yet soothing waters. Almost childlike she started singing and dancing.

She felt her body very very light..."Am I floating on the land too!" She looked at her feet. Were they not a few inches above ground? Suddenly, she saw another pair of feet walking, nay floating, by hers. Never had she seen such perfectly shaped tender feet painted red and with anklets. She looked up to see the face. But everything was hazy. She wondered if she was hallucinating in this magical land. Mira started to run toward her hut. All she heard was the sound of the anklets on the pair of the dancing feet by her side and a gentle laughter, almost like her own musical laughter.

"Have you seen a woman by the lake, Isa?" Mira asked with a puzzled look when she reached the hut. She was nearly out of breath. Isa was sitting by the hut with a vacant look staring at the sky.

"Yes, I see *you* by the lake...often." Isa's voice seemed to come from the beyond.

"Don't make fun of me, I am serious." Mira described the dancing feet and jingling anklets.

"Come, sit here," said Isa pulling her hand. She was practically thrown on his lap. "Listen, this is the land where Shiva spoke of the inner meaning of *Yoga* to Parvati, sitting her on his lap much as you are here on mine now," Isa added with gentle humor.

"You presume you are Shiva?" said incredulous Mira with raised eyebrows and her enhanced musical laughter...

"Mira those dancing feet with you were Parvati's. They are your extension," Isa spoke in a deep sonorous voice with utmost tenderness, holding Mira's hands in his. Mira felt their intertwined hands vibrate at an unusual frequency. She felt a re-awakened awareness in that moment.

Almost in a dreamy tone, she said, "in Vraj Radha worked her magic on me, here Parvati is playing with me." Mira was thrilled.

"As humans, as you know Mira, our vision is limited. We draw three dimensional lines around every object. But just as in your consciousness, you became Radha in Vraj, here in Kailash you are Parvati. In reality there is no difference. You know it, Mira." Isa pressed her hands harder transferring more vibrations.

Soon Isa and Mira were in deep meditation with open eyes. Staring steadily at Kailash for a while, both envisioned a gigantic figure of Shiva: matted hair with the crescent moon, holding a trident in one hand, another on the shoulder of Parvati seated on his lap. The image was huge; it seemed to cover the entire peak of Mount Kailash. Isa and Mary sat totally absorbed...

Time was non-existent.

* * * * * * * * * * * *

A few days later when Sriram materialized, Isa and Mira narrated their simultaneous vision of Shiva and Parvati. Sriram questioned, "You both have had simultaneous visions before. What is different now?" Isa knew how close he and Mira were in their evolutionary growth.

"You mean so far we were having the same vision but were unconscious of it?" Mira wanted to be sure she understood Sriram's enigmatic question.

"And now....?" Sriram's twinkling eyes were still questioning.

"And now, we are conscious of its simultaneity? So we have evolved?" Mira as always was childlike and direct.

"You are and have been *always* evolved. You are perfect, have been. *Your consciousness* now perceives it," Sriram explained. Isa was grateful for Sriram's simple, uncomplicated statements.

"We are grateful, Sriramji for your guidance in our journey. During this time in Kailash, I have thrived on the vibrant energy of this land, the constant play of *purush,* spirit, and *prakriti,* nature in the purest form, unhampered by any interference. This has been the apex of my constant bliss, *nitya ananda.* That is my *living enlightenment,*" Isa's eyes shone with indescribable light.

Mira soaked in its beatific grace and bliss, the emanating divinity.

Sriram closed his eyes in grateful meditation, uniting the universal forces at play in this moment.

Chapter 65

"Do you think you are ready to leave Kailash and Mansarovar to continue our journey, our life's work? Maybe we will travel further south to learn, teach, share, and fulfill ourselves." Isa asked.

"If that is what *you* desire, I am ready." Mira spoke with a gentle smile.

"You do not have to follow the example of accommodating Parvati and follow *my desire*. I rather like your ferocious Kali phase when you crush Shiva under your feet and wear a garland of skulls." Isa joked about Mira's unusual compliance.

She said, almost challenging Isa, "Teasing me is asking for trouble, Isa! Let me ask you. Why do you have a *desire*? You are not supposed to have it. Remember what you taught our companions back home in Capernaum? You taught what was at the core of Krishna's teaching, not to have a *desire*."

Isa knew he initiated this attack when he invoked Kali in Mira. How many times he had seen that? But, as he said, he really enjoyed that aspect of Mira, challenging, questioning, yet always loving. "My work, our work, is what we agreed on before we incarnated this time. All we need to do is what is necessary. There is no *desire* to achieve anything, gain anything, certainly no desire *for the fruits of our actions*. That is what Krishna told Arjun. Isn't that true?" Isa waited for Mira's answer.

"When you wish people would hear you and follow your advice, isn't that the *desire for the fruits of the action*?" Mira had her lawyer father's genes or of her free spirited mother's. Isa could not decide.

After a few seconds of deliberation, Isa said, "Yes, my *intent* is to instruct them about the true nature of life and show them the way to direct their steps. But I am not *attached* to the outcome. I do my work, and leave each to his or her *choice*." Isa was truthful in his approach and attitude. Mira could not argue with that. In fact, she had admired Isa's lack of attachment in his dealings with masses of people for quite some time...

"What about your *desire* for *me*?" Mira totally took Isa by surprise; he was off guard.

He kept looking at Mira intently for a few moments focusing his eyes into hers.

Isa then spoke with utter simplicity, "You are the real love of my life. I breathe you, live you, I am you. There is no distinction. Hence *desire* is irrelevant." The words seemed to flow from another dimension.

* * * * * * * * * * * *

Leaving the snow clad terrain, going south through the hills of the Himalayan ranges, treading the land of the Brhamaputra, Isa and Mira were headed toward the famous Jagannathpuri, literally, the city of the Lord of the Universe (modern Puri which also became the origin of the term, 'Juggernaut').

Sriram was curious what Isa would feel in this ancient place. Isa knew that yet another exploration in another dimension loomed ahead...

"How energetically the Brahmputra is gushing to meet the ocean, her lord?" Mira was astounded by the brown waters of the river that had carried much of the mountain soil over hundreds of miles...for millennia, "Nothing seems to stop her. Such is love. I wish I could flow, rush mindlessly like these darkened waters." Mira was lost in the roaring sound of wild currents. A while later she looked up to see where Isa was.

A few yards away Isa was sitting on a rock, eyes closed, spine erect, in deep meditation:

It seemed their journey was long. He was with two companions, a male and a female in this celestial vehicle. All three were intently looking at their new destination earth, Prithvi, as it came in view. They were assigned to explore the wide inlet of the ocean south of the tallest snowy mountain ranges called Himalaya, the snowy abode. Evidently three large rivers originating from the Himalayan Mountains flowed into a bay at the delta. All three occupants of the

flying contraption were young, full of curiosity, excitement and vigor.
Their inter-stellar flying machine softly landed, almost gliding, on the
huge river delta. Their home star did not have such lush garden land.
They admired the magnificent terrain. Then they saw a group of local
inhabitants gawking at them. The earthlings had long, uncouth hair,
fierce looks, and hairy bodies. The interstellar vehicle and its three
strange visitors scared them. Some natives stood ready to fling their
long spears. The visitors had heavy bags of gifts, heavenly waters and
manna. The female visitor carried sparkling gems in a transparent jar.
Their rounded white viewing glasses, white rounds with huge black
circles in the middle, must have scared the locals. Most of them
started running away, except the chief warriors and the wise men
standing behind the warriors.

"We come in peace from Brahma Loka, most advanced planet
in the galaxy," the young visitors declared in the language the natives
did not understand.

Isa felt the cool breeze on his body; opened his eyes; and saw
Mira with a jar resting on her hip staring at the waters. Is that the
female with a jar from his vision? Isa smiled. He knew.

The tremendous shift in Isa's awareness since the crucifixion
had shattered his ordinary notions of space and time. The new
awareness allowed him to feel all that his essence, his self, had
experienced in the past or will experience in the future. There was no
distinct past, present or future. All was total awareness, ever present.

Mira turned, looked at Isa. She walked toward him; placing the
jar on the ground, she said, "Did you see all those people looking at
us like we were alien creatures they had never seen before? I was
amazed. Within a wink they were no more. Am I hallucinating?"
Mira had a puzzled look.

Isa knew once again Mira and he were simultaneously
experiencing the memory of the same ancient lifetime. His loving
eyes deeply stared into hers, "What do you feel now, Mira, troubled,
puzzled or at peace?"

"Oh, I am utterly joyful, feel very light, though I know not what
it is all about. I see this huge bright ball of light in a gigantic violet

triangle that vibrates like it is breathing. Don't laugh, Isa." Mira gently slapped smiling Isa's wrist.

"If you saw me laughing...well, it is out of absolute joy. It is the *ananda* of *satchidananda*: *sat*, truth *chit*, consciousness, *ananda*, bliss. You know it, Mira. Let me share with you something I have felt for a long time." Isa's voice was measured, deliberate, deep. It matched his intent eyes. Didn't Mira know that look? She was all attention, her eyes interlocked with his.

"In our cosmic selves our spirits have often travelled together in different parts of the universe. You know that. In our countless journeys we experience life individually and together supporting each other. Both of us walk to fulfill our self-chosen assignment in each incarnation. This time it is as Isa and Mira, the twin flames to manifest absolute love. Love for each other and also for all humanity. Just to feel that love, transformed into bliss, is a divine experience."

Mira had experienced such transformation; Isa and she had often witnessed it before. What is new now, she wondered. But she remained quiet, not wanting to interrupt Isa.

"This time, the culmination of our twin experience on earth has reached another peak. Both of us simultaneously experienced the interplanetary travel made eons ago. That is what you saw in that gawking crowd staring like we were aliens. That is who we were for them. I had a full vision of that experience in my meditation at the same time you saw yours. Mira, you and I have individually arrived at that level of consciousness, of total Oneness with each other."

"So that is what you call *integrating the dual and becoming non-dual?*" Mira was referring to the endless *dvaita/advaita* debates that she did not care for much. "Krishna-Radha confluence of love is the ultimate integration of duality for me. You know that Isa."

"What I am pointing out goes beyond such integration. In fact, time and space disintegrate as you and I remember all lives, past, present, and future simultaneously. That is a giant step forward in our three dimensional world on earth this time, Mira. I am utterly pleased with it."

"Isa, do you feel that our stay in Kailash-Mansarovar triggered another level of consciousness?" Mira asked reviving the memory of that simultaneous vision of Shiva-Parvati as large as the top of Mount Kailash. Isa knew that for Mira *that* was the moment of enormous significance.

Before that, Isa had had his transformation on the cross on Golgotha, which was the most important experience of his self-chosen assignment in this incarnation.

Isa remained quiet, continuing to look deeply into Mira's soul, soaking it to its core with Love. She was ecstatic.

Moments turned into eternity...

Chapter 66

Arriving on the day of the chariot festival, *Rathyatra*, in Jagannathpuri was challenging. Enormous crowd resembled the force of the flooded river Ganga rushing mindlessly. Mira felt she was vigorously swimming against the currents to reach the bank. She was breathless and lost Isa's hand several times as people pushed them apart. They found each other again and again.

Loud cymbals, the deep sound of conch shells, deafening bells, and the *Hare Krishna* chant energized all, almost intoxicating them. Mira too was getting caught in the spirit. Isa was immersed in it balancing his consciousness of the dual world. He experienced all the commotion; moved with it; but felt only the unity of both. Immense stability pervaded his being, inner and outer, effortlessly.

As they approached the renowned ancient temple of Lord Jagannath, the Lord of the Universe, they saw thousands of devotees pulling a gigantic chariot with thick ropes. The top of the chariot was higher than the top of tall houses nearby. On the center altar in the chariot were three idols of: Krishna, his brother Balaram, their sister Subhadra. Isa led Mira to a nearby stoop of a house to be able to view the idols way up in the chariot.

Isa's eyes were fixed on the idols. His body vibrated with intensified energy. Mira felt it in his tightened grip of her hand. In a moment Isa saw it clearly:

The three idols had exactly the same look of goggled eyes he had seen in his recent vision of the crew in the space craft. He knew Mira and he were two of the occupants of the interplanetary flying machine. These idols looked exactly like the astral flyers the local inhabitants had seen, eons and eons ago. Isa *knew*: the benevolent beings from another planet eventually became "gods" because their gifts transformed people's lives. Earthlings evolved as humans, casting off their animalistic existence. A religion grew after the event. Later when civilization evolved, people built a huge temple in adoration of these astral "gods." At the altar they placed three idols resembling the alien visitors: goggled eyed, arms outstretched, no torsos or legs, exactly as hairy natives on the gorund saw them up in their space craft.

As rituals grew, people built a huge chariot to mimic the flying space craft. Every summer people would celebrate the descent of gods among them by taking the gods for a ride in this chariot. The only way they knew to move this giant vehicle was to pull it with ropes. No animals would do. Thousands of devotees would use all their *energy* to propitiate their gods. It was their act of ultimate *surrender*. If they died in the process, so be it. It brought them straight to their gods, a real liberation, they believed.

Isa looked at Mira, loosening his grip a little. "Are you feeling alright, Mira?"

She took a little while before coming out of a trance, "Don't those idols look familiar? And they are totally different from anything we have seen in other Krishna temples over the years. Amazing. What do you think Isa, why do these strange images look so familiar to us?"

Isa was pleased with both the comment and the question. Millennia after the adoration of the visiting aliens began other traditions grew, introducing new gods, names and icons. People merely changed the names of gods. But the ancient figures remained. Isa knew all this in a moment. He knew Mira and he resonated in their conscious journey, though each had a separate trajectory. Joyously he drew Mira close, putting his arm around her shoulder, their heads touching in repose as they continued to look at the gods in the chariot. Were they looking in the mirror?

Despite the crowd, the noise, and movement all around them, they were immersed in total silence.

Chapter 67

"Oh Isa, look who is coming in that boat?" cried Mira pointing at the boat approaching the river bank.

Isa and Mira were lived in a small hut on the delta near the confluence of three holy rivers into the bay.

The boat neared the bank. Isa and Mira went to receive the guest, "Hello brother Thomas. At last you are here," said Isa hugging his dear companion whom he had not seen in nearly seven years. Tears of joy shone in their eyes. Thomas bowed to Mira with joined palms. Mira laughed her mature musical laugh, held Thomas' joined hands and bowed respectfully.

The three walked to the hut, chatting. Mira and Thomas were speaking almost simultaneously, eager to know all about each other.

"You look at peace, Thomas. I am very happy," Isa spoke with utter contentment as they reached the hut.

"Yes, Master..."

"None on earth is thy master, Thomas, only God is. You know that."

"Old habits die hard, brother. I now address all as *swami*. People call me *swami* or *appa,* father, in Mayapur," Thomas joked about his status in his new place of worship in Mayapur, a small town further south by the river Kaveri. People called the center *ashram.*

"So are you happy you came to India, Thomas, although you were reluctant at first?" Isa was curious.

"I opted to come when you decided to come to this land, brother. I was hoping we would meet some day. Sriramji has guided me in my work over the years," Thomas was grateful.

"Sriramji has been of immense help to all of us. That is how we meet today, I guess," Isa speculated. "How is your work? You look happy."

"I find people in this part of the land are receptive. Scholars are well versed in scriptures. Most lay people adhere to their rituals but some of them are eager to listen to new ways of thinking. And there are many who are in between, ready to accept new ways of worship," Thomas was pleased with the devotion and integrity of his followers.

"Mira and I are eager to travel with you to both of your centers." Thomas had established his first center on the eastern coast (in modern Kerala) and more recently another center on the bank of the river Kaveri on the eastern coast of the peninsula.

Mira noticed a remarkable change in Thomas. "You look happy and fulfilled, brother Thomas. This land has helped you evolve. Isa and I grew immensely in our younger days in this land too," said Mira looking at Thomas with loving tenderness.

Mira's words and tone evoked a streak of memory on Isa's mental plane: he *knew* Thomas was the third interplanetary traveler on the space craft several millennia ago!

Isa was pleased, but kept the thought to himself.

* * * * * * * * * * * *

Three old friends talked and talked and talked. Each realized they had experienced life deeply, and each had evolved independently. The doubting Thomas had grown into a knower. Thomas recognized his self-assigned work. Isa sensed even more about the connection of the three as interplanetary visitors. Intuitively Mira felt a deep connection with Thomas.

On his part, Thomas had learned to deal with his connectedness with Isa in a more detached fashion. He had felt Mira's depth before in Jerusalem, but now he recognized how intuitively wise she was. More than anything else, Thomas felt the palpitating love in her actions and words. He would not be surprised if the three had a role to play, or maybe they had played it already. Oh, all these thought processes are a burden, Thomas thought, and smiled....

"You have not given up thinking yet, Thomas?" He heard Isa approaching. It was the day after their reunion. Thomas was ruminating by the mouth of three rivers flowing together. In this delta the three rivers, the holy Ganga, Yamuna, and a tributary of Brhamaputra flowed as one river and merged into the bay.

"Yes, the three are one. So we three meet here," continued Isa knowing what Thomas was thinking.

"What three?" Thomas was surprised.

"The rivers. Weren't you thinking about the three holy rivers?" Isa asked.

"Yes. Do you know what is in my mind? What my thoughts are?" Thomas was surprised by this new phase of Isa. Isa was cautious not to reveal his recent attainments.

"Yes, and much more," said Isa smiling gently, "Those who are connected at soul level are like parts of each other. We have connected memories, obligations, perceptions, above all consciousness. Some of us are aware of that, most are not. But whether one knows it or not, the connection exists. We can grow consciousness, we can evolve, we can see connections, and we know how to cultivate them. Whether we would or not is our individual choice, Thomas. I went through all these stages of struggle, reasonably quickly, often effortlessly." Isa waited to see Thomas' response.

"Beloved friend Isa, you often spoke of similar concepts to us in the past. But I guess I was not ready to see or hear the full meaning of your words then. Today, it seems I am hearing them clearly for the first time, and understanding them too." Thomas' face lit up.

The sun was to set soon. Isa was mindful of multiple realities as they walked by the sacred site of the confluence of the holy rivers.

"Let's sit closer to the water," Isa suggested. They found a flat stone slab and sat facing the setting sun. Mira, who was lost in her own reverie, was walking a few yards behind them. Now she caught up and sat leaning against a tree not too far away. The sun was whirling fast, descending.

After a few silent moments Isa cupped his hands in the water, raised his water-filled palms above Thomas' head and let the water fall. Thomas felt the water run down his head and face; he closed his eyes, joined his palms, and bowed to Isa. He placed his hand on

Thomas' head transfusing energy, unlocking his deeper awareness. "What do you see, Thomas?" Isa asked.

"Light... light...bright light. Now I am floating in the air. Almost flying like a bird... But I have no wings," Thomas was speaking slowly, as if he were watching scenes in fragments. After a short pause he continued, "It feels like I am in a vehicle...I am not alone. It looks like a ship, but it is flying!!!...." Thomas was shivering.

"Not alone? Who is with you?" Isa asked.

"I have two companions with me, it seems."

"What are you all doing?" Isa asked.

"We are...kind of...operating this vehicle. We have some assigned work. It seems we know what it is. And we all are enjoying it," Thomas replied as if he was 'seeing' things gradually as they opened up.

"What happens next?" Isa nudged Thomas.

"Hey, it seems we are descending...we land on some marshy land. Earth is our destination," Thomas was elated.

"Where are you coming from?" Isa asked.

Thomas knew, but could not name the place, "A planet in outermost galaxy...a very powerful world, it seems. But I do not know its name."

"Do you see anything else?" Isa asked.

"It seems we scared the local people. They look uncouth, almost like wild animals. Some run away, others stand to attack us," Thomas was unsure...evn a little confused.

"Where on earth are you? Do you know?" Isa asked.

"No, I don't...wait, wait...It was right here, not far from where we are." Thomas was almost laughing, all confusion gone. He opened his eyes and looked around. "What was that brother? Was I in some kind of trance?"

Isa was happy. He was hoping to evoke Thomas' memory of another lifetime. This was the sacred place where it happened several millennia ago, when man began evolving from animalistic existence into becoming civilized.

"You just saw one of your former lives in antiquity. That life is relevant to your current life." Isa continued, "Keep it sacred. Evoke that memory to get more guidance. In that life Mira, you and I were together, and now once again, several millennia later, we are in this land together. In those days humans were still not fully developed. Our gifts triggered their next level of evolution. Now we are here for another shift in people's awareness. All beings are reborn to continue and or complete their chosen assignments."

"Chosen by whom?" Thomas' curiosity was persistent.

"What do you think? Correction, what do you *feel*, Thomas?" Isa smiled, using his characteristic mode of questioning. Thomas smiled. Of course it was *one's own* choice.

Mira was elated by Thomas' recall of an ancient lifetime when all three of them were together. Their mission was exploration of the Earth then, and bringing gifts.

"Can you believe those people with their un-evolved minds thought we were gods because we brought them life sustaining gifts?" Mira was surprised by their simplistic minds.

"In fact, several millennia later when their religious practices became more sophisticated, they kept those old idols giving them names of the new gods," said Isa referring to the temple in Jagannath Puri having the same ancient idols in its sanctuary, now called Krishna, Balaram, and Subhadra.

"You mean they intertwined our visit in space craft with Krishna worship? But Krishna manifested at least a millennium or two later. How amazing is the human mind constantly weaving ongoing experiences," Thomas was thrilled by this constant interweaving.

Mira said, "It is like a cosmic loom as it were. You know, Isa, I could not help being a weaver. I am part of this cosmic process." Her musical laugh reflected the joy of her new perception.

"Yes, we all are a part of this endless process of learning and interweaving. But few recognize this fundamental truth of life," Isa spoke. Was there a tinge of sadness in Isa's tone, Thomas wondered.

"Why do you sound sad, brother? Do you feel people remain ignorant despite the knowledge that is available to them?" Thomas asked a rhetorical question.

Isa looked at him, smiled, and remained quiet. He could look into the future and knew more.

Isa knew of the constant cycle of conflict, upsurge, destruction and awakening. The process was continuous, endless. Even after an awakening, the conflict between the forces of light and darkness continue; but now on a different level. Former contending forces join hands and fight against another force. It seemed the conflict persists in a renewed form. Is this cycle of conflict interminable? Isa saw that the Divine Source had to intervene again and again to redeem humankind. Was it not Krishna who said to Arjun that whenever chaos prevailed on earth, to protect the good and destroy the wicked, to establish *dharma*, Krishna descends on earth again and again?

Isa envisioned his own future; facing challenges of yet another time.

Mira was still basking in her newfound joy of the ancient memory.

"What is the meaning of the three of us working together in this incarnation, brother? Are we completing 'unfinished' work?" Thomas continued his query despite Isa's silence.

"It is not about completing unfinished work; it is more about recognizing the need of the time. Our intervention was needed then, as it is pertinent now. So we came," Isa explained the purpose of the descent, *avatar,* of liberated beings.

Mira had a different perspective, "But life is not all about duty to be performed to save others. It is about the joy of living too, isn't it? I find living self-fulfilling. Haven't you often spoken of utter bliss, *ananda,* Isa?"

Isa's smiling eyes touched sheer joy in Mira's. He admitted, "Mira, you always complete my thought. The trinity of Cosmic Reality – Truth, Consciousness and Bliss, *Satchidananda,* is one cohesive whole -- inseparable. Mira, you are Bliss, Joy, *ananda,* incarnate. I heard it in your first laughter by the well," Isa was once again cheerful; he was laughing.

Thomas had to ask, "So if we constitute a trio, what about all others who play a similar role on earth right now? We have our brothers and sisters in Galilee and Judea who are serving many. Isa, you learned from so many masters in India, Persia, Greece, Alexandria, Egypt before you started teaching in our land. And what about the roles of people like Sriramji and Maniji in this rescue mission, redemption, of earth, if I may use such terms? Where and how do they fit in this cosmic net?"

Thomas's inquisitive mind kept Isa's own intellect alert. Although in his heart Isa knew it all, Thomas pushed him to translate the abstract truth into words. After all, language is the most accessible tool for humans to express thoughts. Music and painting and other arts may capture feelings and awareness, but the *word* is the ultimate for thoughts.

Isa spoke in a measured tone, "All living beings are atoms. Their source is in the Cosmic Energy Consciousness we call God. Thomas, you know that. We talked about that in our companions' gatherings in Capernaum. All these atoms keep moving, propelled by their subatomic parts – their thoughts/actions/spirit in their individual bodies."

"So are our companions helping others, or are they completing their own desires?" Evidently Thomas had struggled with this thought for a while. He could not resist asking his teacher for an explanation.

Isa knew and felt Thomas' need at this time, more than Thomas was aware of. Intently looking at Thomas, Isa began, "At the time of death, as the Jain and Buddhist monks upheld, the *unresolved* atom clusters – issues, desires, obligations, and such -- are reborn. Those who are struggling with basic lower level desires may choose to be reborn right away for yet another cycle of birth to fulfill those desires. Each soul evolves at individual pace. All do their work and accomplish according to their self-ascertained intent."

"What about our intent? Do you think we three will decide to be reborn at the same time?" Mira was always focused on specifics. Theories left her unfulfilled and dry.

"We might," said Isa. "Advanced souls choose to be reborn when humanity needs them."

"That sounds so much like descent of god, *avatara,* people here in India speak of," said Thomas. "For them there is no contradiction between human free will and God's will. They are two sides of the same coin. God wills it, but so do humans, as parts of the same divine."

Thomas admitted how many of his earlier questions were answered when he worked with people in this land, be they farmers, artisans, teachers, pundits, or business people.

"Above all Mira," he continued, "my talks with women were most enlightening. They had an easy way to explain this complex phenomenon. They say each person is a child, a manifest divine whom you nurture, protect, train, and serve with love. Love is everything, they say." Thomas was pleased with this lesson which he once found too hard to accept.

He added, "I asked them how they would deal with their neighbor's son who would have hurt their own child? With love, I asked?"

"What did they say?" Mira was interested.

"First they laughed and said, '*Appa* that is so simple! You are a learned master, why do you ask? Love is not about always being soft or kind. It is about *knowing* what is right. You are guided to help, not hurt. We know we all are a family, and therefore connected. If we scolded the neighbor's son for his wrong doing, my neighbor would not mind. Because he knows we love his child as much as he does.' And they would be puzzled by my intrigued look." Thomas described the difficult lesson.

Isa said, "Thomas, I have always emphasized *love is not an emotion; it is the recognition of connectedness of all.* These women have intuitive knowledge of it, but perhaps have no adequate words to explain it. They transfer their inner knowledge into action, easily, naturally, intuitively. No need to explain what, why or how."

Smiling and looking at Mira, Isa added, "I learned it from Mira."

"From me?! I never knew you learned anything from me!" Mira protested, "Though I always wished you had, especially when you were so stubborn."

All of them laughed heartily.

Chapter 68

Sailing down south in a large boat on the bay along the eastern coastline of peninsular India, Mira was ecstatic. It had been many years since she had been on a large boat. They were headed toward Thomas's new center on the bank of river Kaveri. Thomas had waited for this moment for a long time. This visit of Isa and Mira was dream come true, for him.

The next day at early dawn Isa was standing on the deck facing east. A gentle breeze flapped his flowing white robe. He was contemplative.

Up in the sky the dark Night was collecting sparkling stars in her mantle. She was receding gently, ushering Dawn. A streak of light tinged the solitary roaming cloud. Dawn eagerly got busy: touching the morning lotus, tickling the sleepy singing bird, waving the tender blades of grass, nudging the leaves on trees. Sweeping along, she saw Isa on the deck and smiled. She knew Isa was awake though his eyes were closed. Now all was ready for the Sun's arrival. The first ray of the Sun touched Isa's eyelids. As he opened his eyes, these words intuitively flowed from his mouth:

Om bhur bhuvah swah
tat savitur varenyam
bhargo devasya dhimahi,
dhiyo yo nah prachodayat. Om.

I meditate on the effulgent Light,
The power of It who is worthy of worship
And who has given birth to all worlds.
May It direct the rays of our intelligence
To the benevolent path. Om.

Isa glided into total absorption, trance. He knew this was another recall of a past life when he was a *rishi*, seer, in some remote antiquity. Such was Isa's constant state now, knowing the past, present, and future simultaneously. Gratefully he embraced this vibrant awareness.

Thomas came on the deck to pay homage to the rising sun with *suryanamaskar*, salutation to the sun. He had learned this yoga from Isa and often they used to practice it together. Thomas had made it a daily practice for all residents at his centers. In fact, he told Isa, *suryanamaskar* being a familiar practice for Indians, made Isa's teaching less intimidating. It was even helpful in attracting many more to his teaching.

Both of them stood silently on the deck.

"What a glorious day: the bright blue sky, the quiet bay stretching as far as eyes could see, and the balmy breeze caressing our bodies. Such kind gifts from God!"

They heard Mira's musical voice as she emerged from the interior singing a morning hymn to the Dawn. Sailors paused to listen, holding their oars steady. The ship's sail caught the wind and flapped in rhythm....

* * * * * * * * * * *

Mira was now standing next to Isa, "Why would every moment of life not be divine?" She asked, "Why should it change?" Mira's words were innocent, childlike.

Isa said in a teasing mode, "Because nothing is permanent!"

"Yah...yah, *punditji*!" Mira said laughing loudly, "but I know, you too wish these moments would last forever."

Thomas, "I do not know about you, brother, but I am with Mira. I wish such moments would last forever."

Gently looking at Thomas in deep contemplation, Isa kept quiet. Then he slowly uttered, "You know Thomas what the Buddha taught. Life is impermanent, *aniccha*. We do not step in the same river twice, nor is the burning flame the same the next moment. Many who come to your center have this knowledge, don't they?" Isa asked.

"True. When I talk about many of your teachings, they find them easy to comprehend. A young student once questioned me if I wasn't a hidden Buddhist." Thomas gave a hearty laugh and continued, "Even some Brahmins are suspected of being hidden Buddhists. You know there are now hundreds of Buddhist schools, unfortunately with deep friction among them." Thomas was facing problems of religious competition.

"So do you feel uncomfortable teaching them our Way?" Isa was curious, but not concerned, because he knew the pattern of recurrent human behavior.

"Oh no, on the contrary many older people readily accept our Way. They say it seems so familiar. And then they say 'All saints come to teach One truth; they use different stories, different gods or goddesses. People and places differ, so do their trials. But their teachings are similar and are equal in strength.'"

Isa was happy. "Do they not tell their stories?"

"Oh they do. But even more interestingly, they draw parallels. In fact, one time I narrated the story of *your* sermon on the hill by the Lake of Galilee. I still remember it vividly. It was my first day with you; my first experience with our community. You may have forgotten that day. But I will always remember it fondly. I tell them about that little girl who saw a king and an eagle flying out of the sun taking her on a ride. I then asked them if anyone would want to share a story."

Thomas continued looking at the flowing waters, "One of the assembled said, 'That eagle must be Lord Garuda, the vehicle of Lord Vishnu. Maybe the girl saw Lord Vishnu as the King coming out of the sun and taking her on a ride on Garuda.' Another man said, 'Your Isa is just like our *sants*, our holy men. He has similar stories. Lord Buddha spoke of the poor widow's two sheckles that were mightier than the king's donation of thousands. Isa also spoke of the widow's mite, didn't he?'"

Isa was once again pleased that Thomas decided to come to India. He was thankful to God that he returned to this land with Mira. Something in this place allowed people to integrate differences, despite their constant confrontations. That's why they have so many deities, theories, traditions, and yet they can see confluences everywhere. That is their strength, Isa concluded.

But in the dualistic world there cannot but be conflicts.

Isa asked, "Do you not face any opposition? People can be divisive, devious. How do you handle that?"

"Sure, I faced resistance in my early years. But I soon understood their thinking. They resent claims of superiority or exclusivity. Either they stop coming or they challenge you. So I prefer to not claim any exclusivity for our Way. You always alerted us not to make any such claims, brother. " Thomas reiterated what Isa always reminded the companions back in Capernaum.

"I commend your ways, Thomas. Many of our companions may carry their sincerity and affinity passionately. They may speak of our teaching as exclusive or superior. I never encouraged that. I am pleased with your approach," said Isa who had no direct knowledge of what was happening after he left Jerusalem. It was his intuitive knowledge of human behavior, his deep awareness that enabled him to know what could transpire.

"I am grateful, brother, for your appreciation. One has to be wary of the prevalent factionalism in many kingdoms here. Brahmins, Buddhists, Jains -- all teach higher truths. But the followers in each tradition often get entangled in rivalry and politics. This confuses gullible lay people. Some of them admire the simplicity of our Way." Thomas was pleased with his progress without ignoring the inevitable strife between religious schools.

"Why are you so quiet Mira?" Isa noticed Mira was standing a little bit aloof soaking in the beauty of the sky, the flowing water, the solitary bird flying under the rain clouds.

"Oh...this beautiful world is blessed with grace and sheer joy! Any idea of conflict seems an unnatural state. I am thoroughly soaking in this pure joy, bliss, *ananda*. I can then manifest it whenever I face conflict, strife, or sorrow," Mira shared her creative strategy, her dream.

This childlike wish impressed Isa, "May that child in you be our redemption, Mira."

Mira's laughter resembled a soaring serene flight of a blessed bird, "You know Isa, it seems the worship of *baal* – child -- Krishna captivated me even more than that of Radha-Krishna. And I did not realize that till now."

"Nonetheless it is the *same* Krishna, the child or the lover," Thomas added laughing.

"We have to find the language to convey that all creation carries the same divine source, energy. And still as Zarathustra said a long time ago the conflict between dual forces is a natural human condition. We continue the dance of life, like *raas lila,*" Isa said.

"Did you not say one time that the balancing Tao of *yin-yang* that Sriramji first heard from the Chinese traveler could be our ideal objective?" asked Mira.

Mira's perception, Isa realized, synthesized diverse trends. Without rejecting any specificity, she expanded them to embrace the seamless whole.

Chapter 69

Holding yellow flower garlands, the members of Thomas' center were waiting at the port to receive their teacher coming home with Isa and Mary. They knew her as Mary, not Mira, since Thomas had always spoken of Isa and Mary. Despite the gathering rain clouds that might break into thunder showers anytime, people were cheerful.

As they saw the boat approaching, men, women and children with bright smiles hailed the trio: "*Jai, Sant* Isa," "*Jai* Mary-ma" "*Jai* Santom*," short for *Sant* Thomas.

"Why are they hailing me?" Wonder-eyed Mira was surprised, though delighted and excited.

"When I told stories of Isa's life, it tickled them that Isa's mother and sweetheart both were named Mary. Many have named their newborn girls Mary. One enthusiastic family had three Mary's in their house: The first girl called Mary became 'Older Mary' when the second girl was born. Third Mary promoted the middle one to 'Middle Mary'; the youngest was '*Munni*, little, Mary.'" Thomas gleefully described the enthusiasm of the new converts. Many followers came from the underprivileged class, commonly known as the untouchables, and now were part of the social structure because of conversion. They used *foreign* names to wear their newfound respectability visibly.

Isa was listening quietly. He was pondering over the psychological and sociological layers of transformation in religious systems. Do they become political? Of course, look at Buddhism, so many schools and sub schools arose even before Buddha's death. On the positive side, politics may be a plus. Without King Ashoka's conversion and promotion, Buddha's teachings would have remained confined to India, like its contemporary Jainism.

Politics is a two edged sword for all religions. Isa wondered what would happen to his own teachings. It could be politicized in the future, centuries after he is gone, if at all the teaching survived. He could see a bleak future in his deep consciousness, but he preferred to ignore it right now. The secret is to continue the *lila*, dance, of life.

The boat was docked. As Isa, Mira, and Thomas walked down the rampart, people rushed to welcome them with garlands. Today, their chief master, *Sant* Thomas' Master, *param guru*, *Sant* Isa had come to visit them with *Maryma*! It was a rare occasion for them; once in a lifetime you get to be with such holy beings, they said.

All three descended with cheerful smiles. Some touched their feet or bowed in traditional Indian way; some shook hands or gave hugs. They were singing hymns, smiling, chatting. All were joyful. Mary was ecstatic. People's enthusiasm deeply touched her. Isa was much delighted. He applauded Thomas for his immense success with people.

The dark looming rain clouds did not bother anyone. The sailors were happy they docked just in time before the storm.

* * * * * * * * * * * *

That evening for the prayer meeting, the center room, the largest indoor area, was full. Thomas ordinarily held his meetings outdoors following the traditional *ashram* practice of having classes under a banyan tree. But today the impending storm prevented that.

Those assembled were not all members of Thomas' center. Many came for *darshan*, to see a holy man, *Sant* Isa. After hymn singing and traditional welcoming *aarati*, waving of lamps, an elderly man Matthew, former Mutthu and the leader of the congregation, started to speak.

"We are fortunate to have you among us, *Sant* Isa," he said, "We have total faith that seeing you and touching your feet has liberated us. You have washed off our *karma* of many lifetimes. We bow to you a thousand times." He touched Isa's feet and then touched his own head in the traditional Indian way.

"Blessings brother," Isa joined his palms and touched Matthew's head pressing it on the top. That magical touch triggered a shift in

Matthew. Tears of joy trickled down Matthew's cheeks as he sat, his palms joined, his eyes focused on Isa's face.

Sitting next to Isa, Mira was moved by the dedication of people. It's all love and joy, she mused. Thomas was sitting on the other side of Isa. He had not expected such a big gathering. Evidently people from his center had spread the news of the holy couple's arrival.

An old woman, bending on a cane, with failing vision, came closer to view the three, and spoke, "When I was a little girl, *Bhagvan*, the supreme Lord, Rama told me in my dream that before I die I will see him in person. Now I am a hundred and one years old. I can die peacefully because my dream has come true. You are *Bhagavan* Rama with Sita Devi and Lakshman by your side." She pointed at Mira and Thomas sitting on either side of Isa. Traditionally each Rama temple would have three figures: God Rama, Sita, his wife, and Lakshman, his brother. Everybody knew that old Iddima spent hours in Rama's temple every day. She then prostrated herself in front of the trio as she would in the temple of Lord Rama.

Shankar who brought her at this gathering said, "Iddima insisted she wanted to come here today. We were all surprised that she wanted to go to a *videshi*, foreign, center when she is a strong Rama devotee. We explained to her that it was a different God they worshipped in this temple."

"'You want to teach me about god?' she scolded my husband," said Shankar's wife, "'You were not even born when *Bhagavan* Rama came in my dream. Keep your mouth shut and take me there.' she said."

Isa closed his eyes and touched Iddima's head, who was bowing with her head at his feet. Isa bent to raise Iddima. Her body remained motionless.

A young beautiful woman clad in a red sari arose from where Iddima's motionless body lay. Isa touched her head, hugged her tenderly, and walked with her to the doorway. She smiled gently, turned, and her spirit glided heaven ward.

Mira could see the inner play of the spirit. She blessed Iddima's spirit. Everybody else was quiet. All the rest of the group saw was that Iddima had died and *Sant* Isa was sitting with his eyes closed blessing her. It was time for Iddima to go. No surprise there. But that it should happen in this way, so unexpectedly away from the Rama temple. That intrigued ever one.

"Iddima is in heaven with Rama, Sita, and Lakshman," said Isa, "Her life's work is over here on earth this time. She realized the dream of her life. And will reside in heaven peacefully as long as she wishes."

"Will she come back?" asked a little boy crying. Everday he brought flowers for Iddima to take to the temple for *pooja.*

"She will be with you whenever you need her, young boy," said Isa, "She can show up anywhere anytime. So do not cry little one. Think of her, call her, and she will be with you."

Thomas led a prayer for Iddima. After that Shankar's wife started a chant in honor of Lord Rama, "*Raghupati raghava raja Ram patitapavan Sitaram.*" All chanted '*Jai Rama, Jai Rama*" together as Shankar picked up Iddima's frail lifeless body and started walking toward her home.

Chapter 70

"You have so many peacocks, Thomas," Mira was admiring these colorful birds strutting around. They 'te..hooked' vigorously when enamored and the vain male would display his colorful feather fan.

"Your center is flourishing. You have such loving and caring people, brother," Mira was enjoying her stay. Isa talked to the group every evening drawing larger crowds. Some of those became members of the center adopting the new path. But many came to listen. They were from other religious traditions and castes, high and low.

One day a successful businessman, Putthuswami, came to listen to the now popular *Sant* Isa. He was a well travelled man and had heard of the crucifixion, now an almost twenty-five-year-old story. He wondered if there was any connection between this Isa and the crucified one. Topic on this day was death. Isa described death not as an end of life but a new beginning.

Putthuswami asked, "Do you think one can be revived after death?"

"Many *rishis* and ascetics have revived the dead in this land. Why do you ask?" Isa was curious.

"I do not believe in those so called magical stunts of ascetics. But you are a learned *sant*. What is your explanation?" Putthuswami seemed a rational inquirer.

"Do you believe in reincarnation?" asked Isa.

"I am not sure. I need more authentic proof."

"Do you believe in God?" Isa persisted.

"Ummm...I am not sure. I need proof. It seems the Buddha could do without a god. So could the Jain *muni* Mahavir. But, I am still not sure." Thomas thought Putthuswami was a skeptic more than a seeker.

"Nothing is wrong with your belief. Do you think there is an operative power, a kind of energy that prevails in the universe?" Isa asked.

"Yes...I am sure there is something that keeps the natural order in place. Yes, I believe in that," Putthuswami conceded.

"For convenience some call it God, Shiva, Krishna, Rama, what you will. Such names and images make it easier to relate to this *principle force* of life, its natural order. I call it my Father because I emanate from it," Isa explained.

Thomas liked this man's questioning, even though his intent seemed dubious. Had he come to create a disturbance? Thomas wondered.

"So we all are a part of this energy force, life force?" Putthuswami needed a clear statement.

"Yes, and that is an indestructible force. Since nothing is destroyed, everything is transformed."

"So there is no real death, only rehashing of energy, so to say," Putthuswami was oversimplifying.

"If you say so, yes," Isa conceded.

"So you teach that after death those who follow the commandments of the Father are placed in his proximity. And others who transgress are punished for ever?" Had Putthuswami done his homework correctly, Thomas wondered? Where did he get this idea? Neither he nor Isa had spoken of everlasting hell.

"It is only a simplified version for the common masses to understand an abstract concept of afterlife. For those like you who can conceptualize abstractions, I would recommend Pythagoras, Cicero, Plato and many of the visionaries who spoke of the soul, its transmigration and reincarnation. Among the best are the Vedic *rishis* of this land," Isa said.

"So your teachings change according to the audience?" was there a note of sarcasm in Putthuswami's question? Thomas looked at Isa to see his reaction.

"Why should that surprise you? It's so common in the culture of your land. All variety of gods and goddesses are nothing but diverse answers for different audiences at various times. I think that is the most natural way to bring information to people: teach each according to one's level of comprehension. It's common sense. What I teach my close associates is different from what I say to large masses of people who may not comprehend it." Isa was laughing loudly. He thought he had said enough to deflate the skepticism of his educated questioner.

"I am grateful to you *Sant* Isa. I have questioned many of our ascetics, but they do not have your clarity of perception. I will come here often," Putthuswami was convinced by Isa's uncluttered logic. "Quite interestingly, currently I am studying teachings of Pythagoras and Plato." He bowed to Isa respectfully and left.

Mira came in after feeding the animals, especially the peacocks. She thought they understood her talk. "That was a long dialogue with the man. My peacocks learn faster," she said.

Thomas laughed, "Learned thinking nuts are harder to crack. Don't I know that?"

"We all go through that process, Thomas. Once the heart softens one evolves fast," said Isa, looking meaningfully at Thomas.

Chapter 71

A month went by. Isa and Mira enjoyed the food, almost all cooked with coconut milk, yogurt and cream with rice, vegetables, and lentils. The weather was comfortable, though for the Kashmir residents from the north a little too hot. The bank of the river Kaveri became Isa and Mira's walking path for their habitual sunset walk. Thomas was busy with his administrative work, teaching, and service in the school and the health center. Most afternoons Isa gave talks, told stories, answered questions, and counseled those in need.

Mira spoke to her female audience of the joy in the everyday activity of life by surrendering to God. That was *seva,* real service, she said, but she was learning a lot from the women as well. Their interests ranged from child care to sewing to dancing. Most girls learned to dance. Dance, music, and daily *pooja* practice constituted upper class girls' education and upbringing. Unprivileged women's focus was working in the fields and child rearing. But they knew a lot about herbs and potions, and handicrafts. Mira thoroughly enjoyed working with all of them.

Isa and Mira visited homes of many poor and disregarded families.

* * * * * * * * * * * *

Sudarshan was a *brahmin* grain merchant and an orthodox devotee of Shiva. He did not care much for Thomas's *ashram,* especially because it accepted untouchables in its fold. His wealth had made Sudarshan a well known community leader, but he was arch conservative.

Two days before Isa and Mira had planned to leave Thomas' center, they were in an untouchable neighborhood visiting a poor old man, Gopak, in his hut. He was alone. His wife and sons had gone to work: cleaning streets and latrines, getting dead animals and disposing them – the work his family had done for generations. Both his daughters were married and stayed two huts away. Their husbands' families were of the same caste and were engaged in similar work.

"Shall we sing some hymns, *sriman*, (sir)?" asked Mira in a sweet gentle voice.

"You called me *sriman*? Are you making fun of me? Nobody in my entire life has ever shown such respect to me." Gopak's voice broke; he was nearly in tears, "All I get is a hateful look and dirty words. Even gods do not care for us. Their temples are closed to us."

"God loves you, *sriman*. You know that. Maybe someday you will want to come to where we pray, and you will see all are welcomed and loved," Isa said. "Would you like to come this afternoon? We can take you."

"I will have to check with my family when they come home," said Gopak with a face that could hardly suppress a smile at the prospect of going to a temple – all places to pray to gods were temples for him.

Isa and Mira walked out of the house and proceeded onto a wider road around the corner. From his store, Sudarshan was watching their movements. Now it was safe for him to approach these outsiders, he thought, away from the polluted untouchable neighborhood.

"What is your business in this part of town?" Sudarshan was curt and direct.

"We came to check if we could be of any help to people living here," Isa replied and continued, "Could we help you in anyway, *sriman*?"

"Yes, you can. Do not go into the untouchable neighborhood and then come into ours. We call that pollution." Sudarshan explained to these foreigners how things were done in his town.

"What gets polluted, *sriman*?" Mira asked.

"If you touch them, you are polluted," Sudarshan was forceful.

"How so?" Isa spoke.

"It's so, because our *pundits* say so. It is an ancient tradition. We do not ask questions. We just follow traditions. These untouchables deal with dead bodies and dirt. They are polluted and we are not allowed to touch them, lest we get polluted. They are untouchables," Sudarshan was clear in his belief, and could repeat dogma like a parrot.

"Don't they clean your streets, collect feces, and keep you clean?" Mira asked.

"I just told you they deal in dirt and filth and carry dead animals." Sudarshna raised his voice; he had no patience with thinking listeners, especially not women.

"Should you not be thanking the untouchables for keeping your surroundings clean and healthy for you?" Isa asked.

"You outsiders don't understand our ways and create problems for us," Sudarshan's suppressed anger was slowly thickening. "You seem to be newcomers and are ignorant of our ways. That other tall fellow who runs an *ashram* at the end of town has been busy for a few years. We see his activities and we do not like his fancy ideas upsetting our system."

"But many of your scholars and *pundits* have come to talk with the tall brother Thomas. And some have even left their earlier worship to join his group. Don't you think they are knowledgeable?" Isa was trying to hold a polite conversation.

"My guru said that Thomas bribes people with food and shelter, medicine, and promise of heaven. Sweet words, that's all." Sudarshan was convinced this new teaching was no good. He continued, "At first there were those Buddhists and those... Jains, now these are Jews of another kind. They worship some messiah."

"They worship the same god in heaven that you do, brother, they call him God – only the name is different," said Mira.

"I have no time for you. Stop your activities or..." furious, Sudarshan walked away in anger.

Isa and Mira quietly left the neighborhood. They knew Thomas could face a challenge from the orthodox community in town.

✳

Chapter 72

It was Friday the Sabbath, time for Isa, Mira and Thomas to relax from other activities of the center. They could engage in deeper inquiry, meditation, and contemplation.

In the morning Isa was in the sanctuary. Through a small barred window above the altar facing east sunrays filtered in, and the floating air particles displayed a hazy path of light. Isa's eyes were fixed on the vibrating light. A deep gaze awakened a perception:

Innumerable circles of varied colors floated in the air. Isa focused on each particle, and saw many beings swirling around in each. Who are these beings he wondered. In one he saw himself floating with masters of yore, each connected by an invisible thread. Immense light emanated from that circle. Another circle, that of darkness, floated by. Both circles vibrated some as they touched each other and moved on. In that moment of friction each increased its element; the lighted circle looked brighter, the dark intensified its darkness.

Next he saw a noisy circle of life intersecting the path of the silent one of death. Life exuded many colors, and he could even hear the hum of music. The circle of death emitted only the hum of silence. It was crystal clear – Darkness is another color of Light; Death only another shape of Life.

One is meaningless without the other.

The h...u...m...kept ringing.

With the *h...u...m...* mingled Thomas' 'Om' as he entered the sanctuary. Isa's eyes were dazzled as he turned his head and saw a brilliant light suddenly extinguished. On that spot stood Thomas. Isa heard him say, "Brother, I saw a violent storm in my vision as I meditated under the banyan tree. It's surprising since it is a beautiful day, not a cloud in the sky," Thomas was puzzled.

"Did you hear the peacocks screaming wild? Do they smell the storm? They flew up into the trees for shelter!" Mira came running into the sanctuary nearly out of breath.

Isa was silent. He had not uttered a word since the morning. Slowly, deliberately, in a measured voice he said, "Life unravels mysterious happenings. Death is but a sleep. One awakens in another phase, a new spin, a new journey: constant flux; no certainty."

Thomas kept his eyes on Isa's, his mind on Isa's cryptic sentences. Was Isa really in the room or in some other reality? Mira knew at once; this was the time to silently connect with the other reality. All three sat with their eyes closed, minds focusing on the center of the room.

After what seemed to be a long time, Isa opened his eyes and said, "Brother Thomas, we leave early tomorrow at dawn. You have done the Lord's work admirably. We may not meet again in this lifetime, but there will be others. Our journeys have crisscrossed over several millennia past and will continue in the future. Only in earthly linear time there are three phases – past, present, and future. I see all of our lives right now. Be at peace."

* * * * * * * * * * * *

The next day, before dawn, when it was still dark Isa and Mira left Thomas' center. Thomas was extremely sad. His wisdom was no match for his emotions -- his pain of separation from Isa. For the first time Thomas admitted to himself how much he loved Isa; tears were flowing down his cheeks.

He sobbed as he stood watching the bullock cart carrying Isa and Mira down the alley. He stood there till he could see the dim lantern of the cart no more. So uncharacteristic were his feelings. As soon as he entered his room he threw himself on the mattress and wept bitterly. Were the tears of surrender or separation?

A little later Thomas was quiet, at peace. The sun had not risen yet. He gathered his robe, his water pot and headed for the river to do his routine bath before the ritual *suryanamaskar*, salutation to the sun. The gentle breeze touching his body infused indescribable peace within. It seemed his tears had lightened his heart. Walking to the river he wondered if he was floating. Thomas' eyes caught the first rays of the sun; he smiled and said, "How glorious is the day. Thank you O Lord for this day and this life! Oh... Lord..."

He screamed and fell on the ground. Somebody had jumped from behind the trees and stabbed him in the chest. Warm blood flowed out of the fatal wound.

Thomas was dead before the grateful smile on his face could vanish.

Chapter 73

Isa and Mira were headed toward Thomas' first center in Mayapur in the back-waters of Kerala on the western coast of peninsular India. They wanted to submerge themselves in the lush, misty greenery of the rainforest and shady water ways before starting the northward journey back to their home in Kashmir.

"You are unusually quiet this morning, Isa," said Mira. The cart-driver was singing early morning hymns to lord Shiva. Isa looked blankly at Mira; he was lost in his thoughts. Mira continued, "Thomas got very emotional when we left. Do you realize how attached he is to you? He loves you immensely."

"Thomas is at a crucial time in his life," Isa spoke after a long vacant gaze at the sky. "I felt his unusual energy when we first met him in the delta in the east. It intensified when we were in his center. Mira, Thomas' heightened level is both transformational and transitional. And it was magnified this morning," Isa sounded very serious.

"What do you mean transitional?" Mira was intrigued.

"We will know...soon," Isa said and turned his sad eyes up to the sky once again.

Mira was thoughtful; she closed her eyes. She began humming a prayer.

Open your doors, O Lord
A devoted child has arrived
After journeying a hard long path
Gently receive him in your loving lap.

The sun arose gently touching Isa's closed eyes. The tears in Mira's eyes captured the golden shine of the first ray.

A few days of sailing through the peaceful heaven of the back waters in Kerala allowed Mira to be in deep quiet. Isa's equanimity was undisturbed, although he laughed less. He was not disturbed since he knew of Thomas's journey beyond.

This quiet meditative journey through the waters opened up yet another dimension in Isa's inner world. He saw his future lives. The whole panorama of past, present and future unraveled.

At once Isa saw all that had happened, even before his interstellar flight to earth countless millennia ago. In that deafening bang of violent explosion, the moment of earth's Creation, he had felt the emanating sound, light, vibration, in his essence self. He still carries all three – the first sound, light, and vibration – in him in this moment. In between he had been an invisible particle in a crystal and a plant, a giant tortoise, a fish, even a boar, and a half lion half man. He simultaneously saw all phases of his journey.

He was breathless as he witnessed his essence infused into uncountable bodies of strange shapes and sizes— human/animal/vegetation, minerals...all at once. Total connectedness like in a complex network: each particle, each cell, still humming the original sound, oozing the first light, vibrating the primordial energy.

And then he reincarnated as a teacher often called 'savior' over and over. Times and places seemed varied in linear sense. But all was now. There was no end. Good and bad, joy and pain, happiness and its lack, light and darkness, life and death looked paradoxical, but were not.

His essence was stability, though as a human he passed through varied experiences. When people called him by different names, in varied places and diverse times, he was the same one essence. He felt, knew, and became that One Reality.

Isa heard the sound of the oars, saw the orange setting sun, and turned to Mira, "This is the moment of revelation, dear Mira." He reached out for Mira's hand as she sat on a plank across in the small boat. They looked at the red-orange sun quickly going behind the stringy palm leaves. The hanging clouds turned pink. Two temple steeples, standing close -- one higher than the other, caught the sunshine and turned golden. Temple bells from the Shiva temple started ringing for the evening *aarati.*

"Isn't the whole universe celebrating life?" said Mira, "All creation breathes one breath, varied and yet the same."

Isa tightened his grip of Mira's hand. *In this moment the time melts, the space disappears, you are aware of One breath. Be it,"* Isa muttered in a whisper.

Mira was speechless; her un-blinking gaze knew not anything else. The boat arrived at its destination.

Chapter 74

Thomas' chief student Paul was addressing the congregation,

"Our dear *Swami* Thomas left his corporeal body a few days back on his way for *snan,* the morning bath in the holy river Kaveri miles away form us. We feel his loss in our everyday life. He raised this *ashram* inspired by his teacher *Sant* Isa. *Sant* Thomas was our guide on this new Way he brought to us. In its simplicity and directness we flourished, our awareness evolved. We learned to base our acts of charity and compassion in Love. We mourn the departure of our *Swamiji.* We also pray for his heavenward journey and God's loving mercy. Today we are fortunate to have our *Swami's* guru, *Sant* Isa among us with his consort Mary-ma. I will request them to give us guidance and comfort in our loss." Paul concluded his announcement, hardly able to control his voice. He respectfully bowed to Isa and Mira.

Isa looked at every member of the congregation, feeling the vibrations of each. Then in a somber note he began, "In our loss we are connected. Brother Thomas is present in spirit witnessing our gathering. He feels your love. In love and service he will be always by your side, as he was in person. Seek his guidance and he will be with you. Do not bemoan his passing. Death is but a sleep, only an interlude. You awaken next morning from your sleep, and life continues.

"Some of you have heard similar words or used them to console the bereaved. I know they may even sound hollow when the god of death snatches a dear relative or friend. But I promise, you will be stronger tomorrow. When I left my home in Galilee, I promised my companions including brother Thomas that I would be with them even from miles away. Today I am promising you the same. Open your hearts, minds, and you will awaken inner consciousness. I will be with you, always," Isa concluded. With tearful eyes, somber faces, and bowing with joined palms all gratefully acknowledged him.

Mira's gentle voice reached each heart, "There is joy in heaven today as God receives dear child, Thomas. Lovingly he lived, cruelly he was taken. Where is justice, we ask God. Gently God smiles and says 'Trust me. I see the whole picture, you see only a part.' *Swami* Thomas' work on earth is over for now. He continues his work from heaven. He is in spirit now. He may be in body again and you may not even know him. Such are life's ways. If we love and be merciful, much of God's world will be revealed to us. God bless you all."

The congregation was overwhelmed. The loss of *Sant* Thomas grieved them, meeting *Sant* Isa elated them, and listening to Mary-ma's gentle words, they broke into tears.

Each member came to touch Isa and Mira's feet. Gently each was held in a loving embrace.

****

The next evening Mira was sitting by the window ruminating on the sad surroundings. The center seemed to be mourning.

"Where do you think Thomas is now? Is he sitting with God?" Mira was curious.

Isa intently looked at Mira. In a deep voice he began, "Each one of us has a different concept of being with God, Mira. You know that life is an energy force pervading the universe. After the soul departs, according to each soul's level, it traverses to a different energy field. People know them by different names and concepts. Hindus name the levels as *loka: Brahma loka, Hiranya loka, Go loka,* and such. They are varied stellar or planetary cultures. Each soul finally evolves to perfection after many incarnations and is liberated from the cycle of life and death. Buddhists and Jains have similar concepts. We speak of the afterlife as being in heaven or hell as do those following Zarathustra. The Chinese describe the perfect stage of balance by the yin-yang image. We call the attainment of that balance being with God."

Mira was astonished, "You mean God is a state of the soul's awareness?"

"Not just any state of the soul. That is not God, though God's essence is present in each. When a soul after countless journeys in the universe -- earth, other planets, *lokas* – finally resolves all issues, conflicts and is devoid of all bondage, it attains perfect balance. It is known as *nirvana*, liberation, salvation, or being in heaven with God, better still, be God," Isa thought this should clarify various concepts.

"So...each soul can be God? We adore God as a helper while we are trying to reach perfection. When we attain the highestl we become God, and are not separate anymore. How fascinating. When I have been crazy about Krishna-Radha, in essence, I have been trying to become them. Isa, it's a powerful revelation for me!" Mira was joy, *ananda*, incarnate; she was all smiles, light, vibrancy.

A bright smile shone on Isa's face, as the setting sun colored the loving pair orange gold.

Chapter 75

Isa and Mira were perpetually at the water front in this dreamland Kerala taking long walks to witness the sun rise and set almost every day. The surroundings were a veritable mixture of tropical colors - countless greens against the dark smoky grey waters and a riot of yellow, white, pink, orange, violet flowers. The splash of multiple colors of birds and butterflies dazzled their eyes.

Today they were walking quietly lost in their own thoughts.

"What are you thinking, Mira? You are very quiet," Isa broke a long silence.

"What an amazing life we have lived, Isa? Do you think we have completed our work of this life? Thomas did." Mira wondered.

"Work of this life?" Isa spoke looking at a little fish jumping in the water, "When you reach total awareness of both worlds, the inner and outer reality, it is a moot question. Whether we are alive or dead does not matter. We continue being in universal reality. We keep going; we do not stop – till we attain perfect balance. We may decide to come back of our own free will to be on the rescue mission, as we are doing in this lifetime. We may change the direction or the modality of our humanitarian work," Isa was matter of fact after their recent dialogue about souls reaching godhood.

"Do you think our time has come to change our path?" Mira was fine tuning her question.

"Do you presume we both will do it together? We may not. I almost did not make it, remember on Golgotha?" Isa spoke with a twinkle in his eyes.

"Oh, stop it. I don't want to recall that day--- you on the cross." Mira slapped Isa's wrist.

Isa was musing. Lately he had been having glimpses of his future. They were as clear as the present. But he was not sure of

Mira's readiness. Her awareness was certainly vibrant. Their male female divergences -- his *purush*, spirit, Mira's *prakriti*, primordial nature -- had to converge. Both principles needed to be seamlessly conjoined for a simultaneous journey on earth and beyond. Isa felt, but did not know yet - if Mira's awareness was totally attuned to his.

"Mira I do want to talk about us," said Isa, "Do you think our personal love has touched a deep level of oneness like Krishna-Radha's or Shiva-Parvati's?"

"Haven't we touched identical levels of awareness often, even simultaneously? Is that not an indication of our perfected love?" Mira wondered.

"Certainly, that is a sure sign. But I have *felt* the vast physical universe with all its planets, stars, constellations, and galaxies within me. I would love to traverse the cosmos with you to experience it fully, physically. Does it stir you in anyway?" Isa looked at Mira to see her response in her body language, not just in her words.

"Ever since I was a little girl I have dreamt of scanning the cosmos. I *knew* it then, there was a huge universe out there, in fact, countless universes... Sitting in my balcony I often saw colorful crystal globes -- floating up in the sky. They intertwined, changed shapes as if they were bubbles in the air." Isa saw in Mira's eyes the same childlike shine he had seen in the eyes of the little girl at Granny's years ago. He admired that almost unattainable innocence and sustained childhood in Mira.

She continued, "I was thrilled when years ago we rode the unicorn into the universe in a dream vision. And do not forget that was our simultaneous dream."

"I never told you I had the same dream," Isa protested.

"You never spoke of your dream, not in so many words... But you said you dreamt at the same time. The unicorn even showed us our home. But in the dream we had no knowledge of that snow covered terrain." Mira was thrilled by the memory of the simultaneous dream on Lake Galilee, years and years ago.

"I have an idea, Mira. On our return path we shall pass through Panchvati, where Lord Rama lived with Sita and Lakshman during their exile." Panchvati was a magical place of Lord Rama's exile with his wife and brother.

"Don't I know of Panchvati? I am eager to bathe in all the *kundas*, tanks, and rivers Sita did." Mira was excited; her childlike laughter resurfaced.

Amused and lightened Isa joked, "But don't plan on being abducted by the demon king Ravana who kidnapped Sita from Panchvati and took her to his kingdom, Sri Lanka. I do not have Rama's friendly monkey prince Hanuman to jump the ocean to help me rescue you."

Mira's laugh was so loud some birds in their nest fluttered.

Chapter 76

They passed across mountain ranges, rivers, forests and farm lands. On the way Isa told life stories of God's devotees, advised villagers and townspeople on social issues. A visiting *sant* was a part of people's lives everywhere in this land; people adored Isa and Mira.

His teachings of love and charity were not new for them. Even when Isa spoke of One God, they did not find it so different from their belief in many gods. They knew all three million and some gods and goddesses were only different forms of the One Divine. Devotion, love, concern for each other, animals, and plants was the focus of divinity within. Each person comprehended the most he could, and did the best he would. Centuries of perception prevailed. However, Isa's words were easier to understand and implement than many pundits' heavy discourses. And they absolutely loved Mira as the mother goddess Amba.

Isa was drawn to places that Rama had visited during his exile and felt the magic of the land.

One evening, a learned *Brahmin,* Vishakh, who had recognized Isa's essence from his talks, approached Isa, "Would you be interested in witnessing an *avakash yaan,* a celestial aircraft, landing on earth? I could take you to that area where perhaps Rama often landed in his Pushpak *viman,* aircraft. I have seen a couple of landings there." Isa was waiting for just such an opportunity.

"When can we go?" he eagerly asked.

"Tomorrow is *purnima,* the full moon, of the fall. It would be an opportune time to see a landing. It may happen if you are lucky." Vishakh evidently was equally excited, but unsure, "I will meet you at the Rama temple after supper," saying that Vishakh left.

That evening Isa's unusual silence drew Mira's attention, "Has something new happened?"

"Let's be ready for a significant experience. I think that tim... tomorrow night. Be ready to go to the temple after supper," Isa to... her about Vishakh and his offer. Mira could hardly wait.

* * * * * * * * * * * *

The next evening after *aarati* Isa and Mira started their moonlit night walk through the forest with Vishakh. Isa was brooding, walking a few steps behind Vishakh and Mira who were busy chatting.

"The *devayan*, god's vehicle, landed right here, when we saw it the first time. We all were youngsters out for adventure. The oldest among us was fourteen," Vishakh said recalling his childhood venture. They had walked nearly three miles through the thick forest without any pathway.

"But how did you know where to go?" Mira asked.

"We did not. We chanced upon it in our game of treasure hunt. Two of us got lost and ended up here. When it got dark, we could not find our way back. So we decided to sleep in one of the trees."

"How old were you?" Mira was getting excited.

"I was eleven, my friend was twelve, I guess. It was a full moon night, like today. We found a high branch of a huge tree. No wild animal could reach us that high. Of course we made sure no large snake was hiding on one of the branches either," Vishakh said with wry humor about that rather scary time.

"What happened next?" Mira could hardly wait.

"We were so tired we fell asleep as soon as we found a safe branch for each of us. It must have been hours later, a dazzling light woke us up. With squinting eyes we saw it was coming from something a little above the tree line. It was approaching fast in our direction. We huddled on the same branch, gawking. The thing landed noiselessly. It brightened the whole area. Two figures came out of the thing and then the huge thing arose from the ground and flew away, just as noiselessly as it had landed." Vishakh completed the story.

"What happened to the two figures who stepped out of the vehicle?" Isa, walking behind, was listening to the story.

"The two quickly started walking through the forest, as if they knew where they were going."

"What did they look like?" Isa was curious, as he knew they came from another planet.

"What do you mean? The usual man and woman -- what else could they look like?" Vishakh was not sure what the question implied. "The next day we had a new *poojari*, ritual priest, in Rama temple. Since then my friends and I came here often. We even cleared this narrow pathway we are walking on," Vishakh was proud of their young adventure. "Over the years some of us have seen at least two, some claim even more, *avakashyaan*, space-crafts."

Suddenly, Vishakh's eyes brightened as he spotted the fast approaching space-craft before he finished his narrative. Isa was prepared. Mira, dazed at first, was eager for this novel experience. Her eyes wide open, she seemed mesmerized. All three watched the celestial vehicle up in the sky headed in their direction. It landed right in front of them, noiselessly.

The doors opened. Smiling Vishakh turned to face Isa and Mira only to see a beam of light swooping them into the opening of the celestial vehicle. Vishakh was transfixed; gaping mouth, eyes wide open, he stared at the vehicle receding into the deep dark blue sky with his new found visitors.

Soon there was nothing but total silence, windless darkness.

The full moon shone in its gentle glory.

Chapter 77

As Mira watched the cosmic reality unfold before her eyes from the spacecraft, she remembered her childhood reveries as well as her dream ride on the unicorn with Isa a few years ago. Now the reveries and the dream were transformed into a real live experience. She actually was *witnessing* the cosmos complete with galaxies, stars, planets, and gaping black holes swallowing all in its vicinity.

"Do you realize Mira, we talked about a cosmic ride not too long ago and here we are," Isa's voice was balanced and deep. He was peaceful; it was like coming home.

"Did you ever imagine that the cosmos would be all dark?" asked Mira, her eyes riveted on the expanse beyond. "Innumerable suns look like mere shining bright spots with their halos of galaxies, stars and planets. The immense sky looks like black silk with sparkles," spoke Mira with dazed eyes, "I always thought there was light all around in this heavenly universe, Isa. Instead it is all immense darkness. Who would have thought such darkness, blacker than black, pervades the cosmos?" Mira's dreamy eyes were fixed on the cosmic-scape.

Immersed in a trancelike state, Isa spotted ethereal floating matter. "See this cloud-like matter passing us? That is the birthplace of new stars. Do you realize how many stars are yet to be born? And we do not know even a fraction of the existing universe," Isa said calmly.

Viewing the scene as far as she could, Mira nearly screamed, "Isa, look at our dear earth, we can hardly see it. It hangs like the tiniest dot of sapphire." She could not believe her dear home could vanish into nothingness.

In his balanced voice, Isa said, "This vast universe is endless and perpetually expands!"

"And we think we are the center of the universe!!" Mira was laughing so hard she nearly fell, or so she thought. Isa had to hold her weightless body. Losing gravity, they were nearly floating.

"Not at its center, but we still are a part of that marvelous universe, Mira," Isa's voice was even, emotionless, matter of fact.

Why were they talking about earthly existence on their space flight, Isa wondered? Looking out of the window to the horizon of eternity, Isa felt a new vibration in his body. He realized it emanated from the silent, nearly invisible, crew of the spacecraft. The two crew members never spoke a word, but Isa realized they were communicating telepathically. Isa recognized the origin of his equanimity and balanced perceptions on this extraordinary flight. He looked at Mira and continued his conversation.

"Despite the high level of universal God-essence in us, on earth we are limited by its three dimensional reality," said Isa.

"Shall we keep coming back to earth to help the repeatedly floundering humanity?" Mira was curious, "In fact, I don't mind it. It's a fun place, the earth is. Once you know it is all a play, *lila*, what does it matter? Pain and joy are all the same." Mira's delightful laugh was in her eyes, audible in her tremulous voice. "Isa, what will happen when all humans reach their potentiality, their divinity, their god-hood?"

Silent Isa admired Mira's fanciful speculations. He was submerged in another process of telepathic communication and kept gazing at the swiftly passing universe. Mira too remained silent, watching the splendor of the ever expanding sky that was enlarging beyond her wildest imagination.

After what seemed to be eternity, Isa spoke in a measured tone, in answer to Mira's question, "There have been such times before now, in distant antiquity, when all beings realized their divinity, and earthly people will experience it again. Existence is cyclical and spiral. All humans will be in their godliness, a perfect balancing of dualism of *yin* and *yang* will prevail. Humans will endure much turmoil before that. The end of one age is scary for people, but it also heralds a new beginning." Isa tarried.

With her dreamy eyes set on the cosmic horizon, the fa spot she could envision, Mira said, "What a wondrous universe! I r it in my veins. I feel light, very light, Isa." She looked down and screamed "I am diffusing, look, Isa!" Her feet were dissolving, disappearing, literally melting. Slowly the diffusion was moving upward...

Isa, not looking at her feet, kept staring into Mira's eyes with profound peace. He was holding her hands...tightly, silently.

The celestial vehicle continued whirling into the cosmos, literally fusing time and space. Everything known so far in human experience was diffusing, disintegrating, transforming.

"Our 'I-ness' is expanding as we physically diffuse, Mira," Isa spoke after what seemed a long silence. "Our bodies feel lighter because they are literally transforming. We are becoming energy waves."

After her initial shock, Mira began feeling the force of transformation. Receiving information telepathically she said, "When our physical boundaries melt away, our bodies will transform into swirling energy strings!" She laughed her sonorous laugh as she watched their bodies becoming wriggling wavy streaks of light.

Starting with their feet and moving upwards, the energy waves were gradually absorbing their bodies. Both kept gazing at each other, trying to hold hands more tightly as they felt lighter and lighter. They kept watching their physical bodies dissolve. The last to vanish were their interlocked eyes.

The interlaced streaks of stringy lights remained floating. In place of Isa and Mira, there were two swirling energy orbs. After a while the two orbs merged *becoming* one dazzling orb, a constantly moving energy of light and sound, fusing in total harmony.

Then even the vibrating sound ceased. Only the indescribable, impenetrable darkness, inscrutably silent and motionless, remained.

That was the absolute silence as it was before the Creation of the Universe.

✳

Chapter 78

All vibration, sound, and light had ceased – the ultimate state of *kaivalya*, attribute-less condition, total emptiness prevailed: so it was before the beginning.

The energy orb began to exude a sound...a...u...m...

Thus began the process of creation after dissolution, once again. Slowly, atoms and particles started vibrating, quivering like waves. Light manifested with its finest strands. The *one* orb split becoming *two*.

The sequence of sound, vibration, light was revealed in cosmic awareness.

The two space travelers began to re-materialize.

The spacecraft zoomed back toward the earth. As the two cosmic travelers started breathing in their re-structured human forms, the vehicle landed. The door opened. The travelers walked out of the craft. And before they would turn around it zoomed out; it was gone.

Isa and Mary had been more than a year in earthly time in timeless space.

Their regained bodies exuded more light, their eyes shone brighter, and their voices had an unprecedented ring of *knowingness*. Both *felt* it in their beings.

"You look radiant Mary," Isa admired the glow on Mary's body. For a moment she felt strange being addressed as Mary, not Mira.

"Look at you, aren't you ready to shine like a star!" She laughed her silvery laugh. "What did we go through Isa? It was like God took us on a cosmic ride. We are literally transformed, physically, aren't we?"

"We travelled deep into the cosmos, lost our physical bodies, reached the highest level of our *essence;* and regained our bodies to return to earth. What an extraordinary experience it was," Isa still seemed partially out there.

"Do you know where we are, Isa?" Mary looked at the clad mountain ranges and the surroundings. Evidently it did not like Kashmir where they were headed from Panchvati, from where they were beamed into spacecraft.

"Let's walk some and find out." Isa saw a man bringing his sheep in their direction. A brief dialogue revealed they were in Gaul, in the south of modern France. There was an old Jewish community in this area, the shepherd said.

"Why don't you come to my house and share a meal with my family," the shepherd offered.

* * * * * * * * * * *

Isa and Mary had not eaten for the whole day, so they thought. Later they would realize they had not had earthly food in over a year.

They ate heartily.

"You must eat well, woman," said the shepherd's wife as she saw Mary getting up from the table.

"Oh no, not anymore; I do not recall having eaten so much in my life. Thank you, it was delightful," Mary thanked the hospitable hostess.

"Where are you planning to go from here?" asked Pierre, the shepherd.

"They can't go too far," said Jean, his wife, "It will soon be winter." Then turning to Isa she said, "You do not plan to take your wife too far, do you? She needs rest and nourishment, now that she will be eating for two."

Isa and Mary were surprised. Eyes wide open Isa looked at Mary with a joyful query, "Is that really true?" Why does the news about the birth of a child in his family come as a total surprise?

Mary was in joyous shock, an incredible surprise. Her eyes popped out, her hand automatically touching her stomach, "What!?"

The two elders were roaring with laughter, "You mean you do not even know you are in the family way?"

Isa stood up from his seat next to Pierre, came over to Mary, and folded her in his arms.

* * * * * * * * * * *

That night when Isa and Mary retired to the comfortable warm ... Pierre and Jean had offered and were alone, Mary said, "Isa, ...en did this happen? And how?" By now from their talk with Pierre they had deduced a whole year in earth time had rolled by. They knew they had no bodies for a part of 'the missing time.'

Elated Isa recalled their cosmic experience to fathom the mystery. "We are immensely blessed, Mary. Among most marvelous visions of the cosmic reality, its universes, life and Creation that we experienced, was this miracle of a new life that we were unaware of. Evidently, our child was conceived when our energies merged into one orb."

Mary was ecstatic, "Isa I cannot believe this child of ours was conceived when our subtle energies fused into one orb! And what's more we were on a cosmic ride in a celestial vehicle!" Mary had to smother her joyous laughter lest she should awaken Pierre and Jean.

Isa reminisced, "These are magical times, Mary. Don't forget my own birth. Mother went crazy in disbelief when the angel of God appeared before her to announce my birth. We are immensely grateful for God's blessings."

* * * * * * * * * * * *

Pierre introduced Isa to his Jewish community which followed simple laws of morality and truth they had learned from a small group of Egyptian Jews of Alexandria. They called themselves *Perfeti Cathars*, ancestors of later Cathars.

Isa soon realized this community was well suited to his teaching and temperament. Pythagoras had learned Zarthustra's dualism and Indian *samkhya*, numbers, both of which were well spread among the Jewish scholars of Egypt. Many of the practices were based in the principle of perpetual antagonism between good and evil. They did not believe God *created* evil. God transcended the conflict; but man had to learn to claim this transcendence, his heritage, his divinity, fighting his way through dualism by living a simple, principled life.

It was decided by the elders that Isa and Mary would stay in this village and Isa would be their new *Perfecti*, rabbi; the old one had returned to Egypt for an indefinite period with a promise of sending someone from Egypt to fill his place. It seemed the timing was perfect for all. Mary would teach women weaving and child rearing. But she knew her mainstay would be to inculcate the joy of divine service through total *surrender* to God.

The news of the crucifixion in Jerusalem had trickled this far west to the Pyrenees. But none knew of Isa's secret revival or self-imposed exile, as Isa's former companions observed total secrecy.

In fact, they were still keeping a low profile back in Jerusalem, Nazareth, and Galilee. They were sharing their knowledge with those eager to learn. Some of them wrote what they remembered of Isa's life and teachings, the way they heard it or experienced it.

Chapter 79

In the valley of the Pyrenees nestled the village Rhedae, modern Rennes-le-Chateau. Gently contoured rolling hills and valleys lent a perfect landscape for Isa's meditation. For the evening sun walks Isa and Mary preferred walking to the ravine by an enchanting water fall. Lush trees, wild flowers, and birds enlivened the gorge.

In his leisure time Isa gravitated to his old passion, making dolls like the one he had made when he was sixteen. Oh, what a long time ago that was, he thought. He fondly remembered the little girl at Granny's in *Prem Kunj*, the Abode of Love, who had sensed the doll in his robe and demanded it.

"Do you know anything about that girl at Granny's, Mary?" Isa asked Mary one morning.

"No, I don't. Unfortunately I lost touch with Granny's wards a long time ago," Mary said with a touch of regret. Life's events had thrown her in a whirlwind.

"I wonder what happened to that little girl. She was a special child, certainly an advanced soul." Isa said musingly while carving the eyes on his new doll. They were sitting on the porch of their new home that the community had helped expand from the one room house of the former Perfecti, who was single.

"Yes, Sophia was special. She reminded me of myself at her age," Mary spoke nostalgically.

Mary saw Adrienne, a six year old neighbor's daughter, coming with a dish in her hand, "My mother sent this for you, Ma'am." She gave the dish covered with cloth.

"Thank you Adrienne. What did your mama make?" Mary lifted the cover to see a dessert, full of healthy nuts and butter.

"My mother says it is good for you and the baby," the girl said, smiled and started walking away. She stopped when she saw Isa chipping a piece of wood. "What are you making, Sir?" she asked, comfortably sitting down by Isa.

"It's a doll. Here it is. Do you think it's coming out well?" Isa held the doll for Adrienne's scrutiny. The girl took the doll, turned it around, looked at it from all angles, and said, "I like her smile."

"That's good. Now I am going to work on her eyes," Isa said. "Would you like me to make her eyes like yours?"

"Oh, that would be precious, Sir. Can you really do that?" She had never seen a doll with eyes resembling a real person's eyes.

"I will try," Isa said looking into the girl's smiling eyes.

"Will you tell your mama, Adrienne, I appreciate the dessert she made for me? Would you take these fruits to your mother for me?" Mary said, returning the dish.

"Sure, I will be careful. My mother scolds me because I always run. She says I do not know walking," taking the dish, Adrienne started running back to her house.

"Be careful, you will drop the fruits," Mary shouted.

"I will wash them, don't worry, Ma'am," yelled Adrienne.

* * * * * * * * * * * *

It was time for the early morning walk over the hilly terrain for Isa and Mary. The ravine at the bottom of the hill was their usual destination.

"Are you sure you can walk the distance with the incline to and fro, Mary?" Isa was concerned about her advanced pregnancy.

"Of course, the baby does not slow me down, Isa," Mary was cheerful as always. That is how she was throughout the seven months since they arrived in Rhedae. No physical discomfort, except for the protruding belly, she was the same vivacious, energetic Mary.

"Is the sky not bluer here, Isa?" She asked looking up at the vault that had an unusual aquamarine hue because of strange light. Nearby trees were ringing with chirping birds' morning songs. They were riotous melodies, Isa thought. As they started on the downward slope, Isa held Mary's hand to support her balance, his other arm on her shoulder. Mary's arm was around his waist.

They saw the ravine at the end of the slope. With blue ripples reflecting the lush green trees and the white foam of gushing water, the earth seemed to be imitating the aquamarine sky and white clouds above. It seemed Nature was creating a magical moment, "As above, so below," murmured Isa, "Isn't this a sacred moment?"

"We are entering a sacred temple, Isa. How perfect is this moment. Wondrous is this earth," Mary spoke in a gentle dreamy voice. "Let's sit near our tree down by the ravine."

Isa helped Mary sat comfortably on a flat spot with her back against the tree. "Look at the ripples Mary. Joyously they flow on to their adventure of life: innocent, vigorous, playful."

"Blessed is this moment. Isa, our child is ready. It wants to come out right now. Hold me close," Mary leaned on Isa. All three of them were pushing in one direction with their own will, their life force. Isa was using his soul-force. Mary was physically pushing the baby. The baby was forcing herself by her will to be born. One combined push of the triple force... and the valley was filled with the first cry of the infant and joyous laughter of her parents.

Birds stretched their necks to look around what the commotion was about.

Isa took the new born to the water and gave her the first wash, with love, prayer, gratefulness, and blessings from the universe. He then brought the child back to Mary. She snuggled her little babe in her bosom.

Chapter 80

Two years had passed since the day of the sylvan birth of little Sarah.

This morning Isa was making yet another doll. His hobby had become a passion. Every child in the community had at least one doll from Isa. It was the unique expression he captured on each doll – male and female -- that made it a special doll for that particular child. Intuitively Isa saw the receiving child's essence and captured it in the face and the eyes of the doll.

Looking up, Isa saw Henrique, the seven year old boy, known for his wild adventures, coming his way with somebody, perhaps a visitor in town, who wanted to meet Isa. Visitors often came to Isa's place for a discourse or advice. As they came closer, Isa identified the newcomer and ran practically shouting, "Is that truly you, Maniji? How did you find us here?" Isa could not believe his eyes.

"Well, young Henrique seems to have answers for everything. And he certainly has an eye for lost souls," Mani joked. Evidently it was Henrique who first spotted Mani in the village square looking for somebody.

Isa said, "I knew Henrique would one day bring me a surprise. And you did it, thank you, Henrique." Henrique smiled, and saying he will stop by the next day, ran in search of another venture.

Hearing voices Mary came out, little Sarah toddling behind her, "What a joyous moment, Maniji! Welcome to our home. This is Sarah," she introduced the child and bent low with joined palms to greet Mani with *namaskar*.

"Oh let me give you a hug, Mary, and to your little daughter here, a special joy," enthusiastically Mani hugged Mary. Sarah steadfastly hung behind her mother's robe; the cautious two-year-old was still measuring Mani.

"Let's go inside. We have much to talk about," said Isa. Isa had many questions. How did Mani know where Isa and Mary were? What has he been doing all these years? What else is happening in the world they once knew so well that is so remote now? What would be Mani's take on Mary's 'miraculous' conception?

It had been almost ten years since Mani last saw Isa and Mary. After the crucifixion Mani had gone to Egypt. When he returned to India, Sriram informed him that Isa and Mary had left Kashmir for Kailash, Tibet, and were going south from there. For the last six months Mani had been in Egypt once again.

"Now comes the interesting part. When in Alexandria, I ran into Joseph of Arimathea on the port. We overheard an old *Parfecti* who was eating at the same table at an inn. He mentioned an 'Isa' who had replaced him back in Rhedea, his native place in Gaul. We both were surprised and asked the man for more details. And here I am. Do not be surprised if one of these days you have another visitor," Mani mirthfully narrated the chance discovery of Isa's whereabouts.

"Joseph of Arimathea was on his tin trading trip to Alexandria, I presume," Isa guessed.

"Yes, from Alexandria he was to go to England. Any day he may show up here now that he too knows of your hiding place!!" Mani sounded happy.

"You made a special trip to visit us, Maniji?" Mary was grateful.

"I needed to check out some alchemical research on the other side of the Pyrenees up north as well. I thought I would surprise you. But you have a joyful bundle of surprise for me, little Sarah," Mani said admiring the little girl who was still staring at the stranger from the secure position behind her mother's robe.

"Well, she surprised us too," said Isa. "Perhaps her unconventional conception may be your next research," Isa was smiling, looking at Mani.

"You mean to say, like father, like daughter? God's angel appeared to your mother announcing your arrival. Did you too have a visitor, Mary?" Mani was joking. But he was curious about Isa's comment.

Mary laughed, "Well, Isa will fill you in. Let me start getting some food ready." She picked up Sarah and went into the kitchen in the back of the house.

With great interest Mani heard the story of Isa and Mary's cosmic journey. Isa described as much as he could of the inscrutable expanse they witnessed. Their transformation into energy and fusion into *one* orb of translucent sparkling waves fascinated Mani. For his scientific mind this was a gold mine, a fresh discovery. But the real surprise came when Isa added, "It seems that is when Sarah was conceived in that integrated *orb*. There is no other traditional explanation since we were up there for over a year in earth time. We were surprised when the old shepherd's wife said Mary was with child. That's when we knew," Isa laughingly concluded the detailed description of their cosmic venture.

Mani was wonder struck. Conceptions through god and human connection were commonplace in Greek and Indian cultures. Extraterrestrial visitors were not new for Mani either. "Isa, your mother Mary remembered only a fraction of what happened to her. And that is usual. Even you cannot reproduce all you experienced in your cosmic travel. So that is usual. No one can reproduce what happens in those extra dimensions. Since a lot more happens than can be perceived by limited human senses."

"What about the birth of the Pandavas, the heroes of the *Mahabharata*?" Isa asked. "Didn't the two queens *themselves* invoke various gods: Surya, Indra, Vayu, and Ashvini Kumar to beget five sons?" *(Respectively: the Sun, king of gods, god of wind, and the twin gods of medicine)*

Mani said, "That's what I am saying. Such yogic practice had been common in India in ancient times. In Greece gods and goddesses begot children with humans. So that is not implausible. That is part of human culture. What you are saying will be clear to us in the future as our knowledge of the universe expands, Isa. This is pushing the energy field into another dimension, another transformational state we do not quite know yet. This is huge, a new field of investigation, a great advancement," Mani was getting excited about this earthshaking revelation. He could not stop, "Mathematics and physics, chemistry and biology, various strands of *vijnan*, sciences, are converging, coalescing." He kept staring at Isa in disbelief that Mary would conceive at the time when they had no physical bodies as we know them. They were energy orbs. And obviously the energies had 'copulated' as it were. Was it yet another aspect of energy fusion that physicist and physiologists had not known yet?

Mani was enviously looking into the distant future when new research would explain more about energy, physics, and creation. Certainly it would not be achieved in his lifetime. He said, "Sarah is a special child, conceived in the cosmos by transformed energies, *your* already *elevated* energies. You and Mary have been miracle workers in many ways. This is the best of all!"

"It was uncanny. We were surprised but incredibly happy. I know Sarah is of highly evolved essence," Isa said in a matter of fact way, without sounding like a bragging father.

"Is Sarah different from other two year olds?" Mani was curious.

Isa heartily laughed, "Maniji, we are like all other doting parents. Of course, for us everything she does is unique," he tried to downplay Sarah's special traits.

Mary brought food on two plates, fish on one, vegetables and bran on the other. They all sat to share the meal. Mani asked Mary the same question if she had noticed anything special in Sarah.

"Yesterday she surprised me. Isa, I have not had a chance to tell you yet. I was in the yard putting clothes on the line; Sarah was sitting on the ground staring into the sky. I watched her off and on while finishing the clothes. For nearly fifteen minutes or so she sat there steadily staring into the sky. I was a little frightened seeing this restless girl sitting like a statue with unblinking eyes. I touched her and called her by name. She turned her face toward me, gently smiled, got up and silently walked in with me. It was so unusual." Mary's narration left Isa and Mani thinking.

"Obviously she was meditating. She must have been an advanced yogi in other incarnations, like you," said Mani with mischievous eyes. "You both watch her more carefully. She is blessed, gifted and may have unusual traits. She will leave her mark in the world. Sarah is the daughter of exceptional parents. Don't forget she didn't choose you both as parents for nothing!" Mani laughed looking at Isa and Mary.

"I feel she is an ancient soul," said Isa. "She was born in nature-- by the ravine, and her birth was unusually easy, nearly effortless."

"Effortless for you, maybe!" said Mary with mischief in her eyes, and continued, "Honestly, Maniji, I have to admit, it was easy. The pregnancy and birthing both were nearly effortless. She is a divine child," Mary joyfully celebrated being the mother of an extraordinary child.

Chapter 81

In the next five years Isa and Mary became the center of their community.

Whether it was a broken roof to be mended, or a child to be admonished or trained, each villager came to consult Isa or Mary. If someone thought God was punishing him, Isa was there to help him figure out what was on God's mind. A teenager asking questions about the meaning of life found Mary's musings meaningful. When Sarah, now seven, walked in a group of squabbling children, most fell quiet.

The new center was built to serve as home for Isa's family, besides being a venue for community gatherings. It all started after the first visit of Joseph of Arimathea five years earlier, soon after Mani left. The tin merchant's generosity initiated the center. Now it was Isa and Mary's home, work place, and spiritual center.

It happened at a Friday gathering.

Isa said, "Our bodies are temples in which God resides. We all have recognized the duality of the body and the spirit. Some of us think that the satisfaction of the body's demands throws us off the spiritual path. But neglect of the body may diminish its capacity to serve the divine in us. Finding the perfect balance between the two is the purpose of our lives. We cannot defile the body. It is as good as polluting the sacredness of the temple."

"Do you have a method we can observe to keep such balance?" asked old Pierre.

"Keeping God's name constantly in my heart during all my doings, running chores or teaching, has helped me," said Mary. She remembered her days in Vrindavan years ago. Internalizing the Divine, she glided through the day's activities.

"Some of you may not be comfortable naming the unnamable divine, YAHVEH. You may visualize the Eternal Infinite without shape, color, or form," Isa added.

"But that is so difficult, the Eternal Infinite is kind of abstract," said Henrique, now a thirteen year old.

"But you can give it any shape you want, like fairies," piped in little Sarah. "It is *your* God, and he is with you always – like your ear or nose he goes with you everywhere." All broke into a peal of laughter. Sarah looked at her parents wondering why everybody was laughing.

"That is a good suggestion, Sarah," said Isa, "I will try it myself. Let's sing our prayer and contemplate before we part."

Soon the evening meeting was over. Henrique's mother, Annabel, brought her visitor over to meet Isa and Mary. A beautiful tall young woman, self confident and elegant, walked toward them. "Do you remember me? Were you not at *Prem Kunj* at Granny's in Gandhar?" the visitor asked Mary. Surprised Mary kept looking at the woman, and then she nearly screamed in total disbelief, "It can't be. Is that you, Sophia?"

"Yes, of course," and the two women hugged, gleefully.

"Are you the wise little girl at Granny's?" asked wide eyed Isa with a broad smile.

"Not a little girl anymore. And wise? Who knows?" said Sophia bursting into gleeful laughter. "I remember you as the man who gave me the doll tied in his robe. I still have it."

Isa, Mary and Sophia were a fountain of joy, holding hands and chatting.

Sarah was watching them, "Mother, why is there a golden thread around you, me and the lady?" Obviously, Sarah saw something none of the adults could perceive.

After a quick look at Mary, Isa said to Sarah, "We will soon find out." Then turning to Sophia he suggested, "Let's go in the kitchen and catch up. I am sure we have many stories to share." Annabel excused herself leaving the newfound friends a time to visit.

The two women's enthusiastic questions and answers overlapped as they shared life stories of more than three decades. Before one could finish a story, or even a sentence, the other would have another question leading to endless digressions. In fact, Isa learned quite a few details about Granny's abode that he had not known before.

Sophia's story was like a fairy tale. When Sophia's mother died in childbirth, Theodosius, her father, was heartbroken. He was a fourth generation Greek warrior and had risen to a centurion's position in the Roman army occupying the region of Gaul. One of his colleagues, a professional caravan leader, suggested Granny's abode for the newborn. Theodosius, always a little radical and ambitious, decided to follow the friend's suggestion, instead of following the tradition of allowing his sister to raise Sophia. The sister was offended, of course.

When Sophia was ten, Theodosius brought her home from Granny's to Gaul to join her loving step mother Helena and a seven year old half brother Philo. Life was delightful. Sophia loved the vibrant lifestyle of festivals and dances, music and songs. Her intuitive ability to see other dimensions of reality made her special among young and old.

Theodosius decided to send both his children to the school for noblemen's sons to get educated in rhetoric, politics, ethics, mathematics, music, literature, and such. Of course these schools were not for girls. Noblemen's daughters had training in music, dancing, art, and were home schooled. But that would not daunt ambitious Theodosius. He sent Sophocles, Sophia dressed as a boy, and little Philo in the most prestigious school in the area.

"That is the most hilarious story I ever heard, Sophocles!" said Mary cracking up into a hearty laughter. Isa joined her in the most raucous laugh he ever laughed. "I am sure young men lined up at your father's abode to claim your hand after you finished school," said Mary still laughing.

Isa concurred adding his own qualifier with a sweet smile, "I hope those young men were compatible in wisdom and insight. Did anyone resemble your namesake Sophocles?"

"Not everybody is as fortunate as Mary, I am afraid," said Sophia looking meaningfully at Isa. "My father became anxious when I turned down all suitors," Sophia said with a serene smile.

"I hope you did not have to take poison like the other wise Greek, Socrates," Mira could not help but be jovial.

Sophia said, "My only *poison* if you call it so, was to give up my desire to have a suitable consort. In fact, I found my calling: teaching. I started a mini training program for boys and girls of all classes – Greek, Roman, Jew, even the children of slaves. Now it is a regular academy with a curriculum resembling that for aristocratic children. It includes science, mathematics, philosophy, mythology, literature, besides crafts, music, and dancing...that is what I do now in central Gaul."

"Did you have to pay a price for being such a radical, an iconoclast breaking traditions?" Isa knew too well such acts would not go unnoticed or unchallenged.

"Well, some people were nervous about it. But having a radical father, who is also an influential centurion does not hurt, I have to admit," Sophia said with a meaningful smile. "Let's not forget, political power has long arms."

"You can say that again," piped in Mary. "Political games can be dangerous."

"So are you here for a visit?" Isa changed the subject, Sophia noticed. No one outside Isa's close circle in Galilee knew that he was the same man who was crucified in Jerusalem. People in this town thought Mani and Joseph of Arimathea came to visit an old friend.

"Well, Annabel is originally from my town and knows about my school. She admires you and wanted me to come and meet you. Little did I think I would meet my childhood friends," Sophia said.

Sarah entered with a little dog in tow, "Are you still talking? I am hungry."

Mary got up to get food ready. Sophia said she will stop by soon and started to leave.

"If you leave our home, do you think the golden thread will stretch up to Henrique's house where you live?" Sarah asked as she still saw the thread around the three of them. Mary, Sophia and Isa kept looking at each other.

"It might, Sarah," said Isa, "because you three are like different color gems in a ring. What do you say?"

Seven year old Sarah looked at her father quizzically, thought a little, and said, "It is possible. I think you are right."

Isa gracefully accepted his daughter's concession to his wisdom with a bow and a smile.

Chapter 82

Years rolled by...

When Sarah was twelve she was sent to study at Sophia's school to explore a new world of learning.

That was eight years ago.

Today Isa and Mary are eagerly waiting for her return, as they had done for a few days in fact, since they heard from Annabel that Henrique and Sarah had left school and will soon be coming home. Journeys are unpredictable. Who would know that better than Isa and Mary?

Mary was tending to her spring flower plants. Pooch, Sarah's dog, was hanging around. As a fifteen year old dog he was not sprightly anymore. Isa was looking at the sky trying to balance a father's eagerness with yogi's equanimity. He smiled to himself: how enigmatic is the struggle between the divine and the human when it concerns one's child. He picked up his flute and started playing his favorite tune. Mary began humming and then burst into her special song.

> *Come along, come along, dear one*
> *My eyes are thirsty, my voice is dry,*
> *I envy your flute, close to your lips*
> *I am so far, so far.*

Isa kept playing 'so far' 'so far' in a plaintive note. Mary kept humming and watering. Chirping birds fell silent to listen to magical music. Gentle breeze tarried some trying to mimic the divine note...

Then suddenly Pooch darted toward the pathway faster than he had in a few years.

Twenty-year-old Sarah, an absolute beauty, was elegantly walking the pathway to their home. Trees with light green new shoots on both sides of the path made provided a picture perfect welcome for Sarah. Isa left his flute and jumped out of the hammock; Mary dropped the water can. Both stood transfixed: their eyes -- their entire bodies -- radiated utter joy.

"Father, Mother...I am back," Sarah started running as soon as she saw them, laughing and shouting in sheer delight. Her voice filled up the valley and her parents' hearts. Outstretched arms intertwined in a warm, tight hug. Up above in tall trees birds were silenced by Sarah's loud voice.

Pooch could not quiet down his uncontrollable barks and shuffling, till Sarah hugged and caressed him.

"Let me look at you. Are you my little Sarah?" Mary held her daughter by the shoulders, viewing her up and down, in adoring amazement.

"Do I know you, young lady?" Isa asked with a gentle smile, love exuding from every cell in his body.

"Mother you do not look a day older. God be praised. Father, only your beard is a little greyer. Both of you must feel great, I am sure. Evidently you did not miss me," Sarah added mischievously. Everyone laughed heartily. They went into the house; there was much to share.

* * * * * * * * * * * *

The next morning after Isa returned from the ravine and as the family was settling for breakfast, he saw Henrique approaching the house.

"Is that Henrique? How grown up he looks. And who is with him?" A tall man was walking with Henrique, "As a young boy he used to bring visitors to our house. It seems he has not broken his habit."

Surprised Mary looked up, "Is that Henrique, the eight year old we once knew? Look how grown up he is! He is like a court scholar or a diplomat. On his first day of home he has already found a lost stranger in town?" Mary and Isa kept looking at the approaching pair.

"God be praised," excited Isa shouted, "It is Demetrius!" He ran to meet his Greek friend he first met in India decades ago.

"What?!" Mary shouted in disbelief and came out into the yard. Over the loud laughter of three old companions, no one could hear what any one was saying.

Sarah and Henrique stood witnessing the absolute joy of the reunion of three kindred spirits.

Going inside the house Sarah said, "Mother, I will get the board ready for breakfast. Why don't you visit with your friend?"

Henrique said, "I will help Sarah." Both young ones went into the house.

Mary, Isa and Demetrius settled to talk. Once again Pooch was restless. Who was it now? Mary and Isa saw Sophia coming their way.

"A morning of dear friends' gathering," said Mary getting up to receive Sophia.

An hour later, after a barrage of questions and comments from the reunited friends and their silent witnesses, breakfast was over.

In essence Isa and Mary learned: Demetrius had been second in rank in his Platonic Academy in Greece for a few years now. Two years ago, a newly enrolled scholar in the Academy spoke about an unusual school run by a woman in Gaul. Platonic Academy appointed Demetrius to check it out. Not only was he impressed by Sophia's school curriculum and set up, but more impacted by her "vision and verve," her daring. Demetrius invited Sophia to come to his Academy in Greece for further deliberations with his colleagues. Meeting brilliant Sarah at Sophia's school was an incredible bonus. When Demetrius heard of her parents - an Isa and a Mary -- he could not return to Greece without checking if Sarah's parents were indeed his old friends.

"So tell me about you two," Demetrius was eager to know more.

"We have a lot of time to talk about it on our sunset walk as we did in Mathura," Isa said. "Here we have our favorite ravine. It is not the river Yamuna, though. Let's get the young people in our conversation. They have been silent witnesses to our ramblings," Isa said.

Chapter 83

The next day Demetrius and Isa went for a long walk in the mountains. Much had happened since their last meeting in Greece nearly forty years ago. That was after their return from India before Isa began his teaching in Galilee.

Isa spoke of his life. It had literally been turned over, he said, giving the shortest possible version of his teaching, the crucifixion, and the resurrection – the life-story he had not shared with anyone else in all these years. Different versions of Isa's crucifixion and resurrection had filtered through in different parts of the Roman Empire. Demetrius had heard some. But none outside of Isa's inner circle knew the real story of his physical survival and self-imposed exile in India. And certainly none from his close circle was speaking of it to another living soul, said Isa.

Absolutely stunned Demetrius stopped in his tracks and kept staring at Isa, "That is inconceivable, brother. I always knew you would reach an extraordinary level of conscious awareness. But what you have been through, and have attained, is beyond me. You have brought new life into the world, brother. Life itself is resurrected." Demetrius was looking at Isa to see if he was real. He could not believe his old friend Isa was the Messiah, the Savior that this man Paul was vehemently preaching in the Hellenic world.

Demetrius continued, "There is a zealous leader, Paul, who has been spreading the teachings of the resurrected Messiah in Galatia, Athens and other areas around. Evidently Paul, formerly known as Saul, never met his Savior, and even opposed him at first, he claims. But the story goes he was literally thrown off his animal by a dazzling light. That was his instant conversion, he says. But I did not know that Paul's redeemer was my old friend Isa!" Demetrius was still excited.

He held Isa's hands and stood staring at him. A deep force of energy flowed from Isa intiating Demetrius, activating his innermost awareness.

When Demetrius regained his composure after a long silence, he spoke in a calm angelic voice, "It was you brother, who years ago awakened me to *experiential* awareness beyond the *intellectual*. It prepared for my transformation in the waters near Dwarka. Today, once again you revive me from my academic submersion with your heightened, nay, perfected consciousness."

Isa was looking at faraway mountains. He envisioned a distant future in great detail. Many of his teachings were misquoted, misrepresented, misunderstood.

Isa turned his face toward Demetrius and solemnly said, "Isn't it ironic that once I critiqued the temple priests' misuse of the scriptures. In the future my words may be misused by new voices in my name? Such is the human saga."

"Didn't we recognize the same tendency when we discussed various commentaries on the ancient texts in Takshashila?" Demetrius remembered their days in India.

It was clear to both, the visionary and the intellectual, that such repeated human behavior is a constant, will be so, till the collective energy of humanity is finally elevated. Each generation will make its contribution to that evolutionary transformation, bit by bit. It is a sluggish process....

They had reached the peak of a small hill overlooking the fresh green valley. The fragrance of new leaves and flowers refreshed the two companions.

After a long silence Isa looked at Demetrius, "Let's go home, Mary must be waiting."

Chapter 84

A few days later, after lunch, Isa and Mary were reminiscing their days in India with Demetrius. The temple rituals, the river walk – and talk, above all the extraordinary *raas lila* in Vrindavan, and their meeting with Mary's grandparents, and then again in Dwarka – all seemed amazing coincidences. They all laughed saying in chorus, "There are no coincidences, of course."

Sophia, entering, said, "Of course not...You all seem to be in good mood today." Looking around, she asked, "Where is Sarah?"

"She went for a walk with Henrique. They will be back when they are hungry," said Mary, her eyes and voice still full of joy.

"She is a vivacious, that girl," Sophia said. After a quick thought, she asked Mary, "Have you asked her recently what she makes of that golden thread around the three of us she saw as a child?"

"No, we haven't asked her. But what do you think that thread is, or was, about?" Isa asked. Then turning to Demetrius he added, "When Sarah was seven and saw Sophia for the first time she saw a golden thread going around Mary, Sophia and herself."

Sophia spoke remembering many of Sarah's exploits, "In my school as a student Sarah reminded me of determined Hera, Zeus' wife, self-assured and ready to strike, even to kill. Self-determination and a sense of justice are vital for her, and she is full of pious rage if anyone violated them." Sophia was pleased with Sarah's rebellious acts, though as the administrator she had to deal with them diligently. Diplomacy required she had to reprimand Sarah, now and then.

"You know brother," Demetrius said with excitement, "ever since I met Sarah and Sophia in school, I saw their complementary characteristics. Sophia is wise, pragmatic and a visionary, ready to achieve the impossible, be a fighter like Athena." His admiring eyes were fixed on Sophia.

Isa was fascinated, "If Sarah reminds you of Hera's power, and you Sophia, resemble wise Athena that leaves Mary to be Aphrodite, the goddess of love, Venus." Isa spoke with fervor and with a smile holding Mary's hand and continued, "And that she is. She is my Parvati. I found that when we were in Mount Kailash years ago," Isa was intently looking at Mary. He then continued, "As I always said, you three are the trinity of the Divine Feminine -- Parvati, Durga, and Kali -- three aspects of the Mother Goddess - or Hera, Athena and Venus. Choose what/who you will," Isa spoke in a jest, but partly seriously.

"Isa, I don't believe it. Are you actually deifying us, making us goddesses?" Mary was incredulous; she was laughing her heart out.

"What is so amusing, mother, why are you laughing so?" asked Sarah walking in with Henrique. "We are hungry," without waiting for an answer Sarah headed for the kitchen pulling Henrique with her.

Isa did not want to let go of this moment to ask Sophia what he meant to ask for a long time, "Are the three Greek goddesses of Wisdom, Love, and Valor relevant to you, Sophia?" Isa asked.

Sophia kept quiet for a few seconds, then looking out at the sky through the narrow window, thoughtfully she replied without moving her gaze, "Often have I wondered about the spiritual aspects of Greek deities and their connections with us...Rather than emulating their divine effulgence as they do in India, in Greece we humanize our gods and goddesses. We do not try to reach gods' divinity; instead our mythologies humanize them bringing them down to our human level." Turning to Isa, she added, "So I am not sure about the spiritual underpinnings of their power for us." Sophia shared her ambivalence.

Sarah piped up from the dining area, "All these stories of gods and goddesses are essentially 'fairy tales for grownups.' Children need fairy tales in the process of growing up. Fairy tales contain truths, but are fictitious. Animals don't talk like humans. So are the stories of multi-headed, multi-armed super-powered gods and goddesses. Similar are the stories of one God, the big father in heaven; or a shapeless entity whom you cannot name...All stories help the human mind to wrap around the abstract concept of the transcendent force. Once the individual self matures...you do not need any of these stories. As long as you remain *spiritual children* you need them. You don't, when you grow up... *spiritually*, that is." Sarah gave her absolute opinion with assertion and clarity.

For a while every one remained quiet. Isa knew Sarah was the new voice, conceived in space, to create a new awareness. Recalling the two year old Sarah staring unblinking into nothingness, Mary wondered if grown up Sarah was getting her knowledge from out there, the world beyond. Demetrius was deep in thought. Old mythologies have to be abandoned, to create new ones. We need new heroes. "Isa is the new mythmaker," Demetrius said to himself as he looked at Isa and smiled. Or was it Sophia? Or could that be Sarah? Demetrius was not sure.

Sarah and Henrique joined the elders. Both young ones with their rosy cheeks and bright eyes looked refreshed after their vigorous nature walk and, of course, food.

Sophia wanted to question Sarah about her anti-deity diatribe, "Sarah, if you say all gods are mental creations, stories, not actual reality, then how do you explain the golden thread around the three of us? Is that also not another fairy tale like those myths? By the way, do you still see it?" Sophia was eager to get her data straight.

"Actually, I see the golden thread more clearly now than ever before," Sarah spoke, "The difference between myth and reality as I see it is *that myth represents someone else's observation or experience of Reality.* Reality for me is what I experience. So the golden thread is real for me. For you it may remain a myth. Both of us are correct from our perspectives."

Demetrius noticed Sarah's logic was irrefutable. There was no ambivalence or hesitation in her words. He saw her as the new mythmaker. He was sure.

The time has arrived for the young ones, Isa thought to himself. He said, "In a sense aren't we all mythmakers, Sophia? When we express our deeply felt truths, our experiences, we need to use words, so we tell stories. Since words are limted, so are the stories. But that is the only way to express our truth, through *words.*" Isa stopped himself, abruptly. He had been trying other means to communicate, but that was his sacred secret. At least so far...Mary looked at Isa, trying to decipher his look, comprehend his incomplete thought.

"But that does not make the stories fictitious fairy tales either," said Demetrius, "We need mythmakers for our times and you are that... *tattvam asi* as they say in India. You young people are the new dreamers, new mythmakers."

Sarah's face was glowing, dreamily she said, "The other day after a long hike, I sat by a boulder viewing the panorama of rolling valleys and snowy mountain peaks at a distance. I was kind of lost, I guess, for how long I do not know.

Out of the golden orb of the giant sun emanated golden strings crisscrossing and expanding into an enormous net. At every connecting point where the strings intersected there was a little shining spot like a crystal. The whole thing grew into a gigantic sparkling golden cosmic net. I kept gazing at it for a while. And then I was in it, I was a part of it. There were many people in each crystal. In one of the formations I saw Mother and Sophia with me. We three kept circling in it tirelessly....

That was it. I do not know for how long I sat there. I kind of woke up when Pooch started licking my feet. We walked back home." Sarah completed her story.

"What do you make of it, Isa?" Mary wanted to know.

"Sarah witnessed *Indra jal,* the cosmic net of Indra. It is no more a Vedic *myth* for her, but a real *experience.* It further supports my vision that the three of you are different aspects of the same feminine spirit, the Mother Goddess. You operate with your individual particularities, as three multicolored gems in a ring...manifesting the same vibrant energy."

Chapter 85

Demetrius went to the community gathering with Isa and Mary. Isa had asked him to talk about Plato's cave. He wondered if Sarah and Henrique, who were teaching at the center for the summer, would want to bring their young students to that event.

"Of course, we will," Sarah, the new teacher, was excited. So it was a mixed group of listeners from age five to sixty five.

"Say, if you never saw a real bird, but you knew of it only by its shadow on the wall, how would you describe it?" Demetrius asked the gathering.

Many laughed at the funny question; some thought it was a trick question; some thought it was condescending, what else do you expect from a grand master of an academy?

A ten year old boy said, "I cannot say what color bird it is. I would see its beak move but could not describe its chirping because I would never have heard it." His seven year old sister sitting next to him whispered something in his ear. The boy said, "My sister says, she would not know how soft its wings are either, though we might see the wing in its flying shadow."

Demetrius was impressed by the children's response. "My teacher Plato believed that there are two realities, one we see, touch, feel, and hear with our senses, the other is invisible. But he maintained that the invisible one is the essential reality – the one we perceive with our senses is like a shadow in a dark cave. We are imprisoned in a cave. The light is outside. Unless we go into the light we will not know the *essential* reality."

"But why are we in a dark cave? We can walk out," said the seven year old girl.

"Yes, we can. You learn fast, don't you?" Demetrius laughed.

"So if we all walk into the light, we learn the truth. Do we? But isn't it true where there is light and substance there must be a shadow," asked a twelve year old.

"You are all very observant, I have to admit. Learn to use light in a way that enhances your vision of truth. Even shadows can reveal important truths about your selves," said Demetrius. He noticed that standing on the shoulders of the old the new generations were getting smarter, more observant.

The young ones were dismissed for their field project studying flowers and butterflies.

Henrique said, "Sir, for Plato there were 'ideal' forms for everything. What we see is a copy of this ideal form. Did he speak of an 'ideal' form for *war* and *violence?* Did he talk about dark concepts?"

"He spoke of the dual world. That is the nature of reality. So with good there is evil. With peace there is war. Without light there would not be a shadow either," Demetrius spoke with some hesitation, anticipating a rejoinder.

"War and violence are facts of life, Henri," said Sarah, "Have you heard of any time in history devoid of war or violence?" Demetrius was happy, but not surprised, to have an unsolicited student assistant.

"So what is your point, Sarah? Are you saying that Socrates and Plato spoke of the 'ideal forms' of violence and war as well?" asked Demetrius. He wanted to know how far Sarah had internalized the Greek philosophers' perceptions.

"Socrates and Plato maintained that the human condition is based in dualism – the *real* and the *ideal.* If *all* concepts have their idealized forms, so must war and violence, right?" Sarah's logic was impeccable.

"So you imply that war and violence also have their idealized forms. They too are aspects of reality, accepted forms of behavior?" Isa wanted to know his daughter's perspective on this moral issue.

"Father, even the bee that sucks the flower is violating the flower. A big fish eats a little fish. You and I also kill a pig or a cow, uproot a plant or consume barley and grapes to sustain ourselves. Violence is intertwined with survival at all levels of living. So are war and violence. They are natural conditions of life, even inevitable, in this three dimensional existence. They are as natural as earthquakes, and floods, and volcanoes. War and peace are like like light and darkness; one is meaningless without the other."

Sarah was clear about this natural human condition. Why would anyone be confused about it? And why was her father, of all persons, asking that question, she wondered? This must be his facile way of testing her, she concluded as she kept staring at him.

"Sarah, are you justifying indiscreet violence and the rampage of killing in wars? What about Alexander's wars of expansion?" Henrique seized a quiet moment to challenge Sarah.

"Of course not...you know that. I never liked that blood thirsty Alexander, so young and so obtuse. But a war may be essential to restore one's honor or destroy the evil-doer. One may call it a just war or even a sacred war. At times it is one's duty to engage in war for collective preservation," Sarah was emphatic. There was no oscillation. It was evident Sarah was distinguishing between wars of profit, expansion or domination and those of defending one's honor, survival, or country. It was an opposition of self-interest against self-preservation, though the line between the two always fluctuated.

"What do you say to that, Henrique?" asked Demetrius.

"U...m... Sarah has a point, there." Henrique looked at Sarah, "But what about the other side of *violence* and *hatred?* What about *love* and *compassion?* In the dual world love and peace, the opposites of war and hatred, must also manifest. Shouldn't they?"

"Sure they do. That's my point," Sarah's response was firm. "Both concepts – compassion and hatred – are real. Humans swing between these two forces, but neither is ever absent altogether. Such is the nature of our dualistic existence. Zarathustra's teachings are based on that as do the *yin* and *yang* of Tao," Sarah's observation was conclusive.

"That's well said, daughter," said Isa appreciating Sarah, "life and death, war and peace, good and evil hang in precarious balance.

Individuals have to be vigilant about what to uphold when and how. That is why masters impart knowledge of right behavior, to balance these dueling forces."

"Often times our choices are not so simple either," spoke Mary in a measured quiet voice, "Nor is the path easy. Our faith is tested."

She looked at Isa meaningfully remembering the days of yore in Jerusalem.

Epilogue

Sarah and Henrique accepted Sophia's offer to teach and supervise at her school while she went to Greece with Demetrius.

Isa and Mary continued their work as a vital part of the community, personally remaining absorbed in another dimension.

Whether she was cooking, sewing, making flower garlands, or advising a child, Mary was always *God-absorbed* – people said.

"Isa's gentle words, in his vibrant voice, 'Your *Self totally fuses with the Ultimate,*' seem to stream from another reality, a remote star – deep, distant, and yet caring," they said.

* * * * * * * * * * * * *

Days passed on...becoming years...yet...*time* did not matter...

One spring day, Isa was in the hammock playing his flute, staring at the sky, lost in his own world. Mary was sitting on the porch making a garland of jasmine. The mellow notes of the flute fusing with the sweet fragrance of jasmine hauled her into another reality.

Isa and Mary were in this world, and at once out on another plane.

Time and *space* were irrelevant...

Joyful bliss pervaded Mary's consciousness merging with Isa's.

The melodious flute revived memories of their younger days in distant lands.

Mary started humming her favorite song; Isa's flute tuned in with her heavenly voice.

I am the flute at thy lips,
Make me hollow
For your love to flow
Through me

The melody rippled over the valley, touching shimmering leaves and tender blades of grass on rolling hills...The fragrance of jasmine whirled with quivering notes reaching the ravine beyond.

As the sun started his downward journey, Isa left the hammock and approached Mary.

Sitting close on the porch, both silently stared into each other's eyes for what seemed to be eternity...

The setting sun tarried to witness the precious moment. The full moon had begun its ascent in the east.

"I was waiting for *our* special time, Mary, to give you a gift," spoke Isa in a soft voice. "Look at the full moon rising up as the sun is leaving us."

"Aren't they magnificent?" Mary looked up at the pale moon greeting her ever-unreachable-lover sun. This moment has been significant for Isa and Mary over the years.

The sun had not yet reached the vanishing point on the horizon ...but he was getting redder as he stared at the elegant fullness of his beloved moon.

"Here is my gift for you." It was a piece carved in wood: a burning flame in a bowl.

Surprised, Mary held her gift against the sun's glow.

"What a marvel, Isa. You have carved a flame of light in a bowl, all in wood! It is incredible," said Mary in a tremorous voice.

As she turned the wooden bowl, she noticed two carved heads, a male and a female, emerging from the flame.

"Is that you and me, Isa? You finally made a doll for me! For us!" Mary's laughter rippled through the silent valley.

The sparkling eyes carved in the faces exuded sheer love and the carved quivering lips pined to touch one another. Ecstatic Mary nearly cried, "Oh...Isa...you have captured our abundant love in this piece. You have etched lines in wood as if it were wax. This is passionate, incredible, fulfilling, fascinating!" Mary was furiously trying to find suitable words...in vain.

With an earnest look, holding the piece high against the deep orange rays of the sun, she said, " *You have carved our twin souls in a flame of love....* This piece is a gentle song, a poem in wood, Isa," Mary's voice quivered. Tears of joy reflected the setting sun.

With a tender smile on his curved lips Isa was intently watching Mary immerse in bliss.

The sun was now a tiny speck of light.

"Words fail to capture the *essence of our love,* Mary. So I carved it in wood for you... for us."

"It *feels* like our love is the *essence* of *all* existence," Mary said softly, her eyes still wet.

Casting the last look at the moon, the sun vanished.

In the splendor of the full moon's ascent, ecstatic Isa and Mary silently gazed at the loving pair within the flame...their mirror.

Wordless moments transport them into the celestial music of silence. They float into the infinite cosmic energy field. They envision their space flights, millennia old and in this lifetime, now. They traverse several life paths strewn with joys, sorrows, trials and triumphs in a flash now. Their **past** *is* **now.**

They remain floating, perpetually inhaling and exhaling the swirling energies. They connect with all That Is. *They are reflected in the crystal knots of the cosmic net of connectivity. In every scintillating knot of the web they envision their incarnations yet to be. Their* **future** *is* **now.**

They witness in every moment a perpetual creation, the unceasing energy flow, feeling its thrilling vibration, *hearing its blasting* sound, *seeing its dazzling* light, **now.**

Manifesting the universal immanence, Isa and Mary are the cosmic Ultimate Love In this moment that transcends time, **now.**

The End

Made in the USA
San Bernardino, CA
14 February 2019